Acknowledgements

To God, who I have not given props to in a while, though he is the real Creator of all. Thank you for your continued guidance in this journey.

To author Terry Brooks, whose characters inspired me to create my own, whose adventures inspired me to live my own, and whose endings inspired me to become utterly frustrated with the world because I realized then that life does not have a fairy tale ending and nor should it.

To the hardships, which never cease to stop and adamantly continue their incessant ramblings in my ear about the past, what I'm doing with the present and how I'm ruining my future. Without your help, I could not have finished this novel in a year's time. Thanks, hardships!

<u>Special Thanks to:</u>

Jennifer Street, who has the creative power of a dozen DaVincis when it comes to graphic arts. Thank you for envisioning Ar Solon as a series with me.

To my scattered family and friends throughout the United States, though you are out of sight, you are not out of mind.

To my family in Baltimore, I may have left there but I have not left you. Much love.

OTHER BOOKS BY RILEY S. BROWN:

<u>The Chronicles of Ar Solon Series:</u>

Book 18: Chains of Solace: (TBA)

Book 19: Forgotten Angel (Released April 2010)

Book 20: The Paths We All Walk: A Collection of Tales (TBA)

Book 21: The Healer, Part I (Released August 2011)

Book 21: The Healer, Part II (TBA)

Book 22: The Plague of the Elves (TBA)

<u>The Wunderlannd Series:</u>

Edward in Wunderlannd (Released October 2011)

Edward and The Enfeebled (Released December 2012)

Writing under the alias Titus Strong:

<u>A Man's Romance Novel Series:</u>

- **The Temptress: Book One (Released August 2011)**

- A Corporate Feeling: Book Two

- Teach Me: Book Three

- How Santa Ate My Cookies: And Other Festive Tales of Erotic Fiction

<u>Available for purchase at:</u>

www.lulu.com, www.bandn.com, www.amazon.com

The Healer,

Part I

- Book XXI -

of

THE CHRONICLES OF AR SOLON

BY

RILEY S. BROWN

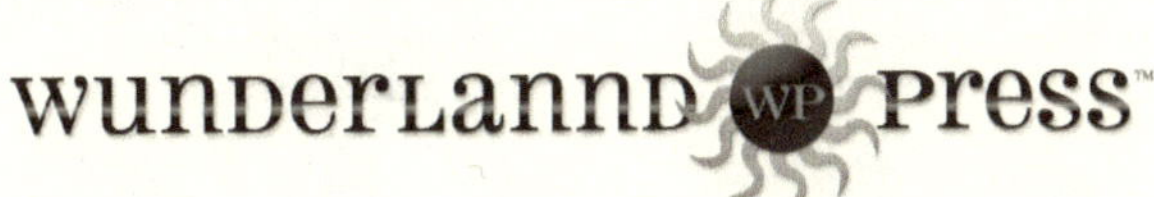

Published by Wunderlannd Press Publishing, LLC

Baltimore, MD

The Chronicles of Ar Solon

The Healer, Part I

-Book XXI-

Map of Kariyl and the Island of Dree drawn by Jawan Brown

Graphic Arts Conversion of Maps by Jennifer Street

Original Sketches by Riley S. Brown

Permission to be used and

Copyright © 2011 by Riley S. Brown

Cover Photo and Author's Photograph by Riley S. Brown

Graphic Arts for Front and Back Cover by Jennifer Street

Copyright © 2011 by Riley S. Brown

All rights reserved

"His father watched him across the gulf of years
and pathos which always must divide a father from
his son."

- John Marquand

Foreword

By Riley S. Brown

This is my first real novel that I've written in years. I started writing and finally finishing most of my old works, but what you are about to see within the following pages is a story that was created after Book XIX: Forgotten Angel was finished. A load of information fell upon me and I couldn't stop writing. Once I got the writing bug, I became engrossed in my work.

There were a lot of problems in my personal and professional life that made me turn to Forgotten Angel, made me complete her; however, once I was finished, I realized I had created another story in the process. This one was more close to home than the last one had been.

In this book, you will find shattered pieces of myself, a world that is dreary and dim yet there is always a light shining. Many times the light cannot be seen at that moment, but it is always there. When I walk through this story, I see that I find what so many around me have been going through over the years: never ending turmoil, battles with friends turned foes, love that blossoms out of the ashes and, finally, an inhabitant who is looking for their one, true purpose, and will not stop until they find it.

To me, this novel rings true that sentiment in many of the inhabitants that surface within this story; there have been so many people that I have known along my journey in life that have slipped and fallen along the way in theirs, on their own journey, looking for their grand scheme, that I feel it is important to show that in my novels.

I can't tell you why the grand scheme is so important in the novels that I write right now. It could be because, behind the eyes of everyone, I hope, there is a grand scheme waiting to get out; there is a purpose that drives them to do things they wouldn't normally do, to speak out against wrongs that they would normally tolerate everyday, to show the world as well as themselves that they are no longer afraid of what is before them and have conquered over what is behind, only letting it be a lesson to them and not their complete downfall.

My heart reaches out to those that have felt this way and I hope that you find your grand scheme the same as do some in my novels. Of course, as we pass through life, being inhabitants ourselves, we know that with the good must come the bad. I know that this is and will always be the case in stories, though the bad outweighs the good is so many cases that I have seen.

For a time, I even thought that much of what had become of me had gone away, never to return; yet, when I awoke the next day, a part of myself, the part that I thought I lost, had returned. Do not lose hope, inhabitants, you are merely on your own journey, though it be riddled with hardships, and you have the strength to find and defeat any enemy in your path.

The Healer

Now, onto the novel. When I began writing this novel, I was terrified that I had left so many of my characters in a bad predicament, that I had abandoned them in some way. Many readers that have finished my book Forgotten Angel were on the edge of their seat, as if I had set out to make Forgotten Angel a cliff hanger. Not the case. As I was approaching the end of Forgotten Angel, I knew that I couldn't give you (the reader) the package deal; you know, the nice, neatly wrapped novel that solves all of life's riddles and answers any and every question you may have had along the way in each inhabitant's journey. But, alas, as I was finishing Forgotten Angel, I was already laying out the groundwork for The Healer. In fact, one night alone created all of The Healer storyline. It was two pages of a single scene, something I had not expected to come to me. Once that single piece came, I knew that that scene was so powerful I had to begin the next book, the follow-up book to Forgotten Angel, and all other projects ceased to exist.

Once that single scene had been reworked during a brainstorming session, I saw the rest of it come together; I saw who was going to be taking their places on the writer's chess board. I saw the "good guys" in their bright armor and the "bad guys" with their grim visages and almost robotic smiles, waiting in the darkness for their chance to strike.

A little bit about Forgotten Angel...

There were moments of excitement for me as a writer when I finished Forgotten Angel; it being my first, real novel. I had toyed around with an older novel, The Temptress, and finished it, but it was for fun more than anything. But with this novel, I knew it was different. It was a journey for me as well. I had traveled across states, changed jobs, been married, finished three different degree programs and had another child, all the while toting this memory of Gabriella and her protectors with me for years.

I knew that, when I blew the dust off the story that I would have to continue until it was finally finished. I also knew that it wouldn't be a problem to finish it because I needed a distraction from the norm of the world for the moment. My first moment of excitement was, of course, receiving the first finished copy of my novel. I had mailed off for an incomplete one just to see what it looked like, but to see the completed one was something of a dream for me. To talk to others who had read my novel about my novel was something special for me, too. For years, I had not spoken to anyone that was familiar with the novel and so, it sat, without being a single conversation piece for almost five years. I had people ask about the novel but, sadly, there was no update. It was a solemn time for Forgotten Angel.

Like many stories that lay untold, they lose their luster, their light, their shine over time. I was scared that Forgotten Angel had done just that. Moreover, I felt that I had lost my writing prowess; what I had always held so near and dear to me ever since high school was suddenly dried up inside. Work, relationships, new responsibilities, career-minded goals for the future; all of this seemed to get in the way of me completing something special to me, something that had been special to so many others for so many years.

So, when I finally started to finish Forgotten Angel, I started where there was a place devoid of hope and happiness, where all life and light had seemed to vanish. I started back with Gabriella and where she lay on the continent of Kariyl and I tried to get back what I had lost so many years ago. It was not painful beginning the novel again after so long like many say; when you return to writing, it is like an old home that has been vacant for years. It holds all those memories; even though the smells and the sounds and the feeling of the warmth have disappeared, it still holds fast inside your mind, as if you never left.

In fact, the memories are the things that kill. It's not the world, it's not the people that undo the strength within you, but it is those memories that no one can take away from you that usually do it. Its not until you're sitting in a place with a person from a time long gone that you realize how far you've really travelled, how far you've come from where you left all those years ago.

It wasn't until I sat in front of my friends, Spencer, his mate Jennifer, and my friend Bobby, that I knew that I had done it. Bobby held the book in his hands and just looked at me with that approving smile; and Spencer, my long-time reading mate and friend of ages; he read the Foreword of the Forgotten Angel and grinned his little kid grin at me and I knew that I had done it. They needn't read the novel; what it contained had not been for them but because of them. All I needed from them was that reassurance that I had accomplished what was impossible for so many others.

I hadn't just sat at a computer and pounded out story ideas and pages or have characters slip in and out of conflict until I was tired and ended the novel; no, it wasn't that at all. It was something more for me, something much more important.

When you look at your realm of space that you inhabit and who you affect in the world, the time you have with everyone is so inexplicably short. To be able to bring something to your friends, your loved-ones, to the masses around you, it does something to you. I don't know about fame, fortune, glitz, or glamour, but I do know that recognition of something completed, not just a job well done, is something that is very hard to find in this world.

It's very rare that I get a chance to say how I feel so, in these few pages of the Foreword, I want to tell everyone something; not just what I told you in the Foreword in Book XIX, which was: Don't stop! This was, of course, in regards to writers writing and completing something within a reasonable amount of time. It's not just that. There's something more behind it.

While writing this second novel, with a small fan base chomping at the bit to follow up on the rest of the story I left out, I found an inner strength that I didn't think that I had. I had conquered the weakness of moments in the past, had fought tooth and nail with the proverbial "wolves" in the world around me. But I found that glimmer, that spark within me. In the moments of solitude and solace, I found understanding.

Of course, I don't mean the meaning of life or anything like that, but I began piecing things together, especially with this novel and its characters, and I saw what makes even the darkest personality shine, even the most tame soul stand up in defense for what they truly believed in once and for all time. And with that said, I want you to experience this also. I want you to see them how I see them. Enjoy this novel, for I have thoroughly enjoyed writing it.

Riley S. Brown

June 13, 2011

-in the comfort of my

1st home in Baltimore, MD

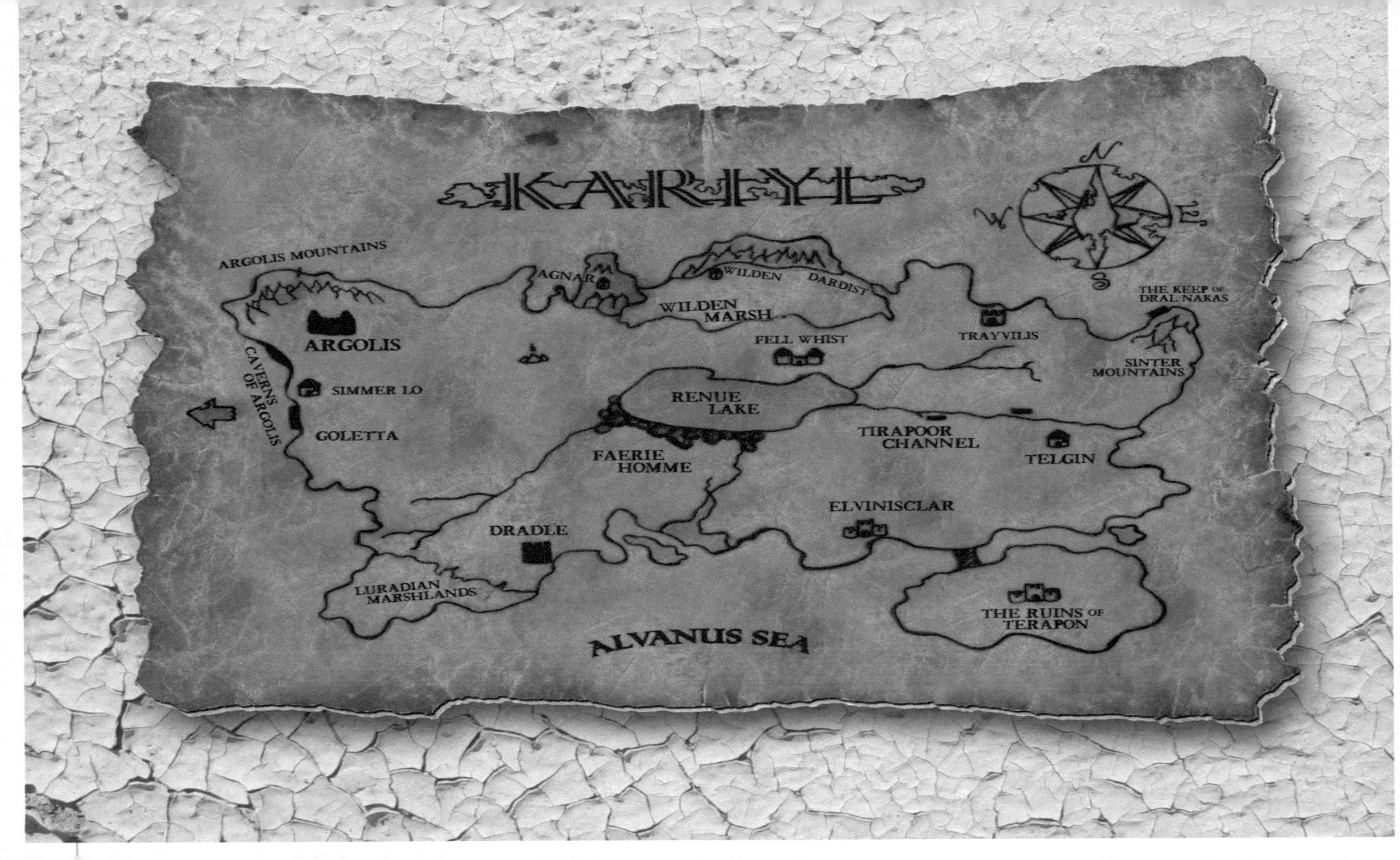

KARHYL
N
W E
S
ARGOLIS MOUNTAINS
AGNAR
WILDEN
DARDIST
WILDEN MARSH
THE KEEP OF DRAL NAKAS
ARGOLIS
FELL WHIST
TRAYVILIS
CAVERNS OF ARGOLIS
SINTER MOUNTAINS
SIMMER LO
RENUE LAKE
GOLETTA
TIRAPOOR CHANNEL
FAERIE HOMME
TELGIN
ELVINISCLAR
DRADLE
LURADIAN MARSHLANDS
THE RUINS OF TERAPON
ALVANUS SEA

ISLAND
of DREE
DRIDDEN TUR
LAKES OF ASH
PASS OF NARNIGGAN
ISLE OF BARTREESE
ISLE OF EMCRIST

THE CHRONICLES OF AR SOLON

-Book XXI-

THE HEALER

Part I

By

Riley S. Brown

Prologue

"There is no one left, Captain Tolver! You must do this! As a Knight of the Treaty, it is your responsibility to lead the soldiers into battle." General Klane stood in front of him now, the layout of the battle plan scribbled on the parchment in front of them. The three officers stared at the map of Kariyl for long moments, trying to decipher the best course of action.

Captain Crin Tolver just shook his head.

"I am not a soldier, General! I was not trained in combat, to lead those into battle, or force others to do so!" Crin slapped at the broadsword over his shoulder. "I have yet to fight with this blade. It was made as a symbol of peace to combat against a time of war."

The General interrupted. "And are you not combating at a time of war, Captain? Is your blade not sharpened and ready for battle like all the other broadswords that were given out to the Knights of the Treaty?"

Crin allowed his silence to be his response, to be his acknowledgement into the responsibility thrust before him. Without another word, Crin stood by as his orders were told to him, his mind collecting the information and storing it for when he stood at the threshold as was asked and to take part.

Three ten day had gone by since those moments in the tents and the battle waged on from the small towns down to the southeastern tip of Kariyl. Captain Crin Tolver lifted his gloved hand and moved the men forward. On the chilly, winter morning, he had been given orders to move his men onto the island which the ruins of Terapon lie and attack what remained of the goblin army that had been ransacking the smaller, less formidable towns.

It was a horror, Crin thought to himself; Telgin had been one of the towns attacked, the captain still remembering the cries that rang out when the goblin hordes rushed in upon them unknowingly. Now it was Crin's and everyone else's chance to fight back at the atrocities that had occurred only a few ten day ago, following the goblins here to their keep.

A familiar voice brought Crin back to his senses.

"See anything you like?" Kalir Ranolf, his brother-in-law, pointed over at the ruins that lay in the center of the island, protected from all sides by the precarious cliffs surrounding it. Kalir was the proud uncle of Crin's eight-year-old son, Ranyll and brother to Crin's wife, Rachel. The young man was just into his twenties and, like many budding fighters, wanted to have a chance at some real fighting instead of the staged pit fighting in Dradle that he had been known to do from time to time.

Soon, Kalir had retired his fighting title and come back to Telgin when he heard that The Knights of the Treaty had returned to service, the small army taking volunteers with fighting experience. Kalir had joined up immediately, however making his service request to be with Captain Crin Tolver as he led an army of 1,000 soldiers to Terapon.

This condition was accepted and both of them stood now, garbed in the colors of the Knights of the Treaty, the blue and silver banners flapping wildly overhead as the winds from the crevice around the island rose up from the Alvanus Sea.

The walled city of Terapon had been created as a symbol of peace centuries ago by a rich, elite family that had taken the political reins of several towns and created a new town with proper defenses if ever there were a problem with attacks. This had been a way of bringing the races together again, prior to the Treaty of the Races, yet it did not work.

Since there was still animosity between the races, trying to maintain peace within one area where three races still held grudges was nearly impossible. Soon, Terapon became a distant memory and all abandoned what it symbolized the most; hope. Now, rotting away yet still a formidable stronghold, the reject race of goblins had taken it over. There was only one bridge on which to cross and the captain and his brother looked out over it; the Katharsis Bridge.

The Katharsis Bridge had been created as one of the most formidable bridges of the age; artisans had been ordered to use remnants from old buildings that had been created with Parthenian bricks to make it. Many laborers had to go to the east and west coasts in order to find the rare Parthenian bricks that had been brought here another age ago, soon finding enough to work with and build the Bridge of Katharsis.

Many inhabitants believed that the head of the family that had begun building was a bit eccentric, a bit withdrawn, yet had come upon a fortune and wished to give back in every way possible. In one ultimate way, they tried to unite the races once and for all on a common ground. And that ground was on the island of Terapon.

It was said that, to walk across the Katharsis Bridge was an experience itself. And, from just looking at it, Captain Tolver could see why.

The bridge had become one of the wonders of all of Kariyl very quickly and very easily; only the towers of Trayvilis and Elvinisclar rivaling it in beauty. Of course, the dwarven cities below Kariyl and in the mountains were majestic, but true beauty they were not. No human had built anything so grandiose in Ar Solon; only the elves, dwarves, and Parthenians had the time and the craftsmanship to do justice to such a simple world. For a human to create such a beautiful thing and, for it to be just the entrance into a newly created site, was something of a feat in itself.

The bridge started simply enough; there were great stones several feet across that had replaced the simple earth of the cliffs for several hundred hands across the ground. To the sides of the stone walkway, even before entering onto the bridge, a small, stone rise had been built, only ten stones high, soon, building itself up to over twenty stones in just a few steps, small columns separating the heights until it connected to the bridge. Once connected, archways had been built, connecting the left column to the right, great carvings of the industry of trade and peacekeeping on each archway, depicting the flourishing of all of Ar Solon and how it came about. There were even carvings of dragons and great beasts from the past in some of the scenes, showing ancient times that many had forgotten.

As the bridge began, the depictions stopped altogether and many of the archways connected in various ways, not just one archway to the other, but a myriad of archways wove themselves across one another, only a skilled artisans hands able to do something so intricate yet still able to stand up against the test of time; which it had, its merely weathered appearance something of a miracle for such a long time that it had stood.

Crin only shook his head.

"I don't see anything I like so far, my brother. I'm trying to see a way across but I don't trust what I didn't make myself. The Katharsis Bridge has been here for years. Who knows it if can still hold the weight of an army. Anyway, I'm not letting a single file group of soldiers move across. That would be suicide for them. We have to go together or not at all." He paused for a moment, looking out and around the bridge itself, trying to see further down into the chasm where the great cliffs of Kariyl held the smell of the seas.

"There's no other way to cross except to build a bridge ourselves or climb down the cliffs and back up again; both will leave us at a disadvantage."

Kalir motioned back to the other groups that had gathered not far from them; the elves and the dwarven races; the elves just to the west of them were four hundred strong, many of them on horseback, giving them a chance at using cavalry if it came to a field war. The elves were dressed in the light armor of elven make; close fitting and very little breaks in the armor at all, limiting the enemy of any chance of finding a weakness. Their silver and white banners fluttered in the wintry morning air, their cold weather fur cloaks sheltering them from the bitterness of the cold as well as keeping their armor warm for battle.

The dwarves were on the opposite side of the battlefield, on the eastern side, three hundred and fifty strong, give or take a dwarf. They did not hoist colors or wear special armor that was made for battle. What armor they wore was what they battled and lived in. They were not in a constant state of turmoil, but they always prepared for the worst, something that Kalir admired about them. He had been around a great number of dwarves early on in his preparation for his trade, when he had been in training in Dradle. Many times, in the fighting pits, he would have to face off against a dwarf. He looked at their numbers, which were small in comparison to the elves and the humans, but knew that size did not matter. Even with their limited height, the dwarves were a strong and feisty bunch. And, from what he had seen in Dardist and in the caverns connecting, the dwarves had managed for themselves for some time without having to have help from the other races.

That says much more about their race than my own, Kalir thought to himself, looking at Crin as he discussed battle plans with the other captains not far from him.

"Do you think the other races might have any ideas about how to get over there?" No more had Kalir said the words then Crin had moved from the group of captains, moving on his own to meet up with the leaders of the other races.

Captain Crin Tolver, who seemed to be a man of the times for many that stood motionless, waiting for a sign to be urged forward into war, made his way over to the dwarven army first. He passed by the rows and rows of his own men, taking a sidelong glance at the snowy cliff that his men occupied. He had seen men before, *but never this many,* he reminded himself, trying his best to keep his eyes on the dwarven captains just ahead of him, standing on the rise of one of the hills near the cliff, their armor much the same as his own, noticing that the Knights of the Treaty armor carried with it the crest of the knights of old, a single gauntleted hand thrust up high, holding in its tightened hand a sword.

Crin patted the sword at his side and knew that it was an honor to have one of them, what the knights of old had cherished so much when finally getting to knighthood. What had been considered a show piece, the broadsword at the captain's hip had been transformed; cleaned, the stone in it replaced with a signet stone of the city from whence he came, almost remade into a war blade over night.

Originally, the blade had been dull at the edge and shiny across the flat of the blade, with a single stone set into the pommel to signify which order the knights had come from. Also, there was ancient writing on the fine blades as well, yet this had all been worn down over time and, as the blade was kindled again in the fires of the Argolis smiths, the writing had soon vanished and the blade then was made into a glass-like surface, which was then sharpened to a point, both sides of the broadsword coated in a glaze the elves had made for the smiths long ago to use on the honored blades of the knights.

Captain Tolver approached the three dwarven captains, his hand out to them almost immediately. The first of the dwarven captains shook it.

"Captain Glenfell Hammerheld, leader of the dwarven army."

Crin could feel the strength in the dwarfs' gloved hand immediately, trying his best to stay his hand until the introduction was done.

The other two dwarves, Delor Griptight and Findle Sharpstone introduced themselves as well and soon the conversation of alternative routes was underway. Glenfell began, his eyes always upon Crin's face, watching as the human took in what he was saying.

"I believe that the bridge is the only way across. In all my years on Kariyl, I've never heard of another way in or over to Terapon."

Findle nodded, his white beard nearly touching the ground as he looked to his captain. Findle was the oldest of the three dwarves that stood with Crin, the dwarf's brows, beard, and hair completely snow white. Even the dwarf's war braids, which were intricately woven with beads and small charms, matched the white of his hair. The wrinkles that creased when he moved his face seemed to cover his entire face from forehead underneath the great helm all the way down to his chin, which was barely visible underneath the white hair of his beard that was braided as well into a number of concentric knots that kept his beard flat across his chest and stomach.

Though he wore the garments of war, his light, blue eyes seemed to soften around the edges, as if the time of war within his body had lessened somewhat compared to the others around him, who still seemed hard and ready for battle.

Delor, however, fessed up.

"I know a way into Terapon without them even knowing we were coming through. Thought you'd never ask! Just thought you humans were going to do all the work for us dwarves!" He chuckled a bit through his thick, black beard; his eyes were alight with a fire from what, Crin could only finally discern, was the great dwarven brew of the North, something that dwarves had a tendency to drink before they went into battle.

To keep the edge off, that's what a dwarf had told Crin years ago when he had first heard of it. Crin had always known that dwarves had a tendency toward the drink since then, though he had always heard stories about them and their "ways" which he never believed until he saw it up close for himself.

It was always best that way, to know your friends, Crin thought to himself later as he walked back to his post at the head of the human army, passing his men again, their faces beat red from the whipping winds that drove up from the cliffs around Terapon, their eyes blinking at him in recognition at his movements, almost as if they could sense that they were about to move into place for the assault. With each step Crin took, he felt that there was an overall sense of impending danger; not like the other missions he had been given since he had been captain all those ten-days ago, but something different altogether.

Captain Crin Tolver had fought this goblin horde back and back and back until there was no other place for them to go but crawling back into the holes from whence they came, which the inhabitants soon found out was located on Terapon. Several of his rangers had come upon the tracks that led to the island off the coast of Kariyl, the goblins not bothering or caring to cover their tracks from anyone, not trying to hide or use surprise as an advantage. Sheer numbers and fear had been their weapons throughout the slaughters they caused and Crin, as well as many others that followed his leadership, felt that this was to be the last time a goblin would set foot on Kariyl without being dealt with.

It had been since before the War of the Races that a goblin had been reported on Kariyl and now, as if by the ancient magiks they appeared again, and in far greater numbers and force than before. Crin had read the histories and knew of their race's blatant disregard of life, using their hatred for the other races their driving purpose behind many of the battles that had been waged between goblins and the other races of Ar Solon. There was only one good thing about the situation that Captain Tolver was in; it was that he would be alive to see the end of the goblin race once and for all; he would never have to worry about his children dealing with goblins in their lifetime.

Already, Crin had tried his best to tame the nightmares that kept him awake at night, wrestling with himself and his responsibilities. He was hard-pressed into this service, he knew, but he kept in sight the image of his son, Ranyll, as well as his unborn child being safe from ever having to fight this kind of evil, that Ar Solon would be free of these kinds of creatures and his children could go on living in peace as he had done and how his own father had done until their grandfather had passed away years ago.

Let us hope that this plan of the dwarves works as well as they told us it would, Captain Tolver thought to himself, approaching his fellow officers, his brother-in-law Kalir standing in with them, his eyes focused in on what Crin was about to say.

"You must be joking, Crin!" Night had spread upon them like a thick blanket as Kalir moved away from the campsite and began pacing back and forth, away from the others for the moment.

Kalir didn't think it was a good idea to go to Terapon at night.

The idea of surprise is not something that the goblins cared about, let alone seemed to mind, he thought to himself, especially since they can see in the dark better than any dwarf.

They were practically raised in the darkness of the world, he concluded, making his way in the dark back to Crin's side, trying his best not to wake the several hundred soldiers lined up just outside Katharsis Bridge, waiting to move onto the bridge itself.

Kalir looked over to Captain Tolver, who seemed to be on the verge of freezing in his boots, the captain pulling his cloak over him as tightly as it would go, rubbing his gloved hands together. Many of the other officers were doing the same, huddling under their blankets for warmth or standing in a circle together, trying their best to keep the cold out and the warmth in.

Indeed, it was cold, Kalir thought to himself, who was only not yet cold due to the amount of brew that he had consumed before exiting his tent for the remainder of the night, his lips and tongue numb from the intensity of the spirits the dwarves had given him. There had been many talks of what lie ahead, across the bridge, what many say had been undisturbed for some time. Kalir was not in the least bit scared of what lay over there or what destiny had in store for him; he knew that he had gone through enough in his life so far he needn't worry about some pesky goblin horde to take him down. Sheer numbers would take him down, but not before he took as many of them down with him as possible.

'We shall use the element of surprise, fellow soldiers! I have word from the dwarves that there is an old secret entrance that has been undisturbed for some time and we can access the courtyard from there, then open the front gates and let the rest of the army in, penetrating their defenses in one, swift strike.' All this and more had come from Crin, which seemed more like a talk to boost morale than anything.

Kalir, however, did not see the resolve in Crin's eyes like he always did. *He doubts this plan*, Kalir concluded, the rest of his gear in hand, waiting for the attack to begin. Kalir, of course, had volunteered to lead with Captain Tolver the first wave of those to get into the courtyard, so Kalir had equipped himself well, yet left enough room on his light frame to move about during battle if needed.

Kalir had always carried a short sword at his left side, a dagger at his right. Lately, however, he had added a small hand axe that he had found on the battlefield. It had belonged to a goblin yet, when Kalir saw it, he took an interest in the primitive weapon. He had a harness made for it that kept it strapped up high on his back so he could slide it out from over the shoulder. That, with a length of rope and a small pack full of supplies, was all that he carried.

His leather armor was light, not like the thicker, metal-plated armor of the Knights of the Treaty, yet he still wore the colors of the Knights, covering most of the leather armor completely.

Captain Tolver motioned to the small group of twenty and they moved away from the rest of the group, Captain Tolver and Kalir the first to cross Katharsis. Their footfalls did not echo on the bridge nor did it make a sound but for the crunching of the soft snow as it began to fall all around them. The cold had somewhat hindered them, but as the snow fell, it seemed to give them additional cover as they moved the rest of the way across the bridge in small teams of four at a time, finally all making it across and on the ground against a slight rise in the land on the other side. They paused for only a moment, then disappeared into the snowy night, getting as close as they could to the fortification's walls without being detected.

The human archers looked up onto the walls and could see nothing, holding their bows tightly to their chests, poised and at the ready. There were five archers; one in each group of four, and their eyes scanned the walls as quickly as possible before the rest of them continued on.

Terapon seemed quiet, distant from the rest of the world on Kariyl. Every-so-often, Kalir looked back across Katharsis, only to see blankets of snow coming down, no soldier in sight on the other side.

They were too far to see us now, he reminded himself, tightening his grip on his short sword, which lay across his body, keeping it close so it would make no noise of any kind as he passed across the outer walls of Terapon's courtyard. He looked ahead of him through the snow falling and could see Crin moving across the wall, one hand against the wall, the other held his broadsword. He kept this close to his body as well, Kalir noticed, making sure it was at least an arm's distance away at all times.

Never know when you can get separated from it, Kalir reminded himself, noting now that the first corner of the outer courtyard walls had come into sight, Crin moving around it slowly once checking the other side. He motioned the others to follow and they did without question. Kalir could see Crin's well-placed steps in the dark even though the snow was swallowing up any thoughts of even ground that were allowed around them, making several of the groups slow a bit before finally catching back up with Captain Tolver and the first group.

Crin soon stopped completely and turned to the courtyard wall, placing his free, gloved hand in front of him, pointing at the markings on the wall.

"This is what they were talking about, Kalir. The dwarves said there were imperfections in the stones, that the stones had been reset in some way, showing an offset to the original stones that were made years ago. See," Crin pointed, "…where the lines do not exactly meet and they seem to pass one another without connecting. That is the place that we start."

Crin sheathed his broadsword at his side and felt at the surface with his gloved hands, trying his best to focus his eyes to see the wall in front of him.

Kalir dispatched all of the archers to watch the tops of the walls and set a group on each side of the remaining groups to scan for anything approaching from either side. Soon Kalir was back and Crin had his gloves off, his fingers deep inside a crack that had been found between the two surfaces. With Crin on one side, one of the other soldiers grabbed at the other side, slowly and as quietly as possible prying the space between the walls apart, a dark cavern way behind it.

Captain Tolver had made a decided stance when taking this upon himself, Kalir thought to himself, watching as Crin was the first to step in, lighting a torch within the cavern itself, soon bringing to light a darkened corridor that dissolved into darkness at the end on both sides. Captain Tolver then made another decision; he motioned to two teams to go south in the corridor while one team went north with his team, leaving one team to guard the exit route so they could make a quick escape if needed.

And Crin led the way. There was no doubt in his eyes this time, no sway in his movements. They were calm and exact; as they had been on the entire journey.

He had come to terms with his mission, Kalir concluded, looking past the captain to the darkness ahead, trying his best to find out if there was anything of substance within these walls besides more and more space.

The corridor was tall enough for all to stand comfortably and was wide enough for all to move through, one at a time, without touching their shoulders to either side of the corridor. It was hewn with smooth stone, the same as the exterior wall, yet the stones on the inside were not as smooth as the exterior of the walls had been. The coldness outside was gone for the moment and all in the corridor seemed glad of that, passing through to the interior of the courtyard within a few more steps.

The corridor suddenly ended with a large, wooden door that blocked exit out into the courtyard for what Kalir could see, noticing some of the courtyard through a small, square hole made in the door, level within eye shot of them.

The courtyard seemed empty as well, Kalir noticed, many random items littering the open space that Kalir was allowed to see before they extinguished the torch they had lit while traveling through the passageway, Crin handing it back to the others, the last man smothering the flame of the torch in the corner of the corridor, coming back shortly, his bow at the ready. Crin moved the archers to the front so they could cover the rest of the group, the two archers moving out first, taking cover positions behind medium-sized discarded items in the courtyard, soon motioning to the captain and the others.

It all seemed to go by so easy, Kalir thought, moving himself out into the courtyard with the others, his eyes scanning the landscape around him for any movement. There was years of items that lay littered upon the ground inside the courtyard, Kalir finding cover behind an old, dry-rotted wagon not far from the door, shoulder to shoulder now with Crin and another from the team. Kalir, once his back was against the wagon, could see the courtyard entry gate, the gate that opened up to Katharsis Bridge, his eyes scanning the ropes and pulleys that were tied to it as a counter weight to lift it up with ease.

They all seemed to still be in working order, Kalir noted, putting up his short sword, his hands now at the two long daggers secured on his belt behind him. He nudged Crin and pointed with one of his daggers at the entry way and Crin nodded, Kalir moving to the gate as Crin motioned to the archers to cover him.

In moments, Kalir was there, not bothering to stop and hide behind crates and vending wagons; preferring to just get to it and get it done.

I guess the goblins took refuge somewhere else, he thought to himself, stabbing his two daggers in the hard earth underneath his feet, his gloved hands grabbing for the levers to pull up the courtyard gate. It took a moment for the levers to lock into place, but soon the great courtyard gate began to make its way up ever so slowly, Kalir's muscles straining in his arms to keep the levers from emanating noises that would give away their position. As Kalir turned around he noticed that, throughout all of the courtyard, for as far as the eye could see, there were no footprints made, there were no clods of dirt upturned due to combined movement of a large force of creatures. It was as if no foot had tread on the courtyard in a dozen years or so.

Kalir had learned several things during his years pit fighting in Dradle. He had learned to parry a weapon and disarm and opponent without causing harm, had learned how to fight back to back with others while taking on over a dozen armed men at a time, this being done while full of dwarven spirits, and he had found that he had many ways that he could kill an opponent, and many without using a single weapon. But, in all his years as a pit fighter, he had never learned to be aware of one's surroundings, to understand and read the terrain around him. And he guessed that many of the volunteers in the group of humans that he was with didn't know how to do that, either, for no one said anything when he returned, his eyes wide with fear, his mouth ready to object to everything else they had decided to do all at once.

He looked at the captain with only the proper amount of concern one could give without being in a panic.

"I think something is very wrong here, Captain Tolver. The goblins did not come through here. They had another way in and it's not the entrance we took to get in. Either that, or they no longer reside in the ruins at all. We are misinformed or we are about to spring the biggest trap of all time."

*   *   *

Second Drez Fistarg, captain of the goblins, couldn't be in a better position for attack than the one he was in at the moment. Only moments earlier, he heard the courtyard gates just above his army of goblins screech open, meaning that there was about to be a small army about to enter, their enemy trying their best to finish what they started on the plains just northwest of here.

But they will get quite a surprise, Fistarg gurgled, a small layer of spittle dripping down his opened maw, issuing forth a stench like none other. The other races that had come in contact with a goblin were immediately in fear at their beastliness, at the purely grotesque features that a goblin seemed to have been inherited with. That is what had made the attacks on some of the bordering towns so successful. The sight of the goblins had sent many into a horrific state of fear.

The anatomy of a goblin was not that different than a human's anatomy; be it that that a goblin seemed to be made in the darkness and purposely misshapen in places that made its body disfigured. All goblins seemed to have a hunch to their gait when they walked, their shoulders jutting up high over their necks as their heads seemed to hang over the front of their chests, almost rolling back and forth across their chest whenever they looked from side to side.

Their green skin seemed to be as much the part of the goblin as the pale, almost marble-like perfection of the elven race's features. The deep-set fingernails that were jagged at the tips as well as the sunken, milky white eyes of the goblins had been something that they had acquired over time through their own progression while living in the darkness, foraging for food within the caverns below Kariyl that no other race would dare traverse. However, goblins were not so much different than the other races when it came to responsibilities and rank.

Fistarg had become captain of the goblins by default after the last Second Drez had been killed after being trampled by a horse trying to escape captivity from the humans. Fistarg was fine with that. He had been a Third Drez for many years, taking orders from Second Drez Belgur without complaint though he would have liked to have been the one to trample over him in the end.

It was a good and fitting end to Belgur, Fistarg had decided, taking the promotion in stride as he was given the remainder of the goblin army by the First Drez Melgoz, a goblin that everyone held in high respect. However, First Drez Melgoz was attending to other matters with the bulk of the army in the caverns below the mountains far in the west, so Second Drez Fistarg would have to rely on his own wits and talents as a leader to lead the goblins into victory. Having a scout come back with a report of the sheer numbers of the armies awaiting entry to the Ruins of Terapon didn't give him much hope in winning the battle, knowing his own numbers barely broke over one thousand.

But my goblins will use their abilities to fight these creatures of the light, Fistarg had agreed when the scout had returned, his eyes on the large casks of oil and the small barrels filled with a quick-acting poison not far from him.

Fistarg motioned to his second in command, Third Drez Mertok, and the goblin moved quickly over to his side. Second Drez Fistarg was a whole head taller than the Third Drez, but Mertok made up for his height with his thick form, which seemed to be almost double the size of Fistarg, who looked down at him with a command at his lips.

"Mertok, prepare your goblins! Have them use the poison; one shot and then move on to the next. Let the poison do its work!"

Third Drez Mertok nodded in response and moved away to prepare his goblins, which were amassed at the corner of the cavern entrance, not far from the courtyard entrance at all. There were a myriad of cavern entrances down on the shores of Terapon, yet there were so many open cavern ways, one could get lost if you didn't know the way. Third Drez remembered only days before making their way into the cavern entry way on Kariyl and down into the chasm that led their goblin army out at the cliffs, just a few paces from their own entry cavern into the caverns underneath Terapon, where many said that the one of the Emcrist had lain in its cradle, undisturbed until one of the faerie clan had taken it, splitting Ar Solon into shafts of its former self.

Second Drez Fistarg smiled, his lips cracking deeply in places from the dryness outside, small trickles of light green blood oozing out of his goblin flesh. He knew that the day would come when he would get his chance to prove himself. Today was that day. It felt good to be a goblin.

*   *   *

"Captain Tolver, we have our chance! Let us rid ourselves of this place and regroup with the others!" Kalir hated to look as though he was pleading in front of the others in their group, but he did not have time on his side. The sinking feeling in his stomach started to get worse as the rest of the army of humans filled into the courtyard, barely enough room for them all to fit, many of them beginning to take positions on the parapets, archers patrolling now the long walkways above the courtyards.

Crin sheathed his sword and began relaying orders back to the others in his army, sending a messenger out to the dwarven and elven armies on the hills just outside of Terapon.

"Kalir, I appreciate your concern, I do, but there's nothing here. There is no sign of the goblins coming through here. Besides, I have orders to occupy this place and I'm going to do just that!" Captain Tolver lifted his hands up to the others in the group and pointed to the northern end of the courtyard.

"I need groups five through nine to move through those doors and secure what is on the other side of those double doors. That must be the entrance to the city itself, to the main hallways and the trading areas of old, from what I am told by the maps we have. Once secure, send a messenger back with word. By then, the dwarven army should be on their way to assist."

The groups did as they were told and the shuffle took place, the four groups making their way to the great double doors on the northern side of the courtyard, just opposite to the entrance that they had come through.

There was a splintering of wood as the axes tore at the double doors, several men in the groups prying at the great door with all their might, using knotted ropes to tear the large double doors apart.

Captain Tolver turned back to his group and rolled out the rest of the map before his commanding officers.

"Since the courtyard is so small, we will have to wait until the double doors are open to bring the rest of our troops in. Once that happens, we will occupy the area and let the dwarves go down into the bowels of the city and clean them out while the elves stay on the parapets and occupy the remainder of the ground around the city so that nothing gets in or out without us knowing about it."

The rest of the command nodded in understanding; all except for Kalir. Kalir knew that he wasn't in any command, only a soldier, and knew that his opinion counted for very little among those elected as commanders of each of their garrisons.

Kalir had that sinking feeling in his stomach again, this time stronger than before. And then the cries began. It was a wailing of sorts, as of many crying out in pain, and Captain Tolver turned quickly with his leaders to see the doors erupt out into the courtyard, crushing a few of his own men under the weight of the splintered doors, sending many others onto the ground as well.

The first volley of arrows from the darkness inside the doors dropped a large number of men, those hit with the arrows screaming in pain as they tried to pull them free from their flesh, which seemed to make their skin wither on contact at the point of entry.

The wailing came from the darkness. And, from the darkness, came the first wave of goblins. They were covered from head to toe in ancient piece-meal armor, all carrying bows and several quivers of arrows that hung down at their hips.

"The first volley was only the beginning!" Crin reached down at his side and pulled the broadsword free of its scabbard, speaking more to himself, though Kalir could hear it echo throughout the courtyard and in his own head as he followed Crin's lead, his own short sword at the ready, picking up a nearby shield from a fallen soldier still shaking from the arrow as it rotted away the skin on his arm.

The wailing had become greater and more pronounced as the second volley of arrows hit their intended targets and a second wave of humans in the army fell before they could find proper cover from the attack.

But Captain Tolver stood, unmoving, his broadsword now held high above his head, a war cry in his throat.

"Men, stand fast! Hold your position and push forward. Archers, on the walls and counter those arrows! Move, move, move! All others, follow me!" And Captain Tolver, with one swift movement, lifted a shield up from the battlefield and positioned it in front of him and moved toward the oncoming hordes of goblin archers, watching as they pressed themselves into the courtyards, firing into anything that moved in front of them, another wave of archers coming out behind them as well, the movement now very limited inside the courtyard.

And all the hopes faded as a single noise penetrated through the battlefield; the metal screeching of the courtyard gates as they closed before the rest of the human army as well as the dwarves and elves could make it across Katharsis, the first wave of humans trapped inside the gates with the goblin army coming out to meet them.

Somehow, the goblins had gotten to the gate controls without us knowing, Crin thought, his eyes trying to focus on multiple enemies at a time, his broadsword dealing death all around him; not neatly, as everything else in his life has been, but scattered, without purpose. Captain Tolver climbed across the dead to meet his enemies, hacking and slashing where he could, plowing through the defenses of the archers with but a swing or a slam of his shield, splintering their bows and dealing a death blow before they could take out their close quarter weapons.

Kalir saw all of this at Crin's side, dealing his own death, working his own fluid form of magik with his short sword and misbegotten shield, soon closer to the double doors than he would like to be, his clothes and armor covered in goblin blood, his face flecked with sweat, blood, and bone. And that is when Kalir saw Crin fall, saw him lose grip on his shield and reach for the wound that opened up on his leg suddenly, trying his best to keep his sword swinging in front of him as he fell into the fallen corpses around him.

One

"You dare **not** challenge me?" Kalir looked across the table at the Happy Traveler at his guards, who sat, not a word passing through one of their lips as he gave his orders. This upset Kalir to no end. He slammed his mug down on the table to emphasize his anger more, which only made his men jolt in surprise. Due to the increased use of the Channel during the winter season, the clamor and bustle of the patrons around them made it hard for anyone to hear a single noise. And, on nights like these, the loudness of the patrons could be deafening. Kalir stared down the five checkpoint guards in front of him, trying his best to keep his composure.

If only Dir'grar were here, Kalir thought to himself. Yet Kalir had sent his friend off on an errand over a ten day ago and he had yet to return.

Tending to my sister and nephew while Ranyll was away should not have taken him that long, Kalir concluded, finishing his mug of ale in one final gulp.

"We have been a team for some summers now, right?" The guards nodded in agreement. "Then I expect more from you! It's not enough just to do as your captain of the guard says; if I say something that you don't agree with, then you must say something to me. Your lives as well as the lives of many others are at stake here; please do not let me be the only one that has words on this!"

Kalir lifted himself up from his seat at the table then, watching as his guards stood up as well out of respect, the captain of the guard grabbing his pack and other equipment, readying himself to be on his way.

During the last winter season, Kalir had been given the title and additional responsibilities of Captain of the Guard. It gave him the master responsibility of seeing over all of the channel checkpoints, namely the western checkpoints, where most of the supplies and boats lay stored away. Many of the council members of the checkpoints had tried to push this title on Kalir after he nearly single-handedly repaired the damage that had been done during the daemon outbreak four summers earlier, yet Kalir pushed aside the idea of being the captain of the guard.

Kalir knew what came with the title; he had always known. When Crin, almost too long ago to remember, had been given a title in the war, Kalir himself had been kept up nights worrying about what lay ahead for the soldiers that had enlisted for the Knights of the Treaty. Of course, he had been one of them, too, but he knew that Crin was a good man and a better leader; he would have followed him anywhere. Now, as he looked at his own men, his own path that he had to follow every ten day, he knew that he regretted taking the job.

But there was no one else to take the job!

In fact, many of the checkpoint guards had left after finding out about the daemons and the deaths of the guards of Checkpoint 19, Kalir remembering the day the bodies came washing down into his men's catch holds to Checkpoint 18, finding a raft with bodies on it as well.

It seemed as though responsibility is something that many do not want now, Kalir decidedly agreed, noticing that the blame for things in the last several seasons had been put upon those with the titles, such as the one that he had been given now.

Even petty squabbling between neighbors and friends had become somewhat troublesome. Kalir had not only been tasked with keeping the channel clean and the checkpoints at an acceptable upkeep level, but also solving petty problems in the towns where he stopped in to give inspections. Life on the Channel had become, in the last few seasons, more volatile than ever.

The crops and other goods to trade had become scarce due to the heavy snow that hammered the continent without remorse during their last few winter seasons.

Every season seemed to get shorter except for winter, Kalir concluded, looking outside now out at the thick blankets of snow that covered the ground around The Happy Traveler; thick layers of ice covering the Tirapoor Channel so it made crossing along it somewhat difficult.

Kalir had become accustomed to the change of seasons at the Channel in his years of service and had prepared adequate supplies for each season. However, now their supplies were more costly and the winter supplies needed to be doubled up due to the length of the season. If this didn't make it hard enough on Kalir, the fact that his right-hand man was nowhere to found only complicated things further.

Dir'grar was due back any day now and his nephew Ranyll had not been heard from in almost a full season; Kalir grew uneasy at this and spent the last few of his nights out on the porch of The Happy Traveler waiting for them both to appear. Of course, he had sent his good friend Dir'grar on his seasonal errand to assist with his sister Rachel and his other nephew Tim. Dir'grar rarely took any time off from The Happy Traveler so Kalir felt it necessary to give his friend something to do throughout the seasons. Along with this, Dir'grar was able to transport goods from the channel to other locations east and pick up any supplies on the way back.

This had been happening for the last few years since Ranyll had left home, Kalir hoping to maintain a further connection with his family in Telgin, yet still wanting to keep distance from his sister.

He couldn't bear to see the look on her face; almost ten summers had gone by, yes, but the look he had seen in her eyes had haunted him that long and continued to do so.

It was the look of loss.

After the goblin horde had been disposed of at the Siege of Terapon all those years ago with Crin, Kalir returned to Telgin with so many others in tow; yet many of those in tow were hauled in bulk and in wagons. Many of the townsfolk called them the wagons of the dead, which had been a saying used years ago when the plague spread by goblins tore through most of Kariyl. Many died from it but those that didn't continued to live on with ailments and deformities. No one knew how it spread from the goblins or how to stop it; even the best healers and most potent potions could not stop the plague.

Crin Tolver and many other volunteers from Telgin had been hauled back to their hometown in Telgin. Rachel was there when the wagons came in, pregnant with a second child, Ranyll close by her side. Kalir had trouble looking her in the eyes. And, when he did, the pain in his sister's eyes cut him to the bone. He didn't want to have to see those eyes again; neither from Rachel nor from his nephew Ranyll, which seemed to be rapidly approaching due to the fact that Ranyll seemed to take on the whole of Ar Solon at once.

Kalir still remembered the night, almost a full year ago, when Ranyll came to The Happy Traveler, bloodied and bruised. He watched as Taleena bandaged Ranyll up, sewing him up as well from a deep gash that had been torn into him, Kalir throwing the bloodied clothes away. Ranyll had been delirious, calling out places

and names of people Kalir had only heard about but never seen.
The one name that Kalir did know of, however, was D'meir.

Though he had never seen a fire fox, Kalir had been told the
story of D'meir by Ranyll when he resided at the Happy Traveler
with him for the first few summers after their ordeal in the caverns
of Dardist. His nephew had told of the magikal creature and how
it had given him gifts, abilities that he had never known of before.
Kalir had seen one of the gifts that the magikal fire fox had given
his nephew in action that night in the caverns all those years ago;
though the dwarven passageways were dark, Kalir could see clearly
within the confines of the caves when he approached Ranyll that
night with the others of his guard at his side.

The broadsword that Kalir had given Ranyll had lit up, as if by
magik, a white-blue flame encircling the blade, Ranyll holding it out
at The One, daring the being to move toward the angel, Gabriella.

Yes, Kalir concluded, *a great gift had been given to him by this creature
D'meir.* Kalir wondered now what Ranyll had up his sleeve; and he
also wondered if it would save the world around them.

So much had passed in that short amount of time, Kalir felt it
difficult to remember the parts and which order they came in;
somehow, the world slowed down during that time. But there was
one thing that Kalir did see amidst the chaos and confusion; one
thing that Kalir saw that he never would forget; the look of loss in
his nephew's eyes the same as Rachel's that night when the angel

Gabriella died. Kalir hoped that the loss in Ranyll's eyes would be the last he would see, but the grown man knew better.

There would be much more loss before this year is up. I can feel it, just the way I felt the dread in that courtyard all those years ago. Something is coming, I know it. And it is far worse than any goblin army would ever be.

*   *   *

The wind and snow had become an obstacle to the lone figure out in the wintry wilderness, which could hardly be called wilderness since nothing wild seemed to be out in this type of weather.

Probably somewhere safe, the figure thought, the gloved hands pulling tighter the thick winter cloak around his snow-covered shoulders.

He has to be here, the lone figure thought, looking ahead through the thick snow to the small glimmers of life that could barely be seen in the snowstorm. Somehow, the snow seemed to cover all of Kariyl at once.

Lanterns ahead, the figure hoped, trying to keep himself steady, though his legs, up to the knee, had gone numb several steps back. The only thing that he could feel were the flakes of snow that rained down on his forehead and in his eyes and the wind that attacked at every exposed part of his flesh, which wasn't much, though it did take a toll on the warmth he had tried to create around himself. The small village laid just a few hundred more steps and the thickly garbed figure feared for a moment that he would not make it. Standing still for a moment, he tried his best to remember the faces in his mind that helped him continue forward.

In moments, there they were; the eyes, the smiles, the tears, the pleasure, the confidence, all came flooding into his mind. He knew what he had to do, had known for some time, yet he had wandered. Like many of the other inhabitants, he had let time in Ar Solon take its toll on his mind and body. The figure had let his time slip away, had let life take him on a detour, moving him away from what he needed to do. He had trained, yes, but for what he didn't know.

There's always a reason for it, he concluded, leaning on the walking staff in his gloved right hand, making what progress he could with the energy that he had left, hoping that the faces would help him along a little more, make him pursue what he knew to be true just a little bit quicker.

To find the truth, that is my purpose. Ranyll knew it to be so. He plowed through the snow and the storm, soon finding the village he was looking for, what he had seen in his dreams only a ten day earlier.

The only way that he knew that this was the village in his dream was from the lull in the valley ahead of him; he had seen this covered in snow, had known that the valley held the village and that the village held answers. Ranyll could feel the weight of the pack on his back, the tome he was carrying nearly the entire weight of the pack itself.

If there is to be more, then let it be done here. I have nothing else I want to see. The human looked up into the clouded world, though he could only see the shifting snow above him as it caught in the wind that whipped at his very core. *Please let this be the final one... I have no need for all of this...I have enough to see inside my own mind....my own visions.*

In the last few summers, Ranyll had left his family to find answers. He had traveled much of the continent of Kariyl, even venturing onto elven territory in Elvinisclar and Trayvilis, keeping counsel with the elders that would see him there. It had been some time since he had seen an elf; even the elves he had seen long ago during his childhood he had never really considered to be true elves. They had been outcasts from their elven race, slowly but surely adopting the other inhabitant's culture around them until what they had been disappeared from sight and they became just like the many others around them. What they had once been seemed to vanish.

However, what Ranyll had seen within the city walls of both Elvinisclar and Trayvilis was something altogether different. He had never seen the customs or rituals of the elves and had never thought he would. But, as he had been accepted as a guest into the home of an elder, he soon grew accustomed to the very strange, almost cult-like aspects of the elves' lives. And what he had seen when he got there, what his purpose was while he was there was….disturbing.

It took Ranyll several long strides to pass through the two lanterns and down into the valley where the small village lay, using his walking staff to test the snows' depth before continuing forward. He could still feel the pain in his leg at his last error and how it had almost cost him his life.

That was too close, Ranyll reminded himself, remembering the fall he had taken a couple of villages back when he had tried to hike ahead without testing the depth of the snow. Now he knew better. Ranyll limped forward, his eyes on the small structures that made their way into his sight as the snowstorm lessened the deeper he got into the valley, watching as the snow drift he was traversing through began to rise up to his waist.

This is ludicrous, Ranyll agreed, remembering a friend who had said that to him not long ago. At this moment, the human agreed.

The snow drift began to make it up to just beneath his armpits and Ranyll had to clear away some of the snow in front of his face with his walking stick, his legs aching from moving almost out of habit, yet the muscles seemed frozen from the waist down. He could see the tops of the structures just ahead of him coming into view and, in another moment, the snow drift just ended, dropping down almost completely to the ground level. Ranyll knocked the loose snow from his shoulders and pack on his back with his staff and looked around, most of the snow cleared around the structures, which were small cottages, Ranyll noticed, after he had a moment to look around. There were small braziers that were hung near the ground next to each cottage entrance that held white hot coals, the barren ground showing beneath in a few places, Ranyll trying his best to keep himself standing.

He noted now that the snow had been holding him up through much of the trip here from the last village and, now that he had to support his own weight, his legs refused to help. Ranyll tumbled to the ground, letting his walking stick hit the ground not far from him. The ground rushed up to him and he was pleased to meet it. His eyes closed for a moment and then refused to open again. They seemed to be as frozen as the rest of him, yet his eyes felt dry and stuck to the insides of his eyelids.

Though the snow was cold as his body lay on it, Ranyll felt comforted that he could finally stop for a moment; that the journey had not killed him after all like the last few villagers had said it would.

When I get a chance to go back, I would have to tell them. Not far from him, Ranyll could hear footsteps crunching quickly across the snow. In another moment, he heard voices.

"Mother, come quick! There's a man fallen on the snow from the other village!" Another voice answered back.

"Flip him over so he doesn't freeze to death! Bring him closer to the heating lantern until I get there with the blankets."

A set of footfalls moved away and Ranyll felt himself being flipped over onto his back, his pack and broadsword strapped across his back making it difficult for the person to help him over. Soon, he could feel the pack on his back being removed but Ranyll was too weak to protest. His arms tried to move but the voice urged him to remain still. Then Ranyll could feel the scabbard on his back being moved as well. Reflexively, he reached back and held it at bay, with what strength he had, he did not know. He shook his head.

The voice seemed to understand. Ranyll's eyes tried to adjust, but all he could see were his eyelids, which still held glimmers of the light that he had seen from the braziers when he entered the village. He strained his voice to speak.

"Water, I need water!" The voice responded quietly, leaning in close to hear him.

"It's not a good thing to give you water right now, sir. Just you wait until my mother gets here. She'll take good care of you. She's the best at these things, that's why they moved her to the cabin at the entrance of the village. She will have you good as new, sir. You'll see." Ranyll nodded without speaking again, trying to take in what details he could of this voice, yet he could not tell whether or not it was a boy or girl. Apparently, the child was only several summers old and not very wise in the ways of Ar Solon.

Ranyll soon felt his body being moved across the snow to a warm brazier not far, his face and hands beginning to feel the warmth from it. In moments, Ranyll could feel the exhaustion overtake him and sleep followed shortly after.

2

That night, Ranyll dreamed. He had had glimmers and pieces of what he could call dreams, but one who knows dreams would simply call them visions. Not many inhabitants would know that, though. In the last few summers, not a single inhabitant had dreamt a dream. After the death of the angel of dreams and visions at her own hands, the inhabitants of Ar Solon slept restlessly. However, the one inhabitant that could dream, the one that did dream, dreamt dreams enough for many inhabitants besides just himself. That one inhabitant, Ranyll Tolver, shifted in his place on the bed that night and for another full night following his arrival at the small village of Sift.

He could not shake it off; the feeling of despair in the village. Something had brought him here. And that something took hold of him now. He remembered the power of Scarwol within the caves of Dardist and knew what the creature was capable of, yet this was not that creature. It was a dream. It was the same dream he had had for the last few ten day. With every place that Ranyll went, this dream seemed to fit itself, seemed to find him and place itself between him and his present course. Yet there was something behind it as well, something more that it wanted to tell him but couldn't. The dream was like a man yelling in a thunderstorm, seen but not heard, noticed but not completely warned by his presence. Ranyll let himself fall into his dream, let it take him over.

He could feel it here; the plague. It came at him, writhing and wrestling with him like the Fog Beasts in the caverns of Dardist all of those years ago. Yet, the plague here did not take a form. It drifted towards him, covering the village in a thick blanket of white, soon turning red, like flakes of blood raining down upon him. The sky spit out the smoldering red and it overtook the village without warning. Ranyll watched as his own flesh was devoured by the red snow, his arms flailing in brief response to the pain and then thrashing about to free himself of the death that overtook him as it splashed across his body in broad strokes, the painter of death using Ranyll's body as a canvas.

Ranyll felt himself hit the ground, covered in red snow, the white snow around him soon being transformed into the same red snow, the blankets of white snow around him now stained with a coat of red. He looked around him, watching as well as the white snow that had been almost as tall as he melted before him, uncovering what had always been there all along; the entrance.

The entrance was simple enough; hand-sized paving stones were packed tightly together, forming little sets of rounded teeth that sat side by side, so many of them showing little imperfect mars across their surface, many chipped and cracked from years of time and age. The entrance was made up of a simple set of columns, three in a row, old ropes sagging in between each set, ushering any in who came. It seemed as though it were a side entrance into what once had been a great city at one time.

Ranyll felt himself drift in and out of sleep, trying his best to retain his composure within the dream, his hands reaching out, searching in the darkness for…. his sword. In another instant, the sword was at his side, in his hand, whether he grabbed it or someone handed it to him, he did not know. All he knew now was that he had control of the vision at that very moment.

He was on a shore, on an island full of ancient secrets and tales that were lost and never recovered. He could feel the waves take him forward and, as he looked down, there was a boat under his feet. It was old and seemed as though it hadn't been used in some time. There were small puddles of water forming under his feet and he reached for the oars so that he could bring himself in on the island ahead of him before the boat filled the rest of the way with water.

As Ranyll lifted the boat out of the water, wading through the sea foam that caught at the sand and drifted its way back into the water, he noticed the ruins. They started at the water, nearly a dozen short stones protruded from the water. It looked, at first, like the ocean rocks that guarded the shores Ranyll had seen before on the eastern shores near Telgin when he was a child; but these were somewhat different. Upon closer inspection, he noticed that they were manmade and they were placed in a neat line across the sand. The ocean rocks were not small; they were nearly the size of Ranyll, just a head or so shorter, Ranyll using one of them as an anchor to tether his boat to; he threw a knotted rope around one of the ocean rocks and tied his boat down, pulling the rope taut so that the boat wouldn't damage itself when the tide came in and out.

Ranyll felt himself jolted awake. There was a firm hand on his shoulder and, in another second, the hand shook him soundly. His eyes fluttered open and he saw a dry, wind-whipped face of an older man staring at him. The man's cracked lips opened to speak.

"Man, wake! Awake, stranger!" Ranyll lifted himself up onto his elbows and scooted back onto the bed to give himself space between him and the man. It was nearly mid-day, Ranyll could see from outside, the light still high in the sky as the sun reflected off Ranyll's sword, holding it out at the man next to him. Ranyll let the blade catch the sunlight and glint once more before speaking.

"Is that how you would wish to be woken by a stranger, sir? Being shaken and told to wake?"

The older man, a little shocked, moved away from the bed in which Ranyll slept, holding his hands up non-combatively, his palms out to Ranyll. The old man's voice crept out of his mouth again, this time a little less urgent and a little more respectable.

"My apologies, stranger. It's just that we have not seen nor heard from the outside villages in some time. You are the first we have seen in a few ten day."

Ranyll lowered his sword and sat up, putting his feet on the ground, the floor ice cold, his boots having been taken off during his sleep. He sat his sword in his lap and stretched his aching limbs. For a change, it was good to feel his feet. They were cold, yes, but they were not numb nor did they retain damage from the cold, which was good for Ranyll since he did not have a horse to travel with.

"There are other ways in which to wake someone. Who is the child that took care of me last night? The child and her mother."

"Yes, stranger. The child is my niece, Debbs, and her mother, Tira, is my sister. I am Talkan and…." the man, Talkan, hesitated, "may I know your name, stranger?"

"It's Ranyll, Ranyll Tolver." Ranyll slipped his boots on, tying them up tightly so that the cold would not get to his feet again. He lifted himself up and, finding his pack as well as his other things; he moved over to them, sheathing his sword back in its scabbard. It was chilly in the room that they were in yet Ranyll could feel warmth somewhere, smell the wood burning in a room adjacent to this one.

Talkan continued his questions.

"Are you the healer?"

Ranyll stopped short in what he was doing, his left hand moving up to the scar on his forehead, within the front of his hairline, then apprehensively to the handle of his sword that sat near him without Talkan knowing.

"A healer, why do you ask that?"

Talkan took a few steps closer to Ranyll. Ranyll's hand tensed on the handle of his sword as he waited for an answer.

"Our village had sent a messenger out to the surrounding villages for a healer and we have yet to hear back from our messenger. We hoped that he had gotten the message out and a healer had been sent. Are you the healer?"

Ranyll's grip loosened on his sword and he put the rest of his garments on, noting that they had been washed by a gentle hand. Ranyll grabbed the remainder of his things, the pack being slung over his back, and turned to Talkan.

"Yes, I am a healer."

They moved their conversation into the other room, the living area, that had a fireplace that was lit and burning well, a bubbling pot hanging over the flames in the mid-morning light. There were several simple chairs in the living area and a thick fur rug of an animal draped in front of the fire, the girl Debbs resting on it, watching the fire lick at the snow on the logs that had just been brought in from outside. Debbs was indeed a young girl, only eight or nine summers old, Ranyll noticing her curly locks hanging from her head, her blue eyes sparkling as she looked into the fire.

Tira was busy bringing in the remainder of the wood for the cooking fire, a thick coat and gloves covering her from view. Once inside, she pulled the small sled loaded with wood directly to the fireplace, motioning to Talkan and then to the door.

"Can you get that, brother?" Talkan moved for the door, his hand reaching out to close out the perpetual blankets of snow that seemed to show just outside the cottage and most of the surrounding areas on the continent. Ranyll shivered in his warm clothes at the thought of having to go back out there.

Tira nodded politely to the awakened visitor, pulling the sled the remainder of the way to the fireplace, Debbs hopping up from her place on the floor to assist her mother. Tira smiled at Ranyll and began to feed the fire, the flames hissing when the snow hit them, the flame dying down momentarily then back up in another second, eating hungrily at the dry, frozen wood beneath.

"Oh, I see you are awake, sir! It's good to know all that care was for something, eh?" Tira continued to feed the fire all the while speaking to Ranyll, her eyes drifting to him every so often.

"Yes, Tira, thank you for your kindness. It's hard to find charity like that around here during these trying times. It is much appreciated."

Tira nodded and moved away from the fire, letting Debbs finish unloading the rest of the wood off the sled next to the fireplace, soon retreating back to her spot on the fur rug after pulling the empty sled back to the door.

Talkan piped up.

"And it seems as though it's the fate of the Creator, too, Tira. Ranyll here is the healer that we sent for. He's going to help us."

Tira's face changed almost instantly when she heard this. She moved somewhat closer than normal to Ranyll, her eyes looking deeply into his, her hands grasping at his own in nervous excitement. She seemed to forget what she was in the process of doing and focused only on him.

"Is it true? Are you a healer?"

Ranyll nodded. Tira pulled his hands close to her mouth and kissed them, squeezing them tightly into her own.

"You must come with me then! You must come with me to see my husband! I'm sure you can help! I'm sure of it!" Tira's voice drifted off from the idea of hope to desperation in a few short words and Ranyll could sense the uneasiness of Talkan and Debbs who had stopped what they were doing as well to stare at Tira who had Ranyll's hands in a near-death grip.

Talkan stepped in.

"Tira, I think the man would like a good meal and maybe a warm bath, would you not Ranyll, before taking a hike back out in that cold to go see Ardris?"

Tira's brother moved closer and motioned to Ranyll to take a seat at the nearby table next to the door where a collection of foods were laid out to eat. Ranyll felt the hunger shift inside of him and it seemed that he could eat the entirety of what was on the table, which was quite at bit; however, the name Ardris seemed to intrigue him a bit more than the offer of nourishment at the moment.

After all, Ranyll had come to the village of Sift with a purpose. He was intent on keeping it, no matter how much he was offered or warned to do otherwise.

This Ardris person might be what my present visions are about. Ranyll grabbed half a loaf of bread from the food in front of him, grabbing several pieces of fruit as well as a few slices of cheese.

"Tira, do you have any meats cooked yet?"

Tira came out of her intense gaze for a moment and turned, pointing to the pot that hung simmering over the fire, which seemed almost to blaze to life as they spoke. The wood Debbs had thrown in was fully engulfed and, for a moment, Ranyll looked at Tira and saw what he thought he had seen in her eyes when she first walked in; a well-hidden dread.

She nodded and moved to the table, grabbing up a bowl from the plates and other utensils lying on it, moving with a purpose to the pot, ladling out a few servings of the soup she had made earlier. She walked back over to the table next to Ranyll, placing the bowl down before him, her eyes becoming intense again within moments of delivering his meal.

"It's lamb soup. We have very little to offer you, I'm afraid. Meat is in short supply but we are happy to help wherever we can."

Ranyll had seen it before in the eyes of the townspeople and villagers that he had visited the last few summers ever since the dreams had stopped with the inhabitants around him. At first, it was the restlessness that he encountered; then the small parades of those that felt the exhaustion of time without dreams would approach him, trying their best to find a way to retain thought and continue on with their daily duties. Ranyll never knew that such a simple thing as dreams could affect towns and villages so easily.

But it did. And, when it did, it was something horrible to see. Ranyll turned to her and put out his hands to her, taking her hands in his own. Ranyll kept the seriousness in his demeanor as he spoke.

"Let us go see this Ardris of yours, Tira. After all, you saved my life. I am indebted to you somewhat and will not deny any request that you make." Ranyll looked at Talkan and Debbs. "After all, I am the Healer that you requested." Tira wrapped up what she had prepared for Ranyll into a small piece of cloth and tied it tightly, placing it into a basket with another serving of the same food.

Tira nodded and grabbed Ranyll's walking stick that was sitting next to the door.

"Shall we go?"

Ranyll grabbed his thick set of garments and began layering himself for the intense cold outside.

Ranyll saw it the moment he looked into Ardris' eyes.

The snow had slowed him and Tira somewhat at getting to the village jails, but they had made it with Tira's sense of direction in the village. Soon, they were inside a small, dimly lit stone building that consisted of a fire pit in the middle of the room and several cots for the guards to sleep on.

The guards nodded when they saw Tira and led her and Ranyll to a door that opened to a basement of the building, the cells for the prisoners located in small cells with a bit of hay and some blankets for warmth. Through the metal bars, Ranyll could see shadows of prisoners. Yet, one prisoner stood out. Ardris, with a blanket over his shoulders, sat staring at them as they entered, leaning his blanketed head against the bars, his hands holding tightly to the bars that held him there.

Ranyll could see in the man's eyes that it was there; the plague that he had seen before. The poor man, Ardris, looked in his forties and to be in good health otherwise. He did not have ailing vision in those dirty, brown eyes and seemed in a somewhat healthy temperament. He stared at Tira as she walked in, nodded once, but kept his eyes fixed on Ranyll's covered form, trying his best to see into the cloak for the new visitor's face.

When Ranyll pulled the hood from his cloak aside, the wildness in Ardris' eyes seemed to coalesce on Ranyll's existence in the same building as he. Ardris gripped the bars tightly in his hands and shook his cage violently.

It looked as if Ardris wanted to say something but couldn't.

Tira moved closer to him and pulled out a loaf of bread from her basket, which she offered him. His dirty hands broke free from the grip they had on the bars and clung to the loaf, ripping it free from her grip, the loaf breaking into pieces as he tried to get it through the bars. He pressed the first few pieces in his mouth and chewed hungrily.

Tira looked to Ranyll. "He hasn't spoken in some time now. In the beginning, all he did was speak, talk about things that haven't happened yet, talk about the end of all the inhabitants as we know it. Say that the Creator hated us, that is why we have to go through so much in our brief lives. After a while, everyone got tired of hearing it. Even the prisoners down here would begin to complain. Ever since then, he's stopped talking completely."

Ranyll just stood for a long moment, watching as Ardris ate the loaf of bread and whatever Tira had left to offer, the man on the other side of the bars never taking his eyes off his new visitor while he ate. Soon, Ranyll sat down a distance from the cell and reached into the basket for his own food, sitting all of it on a small burlap bag that he used regularly, watching Ardris intently as well.

When Tira turned to speak to Ranyll, he simply reached his hand up to her, handing her the empty basket.

"I will need to be alone with Ardris for a while." Tira looked over at Ardris and back to Ranyll, who was eating the remainder of the stew Tira had fixed him, cleaning the wooden bowl out with a piece of bread he had torn from the loaf he had been given. Lines of doubt crossed over her brow but Ranyll continued in his request.

"I'm sure. I'll be fine, don't worry. And so will Ardris. But we need to be left alone. Please let the guards know this also."

Tira nodded silently and took the empty bowl from Ranyll's hand as well, placing it in the basket, her footfalls loud in the impending quiet of the cells around them. Ranyll heard her footfalls for a moment and then they stopped altogether.

"Thank you, healer!" Ranyll could hear Tira's whisper carry through the hallway to his form still sitting on the ground across from Ardris' cell, her footfalls continuing the rest of the way up the stairs and soon Ranyll could hear the door behind her close, the guard going back to his post to relax.

Ranyll could hear the others in the cells around him, too. Ardris wasn't the only one in there. There were two others. One was asleep and snoring lightly in the cell on the left, just next to Ardris, while the other figure was on the far right side of the cells, his eyes a bright white in the dimly lit room as they stared out at Ranyll, watching him eat the food he had in his lap.

The man in the cell, a dingy, grimy form that resembled a man at one time, looked out through his black and grey beard, his hand thrust out through the bars, a single finger pointing to the food in Ranyll's lap.

Ranyll looked at the figure on the other side of the bars and spoke.

"You want some of this food my downtrodden friend?" The form shook his bearded head and tried to reach further with his one hand, his arm up to the shoulder now, jutting out at Ranyll.

"Yes, stranger. I would like some....would like some a great deal! Anything that has flavor to it would be of a delight! Could you spare?"

Ranyll stood up and walked over to the figure and handed him what remained of his fruit and several small wedges of cheese. The figure took them gratefully and devoured the fruit in an instant, taking his time with the wedges of cheese.

Ranyll looked to Ardris then, watching as he stared as well, *and had been staring*, Ranyll noted, Ardris looking hard at Ranyll before he finally spoke.

"Stranger, do you know of the end of Ar Solon?"

Ranyll paused before speaking. He took his time to answer this question. In fact, he reached for his pack, which was not far from him, and pulled out the great tome and his items for writing, sitting the book down in front of him.

"Let us not be strangers, Ardris." Ranyll then reached out his gloved hand to man in the cell who, in turn, shook it, and sat back in his cell.

"My name is Ranyll Tolver. I was told by Tira to come see you. She says you have visions that no one else can see. Is this true?"

Ardris nodded and pointed at the tome in front of Ranyll.

"Is that for you to record the information I give you?"

"It is, Ardris. It is also for me to record my own visions. I see visions as well, my friend. So many that I must have this tome to keep them in."

With that, Ardris' eye grew wide. His hands clamored for the bars that held him and began twisting his hands over and over again on the bars.

"Then you do know of the end of Ar Solon!"

"I do, Ardris. I have seen a number of visions many times in the last few summers. Much of it is symbols, something I've been trying to decipher and interpret for some time. So far, I have done well. As for the end of Ar Solon, what have you seen?"

3

Falwen Sanse closed the Agnar Guild shutters to the large writing room that afternoon, watching as the snow came down in thick layers, blanketing the dwarven village he was in within moments. He looked out through the last set of shutters and took in the simple dwarven village that had been made to fit the simple lives of the writing guild nestled deep within the Agnar Mountains. It looked nothing like what he had known most of his life.

No lake, river, stream or ocean shore could be seen or heard. The dwarves even drew their water from a well far from the village itself, a simple twenty hands across well that had been dug away from the village so there would never be a dry well sitting in the middle of the village, which would make quite an eyesore if it had ever happened.

Falwen sighed a bit, barely remembering the strong smells of the ocean and the shore since his grand scheme had brought him hear nearly four summers earlier. He continued on with his duties.

The dwarven scribes that he had worked with earlier that afternoon had retired to their own daily duties and, since Falwen had stayed in the large writing room by himself, the responsibility to lock up for the night fell upon him once he was finished.

Finished wasn't the word, the scribe thought to himself. He looked down the long rows of writing desks, passing by row after row to check to see if anything was out of place.

Just getting started is more like it.

Indeed, Falwen could feel the story come to him now, felt it stronger since he had stopped his writing duties moments earlier, the story taking the chance to take over Falwen's thoughts completely, occupy his mind totally, the images coming to him in flashes. The Chronicler stopped for a moment and steadied himself at a nearby writing desk, closing his eyes to get the complete story all at once.

Images of those that he knew sprang up into his mind, his heart almost jumping into his throat. He kept his eyes closed a moment longer and more images flooded his mind.

"No! No, it can't be! They won't have the time to get anything accomplished. It will be too late!" Falwen's eyes flickered open and he began to move toward the door when he saw a shadow just outside the building, standing in the doorway. The short, squat figure of a dwarf stood not far from the entrance, poking its head in.

"Get what accomplished, Master Sanse? Who are you talking to?" Falwen was caught off guard by the dwarf, whose voice let him know that it was a fellow scribe, Scribe Ostondilus Frews, one of his fond acquaintances since living here at the dwarven writing guild.

Ostondilus stood a little under a head shorter than Falwen, yet his size made up for it. The young dwarf seemed to fill in nicely all around compared with the older dwarves that had been around for some time, his shoulders and arms thick and full, his beard still well on its way to greatness. The jet black hair hadn't yet come down to his neck, the small bristles still somewhat uncontrollable on his round face.

Scribe Frews waited for Falwen's response for a few long moments, watching Falwen's features change as he tried his best to answer after being surprised.

"Scribe Frews, you startled me! Oh, I was just talking to myself….. about the deadlines that we have to meet in the next few writing cycles, that's all. You know how it is lately with Guild Master Chestfield."

Ostondilus seemed ready to elaborate. "I know what you mean, Master Sanse! Isn't it always the way of things with Thurn, though? One minute, the scribes are trying to find things to do to keep busy, then Thurn has us tumbling over each other with another assignment."

Falwen nodded his head in agreement and moved outside of the large writing room, shutting the doors behind him, his hands moving into his robes for the lock and keys. He withdrew them from the pocket in his robes and placed the lock on the door, a thick rusty scrape emanating from the lock when he turned the key in it to secure it tight.

Ostondilus prattled on.

"But it has yet to bother me, Master Sanse. After all, this is my first assignment and I don't mind the fast yet slow pace of the guild here. My father says, and I make sure I listen because he doesn't say much at all, 'that it is important to learn the skill of writing for future generations. After all, look at Dardist and the mess they left. The dwarven histories still have yet to be written for the past few decades and no one has taken to the walls to write it'. He's a rather funny old dwarf, though. Still believes that the humans are to blame for the breaking of the treaty between the dwarves and the humans, can you believe that?"

It wasn't hard for Falwen to believe anything these days, especially in the world that he lived in within the small confines of the writing guild's gates. The gates were there more for protection from the outside than trying to keep anyone in on the inside, though very few from the guild traveled outside the gates once coming in. The gates were constructed of a thick timber not found in the mountains but down further south, *probably near Reune Lake*, Falwen decided, not too familiar with the wilderness any further south than Argolis, which made for a very limited knowledge on the greenery in Kariyl.

The gates stood just a hand or so higher than Falwen and kept out most of the wandering animals that preyed at night, trying their best to get in by digging down under the gates. This didn't work, however, because the gates were buried at least six hands down in order to hold them steady and Falwen had yet to see an animal that dedicated to dig that far down in the dirt. But Falwen didn't know of the animals that came around here. He hadn't seen many in his time here.

In fact, all Falwen really knew about was the sea; the sea and fishing. That is all that he was interested in until all of Ar Solon changed around him when he came here. Falwen looked at the gates, which were not far from where he stayed, a few lolling hills in between his quarters and the front gates, letting him look out over the gates and into the wild mountain ranges to the south, which seemed to crisscross over themselves in a number of directions, forever leading travelers into a dead end or back around to the same route from which they had come.

On some mornings Falwen would slide out of his bed, his full garb on for the day, and he would stand outside, watching as the sun rose over the Agnar Mountains, watching the guardian of the morning breathe life onto all of Ar Solon until the rays of light touched Falwen's hands and face, bathing him in the warmth that he missed so much back home in the west. Deep down inside, the want seemed to rise up and urge him to go through the gates and never return, to run to his small town of Simmer Lo and never look back.

The exceptions that left out of the gates were, of course, the traders and messengers, then there were others in the guild that had certain duties, namely to gather wood and other necessities that they would need for the winter within the confines of the mountain chain around them.

Falwen came back to the present only when he noticed Scribe Frews staring at him.

"Oh, I do apologize, Scribe Frews. I was just thinking about the work that I have yet to complete in my study. Would you excuse me, please?"

Soon, Falwen watched as his fellow scribe departed from sight, the young dwarf still a little confused about what the old fisherman meant by work, the Chronicler now moving with a purpose towards his own room, letting himself slip in through the hallways quickly and quietly so that no more disturbances would be made.

I need to make it to my room before the visions become too much!

The Chronicler knew of the intensity of the visions and that, when there was too much within his mind, the story would become confusing when trying to write it in the order in which it came to him. In fact, he had a tendency to write the most recent thing in his mind in a notebook, slowly chronicling backwards until he got to what he needed to remember before starting in the blank tomes that were sat out, stacked up in rows by and around his writing desk.

In the last few summers of writing, especially when the snows came and locked everyone into their chambers for a time, Falwen was able to write great histories without interruption. It had become something of a hobby to him; actually, he enjoyed writing them. There had been stories of sadness, of happiness, of endings and beginnings. In fact, in the few years he had taken on this grand scheme as The Chronicler, it seemed as though the continents had calmed down some.

However, there was a rising turmoil within the inhabitants that seemed to spring from the fact that they no longer dreamed. This and the long winters made for a rough life for many of the inhabitants, especially those that required more than just the basics in life to thrive. Many of the inhabitants that had not found their own grand scheme did not seem to lose any sleep from the lack of dreams. Yet, those that knew their grand scheme seemed to lose the clarity and purpose behind what they were doing when they failed to dream. In the mornings, when they awoke, their own grand scheme began to become further and further from them, sometimes even disappearing altogether.

This did not trouble Falwen Sanse that much for the sheer fact he told himself in the beginning that he would not let the stories get to him as they had the previous Chronicler, Gilden Felves. He knew of Gilden's loss of sanity over time and knew that it was from connecting too much to the inhabitants within the stories and not allowing them to live their own lives, whether they lived or died within them.

That was the way of things here on Ar Solon, Falwen thought to himself, taking out his writing utensils from inside the writing desk drawer, all of them wrapped up in a small brown, leather bag, The

Chronicler laying the quills out in front of him. He then laid the corked inkwell in front of him and grabbed a blank tome by his writing desk, sitting it on the desk in front of him. He opened the tome, placed the inkwell close to him, uncorking it, and began to write, the quill dipping in the inkwell almost methodically, calm, as if he had done this all his life.

'That night, the snowstorms blew in from the tips of the Argolis Mountains in the north and seemed to cover the remaining inhabitants still out in several inches of snow, keeping many from traveling, others from their nightly duties. If carts or wagons had intended to move, their owners made it a point to remain where they were, finding a cozy spot such as an inn or tavern in which to keep warm.

Travel was not something that was safe when the last few snow storms had come to pass on Kariyl. Many inhabitants had thought that the storms were the same as those they had seen every winter before, yet the last three winters the snow storms seemed to take many by surprise, ruining crops, burying roadways, and sending many an inhabitant to the grave. Indeed, when the snows drifted in this time, all inhabitants knew that the best place to be was away from it. Yet, some still did not take heed and chose to weather through the storm.

Just east of the hidden dwarven city of Agnar in the Agnar Mountains from the same name, lay a remote town by the name of

MiddleFast. It had been created as a coastal city when receiving supplies from the other coastal cities along the borders of Kariyl yet, when city of Agnar had been completed, it became a small town and the ports had been closed altogether, soon becoming a sleepy nook in the mountains where travelers could get away from the hustle and bustle of the world. It was surrounded by a small chain of the Agnar Mountains yet was still within reach of the small streams and a lake not far for fresh water, being secluded even more by a forest that kept away any unwanted traveling parties that may have a wandering hand into another's pocket.

MiddleFast townsfolk frowned upon wandering riff-raff, wanting more than anything to attract those that wanted to retain anonymity in the small community or start up a business to build trade once again. However, what they seemed to get were exactly the opposite; wanted men, those too lame to work in the real world, or those that stumbled in late one night and just never left, forever retaining a nightly position at the bar, soon becoming a permanent fixture in the town of MiddleFast. Only a few ever left and those that did never returned, citing that, indeed, the town seemed to want to swallow them up permanently. It is here where the story begins, amidst the town of vagabonds and rogues.'

The winter wind whipped through the town of MiddleFast, delivering a shifting layer of snow across the windowpanes of each shop, inn, tavern, and home that resided there, MiddleFast seeming to get the worst tonight than in three winters. The snow was piled up to the windows and, as Mirtra Wells looked out from his tavern, The Salty Gristle, he turned back to his patrons and the bar which he had spent most of his life tending.

"Looks like you all will be staying here tonight if you don't leave now. It is coming down quite hard out there." Yet, no one got up from their chairs to leave.

In fact, the last few nights, the way that the snowstorms were coming, many stayed in the warm and inviting Salty Gristle. It wasn't the nicest place in town to stay, most of the town had agreed upon this in a vote years ago, but the patrons just seemed to spend so much time in there anyways that it became second nature to fall asleep in their nooks, in their chairs, on the floor next to their seats, or curl up on their cloaks and robes near the fireplace as Mirtra continued to feed it the firewood that was stacked up high against the wall.

For the most part, the patrons were human, but here and there, there were a couple of dwarves that littered the room, with its fifteen round tables and twelve smaller, square tables in the corners of the room and along the edges. The dwarves kept out of the way and seemed to go about their business unnoticed, Mirtra only noticing that they were dwarves when they left their tip in the old dwarven coin.

It's all the same to me, thought Mirtra, the bartender smiling at the thought of a good day's work and what it looked like to him. On a good day, the bartender could make a week's wages in one night. It just depended on what he was serving and how many times he was able to remember what the patrons in his tavern liked.

Of course, fine spirits and ales were getting harder and harder to come by, with the weather lessening his supply loads down to almost nothing; nevertheless, he always seemed to manage to get by in a time of need. In fact, he had been one of those tavern owners that prepared for the coming snow after the first two winters were harsh to him, using much of his own wages to invest in several casks of ale that he stored down below his tavern, keeping several of them in reserve for winters just like this.

And anything else that may come up, Mirtra thought to himself, knowing that each day that came to him came with new surprises as well. Not much surprised Mirtra anymore, with the exception of the occasional thief that tried to rob him.

And that was more disbelief than surprise, Mirtra joked to himself, all of the regular patrons knowing Mirtra's abilities with a crossbow, especially the one he kept under the counter. Anyone from the town knew not to try and get anything for free from Mirtra. He was a stingy man and had an even more disagreeable personality when it came to thieves and robbers.

No one had come into the town in more than a three ten day's time, so it was a surprise when there was a knock at the tavern door, the entire room seeming to quiet down to wait for the tavern owner to answer. The partially dying embers in the fireplace seemed to chirp and pop in response to the knock as well, Mirtra Wells looking from the door to the fireplace, trying his best to decide which was more important to him. The thick, overly hairy tavern owner moved away from behind the bar and passed the fireplace, tossing three logs onto the coals before walking to the door, his eyes glancing back at the patrons at the bar two or three times before he finally got to the door. He looked back once more, making sure that none of his regular patrons tried to get comfortable behind the bar, his eyes soon moving back to the present matter at hand.

He reached the door and, as soon as he took the metal door handle in his hand to open it, braced for the cold that was about to hit him full force. Mirtra had kept his front walk clear of snow, yet the snow had come too quick for MiddleFast in the last few days, so Mirtra was slow in keeping it well maintained. He expected the door to be covered completely, with the exception of the person knocking standing there yet, when the owner opened it after drawing back the metal slide across the door, Mirtra noticed that the snow was only up to the knee, his eyes glancing over the human that had been knocking.

"What can I do you for, stranger?"

The voice broke from the cloaked figure with some urgency, the man standing in several feet of snow with several more inches piled upon his shoulder, with more coming down every moment he stood there.

"Just looking for a warm place to stay and some drink to break the cold."

Mirtra hesitated for a moment. The bartender knew that there was limited travel these days, especially when the snow came in from then north as it did, covering Kariyl with blankets upon blankets of snow for ten days at a time. There had to be more to this human's story than just a simple drink and warmth to risk his own life. Whatever it was, Mirtra wasn't interested in getting involved.

It was too damn cold and I don't fancy myself in the mood for it at all anyway, he thought to himself, still blocking the door from letting the human in. The patrons inside started to shift in their seats a little from the cold, but they remained in place, some eyes lifting up from their business to attend to Mirtra's as he stood at the door.

"There's an inn down a few buildings on the left and…."

The human interrupted. "And I'm looking for a dwarf. The innkeeper at the inn you speak of tells me that he frequents here. I'll be no trouble, sir."

Mirtra must have made an expression that the human caught, he thought, because the last sentence seemed to put at ease what Mirtra had been thinking all along.

"Well, stranger, if that's the case, welcome to the Salty Gristle." Mirtra grabbed the shovel next to the door and pushed the loose snow away from the door, letting the stranger in, Mirtra helping the human with the snow that had accumulated on the man's shoulders and pack. Once finished, Mirtra shut and bolted the door, setting the shovel back in its place by the door, his eyes on the patrons at the bar.

"Gendel, put that bottle back!" No quicker than Mirtra had said it then a man at the bar, Gendel, reached into his cloak and pulled from it a large bottle of spirits, replacing it back behind the bar.

"Next time I will bust those fingers, you old buzzard!" Mirtra moved behind the bar and snatched the bottle from Gendel's hands before he had a chance to put it back, the bartender moving it to another location a little bit further from Gendel's sticky fingers.

The new stranger shed his belongings on his back, including a wrapped broadsword, dropping much of it near the bar, his eyes now on Gendel as well. Gendel eyed the stranger's belonging lazily and the stranger pulled the hood off his head, motioning to Mirtra.

Ranyll looked at Gendel eyeing his sword and pack.

"And I won't be so kind, Gendel. Those items aren't worth your life, are they?" Gendel simply shook his head and the interest in his eyes seemed to disappear completely, looking back to the wall behind Mirtra.

"Name is Mirtra, stranger. What can I get you?"

Ranyll slipped his hand into his cloak and pulled from it a pouch, emptying a few coins into his own hand. He handed a few to Mirtra.

"Some warm food if you have any to be had; that and a jug of ale. If you have some place available by the fire so I could warm up a bit; that would be appreciated."

Mirtra looked into his palm and knew immediately that his day would be fine if he continued to wait on this human for the remainder of the morning. Already, he was paid double for what he was about to hand off to this man.

"And the information about the dwarf, sir?"

"My name is Ranyll, Mirtra. And I'll pay for that once I'm a little warmer and fed."

"That will do fine, Master Ranyll." Mirtra motioned to a few empty tables near the fireplace, which he began to tend to more by tossing a few additional logs onto the fire, soon returning to his place behind the bar.

Ranyll lifted his belongings onto his shoulders and moved over to a table that was warm enough for him, dropping his snow-laden gear down, taking a seat to untie his boots. After he kicked the remaining snow from them, his cold fingers felt for the laces and began untying them. He pulled his feet free from their icy-cold grasp and threw them to the side, placing his feet closer to the fire.

Soon, the fire began to blaze from the logs that Mirtra had thrown in and Ranyll was beginning to break the cold that had set upon his entire frame whilst outside. By this time, Mirtra had brought him a plate of cheeses and bread and some cooked meats from the cooking fires in the back and a bottle of spirits. Ranyll nodded his approval after his first taste of the spirits from the bottle.

It was no dwarven spirits, he agreed to himself, *but it will do to break the rest of the chill on me.* In a few more gulps, the spirits were agreeable and Ranyll sat quietly, watching the fire, his mind wandering through the many days that it had taken him to get here.

It has been such a long time since I have treated myself to a moment of peace. Please let me have it. You, who continually give me these visions; let my mind free of this grip that the future has on me. I have seen enough with this last one; this Ardris.

Indeed, Ardris had told him a great many things that were limited in Ranyll's visions of the future. Originally, his visions had began as pieces of his own future, not the future of all on Ar Solon. Once he began to control the amount and intensity of his own visions, Ranyll was able to see further than he had ever seen before. He wasn't able to control the amount of time or what he saw, but he **knew** that it was the future because he could see the ruins of things that still stood this day.

However, Ardris' visions seemed to be the ruin of all Ar Solon. They had come to him so quick, so easy; he carried no special abilities or magik that Ranyll had been given, yet he had just started getting them all of a sudden. Ardris had stated that they began on the day that he and the other townsfolk met at the square before the big snow a summer ago, and he was amidst a crowd of others.

'It just came to me; an immense heat all of a sudden. It started at my arm and then raced along to the rest of my body.' That is what Ardris had said and Ranyll did not see doubt in this man's eyes. Ranyll did what he could for the man and left just as quickly as he had come, making sure to finish up the last of the tome with the explicit vision that Ardris had seen so that he could look over it again later and try and decipher what happened to allow these things to happen. But Ranyll knew what it was that started the cataclysmic events. Ardris had to say but one thing and Ranyll knew what would cause the destruction of Ar Solon.

The Jewels of Ar Solon…that's what Ardris had called him. But anyone who knows, who has studied the histories, had known them by another name… The Emcrist.

There was a movement not far from Ranyll and he shifted in his place, his fingers reaching out almost instinctually to his broadsword, which lay beside the chair he sat in now. Mirtra appeared in the dim light with a tray of food, a slight welcoming smile on his lips.

"Alright, Master Ranyll, I believe this should be to your liking. I had the cook get something together for you."

Ranyll looked over at the tray, trying his best to be interested in the food, but he just took a sip from his mug and continued to sit in the same position, his fingers drifting away to his broadsword and back up to his lap.

"Thank you, Mirtra."

"You are quite welcome, sir. And if there's anything that you need…"

"I will be sure to let you know, Mirtra."

Mirtra took the hint in Ranyll's voice and bowed out somewhat gracefully, which didn't seem to fit the unkempt man very well, moving quietly away from the table to care for his other patrons in the bar.

At least he's trying to make an effort, Ranyll noted, finishing the rest of his mug and preparing himself for another. He sat up, his hand reaching for the jug, his nostrils finally taking in what Mirtra had laid before him on the tray, when he heard it. The sound seemed to carry over the rest of the idle chatter that seemed to go on around Ranyll and penetrate his thoughts. It sounded gruff with much bass, just as he remembered, but there was something different about it. Ranyll filled his mug from the jug of spirits and grabbed his broadsword, strapping the belt around his waist, leaving the rest of his items at his table next to the fire.

He waited for the sound again before moving completely away from the fire, thinking that it might have just been his imagination, hoping beyond hope that he did not let his imagination get the best of him, *which it had as of late*, Ranyll noted, his eyes looking in the shadowy corners of the Salty Gristle.

Again, the noise broke through the chatter of the patrons and he followed it this time to the opposite side of the bar, his eyes scanning, soon finding the dwarf that the voice was attached to. It was Oagthor Axeblade after all!

Oagthor had changed since Ranyll had last seen him, over three summers ago.

In the caverns of Dardist when we got separated. So much had changed since then, Ranyll agreed, his eyes focusing on the dwarf before him. First thing Ranyll noticed is that Oagthor had gotten fat. It would have been simple enough to say that he had put on a few pounds in the last few years, but that would be a lie and Ranyll knew it. Oagthor no longer wore the chain mail he had worn when in Dardist, but an over-sized tunic that was tucked under a great belt as well as a set of breeches that seemed just as dirty as the tunic, which was stained with food and spirits.

And the second thing that Ranyll noticed about Oagthor was that he did not take notice of Ranyll when he came up, mainly because he was drunk. The dwarf's eyes, which had always been hard and focused on the world around him, especially while in the caverns back in Dardist, were now glossy and wandering, a great mug in one hand, his other arm propped up against the arm of the chair he sat in.

He's almost too big to sit in it, Ranyll concluded, noting the size of Oagthor compared to the chair he sat in, which seemed to groan with the weight of the dwarf.

Small bits of his last meal seemed to hide within Oagthor's stringy beard, his lips glazed over with grease and spirits. He smiled at those around him, still in conversation with some other dwarves when Ranyll approached. The other dwarves took notice of the human standing in front of the table and looked up at Ranyll, still trying to listen to Oagthor's story as well.

The drunken Oagthor continued on with his story nonetheless.

"So there I was, knee deep in the Wilden Marsh, watching as these things tried to come at me. I had a load of treasure in a sack on my back and I couldn't see through this fog at all….I mean, it wasn't trying to kill me or anything like that….like earlier…. But it was NOT amusing, let me tell you! And I…."

Oagthor finally noticed that the others had stopped listening and were looking at the human standing at their table. Oagthor cleared his throat, took a long drink out of his mug, and slammed it down on the table in front of him, startling almost all of the dwarves around him.

"Another drink, Mirtra, for me and my dwarves!" Ranyll heard Mirtra sound back in response and heard footsteps to attend to Oagthor and the others, but Ranyll kept his gaze on Oagthor.

Oagthor did not hesitate; in fact, he seemed to feel a bit uneasy at the human at his table.

"What can I help you with, human? You seem to have a staring problem." Oagthor lifted a battleaxe up from the floor and sat it in his lap. "I can certainly help you with that if you can't help yourself."

Ranyll was not in a shadowed corner where none could see him, however, he knew that he had changed in the last few summers on Kariyl. It was somewhat amazing that Oagthor didn't recognize him at all.

"I would like to buy you and your friends a drink, if that's alright."

Oagthor's thick face grew red with surprise.

"Well, that's a first; a human buying a group of dwarves a drink! Mirtra, did you hear that? This human wants to buy us a drink."

Mirtra nodded in understanding and then to Ranyll, placing the jug of spirits down on the table for Oagthor and the others, taking the three empty ones back. He turned to Ranyll.

"So, you would like to start a tab, Master Ranyll?"

No more than Ranyll had nodded and Mirtra moved away that Oagthor caught the name and his eyes grew wide.

"Ranyll! Ranyll Tolver?" Oagthor's voice, however, did not seem excited. Ranyll could also see that Oagthor was trying to decide what expression that he wanted on his face, for it seemed to shift through different ones before Ranyll could even answer.

"Oagthor, it's me, Ranyll. I came to find you. I've been looking for you for almost…." Ranyll didn't expect to see Oagthor's mug flying at him, hit him, or knock him down onto the floor as it did. The floor rushed up at Ranyll and he hit it hard, his own drink flying out of his hand, smashing on the floor somewhere behind him. Then he heard the real boom in Oagthor's voice.

"And what makes you think I want you to find me? What makes you think, Ranyll Tolver, that I want to see your face or hear from you again, human?"

And then Oagthor's thick hands were around Ranyll's throat.

4

"Oagthor, what are you doing?" Mirtra tried to get a grip around Oagthor's arm to pry him off his new patron, but it seemed rather impossible to do anything but watch as it happened. Ranyll could feel Oagthor's greasy hands trying their best to choke him out completely but weren't able to for some reason. Ranyll didn't wait to see if Oagthor could kill him with a grip that seemed to tighten by the second; he lifted his knee sharply up against Oagthor's breeches and felt Oagthor buckle over him, toppling to one side, his hands suddenly shifting from Ranyll's throat to the bend in his breeches that seemed to weaken his ability to move.

The human picked himself up and slipped on the spirits on the floor, trying his best to stay on his feet on the wet floor. The other dwarves stood up as well, brandishing their weapons.

"What in the name of the Creator was that for, Oagthor? I've been looking for you for almost three summers and this is my welcome?"

Ranyll could feel the knot form on his head with his fingers, small pieces of the broken mug still in his hair. Oagthor rolled over, his hands on the wet floor, the gloss in his eyes slowly but surely melting away. He looked over to his dwarves and waved his hand at them, the dwarves putting their weapons away at their seats. However, they continued to remain standing.

Oagthor picked himself up and rubbed his groin in pain, finally standing all the way up. To an older Ranyll, Oagthor was still a formidable opponent. He had gained a thickness that would make him a challenge. Ranyll shook off the dizziness from the assault with the mug and focused on his friend.

Oagthor replied, somewhat out of breath. "I want you to leave now, Ranyll, and never look at this place again."

Mirtra piped in. "That doesn't sound like a bad idea. I don't want any trouble here, Master Ranyll. I think we discussed that before you entered." Ranyll looked over at Mirtra, who now held a crossbow, his eyes darting from Oagthor back to him, trying his best to remain calm.

The patrons around us as well. Ranyll could feel the tension in the air. But a common bar brawl wasn't going to stop him from his purpose.

"I'm not leaving until Oagthor Axeblade is accompanying me out of this town."

Oagthor's eyes grew wide and he clenched his teeth, his thick hand poking out, pointing a finger at Ranyll.

"This is your last chance to leave now without getting hurt, Ranyll. I want no part in anything that concerns you."

"Can we not discuss this in private, Oagthor?"

Oagthor's voice cracked a little, his eyes beginning to water.

"I have nothing to discuss with you, Ranyll! That time in my life has come and gone."

"What if I told you it was back again? What if I told you there was something more than what we were led on to believe in those caves?" Ranyll tried his best to remain calm, but he knew what this was all about for the dwarf. Mirtra didn't seem to want either of them there at this time and the dwarves looked at Ranyll as if he were a disease from long ago they wanted to be rid of.

Oagthor turned to back to his seat, reaching down for his battleaxe.

"I'm through with quests, Ranyll."

"I don't think they're through with you yet, though, Oagthor. Don't let D'meir's death be in vain!"

That's when Ranyll could see Oagthor break into a million pieces on the inside; whatever hard exterior he had seemed to shatter as well, Oagthor's eyes glazing over with tears. Oagthor lunged at Ranyll, his battleaxe at the ready, both hands holding tightly to it, prepared to cleave Ranyll in half, when Mirtra brought his shovel down hard on top of Oagthor's head, dropping him with one swing of it. Oagthor slammed into the floor in front of Ranyll, almost bowling him over as he slid on the wet floor, his battleaxe sliding harmlessly past, the dwarf out cold.

Ranyll looked at Mirtra, then at the dwarves at the table, waiting for the next move. He had yet to draw his broadsword and hoped that he wouldn't have to.

Mirtra placed the shovel back by the door and grabbed his crossbow up from the floor, throwing it around his back with the straps that he had on it. He motioned to the dwarves, who nodded and, reluctantly, sat. He looked around at the rest of the crowd, who still seemed to wait for more to happen. He waved them back to their seats, back to their former conversations.

"Alright, alright! The hustle and bustle is over now. All of you go back to your drinks, go back to your tables." He looked over at Ranyll.

"I don't take kindly to fighting in my establishment! I already have enough work ahead of me trying to keep this place open during the hard winters as of late; now all I need is a rumor going around that this place is unsafe."

Ranyll nodded his head in agreement, trying his best to flip Oagthor over onto his back, which seemed nearly impossible by himself. Mirtra, noticing what Ranyll was trying to do, assisted as well, rolling Oagthor onto his back.

"I'm in agreement with you completely, Mirtra. I apologize for this. I did not expect that kind of response from Oagthor."

Mirtra seemed to understand. In fact, by doing what he just did, he seemed somewhat sympathetic to Ranyll's cause.

"Master Ranyll, Oagthor has been here for three summers. He's done a number of things that I don't agree with, but he pays a hefty amount for me to deal with it, which I do." Ranyll just stared down at Oagthor.

"Three summers? He's been here that long?"

"Yes, and to date, hasn't worked a single day since he's been here. The story he's been telling us is that he stumbled upon a great treasure up in the mountains and brought it back with him. Of course, my job is not to ask any questions as long as the patrons have the coin available."

Ranyll looked down at Oagthor and still found it hard to recognize him at all. If anything, he could still see the dwarf's features in his face a bit, but his face seemed swollen.

"And you're the first to ask about him. Thought he had no friends, well, none the likes of who would come for him."

Ranyll just shook his head.

"I've been looking for him for almost three summers. For a while there, I thought him dead."

"Well, Master Ranyll, you found him. Now what's your plan?"

Ranyll thought for a moment. The human needed to do something, and while Oagthor was still knocked out. He couldn't allow Oagthor to wake up and see him again.

"Do you have an empty barrel I could buy from you?"

*   *   *

Far south of the mountains where MiddleFast lay deep within a cradle of snow, the Tirapoor Channel was busy at work. All of the other cities and villages were covered in snow, in a state of hibernation compared to those that worked the channel. Though, in no way could the channel act as though it were a simple inhabitant; through the freezing and frozen waterways, merchants moved their goods to the places that needed them most, making their way through the treacherous channel to their appointed destinations. Indeed, the channels had become somewhat littered with ice and snow but the checkpoint guards insured their work, many guards maintaining a constant position outside in a set of newly-made shelters by the channel to watch for the possibilities of chunks of freezing ice.

Much had changed since the snows had begun to tax the inhabitants of Kariyl, making even the easiest pathways treacherous, the most worn trails disappearing under the constant-falling flakes. It wasn't until after the first spring that travelers discovered the remains of those that got caught off the path or wandered too far, sometimes full caravans were trapped due to the death of their carthorses or other labor-heavy animals falling victim to the cold and hunger during the trip. Many inhabitants were fearful of departing from the safe hold within their homes in their towns and villages; even the cities had sealed themselves off for the moment, only receiving supplies when they came, never sending anything out but messages back to the merchants for more goods.

However, not all movement was good during this winter age on Kariyl. A dark form drifted from town to town, spilling forth a poison that could not be cured, not be contained, soon bringing doubt and uncertainty to the populace that had already a great deal much to deal with in just living a simple life. The simple life every inhabitant had become accustomed to soon grew more complex with the winter and, as the dark form moved across the land, a single purpose in mind, it ensured that many grand schemes would not be met.

It had made much of its life simple enough, this form of darkness. It continued on its path as it had nearly four summers ago, moving through the snow with purpose. And now, as it broke through the drifts of snow before it with ease, for it could feel no cold, it reached the checkpoint it had heard about a few days earlier. Its purpose had been a good one, of revenge and of play for the creature, all the while knowing the end result once all was done.

He would pay, this inhabitant of mine. He will pay more than anyone I have dealt with as of yet. His pain will be my pleasure, my purpose.

The creature passed by The Happy Traveler and huddled down into the snow to wait for what was to come. It knew that things would come, that inhabitants that have purpose would arrive at this checkpoint; it had become a popular one from the information he had gathered about it.

It was all because of the deaths of the daemons by the hands of Kalir Ranolf and his friend Dir'grar that made this a place of solace and contentment.

Yes, I will wait. Once I get what I need from here, I will move on to Ranyll.

*   *   *

The work of ages seemed to pass by Kalir while he slept. This was the first time in a long time that Kalir Ranolf had slept through a full night. It was good to finally be back in his own cottage, nestled closely on Checkpoint 18, his eyes trying to adjust to the morning light as it filtered in through the curtains in his room. He had pulled them closed, but Alyssia must have opened them once she had awakened in the early morning hours.

He tried his best to get up, but the morning wasn't being kind to him. His arms and back were tired from riding his horse most of the night to get here, his joints still stiff from the cold. He had taken his chance and rode while the snow had stopped falling, bracing himself against the wind by taking some routes that led him into the tree line, already having covered his horse with a series of wool blankets that kept its body warm enough for travel in the snow.

He knew that Alyssia would still be here. He had only been gone a ten day and the thought of her leaving without him saying goodbye disturbed him greatly. The western snows had covered much of the routes west and he knew that Alyssia wouldn't chance going back to Dradle while the storm still continued… at least not without seeing him one last time. After all, he had just come from the west, checking all of his routes. He was only staying for a short while here before he had to leave again and report his findings to the main checkpoint.

Kalir turned around and eyed the room for Alyssia, but he knew she must be downstairs, starting up the fire to bring some warmth into the morning before he got up. Kalir could feel the after effects of the spirits from the night before, his vision still spinning somewhat, closing his eyes for a moment to get his bearings further.

I will do my best not to allow myself to do that again, Kalir promised himself, pulling himself up from the bed, hands grabbing for his breeches on the floor, pulling together the remainder of his clothes as he slipped them on around his legs. Kalir stood up and tried his best to make it to the curtains.

I wish she would keep these closed. Kalir closed the curtains and the darkness of the room calmed his foggy vision almost immediately. He slipped on his light brown tunic and tucked it in as he made for the stairs, throwing on the dark brown vest as well, boots, belt and sheathed sword in hand.

And there she was. Alyssia had made herself quite useful and had already started the fire, which seemed to be warming the first floor of the cottage considerably, Kalir noticed, his bare feet feeling the warmth of the floor under them, dropping his boots onto the floor by the stairs. Alyssia was at the kettle hanging over the fire, a mixture of dried spices in her hands. She almost dropped them when she heard the sound of the boots as they hit the floor.

"So Captain Ranolf is finally awake?" Kalir could hear the smile in her voice though her head was still turned.

"They told you, did they?" Kalir had been reluctant to say anything to Alyssia about his promotion. He didn't know why, he just had never been interested in titles and hoped that she wouldn't be either. After all, the only thing that had changed was that he traveled more.

"Not in so many words. On the way here, I heard a group of traders talking about some new checkpoint captain that was giving them a hard time about securing their supplies prior to transport and I figured that it must be you. You always give people a hard time, Kalir!" She smiled the smile that he always loved seeing; in turn, Kalir approached, trying his best to grab her without agitating the soreness in his limbs. Soon, his arms were wrapped about her waist and she tried not to care much, but then she fell into his embrace, lying against his chest as he held her.

"Is that what I gave you last night, Alyssia; a hard time? I thought I handled you quite gently." Alyssia could feel the slyness in Kalir's tone slip out then, could almost hear the smirk in his words, the surety.

"Kalir, you can handle me how you like, you know that, and I will succumb to your influence every time." She kissed him deeply, wrapping her own arms up and around his neck, pulling him closer.

It had been some time since Kalir had been with a woman; with his many duties as the checkpoint guard and now as the checkpoint captain, he had little time for frivolity such as this. However, knowing Alyssia, and knowing that she was a part of his past, it continued to haunt him. And, for Kalir, this was something that he needed more and more of as he grew older, as his drive to conquer and achieve began to decline; he knew that he needed a companion for the remainder of his life.

Alyssia had always been there, that's true enough, but was she what I needed? As the past surged forward in his mind and brought his hands around his present state, around Alyssia's fair frame, he drew her and the many smells of her body closer to his own, breathing her in, his face buried in her auburn hair that tumbled down her back and over her shoulders. She was wearing one of his long tunics, which barely reached halfway past her thighs so, when there was a knock on the door, Kalir made a move to dismiss her upstairs.

"Alyssia, I think it best that you go change into something appropriate."

Alyssia countered Kalir's earlier sly smile with her own.

"Captain Ranolf, am I to believe that you don't want your men to see you in such a state with a woman? Are you embarrassed, Kalir, because I can answer the door for you if you like!" Alyssia smiled at him and saw his face grow red with embarrassment, her lithe form reluctantly bounding up the stairs.

Kalir made it to the door, lacing his tunic up the rest of the way and tucking it in before he answered. He turned back to the steps before he opened the door.

"And I'm not embarrassed, if that's what you're thinking!" Kalir smiled and opened the door, and suddenly his smile dropped into a look of concern. There, before him, was a face that he had not seen in years, had hoped not to see, especially not with the look that it had on it. In front of him, was his sister, Rachel; and she was in tears. She could only formulate a single word, and that word tore at the very fabric of Kalir's world as she said it.

"Ranyll!"

Soon, Rachel and Dir'grar both were in Kalir's cottage, relaying what had happened a few days prior. Alyssia had made it back downstairs and was dressed in her own attire, which seemed to suit the moment, finishing up the stew in the kettle and dishing it out into a number of wooden bowls she took from the cabinets in Kalir's cooking area.

To Kalir, Rachel Tolver had not changed since he had seen her last, more than ten summers ago or more. The features that had always made her a beauty were still apparent even with age around them, her smooth, tan skin still vibrant and full, her limbs a little thicker than they had been, shortly after young Timothy's birth. Her eyes were the same color as Ranyll's and her and Ranyll looked more alike than ever, especially now that Kalir had seen his sister for the first time in years.

Rachel began, still a bit upset from the thought of it.

"It was all like it had been before; Dir'grar came to bring some supplies and help out around the cottage where he could and was planning on leaving the other night when Ranyll arrived out of nowhere. He looked pale, drawn; not like the Ranyll that I am used to. I know that he's been going through a lot these days but I knew that he had you to count on." Rachel looked at Dir'grar then, who was standing by the fire, his back to the flames. He nodded.

"Dir'grar has been telling me how Ranyll is doing, how he stayed here when the accident occurred and even before that. Dir'grar says that you were doing such a good job being the father that he had lost; it would be hard for Ranyll to fail at anything. Well, that, and with his father's courage."

Kalir looked to Dir'grar then, who averted his eyes for the moment and then looked back, almost urging Rachel for the story to continue. She pressed on.

"It wasn't him, Kalir! It was something else. He didn't say much but, when he did, it sounded false, as if he were hiding something." Rachel began to tear up again, trying her best to control her speech.

"It was a monster, Kalir, one of those things the travelers have been talking about! A daemon! It came at me and Tim in the night, but Dir'grar had stayed over to see to Ranyll to make sure he was doing well before he left. It tried to get Timothy!"

Kalir just then jolted up in surprise. He had completely forgotten about Tim and not noticed at all that he was not there with Rachel! The boy was getting older, of course, but he was in no way able to take care of himself at his age. He would have a few more summers before he was able to do that.

"Rachel, is Timothy…. is he well?" His sister nodded. Dir'grar assisted with further explanation, trying his best to remain calm.

"He's staying at the Happy Traveler, Kalir, in one of the rooms. I have Taleena watching him while we are here, just in case." Kalir nodded.

"Thank the Creator! Good man, Dir'grar!"

"And she's right, Kalir. It was a daemon. It was a shape shifter. I tried to get it but it got away."

"I'll get the pieces of the story that I need from you later, Dir'grar. Right now, I think my sister needs some much-needed rest. Alyssia, could you take my sister up to my room so that she can rest while I speak with Dir'grar?" Alyssia nodded and took Rachel by the hand, Kalir's sister still distraught from her ordeal. Dir'grar looked taken aback. The two women made their way upstairs and Dir'grar moved to Kalir with surprising speed.

"Your own sister comes to you and tells you this news and you tell her to sleep it off? I know you and Rachel have not been exactly close in these last few years, but she is in need, Kalir! She begged me that she and Tim come along because they were afraid for their lives!"

Kalir retorted, somewhat surprised at his friend of so many years.

"Dir'grar, do not think that I take her feelings lightly, but there is an imposter Ranyll out there trying to kill my family. Just knowing that they are safe now puts me in the mind to have to make some difficult choices and send my men out, not just in a snow storm, but into a danger that almost took some of our own men!"

Kalir calmed himself.

Just the thought of Ranyll out there with another daemon tracking close behind, not to mention that it is a shape shifter is too much!

This did not sit well at all with Kalir, who was already formulating possible plans to move on what he knew already.

"What happened? Why didn't you kill him, Dir'grar? You are a beast with your crossbow and you handle yourself well enough with a sword."

Dir'grar waited to answer. He knew that opening his mouth and letting out his first thoughts would be a mistake to Kalir because he would read into much of what he said. He needed to keep the conversation focused on the present matter at hand and not of other things, though they rang in his head like the alarm bells of an attack upon his very soul.

"I lost him in a crowd. He was no longer Ranyll at that point. He must have shifted into someone else. I'm sorry, Kalir."

Kalir brushed his own remark aside.

"It's of no consequence, really. I'm sorry, Dir'grar. I can only imagine what you are going through as well. You must be tired. Thank you again for taking great care of my sister and my nephew. I am in a great debt for your kindness."

"Are you relieving me, Kalir? I don't remember saying anything that would make you think that I can't handle this."

Kalir winced only slightly.

"It's not that, Dir'grar. It's more of a family affair now, my friend. I would never think to get you involved in a situation of this sort. Besides, you have The Happy Traveler to look after."

Dir'grar responded sharply.

"…and you have the all the checkpoints to monitor, Captain, but I know you will find time for this! After all, Ranyll is your nephew and we've already seen what kind of trouble he can get into being out there in the world. It seems as if trouble is looking for him this time, and he has not an angel with him this time."

Kalir, by now, was slipping his boots on and, once finished, moved to the door, retrieving his thick winter cloak and walking stick.

"I don't know what he has with him this time, but now the daemons are trying to kill his family. Who knows where it might show up next?"

Dir'grar retreated from the conversation somewhat, making his way back to a nearby chair next to the fire.

"You are right. I will stay here at The Happy Traveler with Rachel and Tim. I will stay here for your sake, for your family. But you have to promise me something, Kalir!"

"What is it, my friend?"

"That, before you leave, you will spend some time with Rachel and be there for her, Kalir. Be there for her; that is all I ask."

"I will speak with her before I depart on any journey, Dir'grar. Once she is awake, I will speak with her. I will check on Timothy, make some arrangements with the checkpoint, and be back. Then we shall have a talk as well, Dir'grar. I will not forget my friend of ages past."

"That sounds fine. I could use a few good drinks as well."

Kalir smiled at Dir'grar.

"Let me take care of that, Dir'grar. I will be back with that and much more."

Footsteps were heard above and Alyssia came down the stairs, carrying much of her winter gear as well. She smiled at Dir'grar, who had begun eating at the stew in his bowl, grabbing a small loaf of bread and some cheese from the table nearby, placing himself back in front of the fire. Alyssia tied on her winter cloak and already had her boots on.

She smiled at Kalir and he knew this smile more than any that he had known from her. The smile was that of old times, when they had done things that were wrong and they felt right, when he was not embarrassed or ashamed of his love for her and it was fierce, like the pit battles in Dradle when he was younger. The smile drew forth one of his own smiles that broke across his face, something he had not felt a woman do to him in a long time.

"You may be able to get rid of Dir'grar that easy, but I'm going with you. There is no way that I go back to Dradle now. Not until I get something out of this."

Kalir knew that there was no talking her out of it. He opened the door and the let the chill of the air outside rush in on him. Soon, the two of them were out the door and Dir'grar was left with his thoughts and a bowl full of steaming stew.

5

The journey was not far, not far at all for Kalir and Alyssia. They made it to The Happy Traveler and through the snow rather quickly, with Kalir taking full strides, trying his best to slow down for Alyssia but always focused on the large, well-lit cottage not far from them.

"Something is happening again, Alyssia!" She could hear it in his words. He had been concerned about his family, with them being so far off, she could tell in his voice when he spoke of them, especially of his nephew Ranyll, who seemed to be out wandering trying to find some trail of a quest that he had left on some years ago. But the inflection in Kalir's voice was no mistake; there was real worry there. And, as Kalir mounted the steps within the last few strides, Alyssia knew that he would not stop until he felt they were safe; when that was, she didn't know. But she would soon find out, she knew that much. She climbed the steps to The Happy Traveler, stepping inside just behind Kalir.

The Happy Traveler was bustling with activity tonight. Even during a snow storm, the inn and tavern seemed to attract quite a crowd. In the last few summers, Alyssia had heard about the popularity of the fabled Happy Traveler, the tavern that housed the great checkpoint guards that defended the populace from the ranks of daemons that threatened to swallow up the hope of Kariyl.

There were a number of stories that went from inhabitant to inhabitant, none of them the same as when they were first told; always getting more and more fanciful with each telling. When Kalir closed the door behind him, the patrons erupted with a great cheer, clinking their glasses together, chanting the captain's name.

"Kalir! Kalir! Kalir! Hip, hip, hooray!" Alyssia knew now why he took the job as captain. He at least didn't have to deal with this everyday if he were away. She smiled at him as he led her through the crowd of drunken patrons, the bar maids opening a way for him, holding the crowd back somewhat. Kalir smiled at them all, trying his best to nod his approval at the strangers that approved of his valor, though it was all of three summers ago when it occurred.

I've done much more since then. I wish they would see that as well. My life is not that single moment all those summers ago.

But as Ranyll had said to Kalir all those summers ago, 'People believe what they want to believe, Kalir.' His uncle remembered that much at least, trying his best to keep his nerves calm through all that was going on around him. He approached the bar, knocking on it with his fist. The replacement bartender, Marle Fibbs, turned to greet Kalir, his bald head shining in the evening firelight. He had a few mugs in his hands and he was filling them but turned quickly when he heard the knock, finishing up as he nodded to Kalir.

"If it isn't Captain Ranolf here to grace us with his presence! I thought I heard them clamor for you, Master Ranolf! What can I get you and your friend this evening, on the house, of course!"

It was difficult getting used to Marle behind the bar all the time, Kalir agreed, trying his best not to see Dir'grar's place just behind there all the time. He knew that Dir'grar had a life, knew that Dir'grar was worth more to him than just tending to the bar, but Kalir had grown so accustomed to it over the years, it was hard to see something so familiar change so drastically.

Marle Fibbs, though a good tender at the bar, wasn't much to look at and very limited in his conversation, with mostly the constant rabble to use as his informants, forever babbling about the small goings on of the inhabitants in the local areas. Kalir had known Dir'grar to hold very strong conversations with even stronger points on a number of topics, only to tend to the bar and keep the entire bar in check at the same time. But this Fibbs fellow, he didn't seem to be able to do more than one thing at a time.

"Nothing right now, Marle. I just need to see Taleena. Can you get her for me and tell her to meet me upstairs in the spare room, Marle?"

The bartender nodded and passed the full mugs to the patrons at the bar, other ones replacing those that just left, the orders filling up behind Marle to the point where he brought in the second bartender for the night. His shifty-eyed secondary, Gendle, seemed to be a welcome addition to the chaos that raged at the bar, handling many of the patrons with a strong gaze, keeping them moving from the bar yet always coming back for more. He was smaller in stature than Marle, yet he was quicker and seemed to get things done much quicker than the simple Marle, who seemed to stand still for long moments and try to remember what he was doing. Kalir would have to remember to talk to Dir'grar about interviewing future replacements more thoroughly before hiring others.

Marle nodded to Kalir and soon they were moving back through the patrons of The Happy Traveler and over to the stairs, making their way up to the second floor, where the rooms lay, the noise dying down once they made their way into one of the hallways. Kalir stopped short of one of the doors and turned to Alyssia.

"I must ask you now to make one of your promises to me from this point forward. Can you do that for me, Alyssia?"

She smiled.

"Anything for you, Kalir. You know that."

"Alright. I knew I could count on you." He paused, looking around for anyone coming up the stairs. He continued when he saw that there was no one. "I have not yet told you everything about the stories that they talk about. In fact, much of what they say down there in their tellings were not true."

Alyssia just smiled at Kalir.

"Do you take me for a fool, my love? I know that, in every man, there are secrets. I will wait for the time when you can tell me, when you are comfortable."

"There is no time for that, Alyssia! Before you embark on this next step with me, before you even walk inside this room to meet with my other nephew, Timothy, you must know all. And, when I say all, I cannot simply deny the falsities of what others say, but you must know the truth, from myself and all who know it; because that is what I will be telling you from this point on. I told you little in the beginning because I expected you to be gone by now. I expected it very little for you to stay as you are now."

Alyssia was a little surprised in his forwardness. However, she seemed to take all that he said in stride due to the fact that she understood how concerned he was for the welfare of his family. She seemed to feel that he felt the same way about her the more and more he spoke.

"I did not expect to be welcomed so by you, Kalir. After all, it has been some time since I've seen you. I figured that you would have taken another and forgotten about me by now. I am actually somewhat surprised you are not taken; after all, you are still quite a catch!"

Kalir blushed a bit at this. He stared into her eyes a moment longer and then grabbed her hard, pulling her close to him. She could feel his lips press into hers then, her eyes closing, took in the kiss that seemed to break free from its grasp behind his stern eyes.

Alyssia felt her whole body give into him at that moment, letting Kalir pull her up and against him, his hands pressing the whole of her to him. Kalir let the kiss drift away between their lips, holding her face in his hands for the first time since last night, his eyes having grown soft and enchanting all at once in that single moment of the kiss.

"I have been taken by you for some time, Alyssia. If you did not know that, then you must come here more often than you do and you will see."

"I see now." It was all Alyssia could say, because both she and Kalir could hear footfalls on the steps now. Kalir did his best to pull away for the moment, the desire still in his eyes, his duties pushing it back beneath the surface, down deep into the depths that seemed to hold so much.

Soon, the barmaid, Taleena, approached from behind them. She smiled when she saw Kalir and nodded to Alyssia, extending her hand.

"Evening, ma'am. I am Taleena, the head maid here at The Happy Traveler."

"Thank you for your hospitality, Taleena. It's hard to find that around here these days. It's good to know Dir'grar trains his maids so well. I am Alyssia, a close friend of Kalir's from another age ago."

Taleena smiled slightly and looked over to Kalir then, motioning for them to follow.

"I take it, Captain Ranolf, that you're here to see Timothy. Let me show you to his room. It will only take a moment."

*   *   *

Timothy Tolver had long since known that something was wrong. After seeing Ranyll again some time ago for a short time, nearly three summers had gone by since then, not at all believing what his mother had told him.

If that were true, I'd be seeing my brother standing before me and not waiting for my uncle, Timothy thought to himself. After all, his mother was never good at lying. He could see it on her face. Even though he was only thirteen, he knew much more than his mother and brother gave him credit for.

And my Uncle Kalir, for that matter. Timothy had heard about the daemon attacks on the checkpoints; the rumor had surfaced even before they got word back about Ranyll and how he was doing. His mother was near hysterics and he was the only one there to calm her.

That was a lot for a nine-year-old boy to do. But Timothy had done his best, which seemed to work for the moment, soon the both of them getting word from Kalir that Ranyll was safe and sound at the Happy Traveler, at his own checkpoint, resting.

Timothy didn't ever ask his brother where he went when he saw him again; his mother had forbid him to ask his older brother where he had gone all those ten days, telling Timothy that he simply needed to be glad to see him again.

'Everyone has a path in their life, Timothy. It is, however, not everyone's business to know it.', his mother had told him all those summers ago, the first of the winter winds whipping at the young man as he stood at the door, waiting for Ranyll to return home. He did eventually see him, though Ranyll had changed quite a bit when he returned, somewhat more quiet than he had ever been.

And he had this look in his eyes....this look that....

There was a sudden knock on the door and Timothy jumped slightly, his mind drifting back to where he was. And, in another moment, his Uncle Kalir was there, a stranger to him. He had heard the stories from his mother and his brother, but nothing prepared him for Kalir, who was larger than life. Besides Taleena, the bar maid that Timothy had met earlier, he brought someone with him.

"Timothy, Captain Ranolf is here to see you."

It was dream-like. Ranyll had told him the stories, but Timothy was not prepared for his Uncle Kalir. Kalir turned into the room; it was dimly lit in Timothy's room, but Kalir seemed to be bright enough himself that he didn't need much light at all to be seen. Uncle Kalir, Captain Ranolf, or whatever he was called, seemed to make it a point to dress well and look the part of captain of the checkpoints, as many patrons of The Happy Traveler called him when Timothy had been brought in with his mother and Dir'grat earlier.

He wore a bright green vest that hugged his slim frame, a dark black tunic underneath. Amidst a belt around his waist that carried a sheathed short sword and dagger, he had a few small pouches and a simple grey cloak. It didn't seem like much until Timothy noticed the intricate designs on each piece of clothing. Around the collar of the tunic, small markings and designs were sewn, as well as on the vest, the cloak itself having fine traces of silk woven within the edges of the garment, magnificent designs traced in and between the fabric. Kalir also wore some thick winter boots, but they were still covered with snow and dirt from outside, so Timothy couldn't get a good look at them. He would have to later; he was sure that they were amazing as well.

It was not so much what he wore as how he wore it, Timothy remarked to himself, watching as Kalir rushed up to him, closing his arms around young Timothy tightly.

"It's good to see that you and your mother are safe, Tim."

*   *   *

Kalir held Timothy for some time, letting his sister's youngest son know that he was cared for in this world of chaos that seemed to be just brewing. Indeed, it had been some time since a man had comforted Timothy; his father had died before he was born and his mother Rachel never took another husband in all the years since Crin's death. Recently, Kalir's good friend Dir'grar had been coming by to drop off supplies and help with the labor that Timothy wasn't able to do on his own yet; but that was it. Dir'grar had shown an invested interest in Timothy and his mother, Rachel, but it mostly seemed to stem from the care that Kalir took to make sure that they were safe. Those in Telgin had their families and were connected by their own ties and troubles, so Timothy's trouble of not having a father seemed to go on without ever being addressed.

The Chronicler stared at the page for a moment before continuing. He had put down his quill to rest his aching hand, which seemed to knot up every so often after writing for long hours, which he had just done, while all the other scribes were asleep. He was deep inside his chambers now, in his own personal library that he had found by mistake and made shortly after arriving in Agnar, his eyes panning around the room at the stack of tomes that filled the room, some of them his, but the remainder of them the three previous Chroniclers before him.

It is not the end, Timothy. Have faith, inhabitant!

Falwen wished that he were there on the Tirapoor Channel right now so that he could reaffirm to Timothy that he was wanted, needed more than anything right now, but that was not the case. Falwen knew that he was needed where he was now, needed more than ever, so Timothy would have to grow up somewhat like Falwen's own two sons off in the west coast, taking great care for their mother, their father was most definitely sure, not allowing any harm to come to her at all, be it physical or emotional pain.

In looking at the situation from the point of view of the Chronicler, Falwen was able to distinguish the similarities in which his wife and Rachel were very similar; two children, a simple life, a sudden turn with their husbands accepting responsibility and having to leave the family to work for a greater power. It all seemed so easy to say yet Falwen never felt the ease in his heart like he had hoped after almost four summers away from his family in Simmer Lo. Be it that he was in the west, nestled up north in the Agnar Mountains with the scribe's guild, he had not heard any word from Goletta or from Simmer Lo, which never had much traffic of information flowing in or out of it for that matter.

There are too many similarities in these situations for them to be coincidence. The Chronicler knew that The Creator, the great power that seemed to take control of his mind and body, had a grand design in the happenings on all of Ar Solon, but no great collection of ideas had come across Falwen's visions that made him connect the situations together. It was all his own thinking that did it.

What was all this about? Am I supposed to do something, follow a certain path or something besides what I am doing now?

The wave of questions began in his mind again and he knew that it wasn't the best time for them. He tried to get back to the writing that sat before him but the questions did their best to continue without warning, blocking his train of thought on the visions completely. His mind was soon on his children's faces, which were but mere phantoms floating in his head, it having been so long since he had seen them in person. He had no picture, no trinket or item to remember them by. All of this knowledge on things that didn't pertain to him and not knowing anything about what was most important was beginning to get to him.

It has been getting to me for some time now, really, Falwen concluded, lifting himself up from his writing desk, his hand now reaching out for the lantern connected by the hook on the wall, his shod feet shuffling quietly back up the small staircase and into his quarters. Indeed, it had been several seasons and Falwen's family had been on his mind. He didn't know if something was happening to them that made these thoughts come into his mind or if it was just the general worry that a parent has for his children over a period of time, but Falwen could feel the dread well up inside of him, almost fill him up to his throat, making it hard to breath, his feet suddenly heavy and difficult to move.

Something is happening and I can't do anything about it. They are out there all alone, without me, without their father, without her husband. They are naked without me!

Falwen made it to his bed, placing the lantern on his bedside table, adjusting the light so that it was just a sliver across the small room, only shards of what it had been downstairs in his study.

My writing is done for tonight, the Chronicler thought to himself, his mind raw and suddenly unprotected, his eyes closing immediately.

I must meditate! I must clear my mind of the troubles of Ar Solon, of those out there without, of those being chased, of those struggling within themselves. I must make my mind my own for this time.

Falwen felt himself drift off to sleep in moments, his hands falling down at his side on the bed, ink still stained on the edge of his palms, his fingers still twitching slightly from the long work he had made them endure.

I will let you rest, he could hear a voice in his head say, whether it was his own or another's, he did not care too much because the world around him disappeared, his body collapsing down into the bed completely, the lone figure in his room standing still in the corner until Falwen Sanse was asleep and they could make their way down into his secret writing chamber. The figure did not make any noise; in fact, the form seemed to float through and past the shards of light from Falwen's lantern that none would ever see a thing; that was unless the figure wanted to be seen. And then that was usually the last time anyone would see the figure, for they would be dead within moments of seeing them.

The assassin was on a special mission this night, though, so there would be no killing involved; unless, of course, the assassin was detected.

Then they would all have to die! But the figure wasn't detected, neither entering the Agnar Scribe's Guild nor exiting it, which the form did without detection, even using the rooftops of the cottages to keep himself from leaving footprints in the snow.

6

The snowfall on the eastern half of Kariyl seemed to continue throughout the night and all of the Tirapoor Channel checkpoints soon had to be cleared before sunrise, many of the checkpoint guards working double shifts to do so, knowing full well that the morning trading boats would be on their way south through all the channels on time. Once done, the checkpoint guards and other volunteers worked to unearth the pathways that connected each little cottage to one another until a steady path all the way down through the checkpoint areas could be made.

Dir'grar tread along that path, nodding and smiling through his beard the best he could at the others that he had grown so accustomed to, many he had practically raised since he had been here at Checkpoint 18. Although he did not know all their names, he knew their faces. But he had other things on his mind. He was trying his best, in his best possible way of course, to tell his best friend of so many years that he was in love with his sister.

It's not an easy thing to do, but I just have to say it. Come right out with it and tell Kalir how I feel about Rachel!

The thought in Dir'grar's mind seemed to boggle him, send him swirling into a vortex of situations in which Kalir would try to strike him, disown him as a friend, take Rachel away from Dir'grar, and a great number of things, knowing how Kalir felt about her for all of these years.

It was always a sensitive spot for him. It always was… ever since…

Dir'grar had grown as a man and as a true friend in many ways since parting with his past and joining with Kalir all those years ago, leaving Shinol and Dradle behind completely. Of course, Dir'grar missed a lot of his past, but he also knew that was just a part of growing up, *of growing out into one self*, he liked to call it.

The snow crunched under his feet. Kalir's cottage came into view just ahead. There were several checkpoint guards and others working on the path to it. They were finished but were still shoveling the snow away and packing it against itself, making a wide enough berth for a cart to get through. Dir'grar could see all of the checkpoint guards nod to him in respect and he nodded back as well, forcing a smile from his scenario-filled head, his hands sliding into the pockets of his breeches nervously. He approached the cottage steps and made his way up to the door.

*   *   *

Kalir woke with Alyssia at his side, still nestled against his chest, her shoulders rising and falling with every breath. He hated to wake her but knew that he needed to get ready and be on their way if they were to get anything done in a reasonable amount of time. He moved quietly, so as not to disturb her when she shifted in his arms, sitting up on her elbows. She stared at him.

"Do you really think you would wake before me? I've been awake for some time now. I was letting you get your rest."

"Really? Is that not sweet of you, Alyssia?" He lifted himself off the bed, up on his own elbows. "Well, I believe I have enough information from Timothy and my sister. I think it is time we leave." Kalir could feel the warmth of Alyssia's form against him in his bed, her whole body pressed up against his own, the smell of her skin thick in his nostrils. It was difficult for him to leave, he knew this, but his body moved anyway, out of force of habit or the urgent situation, which one he did not know. Actually, he did not care which.

As long as she comes along with me, Kalir thought to himself, looking back at her lithe form on the bed, his eyes lingering over the exposed parts of her skin that seemed to escape from underneath the fur blankets that lay strewn across his bed almost haphazardly. Kalir reached for his clothes and felt Alyssia's arms across his shoulders before he could get up.

"Captain Ranolf, you think you're going to make your move before I do? Maybe you don't remember, but I am not your everyday woman. I run with you men and beat most of you at your own game."

Alyssia's grip tightened around Kalir and the captain soon found himself back on the bed, Alyssia moving over him, tossing the boots aside that he had in his hands.

"I know that, Alyssia. You don't have to tell me. The years have not made me forget." Her lips pressed against his and he released the rest of his clothes from his grip, letting them fall onto the floor, his arms moving in for an embrace around the soft-skinned enchantress he had met all those years ago, *in the days of my youth*, he reminded himself, trying his best to keep up with her passion. It had been years since Kalir had felt the passion of Alyssia; none he had met in those years between her were able to conceive of the desire that they held between one other.

Or compare to it, he reminded himself, his hands pressing Alyssia's form closer and closer to his own bare body. Suddenly, Alyssia slipped away from him and darted from the bed, carrying a single fur blanket over her, moving to her things that had been left at a bedside table nearby.

"Try to keep up, Kalir! You know how I like to cheat to get my way!" Kalir, still grabbing at his clothes that were now scattered on the floor, looked at her with a slight scowl.

"Like I said, Alyssia," lacing up his breeches, "I haven't forgotten you in all these years." After grabbing up his things, Kalir moved quickly past her and snatched her boots before she could put them on.

"And I've learned a few new tricks just to show you as well!" He threw her boots down the steps to the first floor and smiled as he walked down past them.

The living area was still warm from the fire that blazed in the fireplace, Kalir having stoked it with several logs earlier in the morning so his skin did not feel the cold as it had so many of the other mornings before. He slipped his tunic on and began lacing it up when he saw Dir'grar standing by the door, his friends' eyes on him as he approached.

"Morning, Dir'grar. I guess I should be expecting you down here at some point in time before I leave."

"Aye, Kalir. And where would you be setting off to now? You just got back from the journey southwest on all the checkpoints. You need to rest before you depart again."

"I've rested enough." Kalir was finishing lacing up his tunic when Alyssia barreled down the steps, still dressing, a great smile on her face.

"Alright, Kalir, where did you put…." Then she saw Dir'grar and turned to go back up the stairs, still half-naked, her eyes darting around for her boots. Kalir just turned to her and smiled, then turned back to Dir'grar with a solemn expression on his face, as if nothing had occurred.

"Hello, Dir'grar." Alyssia's voice drifted downstairs.

"Morning, Miss Alyssia." Dir'grar simply nodded to his friend.

"I see you've had a chance to rest, among a great many other things. Maybe when you get back we can have a chat."

"That will be the first thing on my list. Personally, I think you should take Rachel and Timothy away from here for awhile."

Dir'grar looked confused. "But they just got here."

"All the more reason to have them go; as you said, there is a daemon trying to get at Rachel and Timothy. Do you not think they will not try to strike here, too? The daemons that came for Ranyll before knew no boundaries, or do you not remember?" Dir'grar could hear the sharpness in his friend's voice, coupled with small slivers of regret.

Indeed, thought Dir'grar, *there are a great many reasons for Kalir to be angry about this. After all, his family seems continually under attack in some way; he is right to be angry.*

"I'm sorry, Kalir. I'm sorry that all of this is befalling your family." Kalir was still lacing up his boots and he looked up at his friend. The anger had subsided in his eyes somewhat, replaced with a concern that Dir'grar had seen all too often in his years with Kalir.

"It's not that, Dir'grar. What we saw all those summers ago, in those caverns, what the angel told us, it's all coming to pass. He was not wrong. He was very much true in his words. Take them somewhere nice, somewhere safe; take them to Goletta. Spare no expense. Take what supplies you need, a wagon if you need. And take Ermoor and Rynen with you. Drop them at the southernmost checkpoint. I will rendezvous with them there in a ten day or so, if the weather permits. Whatever you do, don't let anyone else come along with you, travel with you, or stay near you."

Kalir reached for his thick winter clothes that were hung against the wall and began to put them on. Dir'grar assisted him.

"Kalir, there is much I must tell you. Can we not travel with you to where you are going? You are done with your reports, are you not?"

"Yes, I am finished with my reports of the southern checkpoints, but I go to Fell Whist to take my reports there personally as well as a few words of my own and I think it best that the trip be made quick. Taking Rachel and Timothy will only slow Alyssia and me down. Also, I think it best that they stay as far away northeast as possible. That's where the daemon was, that's where the daemons had come out from before, and that's the last place that I want my family to be."

Kalir tied the rest of his winter garb on his own and Dir'grar held Kalir's belt and sword out to him.

"So, I guess we are parting ways again, my friend?" Kalir could hear Dir'grar's reluctance in his voice, the large creases in his friend's brow forming just above his eyes, making him look almost mad. The checkpoint captain always thought of it as sulking. Kalir clapped him on the shoulder.

"We will be back in The Happy Traveler in no time, my friend, you'll see. I'm off to find Ranyll and bring him back. He was safe when he stayed here with us before a few summers back and lived with us, wasn't he? Enough of this quest rubbish, my nephew needs to have a normal life. He's been gone too long from his family now. He needs a break anyway, don't you agree?"

Dir'grar countered, as he always does.

"I could say the same for you, Kalir. This is the first time I've seen you act like a normal person in some time."

"This is the first time I've felt like one, truth be told!" Kalir strapped his belt onto his waist, taking great care at adjusting the sword at his hip. He opened the door to his cottage and looked outside. The paths were clear to get out of the checkpoint area, but he had no idea how they looked any further than that. Kalir noticed, too, that his checkpoint guards had also prepared his horses and, once they saw his face from behind the door, they began to untie them from the poles in front of the cottage. Kalir waved them away for a moment and shut the door. He looked back at Dir'grar.

"What is it, my friend? What? If you need to talk with me, please, do so! You know we are very busy men these days. We cannot afford to dally and play all day, especially since so much has changed and befallen us as of late."

Dir'grar just shook his head.

There was too much going on right now to say anything. Better I just wait.

"It can wait until I see you again. If I don't see you or hear from Ermoor and Rynen that you are safe, then I will be on my way to find you, you know that, right?"

"I wouldn't expect any less, Dir'grar, especially from you!"

"Neither would I. I know how inseparable you two are." Alyssia's voice broke from behind the two of them and they both turned to see her as she strode down the stairs, Kalir walking over to retrieve her boots for her.

"Alyssia, my dear, we must depart. The horses are ready."

"Let me say my goodbyes to Dir'grar as well." Alyssia patted Kalir on the shoulder and let her hand linger there for a moment until he moved away, making his way back up the stairs.

Dir'grar stared Alyssia down. He did not hate her or dislike her, he just knew who she was and where she came from; in fact, they were all good friends at one time or another in their younger days, over ten summers ago or so, Alyssia staring back at Dir'grar.

"I know how you feel about me, Dir'grar, but I have nothing but the best intentions for Kalir and how he feels about me. Whatever happened in the past, whatever pain she caused you, I assure you, I'm not her! My sister lived her life her own way and never listened to anything I ever told her, even when I told her to stay with you."

Dir'grar had tried his best to forget about the past but, as he looked at Alyssia, he could make out small details of her face and could almost see her sister with every word she spoke. He pushed the thoughts of Alyssia's sister out of his mind and smiled at her.

"It is fine, Alyssia. I know how you feel about Kalir. And I most especially know how he feels about you. There is nothing to worry about. I just worry about him. He forever will remain a fool in regards to adventures. Bad luck seems to follow Kalir."

Alyssia gave Dir'grar a hug, reaching her arms around his thick shoulders.

"There is nothing to worry about, Dir'grar. I will have Kalir's back until he gets back to you and then you can worry about him all you like!"

Kalir returned shortly after, carrying a large sack full of armor, the clanking breaking any further conversation that they could have.

Alyssia looked at the sack and then back to Dir'grar. Dir'grar just nodded back to Kalir.

"Didn't you know, Alyssia, that Kalir is an official now? It's not just the title, but he also gets to wear the Armor of the Guards of Old!"

Kalir gave Dir'grar a dirty look.

"It's not so much the title as it is formality, Alyssia. I can't walk in to Fell Whist dressed as Kalir Ranolf. I am more to them there. I have been given a title and a great responsibility."

Alyssia gave Kalir a little half smile, grabbing her winter cloak and other layers of clothes she would have to put on before she stepped outside.

"I would not expect you to deny that responsibility at all, Captain Ranolf. All I want to know is, will that slow you down, cause I will not be waiting up for a captain that cannot keep pace?"

Dir'grar just laughed.

*　　　　　*　　　　　*

The western half of Kariyl had not been hit as hard with snowfall as the eastern half of the continent had been, which made traveling veritably easy for Ranyll, who sat on the seat of the simple wagon he had purchased in MiddleFast, a broken-in horse named Bingham pulling it forward in the light snow drifts that had been the only sign of the snow since his leaving MiddleFast almost two days earlier. He had been wary about getting a wagon; he had always been told that it slowed one down. But as he cracked the whip and felt the wagon move forward without hesitation, Ranyll did not mind it so much. It felt good to have a rest from walking for a change, and a flat seat compared to an ice-cold saddle or the wind and snow against his back would benefit him greatly any day.

I should do this more often, Ranyll thought to himself, knowing at any point in time he could stop and rest in the back of the wagon, underneath all of the blankets and other supplies he purchased, keeping warm the whole night without having to build a fire. This, too, pleased him greatly to no end, thinking for a second, that this may not be such a bad trip to Goletta at all. Then he remembered the dwarf he had stored in a great barrel in the back of the wagon, and his thoughts went to other things.

I wonder if Oagthor is comfortable in the barrel. I wonder if he's awake. I have a sinking feeling in my stomach that he will be none too happy when he gets out.

These and many other ideas popped in and out of his mind as he watched Bingham move through the snow just ahead of them, Ranyll not knowing what to expect from the dwarf once he let him out of his enclosed prison. Ranyll snacked on what he had out available, which were some dried meats and a few pieces of fruit that he had left from Tira's items she had given him when he left the town of Sift.

Her family was very grateful that I had come there, Ranyll reminded himself. *Maybe it won't be like every other town that I've been to after all. Maybe they won't be after me like the last few that I've been to.*

The wagon continued on throughout the night until the early morning, soon stopping for a brief interval just before sunrise. Ranyll hopped off the small wagon, grabbing the feed bag from the bed of the wagon as he walked around to check the wheels and axles for any damage along the way. He had to kick aside a bit of snow around the wheels, but it was not so much work as walking through the northwestern half of Kariyl by foot, Ranyll looking at Bingham, the old horse nuzzling up close to him as he approached.

This was Ranyll's first horse that he had ever owned. Years ago, he had taken care of another neighbor's horse while they were away from Telgin, but he had never truly cared for a horse all on his own. This was his first time caring for something since caring for Gabriella all those summers ago.

And look how well I did that! Ranyll scolded himself over and over again for his inability at the situation, his eyes tearing up somewhat when he thought of that awful moment that reared its ugly head in his mind. He tried his best to block out the memory by putting himself to work.

Ranyll gathered what firewood he could find around the area and lit a small fire to cook over, returning back to the wagon for a blanket to put down so he could remain dry while he prepared a small meal. After clearing a small spot in the snow to sit, he pulled out his cooking utensils; a small boiling pot, a few forks, a small iron shelf on which to hang the boiling pot, and a few wooden bowls that sat unused in the bottom of the sack he had pulled from the wagon. With a small carving knife from the bag, he began to prepare a stew.

Soon, there was a boiling pot of vegetables and a few slices of meat, as well as some spices from a few spice bags he carried with him. In a few more minutes, he could smell the food cooking and he remembered how hungry he had really been.

He then turned his attention to Bingham. Once he hooked the feedbag to the horse and checked the horse's hooves for any injury, he strolled to the bed of the wagon, staring hard at the barrel that sat in the back, tied up tightly with a number of ropes.

It was only a few mere seconds and the barrel began to shake, the mumblings of Oagthor coming out.

"Ranyll! Ranyll! I know you're there, Ranyll! I didn't spend most of my life in a cave for nothing. I can sense you out there. Let me out, damn you!"

Ranyll hesitated at first, then slipped the dagger free from his belt and cut the ropes, the barrel slowly rolling off the wagon, soon tumbling down onto the ground in front of him, splintering into a number of pieces. Oagthor's thick body lay within the fractured pieces of the barrel, not moving at all. Another moment went by and Ranyll watched as the lid of the barrel popped off completely and Oagthor pushed himself out, hands still tied to Ranyll's sword. Oagthor lifted his head up to voice a complaint when he ended up emptying most of his last few meals onto the ground in front of him, doubling over in pain as convulsions wracked his thick frame. The dwarf did not move until the convulsions stopped.

Oagthor tried to lean forward and tumbled onto the snowy ground, rolling to the side, his bonds still as tight as when Ranyll had tied them almost two days ago.

The dwarf rolled onto his back, staring up at the morning sky for a moment before speaking. Small pieces of vomit and snow lay mixed into his beard and hair that spilled out around his head. The dwarf didn't seem to care about the snow. In fact, he grabbed handfuls of it and shoved it in his mouth, chewing it up.

The overweight dwarf breathed a couple of deep breaths and a sigh of relief, patting his large chest.

"If I had the energy to kill you, I would. But I'm not going to ask you why you did that, Ranyll. All I know is that you've got my attention." Oagthor held up Ranyll's sword still tied to his hands.

"What is all of Ar Solon is going on?"

*   *   *

Later that day, after Oagthor had bathed from a barrel of water stored in the back of the wagon and changed into the garb Ranyll had purchased for him before they left, Ranyll sat next to him in front of the fire. The boy had changed a lot since Oagthor had last seen him. The young human boy that had wandered into the caverns of Dardist, dodging daemons and trying to save an angel had disappeared inside the young man that now sat next to Oagthor. His hair had grown to his shoulders, his face managed a beard; not thick like a dwarf's, but a nice, well-groomed beard that lay against Ranyll's face evenly. The beard was brown, the same color as his hair, which seemed to make his eyes stand out even more in the afternoon sun.

Oagthor had fed himself several times over with Ranyll's stew, which seemed to set light on his stomach compared to all that he had eaten in the last few years, which was good for the moment, especially since he was still a little weak-stomached from traveling in a barrel for two days. The dwarf was not accustomed to being out in the chill of the air but he did not mind it now. Being in that barrel made him appreciate the cold air on his face; it whipped through his still wet beard, drying it with small flakes of ice forming on the ends of many of the hairs.

The dwarf admitted that it was cold, but not cold enough for him to hide from the morning sun, which seemed itself to rise in the cold of the day and try to maintain its own warmth on the face of the snow-covered continent. There was a long moment of quiet between the both of them until Oagthor could get his bearings on where he was. As he cleaned up after the meal, he took note of the location of the Agnar Mountains. They seemed so far from them now and not much was around them, save the small brush and a few forests to the east of them, which kept the wind from tearing at them completely, which was good because it would take Oagthor some time to get used to the cold again.

Mirtra always kept it so warm in the tavern. No wonder I gained so much weight. Oagthor looked down at his huge self, embarrassed now that Ranyll was here, knowing that he could be so much more for the boy, a dwarf that had been counted on at one time. But all that was gone now. The dwarf tried his best to keep a positive perspective, not something he had done in some time because he hadn't needed it for anything. Suddenly, Ranyll was next to him and the human's voice broke his train of thought.

"Oagthor, if I told you that I've been having dreams, what would you say?"

Oagthor didn't have to wait to think on it. He gave his answer, sipping on a water skin in between breaths.

"I'd say that you were somewhat crazy. Everyone knows that once Gabriella passed on, there have been no more dreams. Not a one."

Ranyll continued. "And after two days in the barrel with the sword?"

Oagthor hesitated for a moment, then spoke up. "I'd say you were right, Ranyll. I saw things while I was in that barrel that I'd never thought I'd see. I thought, at first, that it was visions from the drink; that I had drunk too much. Mind you Ranyll, back in my earlier years, I had seen a great number of visions with drink." The dwarf took a long pull from the water skin, emptying it and tossing it to the side.

"But what I saw in that barrel, I knew it was because of that blade of yours."

Ranyll said nothing.

"I take from your silence that you wish me to speak on what I think it means."

Ranyll nodded. "I would like to know that I'm not the only one."

Oagthor nodded in response. "….then you're not the only one, Ranyll. I saw much."

"Then I'm not crazy!" Ranyll stood up and began to gather the scattered things on the ground and put them back onto the wagon.

Oagthor, with great effort, stood up. "Ranyll, what makes you think you're crazy? These are just dreams. Only a few summers ago, all of the inhabitants had them."

Ranyll unsheathed the sword from his back, holding it blade out at Oagthor.

"Maybe the drink has made you slow, Oagthor! Don't you get it? Gabriella is here, in this very blade! You weren't there when she died. She passed on this very blade. I don't know how it happened, Oagthor, but I see her, too, in my dreams. She is always there, in the background, guiding me in some way. She guided me to you, Oagthor. I had been searching for you for almost three summers!"

Oagthor reached out at tapped the blade down with his hand.

"Don't brandish a blade at me like that, Ranyll! I'll forget what we've been through and take a swipe at your head, human!" Ranyll nodded and stabbed the sword into the ground in front of them.

"Something's happening, Oagthor. Something awful, something that scares me to the very core. I've seen things that I thought I'd never see in all my life. I can't go home, Oagthor! I'm being hunted!"

Oagthor could see the hurt in the human's eyes at that moment, the glossing over, the eyes averting to somewhere he couldn't see. Oagthor knew that Ranyll would not lie. He knew that he would not lie but Oagthor needed to delve further in order to know more.

"Hunted? Ranyll, do you hear what you're saying; that's mad!"

Ranyll lifted up the long hair over his forehead, revealing a jagged scar across the edge of his hairline. He pointed to it, tracing the scar from one side of his forehead to the other.

"From a rock a child threw at me in a port town, just outside Dradle! The entire town chased me out, Oagthor! I was called a curse and they chased me out!"

"What did you do while you were there, Ranyll?"

"I never made it inside the town! Someone recognized me and started to gather others to stop me from entering."

"How did they recognize you? Had you ever been there before?"

"I don't know how they knew me! I had never been there in my entire life! It had to be someone from another town that told of me and gave them a description."

"Are you making a name for yourself around Kariyl, Ranyll? Is there something I need to know?"

Ranyll nodded and turned away for a moment, thinking.

But Shilinda's statue seemed to stand out in Ranyll's mind then; the smooth, white curves of the angel's face, somehow reaching him from that distance past the lake, holding him steady.

"I have the power to heal, Oagthor. I inherited it the same time I got the other magikal powers from D'meir. I didn't know about these until after Gabriella had passed. They didn't manifest themselves right away. I had to learn how to use them over time."

Oagthor was silent for a time behind Ranyll. He had begun to gather the rest of the supplies as well, which he continued doing, packing the remainder of the supplies away, his steps heavy on the ground as he passed by Ranyll.

"Anything else I need to know, Ranyll? This past of yours just seems to get worse and worse. I'm glad I stayed away."

"I know what I have to do, Oagthor. I've known what I've had to do for some time, but the dreams keep taking me back to you. You were always in them, helping me in this quest."

"I'm not a follower of quests anymore, Ranyll, I'll let you know that right now! I've had my fill."

"You know I'm not going to take that as your answer, Oagthor. I've come too far, prepared too long. It's all coming together now!"

"What is, Ranyll? What quest is this you talk about? You know you speak in riddles, my friend? Every time I hear you speak, even when I was drunk back there in MiddleFast, you spoke as if you were in a daydream, as if you were somewhere else. No one can understand you when you're like that, you know this, right?"

"I'm sorry, Oagthor. I've been haunted by these dreams, these visions for far too long. They have taken over my waking moments, making me think that I were in a dream when, in fact, I was awake. I can't help it."

"Well, try your best, for me, okay?" Oagthor climbed up onto the wagon, untying the reins in the process.

Ranyll grabbed his sword from out of the ground and slipped it back into its sheath over his shoulder, looking up at the old dwarf as he tried to get comfortable on the front seat.

"Don't you want to hear what the quest is?"

The dwarf gave an annoying nod. "Can't you tell me on the way to where were going?"

Ranyll smiled and climbed up into the wagon seat next to Oagthor and sat down as they pulled away.

7

"So, let me get this straight, Ranyll! You are telling me that The Chronicler, the great scribe that writes of all that happens here on Ar Solon, is nothing more than a simple fisherman!" The dwarf almost felt faint. He wanted nothing more than to drop off the wagon and roll into obscurity and vanish in the snow. The only thing that stopped him is that the wagon was moving and this was his only pair of clothes until they got into the next town. That, and Oagthor wanted to know more.

"How do you know all this? It can't all be just the visions…er, dreams, or whatever you call them. I take it that you have not been spending your time in Telgin, as you had before your adventure."

Ranyll related the events that happened after Oagthor disappeared from everyone's sight and how Dardist came back into existence again and was, for the moment, protected from the daemons. And the human related more, much more than the dwarf had ever thought possible.

"I stayed, for several seasons, with my uncle, Kalir, and his guards at the checkpoint. He taught me some things, I learned some things on my own, and then I left. The visions had become too strong for me to stay. I traveled up to the Agnar Mountains and then visited the elves in Elvinisclar and Trayvilis, like the visions had told me to, and I found out a lot about Ar Solon from another set of eyes. The elves, they are always watching us. They knew about the trouble with the daemons, they never told me how they knew, but they knew."

Ranyll seemed to drift for a moment, his body still on the seat of the wagon with Oagthor, yet his mind roaming to somewhere else. Oagthor brought him back.

"The elves, did they intend on helping us in Dardist? I mean, do they care about the rest of us here on Kariyl at all?"

Ranyll returned from where ever he was and looked at the snowy road ahead of them. Not far off, the human could see the slopes of another valley and a few villages ahead. They would soon be to Simmer Lo, Ranyll's first order of business. He had a promise to keep. He answered back to Oagthor, somewhat disinterested.

"They have their own troubles to attend to, Oagthor. I was ready to leave as soon as I got there, noticing that there is something none too well there. It is as if there is a feeling that something is stirring within their race, something that they are trying to hide."

Oagthor nodded.

"I noticed that myself years ago, Ranyll, when I was younger and had the mind for such politics."

Ranyll was almost in disbelief. "You, a mind for politics?"

Oagthor confirmed it. "Aye, Ranyll. I was not unlike yourself, with ideals about how Ar Solon should work. I was even a councilman for several years until I lost faith in the system. It had become so corrupt. I am beginning to feel that the elves are thinking the same way many of us do now."

Oagthor snapped the reins a little harder and Bingham picked up the pace. The paths for the last few hours had been cleaned of snow and it was easier for the horse to tread. The dwarf looked over at Ranyll, smiling slightly through his thick, unkempt beard.

"Do you find it hard to believe that I wasn't always a fighter?"

Ranyll shook his head. "You just have that look about you. Even the way that you speak, it sounds as though you've been fighting for years and love it."

"Love is a strong word, Ranyll. I would never use that word to describe how I feel about fighting. Rathor, on the other hand, could use that word and it would fit. I swear that he was born with a weapon in his hand. I would give up fighting, have given it up, actually, before you barged in on my happiness with talks of dreams and quests again."

"That was not my intent, Oagthor, and you know it." Ranyll could feel the tension in the air again. Something was bothering Oagthor, something more than Ranyll knew of.

It was just getting dark and the sun was setting just behind the shapes of the small villages on the landscape. Much further, far down to the south of the villages, the port town of Goletta could be seen. It rose up, as though coming out from the edge of the water, the lit edges of it carving out a path in the darkness in front of them. It was only tinges of light, almost too far to be seen, yet it was there. Ranyll looked to Oagthor then, his eyes barely able to be seen in the darkness.

"What is it, Oagthor? What must you hold inside yourself that you can't get off your chest? I am Ranyll Tolver, the young man that you saved from the daemons all those years ago. What is it that you cannot tell me? Once I was called your savior, but now, I come to you, ask something more of you, and you act as though I am a stranger!"

Oagthor, now angered, turned to Ranyll next to him on the wagon.

"I'm still not over being put in a barrel by you, Ranyll. I still have the mind to show you a thing or two...." And, in mere moments, Ranyll did not hesitate. Before Oagthor could get the rest of his words out, Ranyll's foot was in the dwarf's chest and soon the ground rushed in on Oagthor. The dwarf hit the ground and rolled away from the wheels as they continued forward, without him.

"Well then, Oagthor, maybe you can just walk your temper off! I'm not the boy you knew all those years ago. I have no mood for the baggage you bring on this quest. Let us rid you of it before we get to where we're going. The town of Simmer Lo is not far from here. Just follow the path west and it will take you there. See you at the tavern."

The overweight dwarf slammed his fist down into the snow, pulling out his axe. He wiped the snow from his face and beard and held up his axe, waving it at Ranyll and the wagon he rode.

"And what makes you think I will be going that way, huh? What makes you think I won't go somewhere else with my time, with my talent?"

Ranyll snapped the reins lightly and called out, "Because I have all of your treasure stored up in the wagon! Mirtra let me pack your things while you were knocked out."

The furious dwarf huffed and puffed his way forward, his axe still clenched tightly in his hand. He followed the path to Simmer Lo, intent on taking whatever anger he had left out on Ranyll once the dwarf arrived there. Soon, Oagthor saw the wagon disappear over one of the dips in the valleys and the dwarf was left by himself in the darkness of the snow-covered terrain.

*   *   *

The sun had set in the west and left a shadow over all the land, especially the eastern half of Kariyl, the moon the only light as it glinted across the snow. Flakes of snow continued to fall on everything east of the Tirapoor Channel and continued to do so for the whole of the night, Kalir and Alyssia making their way further north, to a nearby checkpoint to check-in for the night and collect the reports that Captain Ranolf needed before they moved on. Many of the reports further north of Kalir's original checkpoint were another captain's responsibility, but this was the last checkpoint that Kalir had jurisdiction over, so he thought it fitting to stop here for the night and ask for his quarters until the snow died down a little before moving on.

It's too risky to be traveling in this weather, Kalir reminded himself, glancing over at Alyssia on the horse next to him, covered in snow herself. Both of them were covered, from head to toe, with the snow, yet they continued on until they could see the small dots of light that were the lamps that lit the entrance to Checkpoint 25.

Much of what had been said about this checkpoint was true; it was one of the lesser-tended checkpoints. This checkpoint had very few checkpoint guards and far too much land and water to cover with so few on the checkpoint to do it. It was spaced far away from any village or town, so any person volunteering to work with the checkpoint had to live at the checkpoint in order to maintain it. That meant that much of their own work where they lived had to be maintained by someone else or sacrificed for the greater good of the checkpoint. Many inhabitants did not, however, feel that strongly about the purpose of the checkpoints at all; many inhabitants felt that, if it didn't help them directly, then it wasn't any use.

In fact, what Captain Ranolf had seen had been situations like this; that there was an inhabitant that didn't understand the true necessity of the channel and how it could be used, especially during the rough times in the winter season, and it would be a state of turmoil until the situation was solved or put to rest. Captain Ranolf's job was just that; to alleviate the turmoil that many who didn't see the purpose in this job at all. Some of the checkpoints further north had even closed due to the increased doubt of the populace around them, many of the checkpoint guards going back to their families and homes to tend to the problems that their own families faced, forgetting about the rest of the world. Kalir was lucky enough to not have any checkpoints close on his route.

Lucky, indeed, he thought to himself, taking small strides with his horse as both he and Alyssia approached the checkpoint. Kalir looked over to Alyssia, who had been quiet most of the ride there. He uncovered the thick scarf from his mouth and spoke.

"There are some things that you need to know about this post, Alyssia and I feel that it is of the utmost importance that you know before you walk into the situation unawares."

Alyssia stopped her horse, uncovering her face as well, letting the chill of the cold touch her soft features.

"You decide to stop while we're almost there! Kalir, you cannot be serious! Why not tell me earlier on?"

Kalir had been hesitant. He had made it all this way without saying anything, yet he knew that her being here would be an important factor while here, though there was just a basic plan to rest, water and feed the horses, and get back onto their mission, which was still a day's hard ride through the snow, and that was if the snow stopped falling.

It doesn't look like it's going to stop at all, Kalir taking note to the thick flakes that came down on their forms, already creating a small pile of flakes on their clothes and horses.

"I know you can handle yourself, that's why I said nothing. I am telling you now because I may have to show my authority over these men if it comes down to it."

Alyssia countered. "What is it, Kalir? Is it really that dangerous?"

Kalir shrugged his shoulders. "I guess we won't know until we go into the checkpoint. It's simply this, Alyssia: The checkpoint guards here have very rare instances where they see women. In fact, you will be the first one they've seen in almost a season!"

Alyssia just shook her head. "That's just great, Kalir! This should be an entertaining night!"

The two of them made their way through the thick brush that surrounded the checkpoint cottage and three other smaller cottages not far from the main one, following what they could find of a trail to the stable, which was connected to the master cottage, which stood almost three stories in height, dwarfing them as they approached. Everything was covered with snow that reflected the light from the hanging lanterns on each side of the double doors, Kalir motioning to the stable entrance not far.

"This is a checkpoint that doesn't get many if any visitors. However, it's my last stop to collect the reports to take to Fell Whist. That, and it is the closest place that we can rest before we get to the worst of the snow in the east. After this checkpoint, we will make the long haul, about a day or so, to Fell Whist, just above the Tirapoor Channel."

Alyssia slipped off her horse and dusted the snow from her shoulders and the horse, walking it inside the open stable, taking note that there were several other horses tied up in the stable with snow still on them. She tied hers up next to them and filled the trough in front of her horse up with some of the oats that she had from her pack.

"Don't talk at me like I've never been anywhere, Kalir! You know that I've traveled; I know Kariyl just as much as you do. Please do not forget who I am and what I'm capable of!" Kalir could hear the tinge of anger in her voice. He knew that it was pointless to apologize, for Alyssia would take that as a sign of weakness as well. He knew her very well, better than he would like to sometimes.

Kalir nodded and slid off his horse as well, taking great care with his armor strapped back over the pack so as not to damage any of it, tying his horse up and feeding it, dusting the snow off of his shoulders as well as off his horse.

This is going to be a long night! Kalir tightened his sword against his hip, stretching the soreness out of his joints as he followed Alyssia's footsteps back outside and up to the master checkpoint cottage.

"Can I buy you a drink, fair lady?" The frothy-mouthed bartender poured her the drink she ordered and placed it down in front of her, eyeing as much of her as he could while Kalir was away, speaking with the checkpoint guards. The tavern at checkpoint 25 didn't have a name and didn't seem to need one, the cottage being of a very run-of-the-mill, basic creation; a few tables scattered about, a front bar in the middle, nothing too fancy about the design at all. Alyssia looked around and eyed the patrons.

Not much better than the bartender, I fear. It seemed as if the checkpoint patrons fit the bar just as well; very non-descript, not dressed fancy, with the exception of the figure in the corner. The bartender tapped the bar counter and brought Alyssia back to the present, which she seemed to return to reluctantly.

"Can I buy you a drink, pretty lady?" The thought of drinking out of the mugs here did not bode too well for Alyssia, who was used to, not luxury, but class, looking now at the bartender who seemed to allow a bit of froth to remain at each side of his mouth. The thought of having a drink bought for her by him revolted her. That's when she felt Kalir's eyes on her. Every so often, Kalir would turn from his place at the table not far away and check on

Alyssia, Alyssia catching his gaze, his eyes averting back to the map on the table in front of him, his gloved hand motioning to a number of markings on it.

He's checking up on me! That bastard is checking up on me!

Alyssia never thought of herself as a regular woman; a placating humbled woman without a purpose on Ar Solon. In fact, she fancied herself almost a woman of Parthenian means, a woman with a fierce heart and an even more fierce punch, one that could knock out a couple of men if she aimed just right and had enough spirits in her system. She looked down at her drink and took it upon herself to finish the drink in one, long gulp, slamming the empty metal mug back down, many of the checkpoint guards around her jolting in surprise, their eyes growing wider when they realized that a woman had done it.

I'll show him what I can do!

"I will take you up on that offer! And your name again?"

"The name is Kendel. But people know me around here as The Brute!" The bartender smiled and showed Alyssia his seven lovely, yellow teeth that glowed in the lantern light. The Brute took her hand and kissed it with his frothy mouth.

"I'm sure they do."

It had been but a brief parting between Kalir and Alyssia at the bar before Captain Ranolf noticed that she got attention. The captain had gathered a small number of checkpoint guards, the ones that he trusted the most, and relayed the information of the possible daemon threat, stating that it, indeed, had come from Telgin, so be wary. One of the guards piped up.

"So, you're going to Fell Whist yourself this time, Captain Ranolf? We are not to deliver the reports like we always do?" The checkpoint guard seemed somewhat saddened by the idea, knowing that this was his as well as many other's only chance to get away from the checkpoint for a brief interval, at least for a single night's pleasure away from the duties at the checkpoint.

The captain nodded. "That is correct. I feel that I need to report this situation to the master of the guards directly, so I thought it would be easier to take the reports with me and go myself."

The checkpoint guards around him seemed disappointed, though they seemed to understand the reason. After all, Kalir's checkpoint had stopped the daemon disturbance several summers ago and who would be more qualified to speak on the subject of another possible threat than Captain Ranolf himself?

One of the guards brought up another question.

"Well, can we not escort you then, captain?"

Captain Ranolf did not get to answer the question. There was a loud boom behind him, which made him turn, watching as a patron tried to pick himself back up off the floor. The bartender, whom Kalir knew, leaned over the bar, laughing slightly.

"Looks like I win, you lazy Miftle!" The human on the floor rubbed his arm in pain, steadying himself the best he could with a barstool. The Brute flexed his right arm out to Alyssia, who poked at the muscle with her finger and smiled.

"And that's why they call me The Brute," the bartender roared, several mugs around the bar going up in toast to his success. "One of the best arm wrestlers this side of the Tirapoor Channel! You can ask anyone in here!" The Brute noticed that he had Kalir's attention, who just continued to stare in disbelief at Alyssia. The Brute motioned to Kalir.

"Isn't that right, Captain Ranolf?"

"You are correct, Kendel. Best one in here." Though it didn't sound heartfelt, Kalir acknowledged to his long-time friend behind the bar of his accomplishments, and then turned back to the guards with his answer.

"I think that would be fine. You deserve a few nights away from this place. I need you in your ceremonial armor though. You are an escorting party, that is all. You are not delivering the reports as you usually do. You are on official business."

The checkpoint guards nodded excitedly, many of them looking to one another for approval of the situation.

These guards are still so young in the ways of Ar Solon. So glorified by their station, by their surroundings. Kalir remembered many moments in his life when he was just the way they were, in rapt attention at the situation in which he was put in all those years ago.

But it fades with time, doesn't it? What was new soon becomes old and what was old becomes distant memories of long ago…who again told me that? Kalir had spent many a summer in Dradle once he left Telgin, before the resurgence of goblins, before Timothy was born, before he really even knew Crin Tolver as a man. It was just Kalir and his brother all those years ago, causing trouble for the masses in Dradle. That was when he first met Alyssia.

Captain Ranolf smiled at the checkpoint guards and called over to The Brute, who found it difficult to pull away from Alyssia's attentions at the moment.

"Kendel, get these guards some of the finest spirits my coin can buy. They're escorting me to Fell Whist tomorrow. I want them good and warm for the journey!"

Hoorahs went up around Kalir and the guards moved toward the bar, intent on getting their spirits first. Alyssia caught many of the guard's eyes, yet her eyes were focused on Captain Ranolf, who approached, his own hand out for a mug of ale from The Brute.

Alyssia's stare seemed to tear at every fiber of his being. Kalir knew that there was a fire inside of her; that she had burnt him a number of times throughout their years together, yet his soul seemed to ache for her. He pulled her close to him, feeling his old self returning, his hands grabbing for a hold around her hips to pull her into him.

She smiled at him in return. "So, I guess we have some guests coming along with us to Fell Whist?"

The Brute placed a mug full of fine spirits in front of Kalir and he took it gratefully, breaking the dryness in his throat with the first gulp of the spirits. The ale sent a slight fire through his throat, which burned, yet Kalir knew too well about spirits and their ways. Alyssia wiped off a small amount of spirits from Kalir's moustache with her fingers and tasted the spirits.

"I hope you don't mind. Alyssia. I think we could use a few of them to go with us. After all, these are dangerous times. I don't really know what is out there. And, the last time I saw a group of two venture out on their own, they almost died. I don't want to risk it."

"And you don't think that we can handle what's out there?" Kalir knew where she was going with this.

"Always a challenge, eh, Alyssia? Don't think of them as helping us. They are here to do their job, which is relay information to the master checkpoint. And I'm their captain."

"…and you're their captain." She looked over at the rest of the guards that were still getting their fill of drinks from their captain, then back to Kalir.

"So, where is our room?" Kalir grabbed his second mug of spirits as well as Alyssia's arm, leading her through the throng of checkpoint guards and to the staircase leading upstairs to the guest rooms. They passed several doors down the hallway, Kalir pulling her past them, opening up one of the last doors on the left. They moved inside, Kalir closing the door behind them with his foot, his hands somewhat occupied with Alyssia pressed into them.

Downstairs was lit with movement. The guards began gathering their ceremonial armor and other supplies, many of them leaving for the stables to prepare the horses for departure. It had been some time since any of the checkpoint guards had been on official business. Even the guards that were not going to Fell Whist were excited for the others, some of them making lists of the supplies they wanted while others handed the guards letters to take with them to deliver.

After the bar died down from giving out drinks from the captain, many of the guards moved to their rooms upstairs or stayed in a small group at a nearby table not far from the bar. The lone figure in the corner noticed this, took note of the number of guards that had been with Kalir, what armor Kalir wore as well as the number of weapons that could be seen on him. This was all important information since the figure was going to kill him. It was also important to know how many others would have to die in the process.

Nine others, including the human woman, the figure's mind calculated, the assassin's fingers drifting to the weapons hidden underneath the silky, velvet cloak.

I could take them all out here, yet that would draw attention and then Captain Ranolf might stay and attention must not be made with his death. It must be a secret. None must know until the time comes.

The assassin moved out of the bar without being noticed, snow crunching under the high, soft boots that hugged the thin yet agile legs tightly.

I must wait until the moment is right. I cannot kill him here. I will have to wait until he is alone or at least away from a populated area.

The assassin hoped that it would be soon that this would occur, for the time of a great change was close at hand and his master would be none too pleased if it was known that Kalir and the others had not been dealt with before the great change occurred. The figure moved away from the cottage and waited in the tree line, just outside the cottage, for the sun to rise and his task to continue.

It would not be much longer now. The figure had only been gone a ten day and was able to find Kalir Ranolf at his checkpoint at the tavern they call The Happy Traveler. After that, the tracking was the easy part. Kalir made no effort to hide his tracks in the snow or even double back to delay anyone in finding him. After all, Kalir did not know of the goings on of the organization that had sent the assassin or made mention of the captain's name when giving a list of potential threats that could hinder the progression of the times forward.

Before he dies, Kalir will know of The Emcrist Order and what we stand for!

8

The small town of Simmer Lo, nestled at the edge of the Argolis cliffs and not so far from Goletta, was a lucky lot. The tan-skinned inhabitants had been, sometimes, mistaken for river children due to their skin color, yet they seemed to maintain a dusty blond or strawberry-colored head of hair, opposed to the dark, almost coal color of the river children's facial and body hair. It had not snowed as much on the western half of Kariyl as it did on the eastern side, the wind from the cliffs nearly blowing most of the snow away that they had seen, the only thing now that they protected themselves from was the cold, whipping winds that would come up from the Alvanus Sea.

Ranyll Tolver lay undisturbed in his bed in the inn for hours, his hands resting comfortably on the hilt of his sword as he lay on his side, covered over with a blanket that he had brought in from the wagon as well as the blankets that were given to him by the innkeeper for Oagthor and himself.

We will not be here long, Ranyll reminded himself, his eyes fluttering closed as he allowed himself sleep, the visions now coming to him in the form of dreams. As he slipped into the dream, he could feel himself trying to fight it, knowing that the dream could overtake him if he weren't careful, and he would be trapped for some time, as it had happened before. Ranyll blocked the past out of his mind and let himself move into the dream.

Ranyll stands amidst a great number of people, hundreds of people around him pushing and shoving to escape. Ranyll turns and soon sees what they are running from; a fire, great and powerful like a great sea of orange and yellow, passes over homes and buildings, sending many sprawling to the ground, scrambling the best they can to escape. Soon, Ranyll feels the heat from the flames that are approaching, small pieces of the flames breaking into the figure of an inhabitant, a pair of fiery, red eyes burning within the shell of yellow and orange.

Each step the flame people take make an imprint that is left behind them, their forms almost invisible from the great fire raging behind them. The only way that Ranyll knows that they are there is that he can feel their immense heat as they close in on him and the remaining inhabitants that scream in terror. Ranyll turns to run but turns to see a full circle of flame people that have surrounded him and others, many of the inhabitants around him climbing over one another to stay away from the flames, the inhabitants underneath crumpling under booted foot. Ranyll can feel himself begin to fall to the ground.

Ranyll gripped his sword tightly to his chest, his eyes still closed.

Ranyll held his sword out to the flames, which seemed to hesitate, the great form around him shifting in pain, reeling back somewhat. Ranyll continues with his attack, holding the broadsword out at the flame people around him, igniting the sword with its magikal fire. The figures seemed to melt away before him, soon parting a small opening in front of him, the flames behind them parting as well. And what he sees before him he knows is his destiny.

It is an altar of old, when inhabitants used to give up sacrifices to The Creator, wanting more than anything else to please the great being in the clouds. The dais is bone white with a simple slab several feet wide and only a few feet across. Ranyll moves forward, noting that the other inhabitants around him do the same, following his lead toward the altar, his flame sword still out and continuously waving slowly in a wide arc towards the flame people that stand a few arms lengths away from him. Once he arrives at the altar, the flame people surge in on him, Ranyll's great blade arcing out to meet them. Many of them fall at his feet and, as he stands in front of the altar, he feels a fiery, hot hand grab at his sword hand. He pulls his hand away, accidentally loosening his grip on his sword, the sword dropping down onto the altar.

The blade of the sword touches the altar and, in moments, the sword turns to dust, blowing away in the wind. In the wind, the dust is thrown into the fire people, putting them out and turning them to ash, the ash soon slamming into the fiery wall that surrounds Ranyll and the others. There is a brilliant, white light and then Ranyll closes his eyes.

There is a loud knocking on the door and Ranyll lifts himself off his bed, still very much sleepy, his feet planting themselves on the hard, wooden floor. He moves to get up. There is a click of a key in the locked door and the innkeeper opens the door up slowly, peeking in with his head.

"Master Tolver, I believe your guest has arrived like you said. He is ready to come to the room. Shall I…." And, in another moment, Oagthor burst past the innkeeper and waddled in. His hair, both on his head and his beard, was mussed up, thick flakes of snow and ice stuck within the confines of each, his clothes still covered in snow and ice as well.

Just his general disposition seemed to be not a good one at all, Ranyll thinks to himself, noting that the dwarf is shivering for the first time since Ranyll has known him. Oagthor speaks through chattering teeth.

"If..you…think..I will forget this, Ranyll…you are very sorely….mi…mistaken! I should….kki…kill…you for a stunt….lik…like that!" The dwarf nods the innkeeper away and it wasn't until Ranyll nods back in approval that the innkeeper leaves, shutting the door behind him.

"Glad to see you are well, old friend. I take it you need some rest."

"Rest, warmth, food, clothes that are not wet, spirits, and a warm bath would be nice!"

Ranyll nods and slips his boots on in the process, standing up.

"And those things I will get for you, be assured of that. I will go see to those things now. Just you get some rest until I get…"

Oagthor was already asleep on the bed, snoring lightly, his clothes still on and covered with snow. Ranyll grabs his pack and is out the door, shutting and locking it behind him.

Ranyll did what he said he was going to do; he informed the innkeeper of his friend's needs and to wake the dwarf in a few hours, letting him get some sleep before tending to his needs fully. After that, Ranyll was out the doors and into the small town of Simmer Lo, a few of Oagthor's coins left on the counter for the innkeeper. He was on his way to find Falwen Sanses' family. Once there, he would give them the message Falwen had given him and be on his way.

*   *   *

Far-flung from Ranyll and his promise to be kept in Simmer Lo on the other side of Kariyl, evil purposes moved across a landscape that most inhabitants had forgotten. The small chain of mountains to the east of the elven city of Trayvilis had been abandoned long ago due to the fact that it was so remote and away from everything, but Knall Grist chose it for that purpose alone. Many times, the human had traveled on the continent as well as other continents, when he was still a youth, but he found now that his refuge lay in darker places.

That was so long ago, Knall thought to himself, drawing his left hand across his face, his fingers following the thick brown beard to its tip, which had been grown to mid-way down his chest, the neatly-groomed beard something he had kept every since he had become a man, shortly after leaving the war. There was not a gray hair on his head nor in his beard, and no wrinkles set about his eyes or lips, though what lay in his eyes could tell an inhabitant a fair number of stories in the years that he had lived.

Knall was dressed in a simple garb; a dark red tunic laced up to the neck and a pair of black breeches. His leather armor fit well over this, which kept him warm in the chill morning air as he stood on the parapets of his great keep. He wore no heavy armor today; the cold had stopped him from wearing his armor during practice down in the courtyard, moving the training area to inside the keep itself, down in the bowels of his fortress instead. However, his training would have to wait until he dealt with a problem within his ranks.

He looked out from his keep through the ridges of the Sinter Mountains, looking out at Kariyl as it was, still covered in snow, the clouds above it continuing to send flakes downward on the inhabitants. Due to the closeness of the mountain chain to the edge of the continent, the Keep of Dral Nakas did not get much snow, if any, which pleased Knall greatly. He heard his second in command approach, his light footfalls echoing across the ramparts on which Knall now stood.

Knall Grist did not turn. He kept his place, still looking out over the mountains, the morning wind blowing the cloak around his shoulders up in a sudden gust then back down onto his back, a few flakes of snow making it up through the wind around him to drift in his direction.

His voice broke the silence. "So, I take it from your arrival up here that there is word about the one that escaped."

His second in command, Belter Swen, looked out over the mountains as well. As second in command, Belter knew better than to give false information. Many times, he had seen himself rise in rank due to the ignorance of others ranked above him. He drew in his breath, feeling the bite of cold in his nostrils and down his throat, his thick frame nearly breaking through the plated armor he wore.

"More than a word, Master Grist. I have the one that allowed the scribe to escape in the dungeons. He is unharmed and guarded well."

"Oh, is he? Unharmed, you say? Well, let us change that, shall we?" Knall turned and moved past the great behemoth Belter, making his way down the steps of the parapets and into the warmth and barrenness of the top level of the keep. Belter followed behind him.

"Yes, Master Grist. I await your command. I'm sure this one will talk."

He will do more than talk, Knall thought to himself. *He will be of little use to me as a traitor, if he is one.*

The Great Keep of Dral Nakas had been built years before any of the inhabitants truly knew their grand scheme on Ar Solon. Many centuries had gone by with only few to populate Kariyl when the great keep came into existence. From the histories that Knall had read, Dral Nakas had been an elven magician who dabbled in the dark arts. After being cast out by his own race, he left Trayvilis to hide in the Sinter Mountains, slowly but surely building his fortress in the mountains to protect himself and continue his conjuring of the spirits of the unknown. Originally only slightly interested in the Occult of the Ancients, Dral soon became corrupted by the spirits themselves and began controlling a mass of his own people to erect a keep so the spirits would have a safe haven in which to reside while they escaped, one by one, building an army of the possessed, using the elves caught in Dral Nakas's snare to inhabit.

However, with the help of a human sorcerer, Dral was able to free his mind long enough to enchant the grounds of the fortress, trapping the spirits within a great magikal barrier within the keep so they could never escape. Once complete, Dral slaughtered his own people, sending the spirits back into the unknown whence they came, killing his own self so they would never trap him again.

The walls show no sign of this struggle, Knall thought to himself, looking at the beauty of the architecture of each elven-carved stone, each smooth edge of the tower's stones, Knall's line of sight then going to the great tapestries that lined the third floor's walls; great depictions of elves mapping the valley, constructing great elven cities, traversing the waterways of the Tirapoor Channel. There were even a few tapestries of the War of the Races, the artistry apparently changing over a period of time, the simple lines of old replaced with the complexity of colors and the smoothness of the lines, *so much more different than the tapestries before,* Knall remarked to himself, continuing down the long stairways that intersected one another in the keep, his eyes on the flickering torchlight below him as he made his way further and further down.

Belter was silent behind him, like a golem of old, a great stone creature following him, the towering human in stark contrast with Knall's harder features. Belter was from the south, near Dradle, which seemed to give him a rounder face and a thicker frame, as if he labored much of his life, his thick arms and legs almost twice the size of his leader. That, and the fact that Belter was more of a savage when it came to swordplay, more of a hack and a slash fighter than a true student to the ways of the sword made them opposites when sparring.

Indeed, he was a golem for this age, Knall agreed, watching as the light played across Belter's face and huge arms, casting him in a grayish light that seemed to give him a look of true stone.

Knall and his second, Belter, continued through the keep, soon moving down a set of stairs that confirmed that, indeed, there were others living within the confines of the keep itself. Several armed guards, golem-like as well, stood as sentries at the entryway to a number of corridors that opened up around the two moving through the hallways. The guards, once taking note of who was approaching, stiffened up, their eyes averting themselves from contact with either Knall or his second, looking only straight ahead. None moved from their post, their plate armor heavy on their limbs yet still without movement or a single moan from the metal brackets that held it together.

Knall commented. "You have trained your men well, Belter. They do good to fear us." Belter only nodded at this and the two continued to another set of stairs in an adjoining hallway, passing two more guards on the way down.

The dungeons were somewhat different that what many would think when hearing the word. Dral Nakas wasn't a tyrant at all but a great mind. He build the dungeons as a way of escape; it was simply an underground structure that he could access that contained a great many, smaller rooms, some with intent while some were empty and without purpose. Since he had such a strong workforce building the keep, the ideas that he had started with became somewhat greater in grandeur once it began. In time, the magician had created a complex system of underground tunnels that he could traverse through, keeping the tower somewhat simple, yet the infrastructure underground was something altogether different.

Knall had memorized these many tunnels and underground labyrinths, confining himself to many of the closer rooms of the dungeons than the other ones much further underground, knowing that the air became thicker and much harder to breathe within, he had noted some time ago when first traveling through them. The prisoner was in one of these rooms, one of the closer ones, Knall noticing the extra guards at the entrance to the room the possible traitor was in. Many of the entrances had doors built to house different things in them yet this one did not have a door at all. Knall walked right into it, passing the guards without so much as a look, stepping in front of the prisoner, the jumbled mess of nerves that many called Trin Ganthes.

Trin, upon seeing Knall Grist in front of him, immediately went pale white, his eyes bulging from their sockets, his hands, which were tied behind his back and to a chair with knotted rope, began to shake nervously.

He went to speak. "Mmm.m…mas..ter Gri.ss..tt. It is you….I can…explain…., I." Knall's fist slammed up against Trin's temple, knocking him and the chair over in one blow. The prisoner's head hit the floor and he cried out, which made Knall all the more angry, a swift kick followed by a flurry of blows to the head following soon after. Trin whimpered to himself silently.

Belter moved in behind Knall, standing in the corner of the room. There was nothing in the room with the exception of the three of them. No food, no water, no amenities of any kind were given to Trin until he was seen by Master Grist.

"No explanation is needed, you fool! I know everything already! What I do need to know, however, is what did the scribe take exactly? Was it something I need to worry about? Is it something that is going to cost you your life, me having to waste my time on a miserable wretch like you?"

Trin did not move. He dare not speak. He just laid there, still tied to the chair, bleeding freely now on the floor from a cut on his head that had opened up.

"You will answer me now, you worthless mass of flesh!" Knall kicked him again, this time in the stomach, Trin doubling over in pain.

"Mas…..Mas…master…Gri…sst….the…scribe….she…got…..she got..one of..the maps…the battle plans….."

Knall fumed. "..the battle plans…?" Knall looked behind him at Belter, a look of clear worry pasted across his leader's chiseled features. His jaw clenched tightly, Knall continued the interrogation.

"And this scribe, do you know her whereabouts….or where she is going to?" Knall leaned in close. "…and her name would be helpful as well, Trin, don't you think?"

Trin Ganthes, still in pain, tried his best to keep his calm. He breathed through his pain, trying to keep from crying out from the shooting pains in his left side and face, which seemed now to be swelling up as he spoke.

"Her name….her name is Altina Laese and she is one of the…one of the elven scribes that the guild picked up on the way to Elvinisclar. She was…was one of the best reproduction scribes that we had ever found before. She killed one of the messengers and escaped in his clothes and out through the keep's main doors. She probably doesn't even know what she's got in the scroll case."

Knall looked to Belter, who nodded in return, the thick golem-like human moving forward, his sword out in a moments notice.

Trin saw the flash of Belter's blade and began to grovel.

"Please, Master Grist, no! I will make it up to you. I promise! I will.."

Knall simply stood over him. "Does she know how to translate Parthenian?"

Trin shook his head. "She does not, Master Grist! She only knows elven, dwarven, and common. She took the scribe test like the others and she didn't know the Parthenian alphabet."

Belter's blade flashed and Trin's bonds were cut, the ropes falling loosely over his shoulders and onto the floor. Trin rubbed the soreness out of his wrists and lifted himself up onto one elbow, bewildered.

Knall leaned forward and grabbed Trin by the hair, yanking him eye level with his own dark stare.

"Find her, Recruit Ganthes! Find her and redeem yourself! I want her head and the scroll case along with any other pair of eyes that see that battle plan, are we clear? I don't care if they speak or read Parthenian, it is still valuable."

Knall released Trin and turned, walking out of the room, Belter sheathing his sword at his side, moving quietly behind his master.

"Give the recruit a horse and supplies and whatever else he needs to find her. Send a message to the one I have out there now and have him deal with her if he finds her first."

They moved away from the room, returning back up the stairs to one of the main floors of the keep.

"If the other one finds her first, have him kill Trin as well and bring back his head and the supplies he was given."

Belter nodded and moved away from Knall, leaving the leader of the Emcrist Order alone with his thoughts in the adorned hallways of The Great Keep of Dral Nakas.

9

Oagthor and Ranyll watched through the windows as the snow came down in blankets, covering the town of Simmer Lo in a white, shimmering mess. At least, that's what Oagthor called it when it began to come down shortly after Ranyll arrived back from the other side of town. They sat now, at the local tavern, only a building over from the inn they stayed at, watching as the few patrons that had been there began to disburse, carrying with them reluctant footfalls as they made their way through the snow to their homes.

"A white, shimmering mess, Ranyll, if you ask me! I don't see how you could travel through this stuff, let alone get anything done in the process." The dwarf took another drink from his mug, letting the spirits sink in, letting the drink relax his still-aching body from the walk that had seemed to never end. Oagthor pointed at the last of those leaving out the door of the tavern.

"It must be a surprise to them to get snow so far west. It must hurt the fisherman something fierce as well." Ranyll looked back behind him as the last of the patrons left out, leaving just him and Oagthor and the tenders at the bar in the tavern. It had gotten cold early on, when Ranyll was out, but now the fire pit in the middle of the room was breaking the chill from the outside off of him and one of the bartenders seemed to make it their job to continue to keep it burning bright, dropping a few fresh pieces of wood into it every so often, ensuring that the only two patrons in the place had full mugs as well.

"I'm sure it makes things hard on them, not being able to work their trade, Oagthor; just as it is on those in Telgin right now. I remember the snows and how it had hurt the businesses there a few winters ago. But I can only imagine how it must hurt those here and in Goletta just south of us. They rely on trade for survival."

Oagthor nodded to one of the barkeeps, who approached just shortly after. It was the same one that had been tending to the fire pit. He was well-tanned, almost too dark, the skin on his face and neck tight around his bones, seeming to strangle what was left of his form with rigidity. The bar keep was thin, seemed almost underfed to Oagthor, who looked now at Ranyll for direction.

"What would you like, Ranyll? You got the first few drinks. I only see it as fitting that I get the meal for the evening."

Ranyll didn't seem to care what he ate. He had other things on his mind, Oagthor noticed, looking at the tanned bar keep with a little bewilderment.

"Whatever is your best, I would like two of. And make sure that my fish is well-cooked. And if you have any potatoes or a stew, something thicker, I would like some of that. And a loaf of bread…. and spices if you have any." The barkeep nodded and moved away, soon bringing a fresh flagon of what they had been drinking, which was a light brew of ale compared to what Oagthor had been accustomed to. Usually, he could not see down into the bottom of the mug when he drank ale, but this ale seemed lighter, somewhat fragrant.

It isn't my taste at all, but it does the job. He finished what was left in his mug and filled it up again with the flagon.

"Ranyll, there is a lot we have yet to discuss before we move onto where ever we are going, which I still have no idea where that is!"

Ranyll nodded his head in agreement.

"Oagthor, I sold the horse and the wagon here at Simmer Lo. It is worth more to sell it here that at Goletta."

Oagthor almost choked on his drink. "Sold it? Why would you do a thing like that, especially with this snow coming in? And Goletta, that is quite a slog down there. What is it, a day's journey, probably longer now that the snow is coming down?"

Ranyll nodded. "Something like that. The wagon will slow us down. Anyway, we won't need it where we're going, Oagthor."

Oagthor finished his mug of ale and slammed it down on the table, looking back at Ranyll with a mix of hesitation and slyness that Ranyll could only attribute to a tipsy dwarf. The young human pulled the flagon closer and filled up his own mug, drinking a good portion of it before speaking again.

"I have to go to the Island of Dree, Oagthor. I have known for some time about this."

Oagthor stopped with his mug halfway to his mouth, his lips still frothy from the last long gulp. He put his mug back down onto the table, looking wide-eyed at the human. Oagthor's voice almost seemed a whisper in the quiet tavern, his fingers tracing over his mussed up beard, cleaning the froth off from the edges of his mouth.

"Ranyll, this is no joking time! You bring me out of comfort, into this snowstorm and as far west as we can go on this continent to tell me this?" By this time, Oagthor's voice broke in his throat, grumbling something incoherent as he finished his mug and reached for the flagon, filling his mug again. Noticing that that the flagon was near empty, Oagthor raised it up in the air to the tender at the bar, who called back in return, soon trading the empty flagon out for another full one.

"I've seen it in my visions, Oagthor. It can't be stopped. I have to do this."

The dwarf just stared at him, unflinching. "Is this for glory, Ranyll? Is this for you and your own personal mission that you feel that you need to accomplish, because of what happened in Dardist all those years ago with Gabriella?"

Ranyll matched gazes with Oagthor and did not break it. "I wish it were that easy." Ranyll reached down beside him, pulling a great tome from his pack at his side, clearing out a spot on the table for him to open it.

"Look at it. Look through it, Oagthor. These are the visions and the notes that I have compiled these last three summers. It is because of D'meir why I do this, why I go here, if you must know," Ranyll added, hoping that the fire fox's name would not call forth the trouble he saw in MiddleFast.

But the dwarf did not start when he heard his old friend's name, Ranyll noticed, taking another drink from his mug, watching Oagthor intently.

"And did D'meir ever talk about this island?"

"No."

"Then why the Island of Dree? Why must we go there?"

"Because that where D'meir had come from." Ranyll watched as Oagthor took all of this in, the dwarf finishing the mug in front of him, his eyes meeting Ranyll's a few times before the human continued.

"After the battle with the daemons, I tried to piece together what D'meir had said to me, how he always called me a savior, that he seemed to know how things played out before they happened. I couldn't understand it! It wasn't until I spoke with Triggle, a Miftle from the original party set out to help Gabriella that I learned that D'meir wasn't a part of their group of faeries. He was from somewhere else!"

Ranyll opened the tome and turned to the first few pages in it, marking the place with his finger.

"I had to do some study on it, but I found an old text in a library that spoke about some of the faerie races in Ar Solon. When I looked up fire foxes, they are said to come from the Island of Dree. That is also where they get their power from, the magik ability to control a magikal fire, and that is where fire dust that the faeries use comes from; the volcanic ash is used as a magikal source!"

Oagthor hesitated. He looked at the great tome in front of him. It was larger than any tome he had seen in some time; larger, in fact, than the ones that he had seen even in the great halls in the dwarven libraries.

Ranyll has been busy these three summers, indeed! The dwarf leaned forward and pulled the tome closer to him, turning it so that it faced him. He then looked around, his eyes focusing on an object not far from them. The dwarf then stood up, moving over to a lantern hanging on the wall. He grabbed it by the handle and brought it back to the table, turning it down so that the shutter was somewhat lower than it had been.

The dwarf sat back down, his mug near him, Ranyll's tome in front of him, Oagthor's eyes on the pages laid out before him. He didn't begin reading immediately. In fact, he stared at it for a time, his eyes squinting at the writing on the page. Slowly, he reached into his pocket and took from it a small wooden case, pulling out a pair of old, wiry spectacles. Oagthor cleaned each lens with a small rag from the wooden case, sitting them on the edge of his nose, wrapping the small wire frame over each ear.

"I'm not as young as I used to be, Ranyll! Time has its way of working one over. Of course, you wouldn't know that yet!"

Oagthor looked over the tip of his nose at the tome, staring down with the spectacles to examine Ranyll's writings. Ranyll leaned back in his chair, taking a sip from his mug, a tending girl moving over to their table with their dishes, laying out a myriad of plates in front of them. Ranyll smiled his thanks as she moved away. Outside, the snow continued to fall, the patrons that had been bustling about in the snow had ceased their movements, *probably in for the day,* Ranyll thought to himself, filling his mug from the flagon, his eyes on the flakes of snow as they fell outside, watching through the window as a few random people passed by.

Oagthor huffed. "So you believe that whoever told D'meir about your being a savior resides on this island?"

Ranyll nodded his head.

Oagthor just shook his head. "That's quite a long shot. D'meir told me years ago that where he was from there were no other fire foxes and he had not been around inhabitants all of his life… until he came across Rathor and myself in the abandoned keep in the Agnar Mountains." The dwarf paused. "Still, you have some pretty good information… these dreams…err. visions… when did you start having them?"

Ranyll moved his plate closer to himself, sampling the fish, his hand reaching out for the loaf of bread that sat not far from him. He pulled a piece off and sat it on his plate.

"It started shortly after the situation in the caverns in Dardist three summers ago. I was traveling back home from the Tirapoor Channel to visit Telgin and I camped out for the night. I fell asleep and that's when the first one happened."

Oagthor looked up over his spectacles at the human. "When did you realize that the sword had something to do with the visions?"

Ranyll took a bite from the bread, chewing. He washed it down with half a mug of ale and, suddenly, the effects of the ale hit him. Ranyll had spent some time drinking with Ermoor, Rynen, and the other checkpoint guards a few seasons back, yet he had no formal training in the drink, for he could feel it take hold of him when he put his mug down. He felt his speech slur a bit when he answered.

"It was.. it was a few ten days later when I realized… when I realized it. I had noticed that the visions came all the time, but I was able to control them, sort of sift through them, when I carried the sword close to me. I tried experiments."

"Experiments?"

"I let myself fall into sleep, fall into the dream, without the sword. You see, I continue to have the same dreams and visions for days on end. And every time, they get longer and more detailed. Once I held the sword, though, I could move through them without being completely affected by the things in the dream."

"So, you can control the length of time you stay within your dreams and visions?"

"Not my visions. They have the tendency to occur at random. But the dreams, I can *somewhat* control them."

Oagthor was silent for a time, lost in thought, his eyes scanning the pages in front of him again. He read for a few more pages before speaking again.

"So, Ranyll, do you think it has anything to do with her? You know, ….with…"

Ranyll answered quickly. "Gabriella? I know it does, Oagthor. She's in them **with** me."

Oagthor nodded, sitting back in his chair, his hands sitting on top of his stomach.

"What does she do when she's there, Ranyll?"

"She guides me…she guides me where I need to go. She's always in the background of the scene, like a ghost of some kind. She never speaks to me, she just shows me things."

Oagthor shook his head. "In the time I was in the barrel, I had dreams, visions, too, but I never saw Gabriella in them. And I had several dreams while I was in there."

Ranyll finished what was on his plate and pushed it away on the table. "So, you never saw her?"

Oagthor simply shook his head, his hand reaching for his mug not far from him. Oagthor began working on his meal as well, so Ranyll did not push the matter further, his own thoughts beginning to wander to so many things at once.

It has been such a long time since I've thought about her. Her look, her smell; her presence over everything around me, how it seemed to almost control me and my environment. Gabriella, what have you done to me?

The last thought seemed to float around for a while in Ranyll's mind while Oagthor was busy with his meal, the dwarf finishing off the flagon as well, his thick fingers holding up the empty one to receive another.

There's so much going on at once, thought Ranyll, *what am I to focus on first?*

But Ranyll knew the answer to the question even before he asked it. It would have to be to finish following the visions until there were no more at all for him to follow. This had been something that he had been doing ever since…. Trayvilis.

…Trayvilis. I try to forget about what went on there as well as the other populated elven city of Elvinisclar. Indeed, something had been happening in the world of the elves that none of the other races knew about.

But what could Ranyll do? The young human had little knowledge of the other races, including his own race, and did not know if these practices were happening by all of the races or not. It would be wrong of him to bring out into the open the business of other races, especially since the great way that they had treated him during his stay. He felt as if he were royalty, as if he were an important guest that everyone knew. Ranyll had never been treated that way before.

Being from the small town of Telgin, which had no city walls, no palace guards, no grand sports or other fares that were of much interest, Ranyll knew little of the pleasures of life in a thriving city, let alone the lives of those in a grand castle such as the case was with both elven kingdoms he had visited. Ranyll knew not how to feel when it came to disbursing information about the races on Kariyl. Not many had ever listened to what he said, so to have a crowd gathered in anticipation about the outside world around them and its inhabitants, was something that Ranyll became enthralled with, completely captivated at how others lived their lives compared with his more simple life.

Oagthor finished his meal and scooted the many empty plates forward, away from him, closing Ranyll's tome in the process. He nodded to Ranyll and pulled out a small pouch from the belt at his hip, pulling a small pipe from it and a pinch of dried smoking herbs. He closed the pouch back up and put it up, packing the herbs into the pipe with his pinky finger.

Oagthor took the covering off of the lantern on the table and set it aside, lighting a small piece of the spiced herbs so he could light the rest in his pipe. The dwarf spoke through a plume of freshly blown smoke, the smell of it seeming to waking Ranyll up from his restful state.

"I have a story to tell you, Ranyll. It might take your mind off of all of these things that you think about lately."

"A story?"

Oagthor's lips parted a bit and the human could see a smile on them through the smoke that escaped every so often, hiding Oagthor's pursed lips from view.

"Yes, but this will be the first time I tell the story to someone I know. You, my boy, can truly appreciate it. This story takes place shortly after I parted with the faerie army and went on my own. I think it will be of interest to you. It's about the unicorn, Gwenzel."

Ranyll's heart skipped a beat. He could feel the blood rush to his face, the spirits still taking effect throughout his limbs. He tried his best to not show surprise, yet the name of the unicorn brought back so many memories that he couldn't help himself. After all, he never found out what happened to Gwenzel and the two sprites those three summers ago after they parted when Ranyll dropped down into the chasm with D'meir, one of the many acts that changed his life forever.

Oagthor nodded his head. "Yes, Ranyll. Gwenzel... Gwenzel and his faerie friends, Drigno and Tristle."

Ranyll leaned forward in his chair. "What about them, Oagthor? Please, tell me! I have not heard from the faeries in some time." Ranyll had not seen any of the faeries since days after those ten days in Dardist, just short after Gabriella passed from Ar Solon. He had only seen the faeries as they left through the tunnels in Dardist, following the daemons down into the Dwarven Crag shortly after Gabriella's death.

"They're alive, Ranyll; all three of them. I found them and freed them from Scarwol's captivity after I killed the creature."

"How, but… how did you…" Ranyll was at a loss for words.

The name Scarwol seemed to bring open a wound from that same time as well, the human remembering when Scarwol had reached through Gwenzel's own mind to capture and trap his mind from within.

The young man had always known that there were creatures out there, unexplained ones, but he never knew that he would be part of the awful world that many of the inhabitants ever had to experience. In fact, many inhabitants had forgotten the stories of old because they were told in songs and rhymes, which had seemed to disappear with the death of the angel Greditto as well.

"Oagthor….how did you kill him? Scarwol, I mean."

The dwarf reached down next to him and, with one great swing, brought the great double-sided battleaxe down onto the table, spilling Ranyll's and his own mug in the process. The battle axe was a great weapon, the handle of the axe itself forged of the great steel by the dwarves of long ago. Since then, the battleaxe was a grand sight to see, several jewels set into place along the center of the axe and along the handle, yet not in the way of the bearer's hold spots in which to wield it.

"I did it with this, Ranyll." The bartender moved from his place at the bar and came with another flagon, refilling their fallen cups once he collected the others from the floor.

Ranyll did not take his eyes away from the great battleaxe, something that he had never had a chance to wield himself. He had always seemed to stay with the sword and dagger; they seemed to be the easiest to be trained with, what humans were accustomed to using. Of course, he had seen a great many axes wielded by humans in the little time that he had traveled in the last few summers, but nothing like this.

*   *   *

And, indeed, there was nothing like it around today, Falwen thought to himself, the quill in front of him for the second night in a row, the story weaving itself like that of a grand story telling around a campfire of adventurers. Falwen, himself, felt as if the story was being told to him, as if he were one of the many listeners around that fire, the ever-weaving intricacies of the mind pulling others into the story with them as they told it.

I have traveled quite far with Ranyll, the Chronicler agreed, knowing that he was very connected with this young boy for some reason.

Maybe it was because of the timing in which we both seemed to be tasked with our grand schemes, Falwen thought to himself, his nimble fingers holding the quill in check as it slid over the page of the tome, dipping and dancing, dipping and dancing its way through history, not confined as so many others were, so free to do its will without a single encumbrance.

"And that is how it should be." Falwen had taken a great interest in the last chapter, watching as his family name came into view across the page, of how Ranyll had given his own wife, Larissa, the package from him, how she had carefully opened it, tears streaking her soft face, her muffled cry as she brought the package close to her chest, breathing it in as sobs wracked her delicate frame.

Falwen drew in a long breath and wished himself to be there as well, but he knew she would know he were at least safe by seeing the garments inside as well as the gift and the letters.

The Chronicler had never been a writer. He had spent most of his time, his younger years, at sea, chasing the waves and what adventure was brought in by them, always returning home to an empty room, only to set off again on another ship, bound for some unknown shore, far from Kariyl. That was, of course, until Larissa came into his life.

Once he met her, his life was steady and set into the town of Simmer Lo. He had just purchased a boat for himself when Larissa told him that she was with child, and soon, the boat was sold and his life he chose now he had decided for himself. Of course, he would have loved to get a few more adventures in during his lifetime, but he was content with raising a son, and then soon came another only a few summers later.

Eventually, he was securing his place firmly at the dinner table with his family and his pride was as a father of such wonderful children. And his wife, Larissa, was what made him want to become a settled man. He had no want for another, only Larissa. She had become the sun and the moon to him. They had a routine that seemed to be able to outlast the heaving shores around them.

Falwen shook off the thoughts with a smile and a fluid movement of closing the tome in front of him and moving it to the shelf just behind him. He slid it in place with the others on the shelf and moved his fingers across to the other tomes that lie there, all of the ones that he had finished already in only three summers as the Chronicler. He found the tome that he was looking for and pulled it from the shelf, the binding still new, the covering still fresh as the day that he had made it, which was not so long ago.

Magik. The word seemed to make Falwen shudder when he thought of it, the fisherman pulling the scribe's robes he wore closer to his neck and tightly about his shoulders, placing the volume down in front of him on the writing table.

"I hate the idea that it is gone but loath the idea that it has returned; and in this fashion, no less!" Falwen knew that what Oagthor had in his possession was a magikal item from the old times the moment he wrote about the dwarf and his entrance into Scarwol's chambers all those summers ago. The great creature of old who had become somewhat more of a phantom than a real entity, trapped between the ethereal and Ar Solon realms of inhabitants, had been waiting for an opponent to challenge him. He did not invite as many do the challenges of others, but he did recognize that there would be a number of beings that would challenge him in his ways once they knew that he was working with The One.

Ahhh, Darien! The most puzzling of all the beings on Ar Solon.

Falwen had read many of the histories of The One, of Darien as he was called in the clouded world of Drillidan, far away the suffering and pain of the inhabitants. The Chronicler had read of his troubled dealings with Scarwol and knew that there were other schemes that were being put into place; that Test was somewhere at large at this very moment, moving on Ranyll as he had not too long ago, coming after his mother and brother first.

"But they were saved. Yes, they were saved."

And they were saved by love. This idea alone made Falwen see hope in the land yet. He did not give up hope as Gilden did, three summers ago, his mind filled with these histories and more, Falwen was sure of that. The new Chronicler knew where the previous Chronicler's mistakes lay; it was in the idea that there wasn't something bigger at stake in all of Ar Solon to fight for.

And, to fight for love, and to be saved by love, is one of the best feelings of all.

This is where Falwen's mind was at right at the moment, being saved by the love that was saving others, watching as Oagthor bared his soul for the first time in some time to someone he knew, the burly dwarf slamming down the axe of ages, the great axe that had been a part of history for some time now, yet it had none to wield it in over two hundred years. It had been lost in the caves just north of Dardist, in a secret set of caves, hidden well by Scarwol and his fog creatures, among a great horde of treasure that the dwarves had blamed the other races on stealing.

Of course, Scarwol never cared for the treasure itself, never touched it or let others near it; it was not the treasure itself that he wanted, it was what it meant to others that made him keep it. The creature from long ago had no want for material things or great weapons with magikal powers; what he wanted was ideas.

A memory, ways into others minds, the feelings of the inhabitants is what had kept him silent all these years, is what had kept him at peace. He had taken all of these things and more from those that mined in the town of Wilden for over two hundred years and now his palate needed to be satisfied further. He had just begun extending his borders within the Agnar Mountains, within the caves nearest the dwarven city of Dardist when Ranyll appeared within the caves.

However, the death of the fire fox D'meir at the hands of one of his Fog Beasts was what set the stage for his final end.

And the Chronicler knew this all too well. Falwen read through the scene within the volume over and over again, reading as the dwarf named Oagthor Axeblade, enraged by his close friend's death, tore at the very fabric of creation when he came at Scarwol, soon finding a weapon that could defeat him within Scarwol's own cache of great treasures of an age long gone. This weapon, this battle axe Oagthor had found, was a great power long ago and, to be unearthed, set upon Kariyl now, was something that Falwen had not anticipated. That is why the Chronicler set the book down in front of him again, even after so many reads, wanting much to be able to warn Oagthor and Ranyll of the dangers of bringing a weapon of magik back onto the surface.

There was a reason that many of the magikal items of old were destroyed or hidden, Falwen reminded himself, especially after spending a large amount of time writing of Ranyll's journey with a sword that, though not magikal, could be wielded and used by one that held a magik within them. Falwen had been able to tell Ranyll of the dangers of wielding a flame sword and of using his healing powers on others, for it was a time of great despair on all the lands of Ar Solon, *and there is more despair and desperation to come, I'm afraid.*

The Chronicler looked over at the three empty tomes sitting next to his writing table, the binding still fresh from him finishing them days earlier.

There are many stories to tell now, many things that are coming to pass that shall change history as we know it. It is true, as Divlo said, 'keep close the ones you hold dear to you, because it may be the last time you see them'.

Falwen Sanse hoped that that would not be the case for the many that he wrote about now, hoping beyond hope that he would be able to see his boys grow into men, see his wife grow old and die a happy and content woman with her husband by her side, but many of those hopes that he had within him were fading now, fading as he moved the one tome he had been looking through and sat one of the empty ones on the table, reaching for his quill and inkwell that were placed not far from him.

Falwen looked around the walls at the maps that he collected in the last few seasons and eyed the places that he were to write about this time, that he was about to see with his own eyes, some of them for the first time.

See them with the mind's eye, he reminded himself, Falwen falling into the pose of The Chronicler more easily than he had ever done as of yet; eyes squinting somewhat, left hand tilted with the quill in it, his right arm propped against the side of the tome that was blank, his fingers slowly tracing the first few words on the page…

'*It moved with a ferocity that few had ever seen…*'

Immediately, Falwen knew who the words spoke of.

Or what, I should say.

Falwen had written about Test many times, in many tomes, always small slivers of the great daemon coming out into the stories that The Chronicler weaved nightly. At first, the fisherman had been afraid of it, afraid for Ranyll, for the scribe was able to see a little bit into the mind of this creature, and knew what he had in store for the young human and the others that surrounded and supported him along his journey.

But now, now I do not fear it. I know Test.

In that short amount of time, Falwen had seen the daemon take what had been a vengeful hatred and turn it into a well-laid plan, something even the most skilled inhabitant had trouble doing. In no time, Test was on his way, with a purpose stronger than most grand schemes that have ever been given. And, for a moment, Falwen thought about the idea freely.

Do daemons have grand schemes? Was the One giving purpose to death and destruction, just as The Creator was giving purpose to life and the birth of all over Ar Solon?

It seemed trivial, it even seemed somewhat ridiculous, yet when Falwen had read the histories of the Parthenians, he had always questioned why such a war-loving race of inhabitants could be so blessed. The idea came and went, like the flow of the rivers on the Tirapoor Channel on a sunny afternoon, soon bringing him back to the tome in front of him. He continued.

'It moved with a ferocity that few had ever seen. It could travel both on four legs or on two, which made it easily adaptable to many a situation, be it the wilderness or the city, which it eyed greedily now. The daemon Test had been changing his form for centuries and knew that this time would be no different. He looked just north of him and could see the city walls of the vast port town of Goletta coming into view through the rising of the morning sun to the east.

All of Kariyl was still covered in snow, yet there were patches here and there that had begun to melt. The snow seemed to pass those in the west rather quickly, the storm itself dissipating overnight, leaving a rather hefty amount of snow on the occupants just north and east of Goletta.

Test stood up on his hind legs and felt the snap of the joints as they adjusted to hold him at human height, his sinewy toes snapping into place to form human feet, toes, even small toe nails that were indistinguishable from the real toes that he used as his copy. He stared down at the human he had caught earlier, the inhabitant still half alive, his breathing somewhat ragged, his eyes closed from the pain.

It must be the dagger then, Test thought, grabbing at the hilt of the dagger with his newly-formed human hand. He ripped it free from the human's chest and the eyes opened immediately, followed by the mouth, which let out a great scream of pain.

Test grabbed the human by the throat and picked him up before he could get the entire scream out, pressing him against a nearby tree. An exact copy of the man stood in front of him, staring at him, yet the red eyes never changed. Clothes even formed onto this daemon to match the bloodied ones that the human wore. His copy smiled at him and opened its mouth. An agonizing, grating sound made its way out of its mouth, speaking to him in a guttural voice.

To the man, it sounded like glass being broken over and over again.

"What is your name, human?"

The human stifled a cry and answered back. "It's Savaan! Savaan Eldis!"

The copy turned its head slightly and coughed the words out, trying to say the name.

"Sa…v.a.a.n…..El….d.d.d..is.." The voice began to change in Savaan's ears, began to, in moments, mimic his own. The new Savaan Eldis turned to the old one and smiled.

"Well, Savaan Eldis, I need you no more. And, when I'm done with your family, they will share your fate as well." Test squeezed Savaan's throat until the human breathed his last breath, tossing him easily into the woods before the wagon approached. As it approached, the new Savaan smiled and moved forward slowly, waiting for the occupants to respond to him.

A little girl, looking much like her father Savaan than her mother, smiled out of the tarped wagon, wrapped tightly in a thick blanket.

"Daddy, daddy, did you find it?"

Test responded. "What was that, dear?"

The little girl looked disappointed.

"The rabbit! Did you find the one that I saw?"

Test shook his head and moved closer to the wagon, the woman guiding the horses looking oddly at him.

"Savaan, are you alright? You look a little pale."

Test nodded and made it onto the snowy trail leading to Goletta, hopping up onto the wagon next to her. He smiled at her, the red eyes gone from view, replaced by the sad, almost haunting eyes of Savaan Eldis.

"I guess I feel a little tired, that's all."

His wife laughed a bit and patted him on the shoulder, Test feeling the warmth of her hand on his side. Test enjoyed the ride into Goletta.

10

Jannon and Tamarus Sanse watched as the man that called himself Ranyll Tolver walked away from their home, the snow coming down somewhat harder than expected, blanketing the figure completely until he vanished into the streets of Simmer Lo. Both sons turned to their mother, who was clutching a package to her chest, their father's clothes falling out of the carefully wrapped package.

The oldest, Jannon, went to his mother's side immediately, picking up his father's fallen clothes, his arm out to his mother as she took it for support. Tamarus simply stood there, still shocked to see his mother so upset and joyful at the same time.

"You're father, he's alive! He is alive and well!" Jannon pulled his mother close, the rest of her words inaudible as she sobbed in her son's arms. She laid the package down on the table nearest to them and held Jannon close to her. Though he was taller than her, she still felt a sense of motherly instinct for Jannon. In just a few summers, Jannon had begun to grow into a man. Even though he was only fourteen summers old, Jannon had taken on his father's responsibilities without complaint, spending many of his days during the ten day week at the shores himself, like his father had done since he was a child.

Tamarus simply smiled at the two, walking over to the package on the table. He picked up his father's shirt, bringing it to his nose.

Indeed, it did smell like father. It had been cleaned and packed away with the other things, but father's scent was still there on it.

Tamarus sifted through the package and saw a stack of letters tied with some string around them. The name on each letter was for Larissa, his mother, and it was in his father's handwriting.

Larissa began to compose herself further, sitting down at the table by the package. She wiped the corner of her eyes with her hand and took a few breaths before speaking to her sons.

"This young man, Ranyll Tolver he called himself, said that your father is fine, that he is on a charge of the utmost importance and that he cannot say where Falwen is but that he can continue to visit with things as long as he can. He even left us a wagon and a horse compliments of your father. And this…."

Their mother pulled a small brown sack that clanked together loudly from the package and sat it on the table by itself. She untied the strings from the sack and emptied its contents onto the table in front of her sons. An assortment of gold, bronze, platinum, and silver coins rained down from the bag, more coins than either son had ever seen.

"Jannon, you don't have to work as hard as you do now. Your father has done his part; this amount of coin will last us for several summers. You see, he didn't abandon us! Your father would never do such a thing!" Jannon nodded his head, yet he knew there was something more to the story that this Ranyll did not let them in on.

"What if father has been taken captive? What if he's hurt and needs our help?" These thoughts and many others plagued Jannon's mind, had been running through his mind every day, including the days that he spent at the shores, looking out over the Alvanus Sea at the dots in the landscape that his own father used to stare at, day after day.

'A man can never get tired of looking out at something like this!' his father had told him so many times whenever he was questioned about why he was a fisherman. It was such a simple trade, something that dated back to generations when the inhabitants were just hunter/gatherers and lived in tribes. Jannon had a sinking feeling that his father wanted more, had always wanted more, and just didn't know how his family would play into it.

Tamarus shook his head at the ideas that Jannon threw out to them. "Father can handle himself. He taught us how to defend ourselves and I know he can do better than us!"

Their mother nodded her head in agreement. "Your brother is right, Jannon, your father knows how to defend himself well. He spent years on a ship before the both of you were born. He was a well-traveled man. He knows the dangers of Ar Solon."

Larissa stood up and began putting the coins back in the sack, tying it up once finished. She left the bag on the table and picked up the tied stack of letters from Falwen.

"Boys, I think I am going to sit by the fire for a little while and hear what your father has to say in these letters." Their mother put a few of the coins from the sack into Jannon's hand and closed his hand over them.

"What I would like you to do is go get us some things that we need from the vendors, maybe some spices as well for tonight's meal. And Tamarus," Larissa motioned to Tamarus and then to the axe by the door.

"I need you to cut some fresh firewood for the fire. We will have ourselves a feast tonight in your father's honor!" Tamarus smiled at his mother and then moved for the axe, grabbing up his winter garments as well. He was only eleven summers old, he knew, but his mother also knew that he had become quite efficient with an axe these last few rough winters that had come and gone, and he jumped at the chance to get out of the cottage and into the snow. Tamarus was out of the door before Jannon had even put on his winter garments.

Larissa placed the remaining logs onto the fire in the fireplace, positioning the cooking pot over the fire as well, emptying the pail of water they had into it. The pot steamed and hissed its approval of the fire underneath it and the inhabitant grabbed up the blanket in the chair nearest the fire and pulled it over her shoulders, sitting in the chair with the stack of letters in her lap.

Jannon hesitated by the door. Somehow sensing this, his mother leaned her head out to him so he could see her face. She had tears in her eyes.

"Everything is going to be alright, Jannon, you'll see. Your father loves us all very much. He knows he has duties to this family and takes them very seriously. He has always done so."

Jannon nodded and opened the door and, stuffing the coins in his winter cloak, closed the door behind him.

Now alone with her thoughts and the letters, Larissa's fingers untied the strings, her fingers tracing over her husband's handwriting on each envelope with her name on it.

"My, how you've changed Falwen. I see you in each letter, but you've become so different in your ways. I hope you still remember me in these letters you write, I hope you still think of us here as much as we think of you, wherever you may be."

Falwen's wife of many years began to read the letters. She did not go by a certain order when reading them. It was simply just one after another, her eyes scanning the words, her mind taking them in, her tears welling up and emptying out over the soft features of the lovely woman Falwen had married all those years ago.

It all came together so easily for her. Falwen had been chosen, chosen by whom, she did not know or have the want to delve further, but he was tasked to do a great service for Kariyl. What it was, Falwen did not say, only Larissa noticed that his word choice, flow of ideas, and set path seemed so much different than he had ever been to her, as if whatever he was doing made him more resolute in his purpose here on Ar Solon. Whatever it was, Larissa did not mind, as long as he was safe and followed what he considered his path in life to be.

Yes, she missed him dearly, yes, she cried herself to sleep at night; and yes, she missed him here; his touch, his kiss, and his way with his boys and how he held the family together by, what his wife could only say, his sheer will to do so. Nevertheless, she knew that times like these only tested the family. She looked down at the letter in front of her, wiping the tears from her face, and smiled at Falwen's words.

These times, dear wife, these times are yours now. I can no longer share them with you. Take our boys, make them men, how we had always wanted them to be. Show them that you are just as much part of them as I am. They have much from me already. It is now your time to shine in their eyes. I shall return to you all, as a father, as more than I ever have been in my life here on Ar Solon. Please, know this to be the truth. I will not waver in my path, so you cannot waver in this path we made together.

I love thee,
Falwen Sanse

"I won't, Falwen, my dear! I will show you! I will show you great things! Your boys will be men. One of them already is."

Jannon Sanse moved through the snow with a purpose. The thick blankets that came down around him or the snow that was halfway up his boots did not slow him. He was going to find this Ranyll Tolver and get to the bottom of his father's disappearance!

Tamarus had already separated from him and was off in the woods not far from the edge of town, his wood sled sliding across the snow behind him as he ran through the freshly fallen snow. Jannon ignored the calls his brother made as he made his way into the thick of town, the smoking fireplaces of the inns and taverns showing up as he walked over the hill to the town square, an assortment of vendors and shop owners pressed tightly together between and around the buildings, many of them closing up shop as Jannon came into view. The vendors shot out quick calls to Jannon, who had become a regular customer there in the last few summers since his father had disappeared, his oldest son taking over much of the fishing trade where his father had left off.

I even know my father's favorite spots to catch the freshest fish, he mused, looking at some of the dried up fish on the vendor carts as he passed them by. He avoided much of the smaller vendor carts and went for the bigger, better known vendors that set up small tents with their wares under them. Jannon knew just who to go to.

Mendrik Beals shot Jannon a sidelong glance and smiled at him, the young man gliding in through the throngs of customers looking to look, not looking to buy. The aged man was from a long family of river children and had lived in Simmer Lo for most of his last few summers, so he knew a buyer and a looker when he saw one. Jannon Sanse was definitely a buyer. He knew what he wanted and got what he wanted. The elder smiled at him through the thick flakes that had been pelting him since he set his tent up earlier that afternoon. His darker complexion than Jannon's made him look almost like a statue of old that was told in the stories, those great golems that protected treasures and the tombs of great kings.

"Ahh, Jannon, what can I do you for this fine day? Three finely sliced Alvanus striper as usual?" Jannon shook his head.

"I need some information, Mendrik. I think I might have a lead on my father's whereabouts."

Again, with Falwen! Will this kid never give up? Mendrik smiled and tried his best to appease his long-time friend's son, but it had been nearly four summers and not a word from Falwen.

Probably dead somewhere, robbed by vandals. That or shacked up with some young bar wench in another town, gambling his family savings away.

Mendrik had seen it happen dozens of time throughout his life here on Kariyl. Being a sailor most of his life did not help how he saw things, either, remembering all of the broken hearts that sailed off or were left at the docks when the ships would leave out, many of the men never returning again.

It was just the way of things here, especially on the west coast of Kariyl. And, Jannon, though he hated to think about it, *was one of those broken hearts.*

"Listen, Jannon. How long have we been doing this for; three summers now? And where has it gotten us; nowhere! I suggest that you take what coin you do have and buy you and the remainder of your family something nice to eat for a change, instead of giving it to me to find information on a man that is gone for good!"

Mendrik didn't mind taking the coin from the kid, he really didn't. It was more of the fact that, over time, it was quite pathetic to see the hope in the boy's eyes every time he came for more information and ended up with nothing. In fact, Mendrik had even lied a few times, stating that Falwen had been seen by one of his traders that traveled to the east; that Falwen had been spotted traveling with a group of fisherman to trade in Telgin, of all places.

I enjoyed telling that one; that was a good story, even if it wasn't true, Mendrik reflected, shooing Jannon away with a dead fish he had in his hand at the moment, wrapping it up for a lady just behind the boy.

But Jannon would not be dismissed so easily. Reaching inside his winter cloak, he produced a shiny gold piece, slamming it down onto the counter in front of Mendrik.

"Listen up, Mendrik! My father is alive! We've word from him and a few coin, so I will need some information, and quickly!"

Mendrik took the coin from the boy and eyed it closely, biting on the edge of it.

It was solid!

It had been some time since he had seen some gold of this weight and texture, especially in these hard times upon Kariyl. He nodded to Jannon and handed the lady her wrapped fish, sliding the coin into his pocket on his apron he wore.

"Alright, Jannon. What do you need?"

The young man nodded. "I need some information on a man named Ranyll Tolver. He is staying in Simmer Lo, but I don't know how long he's planning on being here. He could have left already. I need to know where he's going and who's with him, if anyone. He came in on a wagon, that's all I know."

Mendrik smiled and pulled a few coins from his pocket. They weren't as shiny and as thick as the coin that Jannon had given him, but he handed them out anyway.

Jannon declined the coin and pushed Mendrik's hand away.

"That's not all, Mendrik. I'll take two of your best Alvanus blue gill as well, and two pouches of your best spices! And you can keep the change!"

Jannon nodded and stuffed the beat up old coins back into his pocket, busying himself with Jannon's order. Neither one of them noticed the shadowed figure that moved past them, out of sight, making its way back to the tavern which Ranyll and Oagthor occupied.

There are too many around for this, the assassin agreed, noting the increasing amount of interest that Ranyll and Oagthor seemed to bring whenever entering a town or village.

I must take the human and dwarf when they are alone, away from all of this!

The assassin disappeared into the crowd, blending in with the hustle and panic of the heavier snow that seemed to fall without any intent of stopping.

Mendrik Beals could see the figure moving, passing through the crowd, apparently thinking that it was not seen.

But a river child sees all, my friend, whoever you are. Years had plastered themselves across Mendrik's aged face, much as they had with Falwen and the other sailors that lived out their lives as simple fishermen now, their jobs now loosening their joints and making their bones ache whenever the weather changed.

Especially now, Mendrik noticed, his limbs stiffening up even more with the cold that seemed to settle in for the rest of the winter season.

But there was a time, Mendrik recollected, *when us sailors were something to be reckoned with, where we took on the winds and the seas and the pirates and an assortment of unsavory things for the good of Ar Solon.*

Inside, deep within the aged sailor, it ached to escape, to break free. In Mendrik's eyes, which were still as alert as ever, they caught sight of the weapons pressed closely against the lean form of the assassin, watching as this form moved away from Jannon and himself, *apparently getting what he wanted from us without much effort,* the human decided.

Well, no one gets anything from me that easily. Especially some out of town, no-good killer! Mendrik knew that there was something more going on around him, that there had been ever since Falwen had disappeared, but he had sworn an oath to his friend to protect his family at all costs if Falwen were ever to fall upon a rough moment.

"Aye, First Mate Sanse. It seems that you have fallen upon a moment as rough as can be, especially if there are armed figures looking for information on you and your whereabouts." The fish vendor closed up shop early though there were still some potential buyers and more than enough lookers at his tent. He handed off the responsibilities to his assistants, who began to put the fish back into the barrels full of water to keep them fresh and break down the tents shortly after.

But Mendrik was already long gone from the vending areas when this occurred, his medium-sized frame slipping easily past the crowds and out of the vending courts within moments, watching as Jannon moved back onto the path to the way to his family's cottage, Mendrik taking another path. He moved towards the taverns and began his search for this Ranyll Tolver.

Maybe this person can shed some light onto the scene, maybe give me some information on the whereabouts of my friend, Falwen. Or maybe I will have to kill him.

Either way, Mendrik was happy to feel the weight of the gold coin in his pocket, it being much heavier than the ones that he had acquired from his petty fishing tent in the last few ten days.

I could get used to this again, thought the old assassin, his hands already moving to the small daggers behind his back, his fingers resting on the tips of the handles easily, almost gracefully.

I may have to come out of retirement after all. Mendrik smiled at the thought of it all and continued on through the snow.

*   *   *

Falwen looked down at the page, the ink still in the process of drying, his aged fingers drifting over each letter of the name carefully, as one would an artifact or item that holds insurmountable value to them. The word was a whisper of what he once had, what he held at such a value that no treasure in all of Ar Solon could compare.

"Son!" He leaned back in his writing chair and stared at the page from a distance now, still in wonder that such a thing was happening.

No images of this had come to him prior, no series of ideas even came through that would give the Chronicler the slightest inkling that one of his sons would play a part in the journeys that he, Falwen Sanse, would write about, let alone Ranyll's journey.

Falwen knew it would be a long night ahead, as well as the other nights following this. In fact, he would write until he could write no longer, ensuring that his son pass through the tomes in front of him and finish his portion of the quest, *with little or no distraction if possible*, Falwen told himself, grabbing up the quill pen in his hand again, the words spreading onto the page so quickly Falwen's mind could barely keep up.

11

Dir'grar watched as Kalir and Alyssia rode through the cleared trails near the checkpoint into the thick of the snow just outside of the Tirapoor Channel checkpoints. It had been some time since Dir'grar had seen his friend, especially since Kalir had become captain of the checkpoint guards, always leaving on some small mission, 'this or that missions' Kalir had remarked many of them to be, brushing them off easily once he arrived at the appointed destination, returning quite quickly back to his checkpoint once doing so.

The great figure of a man moved back away from the front porch and for the door to Kalir's cottage, shutting the door behind him. Inside, the fire was still lit and a pot sat over it, a stew bubbling slightly over the sides. Both Rachel and Timothy had been told that they were leaving so they prepared for the trip, which would be over a ten day's journey, *probably more,* Dir'grar taking another peek outside at the snow that seemed to never let up around them. Dir'grar looked around at the well-crafted cottage and couldn't help but think things were changing for the worse.

He misses this place, he does, Kalir's burly friend reminded himself. *He misses it almost as much as it misses him. And it's not the same without him.*

Dir'grar looked over at Rachel, who had been busying herself with preparing some foodstuffs for the long trek to Goletta.

For some reason, I can't for the life of me think why, Kalir wants me to take his family there.

Then it occurred to him.

Kalir must know something that we here at the checkpoint do not. It was true that Kalir had been traveling more than his fair share. It was possible that Kalir knew something more, that he had seen something far worse than what Dir'grar had seen in Telgin when the shape-shifting daemon came after Kalir's own sister and nephew.

But what could it be? Dir'grar assisted Rachel with the foodstuffs while Timothy packed away the rest of his and his mother's things in a few sacks, throwing them into a large trunk near the door. The young man smiled at Dir'grar.

How he looked like his older brother, that Timothy! Timothy did, indeed, looked like his older brother Ranyll. The only thing that set them part was that Timothy seemed a little bit thinner, like his mother, very unlike his father in his stature and gait, whereas Ranyll only looked like his mother in his face and hands.

Dir'grar filled several small baskets with fresh fruit and some bread that was available on the table, letting Rachel finish the remainder of the packing while he checked on the horses that were to be hitched up to the wagon.

A supply wagon, of all things! To think I get to travel halfway across Kariyl in the snow with a bundle of supplies and two lazy horses is beyond me. At least I'm traveling west!

Dir'grar had already heard about the awful snow storms that were blanketing much of the eastern half of Kariyl without warning. Dir'grar didn't feel so bad when he thought about it that way.

He stepped outside the cottage for a second and saw Rynen and Ermoor leading the horses, wagon in tow, behind them. Ermoor smiled at Dir'grar when he saw him on the cottage porch.

"Dir'grar, no one told me that you were here! When did you make it back?"

Ermoor had changed his left eye patch to a simple, freestanding patch over his eye, with a few well-placed cords that were tied around his head. Even though it had been several summers, Ermoor's scars looked as though they never fully healed, still leaving great gashes across the left side of his face, almost as if the daemon's claws had kept the wounds from healing.

Dir'grar made it down the steps and grappled with Ermoor, picking him up with one arm around him, dropping Ermoor only to do the same to Rynen, who tried his best to fight back. Soon, Rynen knew he couldn't fight against Dir'grar and he submitted, only to be dropped into the snow on his back.

"I got back just the other night. I know how you checkpoint guards have been busy, with all the snow coming down and all, trying to keep that channel from freezing, among everything else that is going on around here at the moment."

Rynen picked himself up off the ground, dusting the snow off of his winter cloak.

"You're telling us, Dir'grar! We have yet to take a break from this place. I don't remember the last time we left here, do you Ermoor?"

Ermoor simply shook his head, rubbing the horse next to him, patting the horse on its great neck.

"So, I take it that this wagon is for you, huh, Dir'grar? Kalir had us take good care in getting all of these supplies in, getting these horses ready, checking everything. I should have known it was for you. If I would have known earlier, I wouldn't have gone through so much trouble!"

Dir'grar countered. "And then maybe you would be getting a good couple of boots to the skull, too!" Dir'grar picked up a handful of snow and balled it up, tossing it at Ermoor. It missed, however, and Dir'grar took the reins from Rynen.

"But it's not just for me, fellas. Kalir's sister Rachel and nephew Timothy are here. I'll be taking the supplies as well as them on a little trip to Goletta. We'll be there for two ten day or so. Don't really know yet."

Both of them looked a bit surprised. They had seen Ranyll; in fact, he had spent a considerable amount of time with them several summers ago.

Rynen lit up. "Kalir's sister is here? And his nephew, Tim? Oh, this is great! So, he's seen them, has he? Tell me, how did he act? Was he surprised?"

Dir'grar hesitated a moment. "Well, Rynen, he was definitely surprised. He hasn't seen them in some time."

Ermoor chimed in. "I know. He still tells us about his visits with his sister and his nephews when they were younger, as if they were frozen in time or something. So, are they going to be here a while? Did they come to surprise Captain Ranolf?"

Dir'grar hated to start the conversations with these young guards like this, but he really didn't have a choice. After all, Kalir had tasked them with escorting Dir'grar and the rest of the party down south until they broke from the checkpoints.

Apparently, it slipped Kalir's mind to tell them that they were going somewhere, too.

Dir'grar wasn't surprised in the least. He knew that is was somewhat difficult for Kalir to the be the bearer of bad news, especially to Ermoor and Rynen, who had such a difficult time with the daemons a few summers back. But Dir'grar decided not to hold back.

"There's something awful that has happened. They had to be brought here, for their safety."

Ermoor and Rynen both dropped the smiles they had worn and seemed concerned.

"What is it, Dir'grar? Is there some problem in Telgin that we need to go handle?" And Ermoor meant what he said, Dir'grar could see from the look on his face; the serious, stone calmness that he had when he spoke. His words did not seem doubtful and Dir'grar knew that both of them would travel to no ends to help Kalir's family if they were in need.

"The daemons have come back and they tried to kill Rachel and Timothy. It was something similar to what you two had encountered; a shape shifter. It posed as Ranyll and tried to get in close to kill them. I happened to be there delivering supplies and stopped it from happening, but only barely. No telling what would have happened if I hadn't been there."

Ermoor and Rynen looked to one another, both somber yet struggling with something inside, Dir'grar could tell, because they were quiet for some time. Dir'grar continued.

"Kalir left on business for Fell Whist to report this and he has tasked me with taking his family to a safe place. He tasked the two of you as well. You are to meet him at the southern most checkpoint until he returns. And you are to escort our wagon to the checkpoint. He chose you two specifically. No one is to know about this trip. You are traveling alone until we meet up outside of the checkpoint's area. After that, we will travel together."

Both of them nodded in understanding and watched then as Rachel and Timothy came out of the cottage with their belongings, setting them out on the porch so they could take the rest of their belongings. Rachel saw the two young men standing next to Dir'grar and smiled, reaching her hand out to the two of them in greeting.

"You two must be Rynen and Ermoor. Ranyll told me so much about you when he visited last. And Dir'grar speaks well of you as well."

They both shook her hand lightly and helped her with the remainder of her things, loading them into the back of the wagon. Soon, Timothy and Rachel were loaded into the back of the wagon and Dir'grar was at the driver's seat of the vehicle, tying a thick cloak around his great shoulders. He threw the hood of it over his head and ran his fingers through his beard to get the small flakes of snow from it, his hands grabbing up the reins in front of him.

He looked at the two young men who he had seen go on a number of adventures to be so young, knowing that this would probably be their biggest yet.

"Travel light, gentlemen. There are enough supplies on this wagon for all of us. Only take what you need. We will see you shortly. Just follow the channel west. You will see our tracks. We will take our time until you arrive; then the travel will really begin."

Ermoor and Rynen watched as Dir'grar snapped at the reins and the horse, wagon, and its cargo moved forward, slowly but surely separating those that knew their grand scheme from those that had yet to find it. Rynen had seen, as of late, the increasing amount of time that both Kalir and Dir'grar spent away, wondering if it would be wise of them to leave as well, knowing that the checkpoint, though full of checkpoint guards, were still shy of seasoned veterans at the checkpoint. The idea wrestled inside his mind until Ermoor spoke up, jostling his friend a bit.

"You think we should bring the Black Starr cards, you know, in case we stop at a tavern or two?"

Rynen looked at his friend of several years. His sight broke across the gory mark that the daemon left on Ermoor's face, Rynen trying his best to remember a time when he didn't have it. It was erased from his mind. It had been some time since they had seen their own families, always setting about on errands of a greater purpose, putting aside their life for the lives of others. Yet, even now, Kalir was taking care of his family, spending time with them.

But wasn't that what I signed up for: the adventure, the travel, the responsibility?

Rynen looked over at his friend, who still waited for an answer.

"Of course, bring the cards! If we don't stop with Dir'grar, we can stop once they're on their way to Goletta. I'm sure the last checkpoint has a few good taverns with people willing to lose a few coin."

Ermoor smiled in return.

"What are you talking about, a few coin? You lost a week's wages the last time we bet!"

Rynen only smiled and looked away on the road at the tracks that the wagon had made, deep in thought.

*   *   *

Ranyll lifted himself up from his bed at the inn, his body aching and sore and a combination of other things he couldn't rightly think of because his head was throbbing and his vision blurry.

"Oh, my head! What happened?" But there were no voices answering back, just the vicious sun as it shone through the small window in the room, beaming down at the young man, his eyes closing in response.

Ranyll rolled back over, a wave of nausea hitting him full force, his stomach churning. He had a dry mouth and all of his limbs ached at the same time, which had never happened before. Ranyll laid there for a time, until there was a movement at the door, the door soon unlocking, the thick footsteps of Oagthor making his way inside.

"Oagthor?"

Oagthor shut the door behind him and moved closer to Ranyll, standing next to his bed.

"Yes, it's me, Ranyll. So, are we planning on leaving today or do you have plans to stay in the room all day?"

"What time is it?" Ranyll tried his best to roll over but found that the waves of nausea were merciful to him as long as he lay still and kept his eyes open.

The dwarf smiled at him through his well-groomed beard.

"Half the day is gone, my friend. I've been busying myself until you awoke. After the tumble you took last evening, I'm surprised you're awake at all!"

"Tumble? What are you talking about?" Ranyll moved to sit up and that is when he felt the throbbing in his forehead. The throbbing wasn't so much from the ale last night as it was from the knot that had formed on top of his head, from what he had no idea. He couldn't remember much with the exception of the story about Gwenzel.

"You took quite a spill in the snow last night when we were walking back to our room. You missed a step or two and went tumbling. I tried to catch you but, by then, it was too late."

Ranyll reached his hand out to Oagthor, who took it, pulling the young man out of bed. Once Ranyll got too his feet, he knew that the day would be harsh to him; brutal, in fact. His vision blurred and his mind swam all at once. He steadied himself with Oagthor's thick arm, taking a few well-placed steps before he tried walking on his own.

"I brought you something for the ache in your head that I knew you'd have. It's a special brew of tea just for the occasion." The dwarf handed Ranyll a water skin full of a warm liquid and then began gathering their things, throwing all of Ranyll's things in a bag that he then threw over his shoulder, ushering Ranyll out of the room completely.

"I think we should be leaving before you drink that." Oagthor shut the door behind them and soon they were on their way.

A few steps outside the door of the inn and Oagthor stopped them, pulling Ranyll into an alley. The dwarf began to organize Ranyll's items in the bag, soon tying it down properly, handing Ranyll his sword and belt so he could put it on.

"Try the drink, Ranyll. It will do you good." Oagthor slipped his pack on his back, securing his own weapon down at his side, repositioning its belt on his hip for the hike. He also had fitted himself with a short dagger and some new attire. Oagthor's hair had been trimmed and the helm he wore was polished and shining.

Oagthor caught Ranyll staring at him.

"I figured, since we're going on this journey, I should look somewhat presentable. I mean, don't you?"

Ranyll nodded in agreement. "No, you look very presentable, Oagthor."

"Alright, alright! Enough with the compliments, can we please get moving now?" Ranyll went to lift his bag up over his shoulders when Oagthor stopped him.

"Ranyll, I think you should drink that first before gathering your things."

Ranyll looked at the water skin questioningly. "What's in it, Oagthor? Am I going to die when I drink it?"

Oagthor chuckled a bit when responding. "You couldn't feel any worse than you do now. Just trust me and drink it! Quit crying about it!"

Ranyll looked the water skin over one more time then uncorked it and drank from it without smelling its contents. The liquid was warm and somewhat salty, yet there was a fragrance that came from it that smelled like a field of flowers. As soon as the brew went down his throat and hit his stomach, Ranyll felt himself drop to the ground, emptying the contents of his stomach out onto the ground in front of him. The muscles in his stomach clenched and unclenched, making him heave over and over until there was nothing left inside of him to let go of.

The young man's arms shook when trying to pick himself up from the ground, Oagthor patting Ranyll on the back.

"It will be over soon, Ranyll."

Ranyll wiped his mouth with his hand, keeping himself steady.

"Why did you do that, Oagthor?"

"I didn't do anything that you didn't already do to yourself. In fact, I cleansed you of it. You will feel better in moments."

Ranyll shook his head. "Why didn't you tell me?"

"Would you have still taken the drink if I told you what it did?"

Oagthor was right, I wouldn't have taken it. And he was right about the nausea passing soon. Ranyll stood up, feeling a dozen times better than he had when he woke up. Oagthor had his pack in his hand, holding it out to him.

The dwarf just smiled at him. "You well enough to travel now?"

The snow had melted for the most part around Simmer Lo when Ranyll and Oagthor set out for Goletta, which was roughly a full day's travel if they kept up their pace throughout the day. Ranyll didn't seem to have a problem with that and, for the most part, Oagthor seemed to keep up nicely, happily clad in his new attire, the dwarf humming a tune to himself as he stepped through the small patches of snow on the trail south, both of them silent for a time.

Then Ranyll continued their talk from last night.

"What did it feel like to kill Scarwol?"

Oagthor slowed his pace somewhat, his eyes shooting quickly to Ranyll then to the trail in front of him.

"What do you mean, Ranyll? It feels like killing anything else."

"That's not what I'm talking about, Oagthor. You went after him for a reason; he was a mystical creature from somewhere unknown and has seen things we could never see in all our lives. Did you not feel something profound when you took his life?"

Oagthor thought for a moment, his thick fingers plowing through his newly-groomed beard, playing with the small beads that had been braided into it. The dwarf then pulled out his axe, the battleaxe that he had shown Ranyll the night before.

"It gave me the power to do it, Ranyll. I had tried and tried to kill Scarwol with everything I had. I chased him through his lair, watching him appear and disappear as if what we were doing was some sick game. It wasn't until I found the treasure horde he had kept hidden that I found this. It captured my attention, Ranyll. It has something special in it that helped me kill Scarwol."

"It's magikal, Oagthor. It is a magikal weapon."

Oagthor brushed the idea aside. "Oh, pish posh, Ranyll! Magikal? Now you are definitely dreaming, human! What makes you think that?"

Ranyll shrugged his shoulders.

Here we go.

"It is what you say, Oagthor, and how your eyes look when you wield it. I have seen that look before and I know that its magik. If you don't have it in your blood, then it's in the weapon you wield."

The dwarf touched the surface of the battleaxe with his fingers and thought, for a second, that he felt something, a current maybe. But there was nothing, nothing but the afternoon sun glinting off of its surface, a small smudge of the shiny exterior of the axe from his finger.

"Is this from your own experience, Ranyll, or do you know something that I have yet to know?"

Ranyll pulled his blade free from its scabbard at his side, freeing the broadsword from its holdings, the thick blade out in the air for all to see, though there were none on the road with them. In moments, the blade caught a blue fire and continued to swirl around it, wavering back and forth with the wind that came up from the Argolis cliffs just to the west of them. Ranyll moved closer to Oagthor, moving the blade away from both of them.

"Look into my eyes, Oagthor! What do you see there?"

The dwarf moved a bit closer, looking deep into Ranyll's eyes, yet still at a distance. Indeed, what Oagthor saw were not Ranyll's eyes at all. He looked closer.

"What in the name of the Creator is that, Ranyll? Your eyes have changed completely!"

Instead of the deep brown that Ranyll's eyes usually were, Oagthor saw the same blue fire within them that was on the blade, as if he were possessed of the magik itself.

"How long have you known about this, Ranyll?" The human extinguished the blade with but a mere thought and slid it back into the sheath, his eyes slowly coming back to the deep brown that they usually were. Also, Oagthor noticed that, once the magik faded, Ranyll came out from a daze of sorts, the human blinking several times before returning back the way he had been, his eyes changing back gradually to their normal brown.

"For some time, Oagthor. I didn't see it until I saw myself in a mirror. I was not as strong with my magik as I am now. Of course, that was a few summers ago when I took note, so I'm sure there have been changes since then."

"So, if it's magik, what do I do with it?" The dwarf put his battleaxe back into the sheath behind his back, securing it in place with one quick push of his thick, right hand.

"That's what I've been trying to figure out since I've received the magik that I have, Oagthor. It's taken me this long just to find a general direction. Let us hope that we can find someone that can point us in the right direction!"

As Ranyll said those words, they seemed to sink in more than ever. He had, indeed, been searching for someone to show him what to do; that was why he went looking for answers in both the elven cities. He had hoped, in some way that the elves, with their somber and secretive ways, had unearthed what ages had buried behind the inhabitants.

Nevertheless, Ranyll left with more questions than answers, feeling more alone than he had felt when arriving at the great cities.

Let us hope that this path leads us somewhere that I haven't already tread, on some new ground in regards to figuring out why Gabriella is still with me, why I have been having these visions yet others have none, and why I have been cast out by almost all of the towns that I have visited since that unlucky day…

He paused, touching his forehead again, feeling the long scar that the event had left, along with doubt in those around him.

Even Oagthor is in doubt, Ranyll thought to himself. *Why did he attack me back in MiddleFast? Was it just for mentioning D'meir or did he resent me?*

Ranyll did not doubt that there was something within Oagthor that churned about and settled on thoughts of a time when D'meir was alive and his kind did not have so many troubles, but Ranyll knew not what to say on these subjects because they seemed to be wounds that Oagthor was still mending. Ranyll decided it was best to keep at a safe distance until Oagthor was a little more comfortable with the fact that they were back together, moving forward on a quest they knew little about.

At least there aren't daemons after us this time, Ranyll thought, his day brightening a little more. The two of them continued on the southern path towards the port town of Goletta, the sun continuing its sentinel guardianship over them and all the other inhabitants of Kariyl.

12

Jannon Sanse left early that morning from his family's cottage, his mother and little brother still asleep in their rooms. He had planned this easily, laying his things out that he would need for the trip the night before, like his father had always done before his big fishing trips.

The snow had gone just as quickly as it had come, leaving only a slight layer of snow on the ground in shadowed corners of the town. Many of the peddlers and shop owners did well to clear the area of snow away from their locales so the morning customers could tread without hazard, many merchants and fisherman rising with the morning sun. Jannon was one of these fishermen.

He covered his tanned frame with his father's thick winter cloak that he had left behind and, carrying his spear and other supplies in a rough sack over his shoulder as he made his way to the vendors that morning. Mendrik Beals had assured that he would be one of the first there.

He better have some information for me! I'm not playing with that old man anymore! Jannon had been led around Mendrik for the last few summers, but the young man refused to be lost without information now, especially since it seemed to be so close!

If Mendrik can't help me, then I will help myself, Jannon feeling more alive, closer to his father than he had in a long time.

I will find you, father! You can be sure of that!

Jannon found Mendrik and the other vendors right where they had been the day before, setting up for the morning purchases, for the morning demands upon them, several of them still opening their doors, putting up tents for the day, as well as stocking their carts and tables with various wares that they sold.

Jannon moved toward Mendrik's tent, bypassing the other merchants, his eyes on the prize.

Mendrik met eyes with Jannon and smiled at him.

"Morning, Jannon, and what can I help you with today, young man?"

"Cut the sentiments, Mendrik, you know why I'm here! Either you have what I'm looking for or you don't!"

Mendrik did not change his expression, just kept his gaze fixed on Jannon. "Well, I do have the freshest Alvanus Menken this side of Goletta, I can tell you that much! Roasted over an open flame, it is the best fish I've ever tasted!"

Jannon was beginning to get irritated with the fisherman. The young man looked around and took note that the other around them were busy with their own work for the day and took no notice of Jannon or Mendrik's conversation. Jannon opened his winter cloak, exposing the dagger underneath for Mendrik to see.

Jannon didn't even notice Mendrik moving for him until it was too late. The fisherman grabbed Jannon around the head, covering his mouth, and swept his other arm underneath his arms, snatching him up over his fish table, pulling him back into the curtains within his tent. Jannon tried to struggle but felt Mendrik's free hand reach for his sword hand, twisting it slightly so Jannon felt a sharp pinch of pain.

Mendrik followed this with a threatening whisper, which seemed to bring a new breed of fear within Jannon's mind.

"You are just like your father, Jannon, foolhardy and brash! 'Keep the conversation light,' I say, 'maybe Jannon will get that someone is watching us!' But the foolish child brings more attention to us in the process!" Mendrik let all of what he said sink inside Jannon's head, eventually letting the young man go once he stopped struggling. He took his hand off the boy's mouth and continued.

"This person has been following Ranyll and his friend for some time, mind you, so you're not the first person looking for this Ranyll Tolver. I think you should leave and go home, where it's safe! What you're about to get into has no room for children! There's an assassin looking after Ranyll and his companion and they've been watching us, too, especially you!"

Jannon matched Mendrik's whisper. "An assassin, following me? How do you know this?"

Mendrik looked through the curtains, only a small fraction of the material opened from itself, peering out.

"Let us just say, for the sake of argument, that I wasn't always a fisherman. And let's just say that everything I told you about me is a lie, with the exception of knowing your father."

"Then how can I trust you, Mendrik, if all you say is lies?"

"Because your father made me promise him to look after his family if ever there were anything to happen to him, and that's just what I'm doing." Mendrik reached out to Jannon, grabbing him by the collar. He brought him closer.

"If you continue your search for your father with this man that calls himself Ranyll, you have a great chance of being killed, you understand me, because someone with a lot of power is watching him as well. You are nothing to the outside world past these buildings in Simmer Lo, you understand me? Quit your search, Jannon! Quit your search and live your simple life out here, where its safe and you have family!"

But the look Jannon gave the old fisherman as he pulled away showed him which direction the young man would take without him even asking.

Eventually, Mendrik nodded and accepted fate.

Then I must do what I must as well.

Mendrik let Jannon go free and he motioned out past the curtain.

"The assassin is out there, waiting for your next move. I heard from some others that Ranyll and his companion, he calls him Oagthor, are on their way to Goletta. His companion restocked with some supplies and they look as though they'll be leaving some time later today."

Jannon wrinkled up his nose. "Oagthor! Is Ranyll traveling with a dwarf?"

Mendrik nodded his head. "You should be able to follow the path south, along the shores, without being detected. If you are quick enough, you may even make it to Goletta before them."

The excitement in Jannon's eyes was easy to spot. Mendrik had seen it many times, on many faces much younger than this boy's. He only hoped that it wasn't in vain.

"I will try and stop the assassin, or at least delay him, for as long as I can. But there is something you need to know; if there is one, there will be more. That is how it works with assassins. Double back if you have to, several times, while in Goletta, to see if someone is following you. Don't make it clear that you're doing that; just make sure you don't walk into a place void of people. Always have an audience when you walk. Assassins are about stealth. There is little stealth in a crowd. Now what did I just say?"

Jannon nodded and, now somewhat nervous, answered back.

"Crowds offer cover. Keep to the crowds."

"Good! Very good! You'll be like your father in no time."

Mendrik peered again through the curtain, turning back to Jannon one last time.

"I will walk out with you, to go get something for you at a cart nearby. You separate from me when I snap my fingers, saying that you have to go or something, then I will lead the assassin away from you."

Jannon shook his head. "No, we have strength in numbers, Mendrik! We can take him together."

Mendrik disagreed. "Jannon, the key is not to take him! An assassin cannot be taken so easily. He is not wandering about, waiting for you to come to him. You must do as I say for now!"

Jannon handed Mendrik a folded piece of parchment.

"Well, will you give this to my mother, so she knows what I have gone to do?"

Mendrik took the piece of folded up parchment and shoved it into a pocket in his cloak, ushering Jannon out of the curtained area, grabbing up one of his empty crates to carry out with him.

"You are absolutely right, Jannon! I should get a few more Golettan Sea Bass for my selection. Let us go then, to my cart. You can get yours from my fresh stock if you like."

Jannon went with the talk and followed the fisherman out of his booth under the tents and through the clustered vending area, just outside of the vendors market, snapping his fingers as they walked.

Jannon bundled up and moved away from Mendrik, the fisherman continuing on to the cart not far from him.

Jannon turned a corner in between buildings and turned around to go the other way. From behind him, he could see a form huddled on the corner of a building, leaning far down against the roof, covered from top to bottom in black. Jannon turned his head and made his way back through the vending area, heading straight for the Argolis shores, which were only about two miles away. The young man refused to look back. His crystal blue eyes continued to look forward, hoping beyond hope and anything that he had left within himself that this Ranyll Tolver would lead him to his father.

Mendrik Beals kept the crate close to his body with one hand, his other hand slipping just behind him to unfasten the knives strapped to his back. He felt the weight of three of them and pulled them from their harnesses, keeping them deep inside the cover of his cloak, waiting for the assassin. Mendrik soon stopped moving completely, looking around him at the lack of others near him. In fact, he was blocks away from anyone seeing him.

...from seeing me or the assassin. This is the place where an assassin would strike. So he knows now that I am calling him out. And he knows what I am.

Mendrik turned back the way he came, his eyes scanning the rooftops and the alleyways near him. Everything was completely silent all around him. He knew the assassin was near, had watched him out of the corner of his eye as he followed him to this point. He kept the crate in front of him, almost eye level, scanning again the dark areas of the street in front of him.

Mendrik eased the crate down closer to his chest, relaxing it a bit. That's when he heard it. A quick exhalation of breath and there was a whizzing sound coming at him. The old assassin shot to the side, feeling the impact of the blow dart hit the front of his crate, another flying past him. He rolled onto the ground near him and sat back on his knees.

Blow darts! What a slippery devil this assassin is! And what a coward!

But Mendrik already knew the assassin's location from the direction of the darts. He lifted himself up from his crouched position, discarding the crate completely, the pieces breaking across the ground as it fell, his throwing daggers out and at the ready. Then the assassin made his appearance.

It was a thin creature, of grace and stride that seemed to make it appear almost like a wild animal as it moved closer to him. Mendrik made his move and tossed two of his throwing knives as hard as he could, then realized it was too late.

The two small knives barely made it out of his hands before they fell, almost right in front of him, his hands falling limply at his sides. He looked down, ready to retrieve them, when he noticed it; a small dart protruding from his chest. He looked up just as the assassin came down on him, blades flashing.

Good journeys, Jannon. I have done what I can, Falwen; what was asked of me.

Mendrik Beal's body never hit the ground as he died. The assassin caught the limp form of the fisherman and carried him to an alley, discarding him in an empty barrel that was covered carefully so no one would find him right away.

The assassin continued its mission.

*　　　　　　*　　　　　　*

"Mendrik, no!" The words came out as a whisper on Falwen's lips, an afterthought on the subject of his long-time friend falling to unknown assailants, the scribe trying his best to stay on task with the other scribes around him, the dwarves working most diligently, copying ancient texts from the other libraries, the old pages in front of Falwen the last thing on his mind at the moment. He glanced about at the other scribes, noticing all of them deep in their work, looking up at the pages for a moment, then moving their eyes back down to their own blank tome, the quill pens moving almost in unison.

This had been a thing of beauty to Falwen when he first came here, a thing that made Kariyl a peaceful place to him, yet it seemed skewed now, as if what they were all doing was false in some way.

But why Mendrik, Falwen questioned, his quill moving now in time with the rest, looking up at the page in front of him the best that he could with so much on his mind.

I have been writing on my son's adventures for the last few pages in the tomes back in my writing room, on his story as well as Ranyll's yet none of this was brought to light.

Falwen didn't have any knowledge of an assassin within their midst, only of Test and his ways, moving stealthily along towards Ranyll like a serpent towards its prey. The Chronicler flipped the page in front of him in time with the others, his hand now steady, his eyes now focused.

I must press on until our mid-day break, then I will find out what is happening.

So Falwen did this, with much a heavy heart, thinking about all of the adventures, about the number of excursions that he and Mendrik had taken in their youth, how Mendrik had saved him from dangers a number of times. Falwen Sanse would find out what was going on within the land of Kariyl, even if he had to do something himself to get the information.

Much of the day wore on in this way for Falwen, who soon finished a tome, only to take up another, the thickly bound volume in his hand practically falling apart. He knew that restoration of earlier texts were important; that keeping up the continent's history was detrimental in others learning the ways of the previous inhabitants so they could forge ahead with new ideas and new ways about them, but many of what Falwen had been copying with the dwarves was the history of the dwarven people, something long forgotten to both humans and elves, so Falwen seemed to absorb it all with great interest, for he had only met a few dwarves in his life and they never volunteered information about their past.

And here it is, Falwen thought to himself, admiring the grand old tome in front of him, carefully untying a small set of cords that held it together, opening the cover to the first page. He read the title:

The Siege of Terapon, by Knight of the Treaty Delor Griptight.

Very few humans will ever see these tomes within their lifetimes, and I am one who gets to preserve them for later generations, maybe even for my sons when they grow to the point where history is important for them.

Falwen had taught his children much in the time that he was there, yet he could never teach them enough.

'Always be ahead of others or you will always fall behind', was something that he had been taught by his own father, so it was something that he had passed down to his children as well, teaching them everything that he knew, even down to the most base things that he had been taught as a child himself. He knew now that it would come in handy to them while he was away, *so they can help their mother,* Falwen reminded himself, steady copying, page after page passing him by, catching up to the rest of the reproduction

scribes around him, his mind soon letting go of what held his attention early in the morning at the Agnar Scribe's Guild.

It was soon mid-day and the shutters were closed within the writing guild, the scribes leaving out to eat and perform their afternoon meditation, including any other odd jobs that any of them had to do today. They were to report back when Guild Master Thurn Chestfield rang the bell twice in the town, giving all of the scribes time to report back in an orderly manner. Once at the writing guild doors, Thurn would do a quick head count and open the doors once all were accounted for, raising the shutters for the remainder of the day as well as lighting a few lanterns that he hooked to poles hanging from the ceiling until nightfall came and their duties for the day were done.

Falwen took this mid-day time to do some writing of his own. His mind was still fresh with Delor's rousing account about the Siege of Terapon, something the fisherman had always heard about in stories and tales that drifted far west where he resided, but he truly never knew the real story. Soon, the story drifted from his mind, replaced by the visions that he was getting, more and more, which made him, many times, leave during his mid-day break and write some of it out. Today was one of those days.

Falwen could hear the guild doors behind him close and he nodded to Guild Master Chestfield as he passed him by, retreating as quickly as he could to his room to write. He felt a dwarf move to catch up behind him and he looked behind him to see the familiar apprentice dwarf on his heels.

Scribe Ostondilus Frews smiled through his thin beard as he spoke.

"Off somewhere in a hurry, aren't we, Scribe Sanse? I had to practically run to catch up to you." The dwarf chuckled a bit through his beard, his youth coming out in his face, the pale white face of the young dwarf reddening a bit with each step he took. It was a cold morning, *colder than the last few;* Falwen took notice, his robes not covering him completely from the wind that crept up through the mountains around them. Falwen continued on his way.

"My apologies, Scribe Frews. I have some things to attend to, if you don't mind." Most of the dwarves had departed by now, just Falwen and Ostondilus on the small main road that connected most of the town together, Falwen seeing his building coming up in front of him. The visions seemed to be coming to Falwen at a greater strength than before, the images in his head making him stop for a moment to gather his thoughts together. He pressed his eyes closed tightly for a moment and meditated. Ostondilus remained next to him, his breathing a little ragged from the chase down the road.

"Everything okay, Scribe Sanse? You don't look so well."

The Chronicler came back from his thoughts and smiled at the dwarf.

"Thank you for your concern but I will be fine. I just need something to eat and some fresh air. Once I get that, I believe everything will work itself out. Excuse me, if you will."

"Of course, of course. My apologies if I bothered you." Ostondilus moved away from Falwen and watched as the human scribe continued on his way.

Once inside his room, Falwen grabbed a few pieces of fruit on his night table next to his bed and a water skin full of water under his cabinet, moving directly to his closet. In moments, he was moving down the small staircase to his secret writing chambers, his hands finding the lantern hanging on the hook from the ceiling in the dark, setting it down on the writing table in front of him. He laid down the food in front of him as well, finding his tinder box in moments, the light from the lantern bringing his chambers into view.

He looked down at the tome that was already open, already written in, and grabbed for his quill and inkwell, bringing it closer to him. In the flash of an instant, his left hand was on the page, the inkwell dipped and ready, his mind coursing through the ideas that were packed tightly together. The inkwell let them flow out of his mind and onto the tome in front of him.

It began as a single thought, as many of the visions he had seen had done as of late, fragments of a moment coming to him, still undecipherable. Yet, it wasn't until the moment was captured upon the page, when it was written down, that the entire story played out after that. Falwen was pleased to be away from the rest of the guild, at least for a time, so he could let the images play out onto the paper, so he could think a little clearer throughout the day once he had done this.

'The dwarf and the human had no idea what lay ahead of them in Goletta nor what lay lurking behind them in Simmer Lo, the many followers eagerly waiting to get their hands on the man with magik coursing through his veins. While each played a different part in Ranyll's journey, the one that was the most important, the one that would lead Ranyll closer to his own grand scheme had no idea what he was getting into when the sun arose on him in Goletta.'

*　　　　*　　　　*

Captain Aaolos lifted himself up from the bed in his quarters, listening to the early morning banter just outside his door as his men prepared themselves for the day. Being captain of a ship was not something that he set out to do; in fact, never in his life had he ever wanted to board a ship.

But it did have its perks…

Aristotle eyed the two beauties in bed, still asleep from last night's escapades. What he started in the local tavern, the two of them completed in his chambers on the Namiah. The two red-heads had enticed him the whole night through once his ship came in port that afternoon, Captain Aaolos taking his men out to celebrate. What he found within the confines of that tavern he had desired ever since leaving Goletta, almost a full four seasons ago. It was easy for him to take it, both with the strong gait that Aristotle had in his forty six summers of living and what lay within the satchels on his back, loaded with treasure from a site almost everyone had claimed was a dry island.

But it wasn't dry, was it, Meekins? My new first mate had been right. It was far from dry. And it was far from safe as well. Too close for my liking, Aristotle agreed, rubbing the soreness in his left shoulder, the wound still not completely healed all those days ago.

He knew it would be a time before his arm would fully recover, if it ever did all the way. He didn't know the answer to these questions and the many more he had asked the medicine man that night in the woods when he had acquired the wound, but he would never forget him or the others that lost their lives trying to escape. Aristotle did not want the responsibilities left to him when it came to telling families that their husbands and sons would never return but he felt that he had to, knowing that the idea of not knowing for the families was torture enough.

It was time for him to move on, he knew. He had stayed his time and then some as captain of a ship that had, before him, changed hands more than a bottle of spirits changes hands amidst a thirsty set of sailors. He had carried the ship across troubled waters and his crew changed with every stop he made into populated areas. Aristotle carried dozens of scars that carried dozens more stories behind them, his wounded body a set of stories written in his own blood that would take forever to tell another inhabitant.

Nevertheless, sometimes, when shopping at the trade market for items for the ship, he would spy a family moving through the Golettan trade center, and he would catch a glimpse of the delight of the children that followed their mother and father. If there was anything that he wanted, anything that he respected more than his lot and the ways that they had, it would be to have part in a real family. He was not a family man or regretting not being a family man by any means; in fact, he had killed a number of men claiming to be family men in the midst of death, but he always took that as a coward's way out and killed them all the quicker. What interested him the most was the camaraderie between each family member, how they seemed to know their responsibilities, their limitations; how relationships, love, dreams, hopes, and life all seemed to function within this one bond between the family and that it worked without putting so much as a little training into effect as he did with his men.

If only my men worked like they were part of something more than just betraying one another for a moment of pleasure, a chink of coin, or a barrel of wine, my crew would not continually be rotating.

But, alas, the captain knew that it was difficult to find men of any caliber near what he would be asking without offering a payment upfront and not just a cut of the treasure that they would hope to get, knowing that he would be penniless and without a ship if he got what he actually asked for instead of a bunch of untrained simpletons.

This will be my final voyage.

He let those words continue to echo in his head as he got dressed. For nearing fifty summers old, Aristotle had kept the shape of a man in his twenties. He had yet to sit idly by and watch his men labor on the ship. In fact, he carried out many of the harder tasks and did them with ease once he got used to them, continuing much of his work in the same way as he had done when he was just a ship mate, over twenty summers ago. The sun and the sea had tanned him well and he drank little, preferring to remain intact in the mind as a captain and not go raving mad with drunkenness as many of his captains he had known had gone. He was the only one of his kind, the last of his generation left sailing, and he still sailed better than most of the newer breeds of captains with their newer, lighter vessels.

He slipped on his black breeches and a basic white tunic, tying the laces up to the neck, throwing a captain's coat over his shoulders, clipping most of the buttons except the remaining few by his neck. He slipped on some hard-heeled boots that had been shined the night before by one of his shipmen, still sitting out in front of his closed door, tying their laces up as well. The women on his bed shifted in their sleep but they made no move to wake fully, remaining asleep comfortably under the covers.

I will have to leave this lifestyle soon or it will eventually kill me. Already, he had more than his share of close calls and experiences that he would have to classify beyond near death. A moment of him being buried alive with the rest of his dead crew and left for dead came to mind, but he tried to best not to conjure up the details at that moment.

It is better to remember that when I have a drink in my hand. Or maybe more than one would be fitting.

He had more than enough plunder to carry him to the ends of Ar Solon and back. However, there was something else that kept him here, at the shores of Goletta, always waiting for the next message to be sent. He had waited for years for word of this one message to be sent to him, to finally see the penmanship it was written in come across his desk on the Namiah. On that day, he would breathe a sigh of relief. But the sigh or the message had yet to come, so he continues onward, moving onto his next transport mission.

All he had to do on this day, at this moment, was sign for the incoming cargo from another ship with some of his much needed supplies and he would be able to pay his men and they would be on their way to their next destination; Dradle. He hated to say it, but that rat-infested cesspool seemed warm and inviting to him at the moment, Aristotle tiring of pulling into the same docks in Goletta, time and again. In fact, he was getting tired of coming in on a ship.

…*Or being captain of one,* he noted to himself, looking around at what he had made for himself in the last 20 years at sea as the captain of the Namiah. He had begun to amass a small fortune with his vessel, something that not everyone in Goletta were able to say that they did. Of course, no one knew of his riches or treasures that he hid away.

After all, I am in a line of work where it pays to keep a secret, he thought, smiling to himself, fingering the jewel-encrusted golden necklace dangling around his neck.

I would have to tell my last first mate that when I see him, to be sure of it. However, Aristotle did not plan on swimming to the bottom of the Alvanus Sea anytime soon to say this to his dearly departed friend.

It will have to be later on then, when I'm not so busy and still have life in my limbs.

Aristotle did not regret losing his last first mate to a hefty tossing overboard, but he did regret taking the only honorable man besides himself off the crew list. Now, Aristotle seemed to be surrounded by thieves and cutthroats. *But, for a refined pirate, when aren't you surrounded by those things?*

It was a big day, indeed, for the payload was to be a hefty one! Aristotle soon woke the women in his bed, shaking them slightly, looking out his porthole window as the snow came down around them.

"Young ladies, I think you should dress rather warm for the impending coldness you are about to embark upon once you step off the Namiah."

Still half-drunk and trying to adjust their eyes, the two young girls stared up at him through their red, wavy locks. They were younger than the common maiden, but they had served their purpose. The captain ushered them off the bed and into their garments.

"It means it is time for me to depart, which means you must find other arrangements for the rest of the day; see where my coin takes you. That was enough, ladies, was it not?"

One of them spoke up. "Oh, yes, captain. That was more than plenty. Thank you again for having us aboard your ship." Their awkwardness at the situation was somewhat annoying to Aristotle, who assisted them with their garments as well as the way out, which they followed Captain Aaolos with sleep-filled eyes.

His crew that came in contact with him gave him a salute and took a quick glance at the damsels before averting their eyes back to their duties, which made the hallways under the ship buzz with the morning movement.

Captain Aaolos continued through the hallways and up the stairs, soon exiting the cabin area altogether. The exterior doors were opened and soon the three of them were on the main deck, the captain signaling to the plank that connected to the dock the Namiah was connected to by a great many ropes. The young maidens curtseyed and made their way off the boat with assistance from some shipmates already on the planks, helping them down safely. The two redheads took one last look at the great ship in front of them and then disappeared into the crowd.

Now, onto the task at hand.

First Mate Meekins lifted the papers closer to his face, trying his best to see the words written on them. He had made it a point to try and fool most around him with his inability at reading written words, but it didn't seem to affect these two in front of him. The dwarf and the human just remained where they stood, ever looking at the large number of vessels behind Meekins who tried his best to piece together the words on the page.

"Who is this from again?" He looked to the young human for answers. After all, it was he that had given him the documents that he now had in his possession.

"That information is for Captain Aaolos to know when we see him. I have secured the appropriate documents needed to board your ship, the Namiah, so I don't see what the problem is."

The dwarf next to the young man chided in. "It's cause he can't read, Ranyll! That's what we get for dealing with the likes of pirates! We can't trust them no way, so why are we here?" The last question seemed directed more at Ranyll than at Meekins, but Meekins still took the sting from it.

Ranyll turned to Oagthor and did his best to console the dwarf.

"Remind me to answer that later, when we're on board, okay Oagthor?"

Meekins' comments seemed to be ignored completely. He lowered the papers from his face and looked directly at Ranyll when speaking. Ranyll could not but help smell last night's spirits still fresh on Meekin's breath.

"Randall, or whatever your name is, fine sir, you're not getting on board; especially with a dwarf! We're not a transport vessel for inhabitants. We transport goods only. Goods only!" Meekins seemed a bit flustered, but Ranyll held his ground.

Meekins had the appearance of a street beggar or simple merchant of wares in a small town; his simple garb, his unshaven face, the smells that seemed to come from him from all different places. Yet, Ranyll knew that there was something more within his eyes that showed him that he was not someone to be handled idly. Even the rusty sword at Meekins side, however flimsy and unsharpened it may be, offered some threat to Ranyll, who had been trained by the best of the checkpoint guards. Then Ranyll knew what it was.

There are no rules with this one except his own.

Then Meekins piped up again. "I don't know who gave this to you or where you come from, but you will just have to find other transports to take you where you need to go. I'm the first mate aboard the Namiah and I know the rules of the captain. No inhabitants!"

Then a voice from behind Meekins spoke up.

"But rules are meant to be broken, isn't that right, Meekins? Isn't that what we pirates do anyway? By the Creator, we would not be alive if we lived by the rules, now would we?" And that was when Ranyll saw the man Falwen Sanse had spoken of for the first time.

Captain Aristotle Aaolos strolled down the boat docks just behind Meekins, two guards with him, carrying a few sacks over their shoulders.

The captain was clad in a basic seaman's garb but wore the jacket of the captains of old had worn, somehow keeping with the tradition of the shipmen that discovered much of what lay across the Alvanus Sea. He had a cutlass at his side, strapped with a jewel-adorned belt and wore a thick, winter cloak that clasped around the neck, fluttering lightly behind him.

He wore a full beard that was peppered with small flecks of white closely around his face that matched his black hair, which had been shorn close around his head, a small red headband with an unknown set of letters inscribed upon it. He smiled but, when he did, it wasn't a smile of welcome but more of a smile of dangerous intent. And, when Ranyll looked at the captain, he knew that the words he had spoken were not spoken kindly, but with intent to show that there were grey areas to what all pirates did and did not allow.

The two men that followed behind Captain Aaolos were of the same demeanor as First Mate Meekins with the exception that they were much larger in size and stature and seemed to be more of brutes than that of wit which Meekins carried with him.

Which wasn't saying much anyway, Ranyll decided, snatching back his papers from the first mate in front of him, the captain himself now only feet away from Ranyll and his friend. Captain Aaolos eyed Ranyll for a moment, looking at his attire, his features, and then went to the dwarf, which he only took a moment before he turned his nose up in disgust.

"I'm sorry, what is your name?" He motioned to Ranyll.

"Ranyll Tolver, and this is my friend…" The captain did not wait to hear the rest.

"I'm sorry Ranyll Tolver, but you have been misguided, given some wrong information about my vessel, the Namiah, because we do not transport inhabitants to any location. We are a supply ship and that is all. No exceptions. And we most certainly do not accept dwarves as part of our cargo, no matter how nicely you dress them up."

Oagthor grumbled a complaint, only taking a once over glance at the two behind the captain before speaking.

"And why not? A dwarf has got a right to travel just as much as any other inhabitant here on Kariyl!"

The captain moved past his first mate and leaned down, eye to eye with the dwarf. Oagthor did not back up; in fact, he met the captain's gaze, which made the two behind the captain somewhat uneasy, their hands moving to the pommels of their swords as well. Ranyll watched this with rapt attention as the captain said his peace.

"Because, dwarf, whatever your name may be, your race carries maladies that cannot be seen with the eye! In all the years I have been a captain, every dwarf that I have set on my ship has brought something or come back with something that affected the whole of my crew, many times killing some of my men! I will not take that chance nor will I let any other seafaring captain chance that as well." He looked to his first mate.

"First Mate Meekins, make sure that this dwarf doesn't get on a single ship of a captain I know. Make it so."

The first mate was gone in the blink of an eye, a quick salute with his hand over his brow and then he was moving past Ranyll and Oagthor to the other vessels that were docked nearby.

"Anymore questions, Ranyll Tolver? A captain does not dally along as many of the others here on this continent do. A storm is brewing and I want to be out of this dock by nightfall if I'm able."

Oagthor huffed and puffed and was about to say something when Ranyll's hand steadied him.

"Yes, I have these papers that grant me safe passage on your vessel." Ranyll handed the papers over to the captain, who looked quizzically over at the young man.

"Are you an elected official of some sort, a brilliant young man on a mission?"

Aristotle looked down at the papers and almost dropped them in surprise. The sardonic smile that he had suddenly disappeared when he looked at the handwriting that lay sprawled across the documents, one of them a letter to him directly. Captain Aaolos rolled the papers up quickly and tucked them under his arm.

"Where did you get these, may I ask?"

"From your old friend, Falwen Sanse."

The captain seemed to have a dryness in his mouth because it was difficult for him to swallow before he spoke. "I think that we should take this conversation to somewhere more proper, don't you?"

The five of them made their way back to the Namiah and were soon on their way to the navigation room down below the main deck. After a few dirty looks by the crew at the dwarf that Ranyll had with him, the three of them: Ranyll, Oagthor, and Captain Aaolos, were tucked away beneath the crew in the captain's personal room. There were a number of things that Ranyll saw within the room that kept him in awe at such a collection, but he did his best to keep his attention on his purpose at hand, which was simply to get on the boat. Once that was done, he would worry about the rest and, maybe, perhaps ask about the items hanging from the ceilings and walls.

Captain Aaolos sat two chairs in front of his map table and pulled his master chair up to it. He rolled up the maps that were on the table at present and placed them into tubes that were hanging neatly behind him, laying out the papers on the table that Ranyll had given him earlier.

Oagthor sat next to Ranyll and looked at the collection of things around the room as well, his eyes roaming across the walls at many things his dwarven eyes had never come across. The dwarf was about to motion something to Ranyll when the captain spoke.

"Well, Ranyll and…" the captain motioned to the dwarf.

"His name is Oagthor. Oagthor Axeblade."

"Yes, well, you and Oagthor seem to have some mission of great importance from what the letter says here. I am just assuming that Oagthor is with you, because the letter makes no mention of a dwarf or any other inhabitant with you… at all."

"This deal, if it happens, will only transpire if I can take my friend with me. There are no exceptions, Captain Aaolos!"

The captain smiled the same smile as before, looking again at the details of the letter and papers in front of him.

"How is old Falwen anyway? Last I heard he was married and had a boy that he was raising."

Ranyll nodded. "It's two boys, and his family is fine. And he is fine. He is following his grand scheme, just as I am. In the letter, it states that you owe a debt to Falwen. He wishes it to be repaid this way, by transporting me to where I need to go."

"I can read, boy, I know what it says! How do I know that it is real, that you have not just used his promise to get your way here, and that what you tell me and what are in these documents are just lies?"

Ranyll looked over to Oagthor, who just shrugged his shoulders and continued to look around. Oagthor looked over at the captain once, meeting with the human's eyes again. The dwarf's eyes caught the light of the lanterns in the captain's navigation room and seemed to sparkle with fierceness.

"Ranyll does not lie, captain! He is a good man, a true man! One of the truest that I know."

"You know what, dwarf? I did not ask of your advice or what you think! It is a privilege for you to be on my ship without my men throwing you overboard just at the mere sight of you!"

Again, Oagthor was about to speak, about to stand from his seated position, but Ranyll stood instead.

"Captain Aaolos, I understand that you have a problem here in regards to my friend being on board as well as the idea of actually taking him on the ship with you, but I will guarantee you and your men safe passage across the sea with us aboard."

"And just how do you think you can do that, my friend?"

"If you and your men are not safely across to our appointed destination with us in tow, then I will offer you my life and all that I own as recompense and you can choose to do what you'd like with it as you see fit."

Oagthor's mouth dropped open.

"Ranyll, you can't be serious! No mission is that important!"

Ranyll silenced Oagthor with but a look.

"This one is, Oagthor, I promise you!"

The captain seemed to have a glint in his eye once this prospect was laid out before him.

"And just where is it that I am supposed to be taking you and your dwarf friend here?"

Ranyll knew that this was the point where things would change, that this moment would determine whether or not he made this journey. However, there was no easy way of getting out of the truth. He had to tell the captain where he was headed.

"To the Island of Dree, Captain. That is where my destination is and that is where I must go."

Captain Aaolos stared at the two of them for a moment, apparently processing what had just been said.

"You are fools, you know this? The Island of Dree is off limits to all sailors. Even if I supported you in your undertaking, I couldn't sell the rest of my crew on going. The stories, the ships that never came back; it's not going to be worth it to them. What do you have that could possibly make them go?"

Ranyll lifted his pack off of his shoulders and placed it down on the captain's table, untying the strings. He pulled out a small satchel within the pack and placed it on the table in front of him, untying it as well. All the while, the captain kept his eyes fixed on Ranyll's face, waiting. Even Oagthor seemed mesmerized by what

Ranyll was doing, his eyes now on the table and not everything around him.

Underneath the folds of the satchel, there lay a small pile of gold and, atop the pile, lay a great, green stone, completely flawless. Oagthor gasped when he saw this, looking from the stone to Ranyll and then back again. The captain took a downward glance at the items and, without so much as a movement in his face, looked back at Ranyll.

"Treasure? Is that what you hope to sell my crew on?"

"Yes. A great treasure, too! The grandest treasure that you can imagine lies waiting on that island, still unclaimed and unspoiled, with the exception of what I have here."

"And you're willing to share the treasure with me and my crew?"

"Yes."

"What makes you think we won't just cut the two of you out of the equation once we get the treasure and say you were victims of circumstance or you fell overboard by accident on the way back?"

Ranyll had no time to doubt himself or what he was saying. He could see where the captain was going with this conversation, seemed to know that the captain was looking for holes in his story.

But you will find none, captain, because this is a well-made lie.

"I have little to no choice in the matter on that, Captain Aaolos, with the exception of the favor that you owe Falwen. I would hope that would be part of the deal. I mean, what is the point of just delivering me to the island if all you are going to do is leave us there or kill us? If you stand by the debt you owe Falwen, then that will be part of it; a safe return."

"And how will Falwen know that this debt is paid?"

He will be writing it, that's how. But Ranyll did not say this. He looked at the treasure before him, not his treasure at all. He was surprised that Oagthor did not lash out at him at the moment that he realized that Ranyll had laid out the remains of the dwarf's treasure to a stranger, someone that neither of them had met until that day. However, Ranyll put his trust in the inhabitant before him, though he knew he was a pirate, probably a killer, a liar, or worse.

"I will deliver the message to him myself upon my return."

Oagthor had kept silent all this time but continued to do so no longer.

"Ranyll and I are bringing a whole lot of things to this table, captain! What is it that you will be bringing in exchange? We can't exactly have a deal that is so one-sided, can we? At least, I won't allow it to be."

The captain nodded.

"Your dwarf has a point. If this arrangement can be made, I will offer safe passage, the supplies that you need, and protection from anything once on those seas, be it a Parthenian vessel or any other pirate sailing the Alvanus Sea. I can get my men to sail to the Island of Dree, but I will not be able to make them stay. I can supply you with a longboat from the Namiah and the supplies you need to get the treasure, as well as the men that are willing to volunteer. I'm sure there will be some fools on my vessel willing to brave what's on that island. I will give you as much time as is allowed. Once you are finished on the island, you can make a signal fire and we will see it and return for you from a distance away."

Oagthor corrected him. "Ranyll's dwarf! I'm not anyone's dwarf! I hope that you will remember that when speaking to me in front of others."

The captain leaned forward, almost across the table. He began to collect up the treasure, tying the satchel back up.

"I will not speak to you in front of others, dwarf! Consider this the only time I do. Your human friend Ranyll will have to be your friend because I have enough friends already. I don't need a dwarf to add to that list."

The captain looked to Ranyll. "I will keep what you have here as collateral as well as to show my men some proof that there is treasure on that island. In regards to splitting the treasure there, Master Tolver, I recommend you allow me 70 percent of the treasure, with you keeping 30 percent for yourself. I have come to an agreement if you have, Ranyll Tolver."

Captain Aaolos extended his hand out over the table, looking to Ranyll for his answer. Ranyll accepted the captain's hand and the pact between the two humans began.

The captain continued. "I will be sailing out as soon as two ships come in, which should be before nightfall. Is there any reason you cannot leave then?"

"That won't be a problem. I have some supplies that I need and will have them ready to load up shortly."

"Then it is settled. When we sail off tonight, there will be a great feast on this vessel to see the ship and its crew off on a safe journey. I have a few more preparations to make before we leave. Until then?"

Oagthor was happy to be off the captain's ship. As soon as he and Ranyll were away from the port and any probing ears, the dwarf began his rant.

"Your dwarf? Can you believe that human said that? Your dwarf? After all these years of traveling and keeping the peace between races, I have to deal with the likes of him! You don't know what you're doing to me, Ranyll! You really don't!"

Ranyll seemed to understand the situation in which Oagthor Axeblade was going through. It had been some time since the War of the Races and peace had reigned between the races; there were no wars, no skirmishes. Many from the three races on Kariyl had come together to work the land, to benefit all instead of just a few that comprised the land around them, yet there were always those that did their best to keep the races apart. Captain Aaolos seemed to be one of the latter.

"Well, at least you won't have to worry about having discussions with him, Oagthor!"

Oagthor huffed the comment aside. The two of them had made their way out of the ports and were, after entering the western gates of Goletta, now in the traffic of the town, moving through shops and vendors posted outside the streets, selling their wares. They headed into the throng of the main streets at the center of the town.

"And the treasure, Ranyll! That was the last of my treasure! How could you do that?"

Ranyll did not know what to say. He did his best to console his friend.

"We will get it back, my friend, you'll see. We needed something to convince the captain that there was something worth going there for."

"What about the real reason we're going, huh?"

"I don't think the captain would feel too strong about my visions being the reason that we're going, Oagthor. That's not tangible enough for him and his crew. They would laugh at us and probably have me locked up for lunacy."

"And locked up you should be… do you even know how much that stone is worth, Ranyll? I could live off that for the rest of my days. I've never seen a stone of such a size in all my years. And you just handed it over to that…. that human!"

Ranyll lifted a small pouch from underneath his cloak, weighing it in his hand.

"I saved a little bit of your treasure, Oagthor. This is what is left." He handed the pouch to the dwarf, who upon further inspection of the bag, did not seem so angry.

"It's good to know that you kept some coin for us, Ranyll. Maybe we can salvage this day after all. Drinks anyone?"

Ranyll veered through the vendors and shops to a long, stone building just outside the main streets. He looked at the wooden sign hanging on a set of rusty hinges: WEAPONS AND SUPPLY SHOP. The young man made a move to go in when Oagthor stopped him.

"What are you doing, Ranyll? This place has the worst weapons!"

"This is where the captain informed us to go. His credit is good here. I thought we would need some provisions and supplies for the trip."

Oagthor nodded in agreement. "I don't trust that captain's knowledge on the finer things in life, my boy. We only have a short time before nightfall. If we can get to the southern gate markets, I know of a dwarf that can get us what we need at a fair price."

"Then lead the way, Oagthor. But the supplies will have to come from out own coin purses."

"I don't mind spending a few coin on good supplies. We'll have a drink on the way, of course!"

"Of course. I'm sure it will be a while before we have another one, considering we're going on a sea voyage at nightfall."

The two of them continued on through Goletta, Oagthor leading the way, the pouch of gold ringing in his ears, the sights and smells of a bustling town around them in all directions.

Ranyll could feel the grand scheme flowing through him. He looked around him and the world felt different, somehow clearer. So many times throughout his journeys since getting these visions, there were moments where things would blur together in his mind, soon making him jot all of it down within the tome that he carried. He had become confused at times, too.

The Book of Burdens, that's what I have called it since beginning it. That's what it shall be called until it is over.

But Ranyll had no idea when that would be. He hoped that it would be sooner rather than later, so he could rest from the things he had seen, both in his mind and on Kariyl.

His hand went to the scar on his forehead at this thought, of the things he had seen here, following the scar up through his hairline with his fingers. So many nights that moment plagued him. Every town he went to since then, he had an overwhelming fear that it would be like before, when they had come at him, fear and hate mingled together within their eyes. Ranyll never wanted to see that again, not if he could help it.

14

You did not fail, my boy. You did not fail at all. Falwen lifted himself up from his bed, glancing around in the darkness. It was still late in the evening, not yet morning, the candle at his bedside having been extinguished some time ago.

It was meant to happen, Ranyll; all of it. Falwen wished that he could be there in Goletta at that moment, to let the young man only a few years older than his oldest know that he was not at fault, but the veteran fisherman was here, doing what he must do for the time that he was to do it.

And I don't know how long that will be, Falwen thought to himself, lighting the candle on the small candleholder next to him, a large number of shadows reflecting off the walls of his chamber. There were no movements outside in the hallways that Falwen could hear, the scribe pressing his ear against the door to see if he could hear anything further.

All of the scribes were asleep as usual, Falwen decided, making his way for the small entrance in his closet, lifting up the wooden floor panel so he could peer down the stairway to his writing room. Lifting the hem of his robes up from the floor, he took to the small stairway, his sandals making a light shuffling sound across each step, the noise disappearing down into the small tunnel.

So much has happened as of late, The Chronicler continued, *something....*

Something very important is about to happen.

The Chronicler knew that there were sights set on a great many things in Kariyl by a great many people, *yet very few of them would get to the point of even making the attempt,* he had concluded, writing some of the histories with the idea in his head that these stories would be a warning to those that continued in their warped ways.

They seemed to only want to batter and break away at the strength that was the grand scheme.

Falwen Sanse had always believed in something greater for himself. Even at a young age, he knew that there was something that drew him back to the shores of Argolis, something that drew him away from the high seas and the adventure of it all.

His simple writing desk and work area came into view in the dimly lit room, bringing the great tome on his desk into view as well, The Chronicler lighting the small, hooded lantern above the desk with his candle. Soon, the room was well-lit and the scribe could make out the bookshelves, the writing materials placed in stacks, as well as the blank volumes stacked up against his desk, still waiting to be filled with stories.

However, this is not what I expected, The Chronicler mused, laying out his inkwell and quill in front of him. The fisherman was happy that he had found his grand scheme, yet he knew that there were other things that he felt he could do with the information he received from the Creator, or from wherever it came from. He straightened his back a little, stretching the sleep and ache from his tired limbs. The last five mornings he had done this. He had gotten up before anyone else, several hours earlier, and began his writing before anyone else had even stirred from their bedchambers. Of course, it did have its advantages.

First, he was not completely spent from copying the entire day and would not fall asleep in his duties as The Chronicler, which had happened earlier on when he was writing after working so late into the night and into the early morning hours. However, the dwarven scribes had never questioned him about his inability to stay awake during copying hours; they seemed to take it in stride that a human could not keep up with a set of dwarven scribes, knowing that must be the reason and not something else, for they never saw nor heard him copying at night.

Secondly, The Chronicler was able to empty all of the information from the previous night's dreams into a tome, which kept him from having moments during the day where the visions were too much. This Falwen enjoyed immensely due to the fact that it gave him a sense of normalcy to life for a brief period of time instead of feeling as though he were an improper fit for the scribe's guild as well. There was no job or duty that could give him the time he needed as well as the privacy as much as a place like this, safe within the world of another race.

So, it was The Chronicler that prodded on through the early morning hours before the others were woke by the morning toll of the bells, his eyes rested, his spirit awakened and alive by this, channeling the visions he had seen merely a night before through the tip of the quill.

The inkwell never ran dry for him. His eyes would sometimes dart to the tip of the quill as it was dipped in small glass bottle, waiting, half-expecting that the quill would be dry and his writing would cease; then it would withdraw from the well and he would see the small layer of ink hanging onto the quill as though it were freeing itself from eternity inside the well.

As his eyes looked down to the page, The Chronicler saw her. He could envision the young elf in her robes of the writing guild that she was from, but that was not what he took notice of most. It was the fact that she was alone, that she was far from home… and it was the urgency in her movements; her arms pumped themselves from front to back, urging herself forward, always looking back behind her. All of this came into view on the page in front of The Chronicler as he wrote it, his fingers moving methodically back to the inkwell then back to the page, over and over again, until the story finally revealed itself.

What she carries is our last vestige of hope!

The Chronicler continued.

*   *   *

The snows in the east had closed many of the trails down between the towns and cities in Kariyl, all traders using only the cleared Tirapoor Channel as a means for trading and travel. This meant, with the exception of Telgin and the other towns that were close to the Tirapoor Channel, the other towns had to fend for themselves the best they knew how. Many did this well, as had been accustomed since the difficult snows had fallen for the first time several seasons ago. However, there were always some random trader or hunter that would choose to move when all others stayed still within their homes, nestled close to the fire.

Altina Laese fled from her captors with hopes that she would find someone on the Tirapoor Channel that could help her. Behind her, the Keep of Dral Nakas and its occupants could not be seen, though the thoughts of them still haunted her; it had been a full night since she had seen to her own getaway. She had escaped without being detected somehow, the young elven scribe running through her mind the scenarios of what would have happened if she had been caught.

I would have been disposed of for sure, she reminded herself, holding close the small messenger's scroll case, trying her best to focus on what her next move was going to be. Her small form had been shivering for the last few hours since the sun had set far in the west, pulling her robes as close to her body as she could allow, still feeling the dampness of them from the earlier snow melting into her thin garments.

She could feel the flushness in her face and hands and knew that she would not last long within the snow. Throwing the scroll case over her head and shoulder with the straps on the case, she secured it tightly and continued forward to find a place to get warm and rest, even if it was for only a moment. But there was nothing within sight around her. In fact, every direction seemed to hold the same for her; nothing.

Altina knew that she was far from home; and she knew even more that it was a bad idea to try and transfer to another guild, especially so far away from her kingdom of Elvinisclar. Trayvilis had been told to have the most extensive library of all the elven kingdoms in all the centuries that had past and, when she was given the chance to go and see it for herself, leaving the solace and quiet of Elvinisclar to see a new world, she had accepted her fate of the possibilities, even if it could possibly turn out none too good.

But I never thought it would be like this.

Her small, elven frame shook with a strong cough that started deep in her chest, making her stop in her tracks, her arms and legs shaking from the force of it. The elf lost balance in the snow and felt herself tumble down quickly, the coldness seeping into her limbs almost as fast as it had when she first escaped the keep. Altina began to slip out of consciousness as the coughs continued to come, the snow around her almost swallowing her up completely.

The young elf's mind wandered for a time within the feverish dreams her mind had as well as her reality, intermingling the two together so seamlessly that it snowed in her dreams.

She dreamt of staring high into the sky, deep into the darkness; an everlasting wave of snow raining down upon her, flake after calming flake trying to wake her. They melted on her face first, touching the pale, elven cheeks with a dispassionate wintry kiss, then moved to her eyes, kissing both the lids. She felt the flakes then move to her exposed hands and neck, then to her forehead which continued up into her hair. The night seemed to watch this with much envy because, time and again, the night would blot out the flakes of snow that Altina saw with stars that could faintly be seen above her, high in the sky.

Altina could feel the whole of her body begin to go numb and then it was warm, the snow kisses landing on her eyelids again, making her close her eyes to receive them. She smiled when they tickled her cheeks where they could still be felt, yet not so much as a feverish blush was returned by her, her face growing colder by the moment. She blinked one last time and was fast asleep in the embrace of unyielding winter.

*   *   *

"What is it?" The voice spoke as if it were afraid of what it stumbled upon, lifting the torch up over the form covered with snow, dusting off what they could with their free hand. The two creatures had been moving across the snow-covered plains, looking for shelter themselves, when they had come upon the still form of this elf. The smaller, squatter forms, much like dwarves, eyed the elven girl curiously, one of them even dusting off the face and head of the elf with the tip of their cloak.

"Triggle, don't do that! She'll probably jump up and stab us with a dagger!" But the creature, Triggle, continued, turning the elf over so he could see her clearly.

"Ilthen, I think she's sick! Look at her face; it's so pale!"

The other, Ilthen, countered. "All elves are pale! That doesn't mean she's sick!"

"Well this one is! Quickly, find me some daldonga leaves! They're good for…"

Ilthen finished his sentence. "…for breaking a fever. I know Triggle! I'm the one who taught you about it!" The female of the group, Ilthen, moved away from Triggle and was back in the snow in a moment's notice, leaving Triggle to assist the elf all by himself.

He looked down at her, pulling off his own winter cloak from his back to wrap around her.

She is near freezing to death! Triggle reached his hands out to the elf, who began to wake up long enough to see the small, dwarf-like creature coming at her, his hands glowing through the blankets of snow that came down around them.

"I'm not going to hurt you."

The elf shifted in her place and began to pull away, fighting the Miftle faerie, but felt her movements sap away at what strength she had left and collapsed back onto the ground, her breathing ragged and labored.

It was hours before Altina awoke, lying next to a roaring fire, the pain in her chest gone, the coughs having ceased. She lay still, unmoving, watching as the fire crackled and snapped angrily at the snow as it fell, one of the dwarfish figures sitting across from her, somewhat difficult to be seen through the firelight. She was blanketed in several fur goods that kept her warmer than she had been in several nights, including those left in the keep's writing chambers, which is where the coldness began for her. The elf's eyes shifted slightly and she noticed that the ground around her and around the campsite was dry and without snow; even the wood within the fire that burned did not snap or sizzle at the snow that should have melted onto the fire as it began.

The male dwarfish creature, Triggle his named seemed to be called, for Altina remembered small pieces of a dream she had earlier, stayed where he was and didn't notice she was awake, keeping himself busy adding small ingredients from the pouches on his belt into a boiling kettle in front of him. He hummed a little tune while he did this.

"…in the days before my love… the days that were less sweet… I came here from afar… and here it is we meet… a peace be with you, love… and with that, I swear…" The rest of the song was lost in the clamor of movement just outside the firelight, the other dwarfish creature, Ilthen, moved through the high snow around the camp to stand just on the edge of the fire, on the other side with Triggle.

Triggle smiled brightly at her when he saw what she had in her hands.

"Ah, Ilthen, you found it, did you?"

The female creature nodded her head slightly, shaking off the snow that had acquired on her cloaked head and shoulders.

"Aye, I did. And you would not believe how hard it was to find, either!"

Triggle stood up and approached Ilthen, wiping the rest of the snow off her shoulders, taking the cloak from her while allowing her to get warm by the fire.

"Thank you, dear!" She kissed Triggle on the cheek and handed him the leaves, which he took, moving back to the kettle.

"And that makes the broth complete! Just a few minutes with those leaves and she'll be as good as new."

Triggle laid Ilthen's cloak by the fire to melt off the snow and began breaking up the leaves into the kettle, stirring it with a ladle he had, dipping it into and out of the bowl repeatedly.

"Did you find out who she is yet?" Triggle shook his head and continued to attending to the kettle, positioning himself back where he had been.

"Not yet. She has yet to awaken. I did find some things of interest on her though."

Triggle lifted the scroll case up by its straps to Ilthen, who took it and began to open it. Altina reached under the covers and did not feel the straps of the scroll case where she should have.

They have stolen it!

Altina leapt up from the fur covers, surprising Triggle so that he fell over into the snow, coming back up from with a head full of it. Ilthen jumped back but stood her ground, the scroll case gripped in one of her hands.

"Give it back! Give it back, I say!" The weak elven girl reached her hand out to Ilthen, who, in turn, drew the scroll case back to her chest when she saw the elf reaching to her belt with her other hand.

"Triggle, she's armed!" Ilthen was about the pull the dagger from her sheath when Triggle stood up.

"Both of you sit down this instant! Elf, there's nothing at your side because I took it and Ilthen, there's nothing to worry about." Both of the women stood for long moments, unsure of what to do, still excited about the situation before them. Triggle straightened himself up a little taller and stomped his foot.

"Now, ladies! Sit!" Ilthen gave into Triggle's demands first, sitting next to him, and then the elf stepped back to her spot by the fire, sitting down as well. Triggle breathed a sigh of relief and continued with his broth in the kettle by pouring some into a set of small cups by his feet, walking over to hand the elf one of them.

"Now we're not going to harm, you, lady elf. You were freezing and ripe with fever when we found you. I only took your things to find out who you were and because you were delirious. You were mumbling through the night."

Triggle handed the elf one of the cups of broth and waited for her to take it from him.

"Go on, take it! It's made of a special set of herbs that will help that cough of yours. Go on."

The elf took it and wrapped both of her hands around it, warming her fingers.

"Thank you." She sipped at the hot broth as Triggle made his way back to Ilthen's side, handing her a cup as well.

"My name is Triggle and this is my mate, Ilthen. And you're name is, lady elf?"

"Altina Laese." The broth was delicious. Altina began to drink it up though it was still very hot, finishing her cup in no time. Her stomach yearned for more. She looked over to the kettle, which was still boiling with broth.

"May I?" Altina motioned to the full kettle.

"No, no, child! Let me do that for you. You need to keep warm under those furs." Triggle moved back over near her and retrieved the bowl, pouring another for the elf, handing it back to Altina, who began drinking from it as soon as the bowl touched her hands. Ilthen sipped lightly at her first bowl and looked at the elf questioningly.

"My, you seemed starved! How long have you been out here?"

Altina wiped the edges of her mouth with the tips of her fingers, looking to Ilthen kindly, somewhat more relaxed than before.

"A little over a day, though I don't know how long I slept here since being in your company."

Triggle added in, "…only a few hours, Lady Laese. We found you before the snow started really coming down. Lucky we did, too, or you would have been lost in that snow for good!"

Altina nodded in agreement. "Thank you for that, too. I never got to formally thank you since knowing who you are."

Ilthen brushed off the remark. "Lady Laese, you have only been awake for a few moments now. We don't expect anything of the sort from you. My, it seems that you've been through a great ordeal. As soon as you feel up to it, you can tell us what you're doing with a map that's written in Parthenian."

The mood seemed to change immediately. And Ilthen didn't seem to mind at all. In fact, she seemed to welcome the awkward conversation to the table. It's not every day that you see an elf carrying a scroll case with a language that is forbidden through a storm that would kill even the well-trained ranger.

And it wasn't everyday that faerie kind followed their hunches instead of the directions that they were given. Usually that gets them into trouble, Ilthen thought to herself, already having dealings with those issues with the time spent with Triggle, traveling through much of the eastern half of Kariyl, in search of something that few faeries believed existed to this day. Ilthen tried her best to forget about her mission that had been pressing in on her by the day and focus on the young elven woman with a death wish and a forbidden map at the present. Worrying about someone else's problems always seemed to put Ilthen at ease.

Altina's eyes grew wide. "How did you know it was….."

Ilthen finished for her. "… Parthenian? Let us just say that I have seen the writing before and I can decipher it."

The elf nodded and took a few more sips from her broth before answering. Her eyes seemed to be gathering up information around her, looking through the falling snow for something more. Ilthen queried further before letting the elf continue.

"Are you in some kind of danger, child? Please let us know so we can help."

Triggle added. "Yes, Altina, let us know. We can help you!"

Altina knew that it was already too late for her. She had known this ever since leaving the keep without the antidote to what they had given her and all the others when they first arrived.

Altina looked sad as she spoke, the cup laid on the ground next to her, the furs wrapped tightly about her thin shoulders.

"They said that it was a slow-acting poison that would kill you if you allowed it to go unchecked. They had been giving us an antidote to counter the poison's effects. I was allowed to stay alive there if I did their work, copied what they needed, so I did. But when I saw what I copied, I knew it was something awful."

Triggle and Ilthen did not speak. They simply stared at the frail-looking elven girl and knew that what she spoke was the truth. Triggle had wavered in telling her what he saw within her because he had doubted what his magik showed him, simply thinking that she would be healed by a hot meal and some rest and warmth.

That, however, was not the case, Triggle thought to himself.

Altina continued. "Ilthen, what you hold in your hands right now are the battle plans to wipe the slate of Kariyl completely clean and start over again. The Order of the Emcrist intends to end history as we know it and the plans are being sent by dozens of messengers to be carried out as we speak. Now, how is it that you can help me?"

The two Miftles were speechless.

It was Triggle who broke the silence with a question that showed his intelligence.

"What's an Emcrist?"

15

When Ar Solon was first created, before inhabitants populated the many continents, there was one, true continent. And this continent, which is called Dizrael by the early historians, was said to be a barren and simple world. From what was known of the past that was passed down through stories told at small village gatherings, the faeries were the first to populate the world. They were the first inhabitants on the first continent. And the Creator had given them a purpose…. and he had given them magik.

The magik was given to the faeries for them to create the most imaginative world of all; and the faeries did this. For centuries, the faeries created, bringing to life trees, mountains, springs, wells, caves, flowers and animals alike, always giving a part of themselves during the creative process. The world became pure and bountiful, soon ready for the true inhabitants to begin their lives on the continent of Dizrael. There came a time when it happened; when faeries and inhabitants lived among one another in harmony. The Creator had meant this to happen. However, it did not last very long.

Deep within a set of caves that the faeries had made, the Creator had kept the strength of magik within the world. It was within these caves that three great gems resided in their worldly cradles. Each gem was the size of a dwarf's head and could make anyone who carried it powerful beyond belief. The gems were called the Emcrist. They rivaled any treasure that could be sought after with their value as well as the magikal powers bestowed upon them.

Moreover, after Dizrael had been created and life flourished upon it, the faeries had little to do. Their eyes began to wander and their purpose was no longer there. This, accompanied by a new race of beings, the first inhabitants, began to make them question their purpose, their own grand scheme. So the faeries broke into factions, separate groups that began to investigate the world that they were on. In the beginning, the first inhabitants and the faeries lived among one another. This was how elves and dwarves were created as races upon Dizrael. The simple inhabitants of the world became enthralled with the faerie folk around them and, as time passed by, the faeries and inhabitants began to flourish and multiply with one other.

This was not considered wrong or against any rules; faerie kin were passionate and unrivaled in spirit when compared with the inhabitants, which gave a drive to the offspring of the inhabitants and faeries when multiplying together. However, it wasn't until the Creator noticed that the inhabitants he had created were without a grand scheme that he began to get worried; something clouded their judgment over a period of time. By the time the Creator noticed this, several generations had gone by and it was too late. He would have to allow things to run their course, hoping that future generations were filled more with the grand scheme than their parents and grandparents before them had been.

But this was not the case. By this time, the impassioned faerie kind that had been mating with the inhabitants had created races on their own; races that were just as spirited as the faeries themselves but with much more of the grand scheme within them than the faerie folk had ever had. It was here that great men and women leaders were created. With a fire burning within their breast and what grand scheme the inhabitants had within them, kings and queens began their reign.

It wasn't much longer after this that a faerie did something that would irrevocably change the world of Dizrael for the worse. A faerie, hearing the stories of the great Emcrist jewels, went on a search for them. For several years, this faerie that they called Y'tin-eres Maerd went searching for what could not be found. Several had tried and they all had failed. Faeries, inhabitants, and even mixed breeds of them all; the elves, dwarves, goblins, orcs, and kobolds had made their attempts and their adventures had been told in stories by the fires, but none had achieved what Y'tin-eres was soon able to do. He found one of the Emcrist.

…and he took it. Y'tin-eres soon found out that removing an Emcrist from its cradle cost Ar Solon much more than it was worth. The continent split into three pieces and Y'tin-eres died in the process, trapping himself within the caves in which it had been found. He died with the Emcrist in his hands. He had found it, but at what cost? The entire world of Ar Solon would soon begin to shatter, and all at the cost of power and greed.

*   *   *

However, Knall Grist knew all of this and still the Order of the Emcrist continued to thrive because of him. Power and greed had become two of his children that he had birthed with great pride these last few decades, moving his followers into position to strike when the time presented itself.

The leader of the Emcrist Order stared out over his balcony, the snow still continuing to fall around him and the rest of his order. It had been over a day since the recruit Trin Ganthes had left to search after the missing scribe and he had heard no word back. He wondered if Trin was even still alive. The snows had come in strong and refused to leave now, blanketing the ground, the trees, the lakes and streams around him as well as the rising mountain chain from all sides, giving very little exposed areas for Knall to look upon besides the ever-falling snow.

Soon, very soon, Knall agreed, his mind on many tasks at the moment; so many that it was hard for him to think at times. Much had transpired in front of him; he had seen a number of events pass before his eyes, being one of the oldest human beings on Kariyl. At two-hundred and sixty-two years old, Knall didn't look over a day over thirty-seven, which was the age that he had stopped becoming a man and was reborn as a lich.

Of course, I didn't know it at the time, he thought to himself, pondering over all of the mistakes he had made in the past. *Turning myself into a lich was definitely one of my bigger mistakes.*

He had seen so many pass away before him; some of the liches that he had known of on the continents of Ar Solon had even found a way to dispose of themselves, releasing their souls from their bodies with much pain and agony, be it that the soul had gotten comfortable in its mortal shell.

Yet no one that was alive knew he was a lich. Even his right hand man, Belter Swen, did not know he was a lich. Of course, his high-ranking men including Belter knew that he housed some magik within his veins; he was able to do things that no inhabitant could do, yet Knall kept his being a lich a secret.

That piece of information always came in handy when things went bad around him. And several times, throughout the decades that had gone by, the land rising and swelling with inhabitants, Knall had seen the downfall of even the greatest of men.

And all of the other races for that matter. The lich's thoughts drifted then to Parthenia and of the great monuments and statues that had been erected of only their best men.

I will have statues someday soon, Knall mused, thinking of what pose he would stand in for the great artisans to carve him in. Very few on the continent of Kariyl had been immortalized in stone. The kings and queens of the humans had not even been carved in stone.

Only the great elves and dwarves kept their heirs with them, Knall concluded, *with the exception of that statue of the angel.*

Knall remembered a few seasons back when he had received word from one of his messengers that there was a statue that had been erected of, from the story that had been told, Shilinda, the queen of the faeries. Many of the inhabitants from around Reune Lake and the surrounding areas had known her to be a witch of sorts, some creature from an unknown place that conjures up spells and faerie creatures upon you at a moment's notice. But Knall knew that many of the stories that were told around the cooking fires and taverns in Kariyl were nothing but lies.

Nevertheless, there was something that was different about this statue; there was no reason for there to be a rumor about it. Knall had thought through the scenario over and over again, waiting for there to be a hole in the story. But, after careful consideration, he had yet to find one. So he traveled there to see it, this statue that everyone was talking about.

And there was no way that it could have been created by any artisan on the continent, no matter how creative that they were. And so Knall knew the answer to what had been happening around him at that moment.

The others that value this world are coming forward now. It was more of a statement than a thought, Knall reminded himself, remembering the others rumors that had been floating around at that time.

A great voice had stretched out across the land in the west, terrifying everyone within a city's radius from the shores. There had been rumors of a great faerie army moving across the middle of Kariyl, approaching the soggy, unworkable land of Wilden. There they disappeared and more rumors surfaced about the dwarves and their holdings in Dardist. Soon, there were stories about daemons surfacing on the land and attacking those guards on the checkpoint not too long after, sending a chill of excitement through all of Knall's limbs at the thought.

It is happening! All of what I have been foretold is happening. The jewel does not lie!

The secret of the Emcrist he had acquired was kept well from all others. He felt the power course through him when he was near it, the great jewel being well hidden in his grand tower; the uppermost part of the keep. No one had seen it since almost a century earlier and he planned on keeping it that way. Many had died at his hands once they left the grand tower, their secret being kept and sealed with blood.

The lich could feel the Emcrist, even several buildings away, call to him. His body ached for the power; he knew this, which made him somewhat hesitant as he made his way through his chambers to the outer hallways, passing by a number of his guards at their posts. They tensed when he passed them, Knall Grist barely noticing their forms as he made his way to the Emcrist.

This is only one of the Emcrist jewels. I can only imagine what another Emcrist would do to me.

Many times, Knall had theorized finding one of the other Emcrist jewels in his frequent searches across Kariyl and the other continents far away, only to find a dead end to the quest every time, Knall's anger taking over. He killed most of his traveling parties, sometimes all of them, making his way back to the boats on his own, leaving no trail behind him. No one was left to know of Knall's previous failures. Decades had gone by since those days and Knall Grist soon began gathering individuals together to reform the long-since dead Emcrist Order.

Yet, when doing so, the lich found that there was still an order that existed. With the shattering of the trust between the races after the War of the Races, the bond between the elves, dwarves, and human dissolved and severed what centuries had taken to build between them. Knall soon found the true believers of the Emcrist Order within the elven and dwarven races, both of those races living almost double the time that the humans lived.

This gave the other two races far more of an advantage when carrying on an ideal, for it was passed on with pride and time backing it. The dwarves had hidden themselves within the mountains, both the Argolis and Agnar mountains, keeping to themselves, very few of them associating with the other races. The elves did the same. Within their great towers in Elvinisclar and Trayvilis they stayed, keeping far from the other races that had once deceived them.

Ar Solon had become littered with distrust, the races that had once been rejected by the Parthenians centuries ago now did the same thing to other races, never learning from the mistakes that shunned them centuries earlier. And Knall, knowing this, decided that this was the perfect moment to strike.

It had all come to this single moment; of waiting and wanting more than anything to find another Emcrist within its cradle, still waiting to be removed.

Knall moved silently through the exterior of the Keep of Dral Nakas, the cold, winter air cutting through his clothes and armor, his gloved hands bringing the hood of his cloak up over his head as he made his way to the tower. Many of these things he did, these rituals, had become second nature to him, almost as if he were still a human and not an undead creature. The daily preparations of bathing and preparing himself for the day as well as the warm clothing for cold weather were all simply a show for the others around him. Since becoming a lich, he felt little physically and even less emotionally, a new level of understanding coming to him over time. Of course, it was not easy, cohabitating with others that were alive.

Knall had become a conjurer, one of the last on Kariyl, shortly after the demise of his human self in order to try and find a cure to the lich he is today. He had been taken in by a conjurer after escaping the dwarven raids during The War of the Races. Within the abandoned Keep of Dral Nakas, he was restored to health, but not after finding out that he had become a lich. After finding this out with grim certainty, Knall dedicated much of his time trying to undo the curse. He had been unsuccessful up until recently and decided to move ahead with his life…or the lack thereof.

In much of this time, Knall found out about the Parthenians and their ways, the magik of conjuring and earth magik, as well as traveling to many of the far-off continents to see the rest of Ar Solon for himself. What he found traveling had assisted him in knowing that his purpose, his one true purpose, would reset what had been undone for centuries. With the severing of the continents, the inhabitants began to work only for themselves; this was shown in an awful light when he witnessed The War of the Races with his own mortal eyes. Even when several from each race tried to start a sanctuary to begin peace again, with the city of Terapon far from the boundaries of any race, it still failed.

Somehow, the idea of the individual had set hard within the minds of everyone around him and it was locked in place, forever to doom the races until the end. And that end was rapidly approaching. Knall was not ignorant to this. In the centuries that he had lived, he amassed a grand library, first with the remnants of tomes that an old elf had given him to a great collection he had found when Terapon had been evacuated, stashed away in a secret room by the family line that had created the city of Terapon.

Much of this was not simply the rantings and ravings of an imagination gone wild in a time of woe or that of a philosopher trying to make sense of insane times; but they were books of research, of maps and destinations before and after the separation of the continents of Ar Solon. In essence, Knall had become a historian of sorts, piecing together the long-gone remnants from the past, trying his best to recapture the world the way it had been before it had been corrupted. And to Knall Grist, there was only one way that Ar Solon could be righted again. It was the destruction of all that had been created, a simply wiping of the slate of the world and starting all over again.

And Knall knew just how to do it. The lich continued to the tower in which held the Emcrist.

It would only be a few more days, then the battle plan would be put into action. Much had been done, sacrificed, he reminded himself, *for just this moment.*

He would relish in it as it came. The lich smiled as he passed the tower guards and made his way up the winding staircase to the top level of the tower.

This day will not be forgotten; by Kariyl, or all on Ar Solon for that matter.

Knall Grist, the general and head of the Order of the Emcrist, climbed up the stairs slowly, taking his time in the dimly lit corridor. The end of the inhabitants was at hand!

*   *   *

Darder lifted himself up from his place at the front desk at the Fisherman's Quarrel and opened the doors for the morning crowd; mostly drunken patrons from the night before, many of them sailors, making their way in, some of them even being dragged in by their fellow drinkers, finding solace within the walls of Darder's inn.

Apparently, that's what I'm known for, the innkeeper thought to himself, dragging his hands against his grizzled face, trying his best to wake up from the small naps he had taken at the front desk throughout the night. Something had kept him up. It had been years ago since he had seen or thought about him, but Falwen Sanse, the great fisherman and an even great friend, had come to his mind.

Maybe because his son, Jannon, is here, he reminded himself, looking up the staircase at the doors on the second floor, remembering when the same thing had happened years earlier. Darder checked his patrons in and showed them to their rooms, unlocking each door with his thick set of keys at his waist, soon passing by Jannon's room. The aged man put his ear to the door, listening carefully.

Must still be sleeping. And a great right to be sleeping, too!

Jannon had come in late the night before, his face drained of all color. It seemed as though he had walked all night to get to Goletta. And, once arriving, he did nothing more than say a brief hello to Darder and pay him, in fine coin no less, for the room his family usually stayed in. This immediately seemed all too familiar to Darder, who had seen Jannon's father come in almost four summers earlier, the same exhausted look on his face, the same mission deep beneath his eyes. Darder knew something was amiss with the Sanse family, he just didn't know what.

That was why, when Jannon awoke, Darder was going to get the facts from this boy. The innkeeper's mind still drifted to what things he had heard about shortly after Falwen's departure from Goletta. The man that Darder had gotten for Falwen to leave the city, Treese if he remembered correctly, had never returned yet someone had found his wagon and horses on the eastern trail leaving Goletta. The horses had been slaughtered.

Treese loved those horses. Finrass and Tartoll were everything to him. And there was no word of him for miles around, though not many searched too hard for he was a man on his own in Kariyl.

And there were several people like that in Goletta, Darder giving them rooms for the night for the last 20 years of his life.

A few more patrons came in to get rooms, Darder leading them up to their rooms, both his first and second floors now almost booked full for the day. Business had picked up for him since the snows had begun to fall in the east, several families taking it upon themselves, after braving the snows for the last three, harsh winters to finally pack up what they could and move to a warmer climate in the west, many staying within the confines of the walled city of Goletta until they found or built a home, which ever came first.

Of course, it wasn't much warmer in the west, but the east got the brunt of the snow, Darder hearing of several families dying trying to stay alive within the blizzards that kept coming. It had been hard times for everyone yet Darder kept his sights on the big picture. And that big picture was money. He had done well with these snowy seasons, better than he had done since becoming an innkeeper. Being inside the city seemed to help, for he always had the city guards to clean up the snows in the streets and on the roofs of the buildings. He paid for it, of course, but he managed to wheel and deal with those guards that had families from the east and would use his trade of rooms for work and supplies to his advantage.

Becoming one with a little more chink in the pocket made him upgrade himself a bit, wearing a new set of clothes every other day. He even took baths regularly now, which he had to do because his inn was so much busier and he couldn't allow himself to linger with a few day's stink on him when he was conducting business. Yes, the snows had made him a man without a care in the world.

But the few things that he did care for, one being the Sanse family, had come into his life again and he didn't intend on letting it slip away so easily. Darder made his way to Jannon's room, intent now on not waiting until breakfast was served to see Jannon. It would be busy on the first floor and the last thing that he wanted was for Jannon to slip out without Darder being able to say anything to him

Or get any information from him, he admitted, wanting more than anything to know about Falwen and his family since those years ago when the old fisherman came to visit by himself. Darder reached the door and reached for his keys at his belt, finding the key almost without looking. He placed it in the lock and turned, pushing the door open with his hand. When Darder looked into the room, he realized that he wasn't going to get anything from Jannon, for Jannon was already gone.

The innkeeper cursed under his breath for his sporadic sleeping habits and closed the door behind him.

16

Jannon made his way through the high traffic of the Golettan docks, the early morning sun reminding him of how little sleep he had gotten.

Not enough for what I need to do, he thought to himself, still trying to rub the sleep from his eyes. He had made it here before Ranyll Tolver and the dwarf Oagthor had, spending a few hours sleeping before he made his way out into city to find them. Finding them wasn't difficult.

It almost seemed as if it were fate, Jannon remarked, lifting the water skin to his parched lips, watching the two of them as they spoke with a sailor at the main dock entrance. He took a drink from the container, the cool water abating the thirst in moments. He continued to listen.

First Mate Meekins his name was, Jannon overheard, committing it to memory as a few others came towards them. He could only make out some of the things that they said to one another from his vantage point. Jannon moved back further behind the pile of crates he spied from, making sure that he wasn't seen by the others that approached Ranyll and his dwarven friend, still trying his best to hear what they were saying. However, now he couldn't hear a thing. There were several ships being loaded and unloaded and the noise broke the stillness of the morning, making him cover one of his ears to try and hear out of the other.

It looked as though Ranyll and this Oagthor wanted to board a ship, the young boy decided, soon watching as First Mate Meekins moved away from the rest of them, moving past Jannon and the crates he hid behind, passing to the other vessels on the docks. Jannon waited for him to pass before looking again. In another moment, he was back to watching Ranyll speak to another man, this one more regal than the first mate. Ranyll produced a scroll case to this man and, before Jannon could blink, Ranyll and his dwarf were on their way down the docks, boarding a ship a few vessels down from Jannon.

They're leaving! This can't be! I have to get on that ship! He peered as far as he could but couldn't see the name of the vessel. Jannon, looking around and finding no one, moved out of hiding from behind the crates. He made his way to the unguarded docks and began walking to the ship Ranyll had boarded. Soon, he could see the name on the side of it.

The Namiah, it read. The great ship seemed almost double the size when compared with the other ships around it, the masts covering a large amount of height alone, not to mention the bulk of the ship itself, which seemed almost as high as the other ships around it. Then Jannon realized what he was looking at.

It's an old Parthenian ship! The young man had heard tales from his father about the ships that he had seen on all of his voyages on the Alvanus Sea, several of them including run-ins with ships of this very caliber.

But to see it floating on the water in front of you is something entirely different, Jannon concluded, staring up high past the hull of the ship itself to see the rest of the ship. Just as he was about to close in on the vessel, a voice called out from behind him.

"Hey there, boy, what are you doing?" Jannon turned to see the first mate moving toward him, his none too desirable face smashed up in an angry expression as he closed in on the young man.

"I was just looking at...."

"Looking or not, you're not allowed here on the docks! This is for sailors only! Sailors only, boy!"

"But I want to book passage on the Namiah. I have the coin to do so." But the first mate would not hear of it, Jannon already knew from the look on the man's face. The dingy man grabbed Jannon by the arm and walked him over to the end of the personal docking area, pressing him ahead of him.

"Now go! I don't know who's been saying that we take passengers, but we're a shipping vessel, nothing more! Now go tell your source that they're wrong, you here! Wrong!"

And just as easily as it was in finding the two he was searching for, Jannon was just as easily guided away from Ranyll and his dwarf, walking back through the smaller docking areas to the western entrance back into Goletta. Soon, the sight of the Namiah disappeared and was replaced by the smaller-manned vessels, a few fishing boats as well as a cargo boat or two tied to the smaller docks closer to the entrance into the city. He passed them by and stopped just short of the entrance, the great barrier doors in front of him, one guard on each side of the door. The two guards, doffed in a light chain mail suit each and thin leather armor underneath, stared questioningly from under their helms, looking out over the docking area.

One of them nodded out to the docks.

"Boy, you trying to be a sailor?"

Jannon looked over at the guard and shook his head.

"I'm trying to book passage on a ship." The young man was flustered and the guards seemed to take notice. The guard shifted his gaze over to the northern docks, just a few docks past the Namiah, where Jannon wanted to be.

"I'm sure some vessels on the northern side are taking on passengers; it all depends on where you're going. Once they unload their cargo, they'll be taking passengers. You might want to try back a little later in the day."

Jannon thanked the guard and made his way to the northern docks, settling down on a crate that was stacked next to many others, watching as some of the more sizeable ships began to unload their cargo for the drop off. Jannon took this time to eat. In the pack on his back, he drew forth a few pieces of fruit and a small slab of cheese wrapped in cheesecloth. He ate enough to fill his stomach for the moment and looked out over the Alvanus Sea, which was just to the west of him past the docks.

Now what do I do, father? I've come to an end where I can go no further. I will find you, father! But what do I do from here?

The clouds in the sky were quiet as was everything else except for the movement and scuffling on the docks around him, a mass of sailors unloading a great ship not far from him. Several sailors passed him by, unloading supplies onto loading pallets for other ships. First, the sailors brought the used, empty containers off the ship, placing them behind the check-in building where many others of the same variety lay. Once that was completed, sailors doubled up and began unloading the heavier cargo, some of them even using nets, ropes, and pulleys to unload the ship.

Jannon watched all of this with great interest, for he had never seen this process, having been born in Simmer Lo, a much smaller town where they got most of their wares by wagons, Jannon watching now as the sailors unloaded supplies that weighed several times their own weight. Some of it was casks and barrels while others were crates and small wooden boxes stacked up on one another, tied down with netting and ropes that kept the items from moving while in storage on the ship.

A few of the sailors passed the young man, using a small, wheeled cart to transport a bulk of the supplies to a wagon that was already waiting near the docks. The rest of the sailors began loading a pallet not far from Jannon, stacking up the remainder of the supplies on this area.

Jannon could hear their conversation.

"Now when do we get paid for this, because I'm about ready to come ashore, if you know what I mean!"

The other sailor nodded in response. "I know what you mean. The captain says once we get our pay from the first mate of the Namiah and we help them load this up for their next voyage, then we can have shore leave. The Namiah has to leave out shortly, so we should get our wages today."

"It's about time, too, because I've been cooped up on that ship long enough…." The rest of the conversation seemed lost to Jannon who seemed to ponder over all he had heard from them.

Leave out shortly? What if they leave without me? I might not ever find Ranyll again and then my father is lost to me!

Jannon hated to think of coming all this way and not being able to find his father. After all, it had been years since he had heard from his father, with the exception of the letters that his family had just received, which didn't tell him anything about his father's whereabouts from what he had heard from his mother.

Yes, I must find a way on board….and it must be quick. I can wait no longer for them to let me on board. If they won't let me on board….

Jannon looked over at the stacks of empty barrels and supply crates stacked against the check-in building, all the while packing up his foodstuffs back in his pack. He climbed off the crate and moved toward the building.

...I'll find my own way on the Namiah.

*　　　*　　　*

First Mate Meekins made his way past the rest of the crew as they made their way on board; many of them returning from shore leave while others had begun stocking up the ship with the first wave of supplies that had come from the other two ships the captain had been waiting for.

Now we can leave this blasted city, Meekins thought to himself. The gruff pirate had known much about this city at one time, though the thoughts were a distant memory in his mind now, preferring the sea more than anything else in his life.

The less the land around me, the better. The first mate had seen more hard times on land than off, wishing more than anything that he didn't have to even get off the Namiah, but knew that his duties took him different places, required much more than what he was used to. Nevertheless, Meekins didn't mind because he knew that he was well respected by captain and crew. Not far from where the Namiah docked Meekins could see the unloading area of the second vessel, *The Father,* which he had served on briefly, only to find better company on the Namiah, which had been a hard vessel for him to get on at first.

There was only one sailor next to the Namiah drop-off area, which had become somewhat the custom; leaving at least a single sailor to guard the supplies until the purchaser came to verify the supplies. The first mate had done this many times, so he took no notice of the sailor, who looked somewhat ramshackle anyway; clothes dirty and disheveled.

Must have been a hard voyage, Meekins remarked inwardly, pulling out the cargo manifest that the captain had given him, looking to the sailor for his as well.

"Well, here's my papers, sailor. I hope it's all here because my captain doesn't like to wait. We have a voyage to be getting to, if you don't mind."

But the sailor had his back to him, apparently busy with something else. In fact, Meekins didn't see any paperwork on the sailor, the first mate tapping the sailor roughly on the shoulder to get his attention. That's when the sailor turned around and Meekins soon saw what he had been busy doing.

The face of the sailor still wasn't quite formed. A black maw with razor sharp teeth was still in the process of forming into a sailor's nose and mouth, the red slits that were its eyes glimmered in the morning light. The great maw spread forth into a disfigured smiled and Meekins then realized that this would be his worst day of all on Kariyl. The daemon called Test leapt at him and pulled him in between the crates, silencing any scream Meekins could hope to give in warning by tearing into his throat immediately.

Test stared at the dying Meekins as he formed into the first mate slowly, taking the pirates belt and other supplies he had on him as his shadowy form snapped into place, feeling the change take him over as it had done with the sailor and the man in the woods. It had been some time since he had changed and the daemon relished in the moments of pain, though they had become shorter for him because his body was growing accustomed to the shifting into another form.

The new Meekins stood up at stretched his aching daemon muscles, looking out through a new set of eyes. He strapped the belt onto his waist and checked the blade for sharpness, sifting through the pouches and other supplies that the pirate had kept with him. He threw what he had no need of off the docks, each item making a quick plop in the water then vanishing under the murky water of the Golettan waterfront.

Test looked over at the two bodies in between the crates then searched around for others on the dockyard. Most of the hustle and bustle had gone once the ships had been unloaded and the men were gone for shore leave so it was easy for Test to dispose of the bodies. They too made a splash and then sunk under the Golettan harbor, finding a place among the debris lost their at one time or another by various sailors.

First Mate Meekins smiled and made his way back to the Namiah with both the cargo manifests in his hands, motioning for the others on the ship to load up the supplies onboard.

"The supplies are ready to go, captain!" Captain Aaolos leaned over the side of the ship, looking down at the first mate.

"That's fine, Meekins. Go ahead and get the things you need for yourself and I'll make sure the men load up what's there within the hour."

There's only one thing I need, captain, Test thought to himself, handing the cargo papers to another shipmate to hand up to the captain, *and that human has already booked passage on your vessel. I require nothing else.*

For the last three days, Test had waited in Goletta, spending some of his time with the family that had taken him in before departing to the Golettan markets, changing his form again once he arrived in the docks after finding out which vessel Ranyll Tolver was taking out of Kariyl.

I have known for some time where you are going, Ranyll Tolver. I have no intention of you going on your own.

And, as the daemon form of First Mate Meekins made his way onto the Namiah, he knew the plan was in place. He knew that the plan would work, though it had been years in the making, which was nothing to a daemon, for it knew no concept of time but the eternity it was to spend in agony and pain looking to the needs and whims of The One.

Out here was far more freedom than any daemon had ever been given.

First Mate Meekins made his way down to his chambers beneath the main deck and, from the memories that Test had taken from this Meekins, he found the human's bed easily and slept, waiting for Ranyll to come aboard so his game could continue.

*   *   *

Oagthor was the first one to speak once he and Ranyll entered The Tempered Sword, the southernmost weapons shop in Goletta. The dwarf smiled through his beard at Ranyll, pointing in the general direction of the dwarf at the counter, down past the rows and rows of weapons that lined the walls.

"Let me do all the talking, Ranyll. This is my kind of place."

And so the human followed quietly behind his dwarven friend, walking down one of the middle rows of the shop to the shopkeeper. There were four rows of the same length; the outside rows housed shields, armor, and distance weapons such as bows, crossbows, slings, and dart guns. The two inner rows were for close combat; swords, daggers, axes, maces, staffs of all kinds, and a few other weapons Ranyll had never seen before. His hand went instinctively to the broadsword at his side.

They approached the shopkeeper, who was an older dwarf, much older than Oagthor, his hair graying throughout his head and beard; only small wisps of black, what his hair color used to be, were present in both. The dwarf also carried a long scar across his face from left temple to his right cheek, his nose a bit crooked where the scar crossed it. He wore a thick pair of spectacles somewhat similar to the ones that Oagthor carried with him, though they were much thicker. The shopkeeper straightened his spectacles when he heard footsteps nearing him. He squinted through them to see who it was.

"It is I, Oagthor, Hemnil!" No sooner had Oagthor said his name then the dwarf behind the counter bellowed back at him.

"Oagthor Axeblade! My, my, it has been some time, has it not?" The dwarf seemed somewhat happy to see Oagthor, though he still had trouble actually seeing him through his thick spectacles.

"How long has it been, Hemnil; sixty summers since we've seen another?"

Hemnil thought for a moment at Oagthor's answer then shook his head, standing up from his place behind the counter.

"Sixty-four summers, and not a day later!" Hemnil smiled, moving around from the counter, his thick arms wrapping as far as they could around his friend, almost picking him up off the ground. Oagthor just smiled awkwardly, a little embarrassed with Ranyll present for this reunion, patting his friend on the shoulder until he eventually let the young dwarf go.

Hemnil chuckled to himself and just stood there, staring at his old friend, almost in disbelief that he was there before him. It was easy to tell from the expression he had. In fact, Hemnil barely noticed that Ranyll was there. After adjusting his spectacles, he noticed Ranyll.

"Oh, my apologies, sir, I didn't see you there. This dwarf is an old friend of mine is all. The customer is always first. Now what can I do you for?"

Oagthor shook his head and motioned to Ranyll.

"No, Hemnil. He's not a customer. Well, he is a customer, but he's with me. He's my friend. This is Ranyll Tolver."

It took a few moments to settle in but Hemnil understood. Whether he liked it or not was another story.

"Friend? Oh, he's a friend! That's good to hear. I hear dwarves are running out of friends these days. We've befriended some faeries in Dardist, I hear, but as for the rest of the races…" He trailed off, looking at Ranyll.

Ranyll, though, could see where the dwarf was going.

"I'm with the dwarves, Hemnil. That's why I'm here. I fought alongside them some years back and understand your woes."

"Hemnil Redspear II, best smithy and shopkeeper in Goletta! My father gave me his name and his accursed drinking problem! It was only after 135 years that I found the last part out! Any friend of Oagthor's is a friend of mine."

Ranyll shook the dwarf's outstretched hand, feeling the strength still behind it though the dwarf seemed much older than Oagthor, at least by fifty or sixty years.

What is this, Ranyll thought. *Do dwarves get stronger the older they get,* his mind lingering off to the other dwarf Rathor Gronas who was older yet just as strong and spirited as Oagthor was.

Oagthor did his best to keep the conversation focused on their needs, which was to leave before the sun had set, for the Namiah would be on the sea by that time. The dwarf still needed to get his drink. He pressed the conversation on.

"I would love to catch up with old times, Hemnil, but I have a ship to catch and am pressed for time. We need to be leaving shortly."

Hemnil's eyes grew wide with amazement.

"A ship to catch? A dwarf! Now the story is getting interesting!"

"Yes, the fun never seems to end with Oagthor's adventures does it, my old friend?"

Hemnil shook his head, laughing a bit, returning back behind the counter.

"Alright, then. You need supplies; you got them. You want weapons, I have the best."

"I need a good price, Hemnil."

"That…. I will see about. Now, Ranyll, can I interest you in a crossbow?"

If Hemnil Redspear II could offer them his entire shop, he would have. Soon, Oagthor had to have Hemnil send for a cart, for much of what they bought they could not carry themselves. Hemnil continued to walk them through his shop, which was two floors, they soon found out, Oagthor's long-time friend leading them down a stone staircase, torch in hand, to the lower floor, lighting the sconces on the wall as they walked further down the hallway. Hemnil, not expecting many more customers before the close of business, locked the door.

Ranyll looked to Oagthor, who was following behind Hemnil, the shopkeeper talking of old times with Oagthor, who just nodded and grunted in compliance.

"There are just a few hours left till the Namiah sails, Oagthor, and I must travel to another part of Goletta to see about some other business."

Oagthor nodded in understanding and cleared his throat, getting Hemnil's attention. The dwarf turned and, for a moment, Ranyll thought the dwarf reminded him of the statues that he had seen years ago in the caves of Dardist with D'meir. The sudden flood of memories made Ranyll realize that he had come far since that day. He looked at Oagthor for a second, remembering the loss the dwarf had suffered by losing his fire fox friend.

I hope Oagthor has come just as far as I have since that day.

Then Oagthor's voice broke the fevered stories by Hemnil ahead of them.

"My apologies, Hemnil, but we still have some other things to take care of before we depart from Goletta."

The old dwarf seemed confused.

"Leaving? So soon, my friend?"

"Ranyll must depart, I'm afraid. I will stay to finish buying what we need… and to reminisce with you about old times, if that's okay with you."

Oagthor looked to Ranyll, his face almost contorted in pain at the idea of it. Hemnil's laughter bellowed and he clapped his friend merrily on the back.

"I will not hold your friend up, Oagthor." Hemnil looked past Oagthor to Ranyll, motioning back up the stone stairs.

"Ranyll, if you go back up to the upper level, my assistant will let you out."

Oagthor nodded in approval.

"I will find you once I'm finished here with Hemnil."

"It was a pleasure to meet you, my boy!" Hemnil shook Ranyll's hand as he departed, the human following the stairs back up to the upper level.

The moment Ranyll left, Hemnil's expression changed, his dwarven features losing the smile that he had kept since Ranyll's arrival there. He looked at Oagthor in the dimly lit corridor and waited another moment before speaking, soon hearing Ranyll being let out of The Tempered Sword's front door.

"When was it that you started having humans as friends, Oagthor?"

Oagthor knew that this was coming. He had expected it to happen upstairs, with Ranyll present, but was surprised that Hemnil held out until now. Hemnil had never taken the time to understand the other races. The scar he had across his face made sure of that. It was a guarantee that there would never be trust in his heart for any other race besides his own.

"It's a long story, Hemnil. A very long, detailed story."

Hemnil nodded his head in understanding, clapping Oagthor on the shoulder as they moved down further into the shop. They already had a fair number of supplies that Oagthor wanted for the trip, much of it sitting in an empty barrel upstairs by the door. Oagthor had a few things in his hands and more in a rough, cloth sack over his shoulder. The older dwarf stopped them short in the hallway to the next room of supplies.

"Let us finish up here before you have to leave. I have yet to have my afternoon drink. What do you say to a few drinks with an old friend before you leave?"

Oagthor couldn't think of anything better at the moment. The two dwarves continued gathering supplies, Oagthor moving more with a purpose now that the thought of spirits was a distinct possibility.

*   *   *

The dwarf was adamant about Ranyll buying a dwarven crossbow, which the human ended up doing so, Ranyll barely able to hold it with one hand. He had it slung over his back now, carrying with him the rest of the supplies that he could hold without being too burdened. The rest was going to be carted away to the Namiah before departure. Ranyll kept the ones that he thought that he would need.

At least the ones that I think that I will need for this.

The young human had not been very forthright with what he was supposed to be doing, especially with Oagthor. Much of that was because it came to him in moments, in visions, within seconds in his mind, forcing him to consider the possibilities of not being able to follow through with his tasks at hand. This task, which he had known about for some time since him going to the Island of Dree had been revealed, he knew a little more about. In fact, someone had been helping him with this part. Pulling out a small scroll case from the pack he had on his back, he popped the parchment out from it, unrolling it slightly.

There was a throng of Golettans that moved about on the streets, but not as many as there had been earlier. The lamps throughout the city were being lit and all of the shops that were still open ensured that everyone knew which ones that were, for all the open shops kept a small oil lantern hanging on a hook outside their door. The doors were not kept open as Ranyll had heard in the stories about Goletta, *maybe because it was so cold*, he reminded himself, his exposed skin feeling the waft of cold air as it blew through the city streets.

Maybe it was that or things had changed since the stories I heard were told.

Either way, Ranyll set about his task, looking for the set of shops that intersected with five directions instead of the main four, knowing that this was the place that the map started from and was the best way for him to find his way. It was not yet dark and it would be a few more hours before the rest of the lamps were lit in the city, the young man keeping to the well-lit cobblestone walkways so that he made better time. Ranyll still had some time on his side.

Falwen Sanse, please let this map be accurate. Much is riding on what happens in the next few hours.

But Ranyll had no reason to doubt what Falwen Sanse had given him or that it was accurate, knowing full well that the fisherman was true in what he had said.

'With this map, you will find what you are looking for.'

And, with this map, Ranyll thought, *I will find the only map every made of the Island of Dree.*

*   *   *

YEAR 635

Much of what the great historians know about the second separating of the continents is wrong. It wasn't until Ranyll Tolver met the scribe Falwen Sanse that he found all of this out; this and much, much more. When the great continent of Dizrael first separated, it broke into three continents; Parthenia, Kariyl, and Anapsid. That was in the year three hundred and nine. Once the separation occurred, it took hundreds of years for the races to continue on in a life of normalcy.

For one, many towns and cities were destroyed in the process of the separating of the continents. With the shifting of Ar Solon came tidal waves, quaking of the earth below the inhabitant's feet, frequent thunder storms with torrential wind and rain, as well as the opening up of the great caves below the surface. For many on the coasts of Dizrael, this meant death.

The reason for this is not just dragons, which many historians blame for the destruction of a great many coastal cities, but for the other magikal creatures that had lain dormant for several centuries since the birth of the land as a whole. In the darkness during the creation of the world, they had been guardians, protectors of what was created. But, once their job was done, they left the world and burrowed themselves within the land, preparing for a sleep that would only wake them when again they were needed.

Be it that the attempted theft of the Emcrist was the reason for waking the great magikal creatures, they were none too happy to know this and commenced to find the culprits who woke them. Much of what is known by the inhabitants about these times has been lost, but Falwen Sanse had a way of finding things; important things that none other could find. Maybe it was the fact that he was the Chronicler of all of Ar Solon and he was given the ability to know all and see much of what still lies ahead, but the old man had found it nonetheless, laying it out before the young man that had used the visions to find him out.

'...And the second reason that it took so long for things to remain the same,' Falwen had said to Ranyll some years ago, 'was because the trade routes that had been were no longer.'

The Chronicler opened the ancient tome and flipped slowly through the aged pages, stopping at a map of Dizrael before it had split.

'After the separating of the continent the first time, the humans had built a great underground tunnel system that could protect them from the dragons when there came an attack. The dragons could never find them inside the tunnels and, even if the dragons had taken the time to dig, the humans made the tunnels so they could never be accessed by breaking into them. The tunnel rock was made some four feet thick and stacked high enough so the humans could pull a wagon through it without the top of it touching the ceiling. This came very handy when they had to live and travel within the caves. And this is how the city of Goletta was born into Kariyl history. You see, Goletta, in the Parthenian tongue, means *stronghold.* And it was one of the most formidable strongholds built in the time of the dragons and other magikal creatures.'

This and many other things Falwen instructed Ranyll in, showing him the old maps of a time long gone that would take him to where he needed to go.

'There is a place in the Golettan scribe's guild that few of the scribes know of. Only the most trusted know of this place. It is called the Hall of Ar Solon, and this place is home to some of the older tomes and maps when the lands were still young and new. Within this hall, the wisest scribes live out the rest of their life, reading and re-reading the histories of Ar Solon, trying their best to decipher what the next move of the inhabitants will be. Here is where you'll find the only map that has been made of the Island of Dree, of the place that you have seen in your dreams.'

Ranyll remembered this talk and many others that he and Falwen had that ten day that he had stayed, nursing his wounds from his run-in with the harshness that was the Agnar Mountains. But there was one conversation that he remembered the most, and that one pertained to the map that he now held.

'There are only two ways inside the Hall of Ar Solon. One way is to be a scribe of several years, devoting much of your life to the purpose. You haven't the time for this or the means. The other way is through the Golettan tunnels and in the back door of the hall which, without a map, is quite impossible. I will help make the impossible possible, Ranyll Tolver, as long as you do something for me.'

*   *   *

And that is how Ranyll Tolver came to be in the service of Falwen Sanse, delivering both the package to the Sanse family in Simmer Lo and the scroll case to Captain Aristotle Aaolos in exchange for the way to the Hall of Ar Solon.

The young man looked around him now. The cobblestone walkways were full of patrons, vendors, and passersby, not giving Ranyll much of a chance for secrecy, his eyes wandering to the circular metal cover that was located, almost hidden from view, just behind one of the larger buildings in Goletta; an inn that Ranyll had heard of some years back in a story that Dir'grar had told the checkpoint guard about the days during his youth. The memory floated in his mind for a moment then was lost amid the constant anxiety that Ranyll had about his next move. He reached down in his breeches pocket and felt the metal key that unlocked the metal cover, trying his best to get hold on his fear as well.

In no time, Ranyll had crossed the cobblestone steps, moving through the crowd, the metal key in his hand, his eyes on the cover surrounded by a great number of beautiful stones that was said to be one of the great monuments in all of Kariyl. He slipped his pack off his back and, dropping it down by the cover, slipped the key in its place in the keyhole.

It was no regular key; Ranyll noticed this immediately when Falwen Sanse had given it to him. It was not a single, thin key, but a thick piece of metal with a rung at the end to turn once the tumblers were in place in the keyhole. The ridges of the key were on four sides instead of just one, and there were several different ridges on each side. Falwen had stated that it was important for him to line up the key with the hash marks that were inscribed on the metal cover, and Ranyll did this, lining up the key and the cover as had been told. Falwen also stated that, if the key were placed inside the keyhole incorrectly and turned, it would lock permanently from the inside and there would be no way in.

Ranyll swallowed hard, feeling the nervousness inside him coming up in his throat, making the muscles in his neck tighten with tension.

Well, here's to my listening abilities. If what Falwen said and what I heard is correct, then I should be in this tunnel in no time.

Ranyll turned the key counter clockwise slowly. There was a loud click that could not be heard for the noise around him but he could feel it shake within the key. Ranyll grabbed for the handles of the metal cover to the underground tunnels and lifted it, a small layer of debris falling into the darkness below. Ranyll slipped the thick key back into his breech's pocket. Just to the edge of the darkness, Ranyll could see a small set of metal rungs that disappeared down into the darkness. Before anyone could see him fully access the tunnels, Ranyll grabbed his pack and grabbed onto a metal rung, climbing down and into the darkness.

Once down there, he grabbed for the metal cover on the ground and closed it over himself and, throwing his pack over his shoulder, pulled out his sword. He let the magikal fire swirl around the blade and looked for the lever underneath the lid to latch it back closed. Once he found it, he turned the lever and locked the cover back, shaking it once to make sure it was secure. Ranyll looked down into the darkness below him.

It wasn't as dark as it had been. With the light he now had with him, the walls of the tunnels could be seen. However, it wasn't what could be seen that affected him the most; it was the smell. And, immediately, he could hear running water.

The sewer system! That must be it. The city had grown so quick in such a small amount of time that there was no way to control the waste that such a thriving city produced in such a short amount of time.

Especially since the snows had increased. It had kept many in the city without escape out onto the rest of Kariyl. By having a working sewer system using the underground tunnels, this made it an easier working environment for the busy trade that was provided, *particularly when it came to the large amounts of sailors that came into the town from the other parts of Kariyl,* Ranyll reminded himself, climbing the rest of the way down to the stone floor of the tunnel.

What Ranyll noticed immediately, besides the smell, was that there was a channel that Golettan officials had apparently deemed available for the flow of sewage. Not far from him, just a few paces from the entrance Ranyll had just come from, was a pathway of thick stones that had been removed so that there was an area where the sewer line could flow through the tunnels without taking the tunnels over completely.

"This must have taken years," Ranyll remarked to himself, passing his flaming sword down the tunnel hallways a bit, which broke off in two directions; one east and one west.

It didn't smell as bad as I expected it to, Ranyll thought, noticing now why it didn't. The sewage flowed almost like water, which made Ranyll move a bit closer, noting that it, indeed, it had been mixed with water from the sea in order to keep it flowing. He remembered the several buildings that were used for a public out house, looking down further to see that part of one wall ahead had been made to be used as a waterway to keep the drainage constantly flowing.

Kalir and the rest of the checkpoint guard would be impressed by this, he concluded, unrolling the map of the tunnel in front of him, laying it down so he could get a better look at it. He brought his sword closer to the map.

I don't seem to be too far from the entrance of the guild. If I go west a few paces, I will run into another path. That path will take me to the entrance. I'll be there in no time!

Ranyll rolled the map back up and put it into the scroll case hanging out of his pack, using his sword as a light to move through the tunnels, soon turning down the pathway the map had shown.

From up above, in the empty corridor Ranyll had just left, the same click was made and the metal cover was lifted silently up and out, the darkly-clad figure moving silently down the rungs, replacing the cover as Ranyll did, only much quieter than the young man could have ever done.

The assassin moved down the tunnel without any light and without making a single sound with the exception of the slight breathing that they made as they exhaled the thick, pungent odor of the sewer ways from their lungs. But this breathing could not be heard over the current of the water that moved the sewage down through the tunnels, so the assassin had nothing to worry about. The figure continued to follow Ranyll Tolver, intent on its purpose.

18

Oagthor knew that once he stood up he would feel the ale even more, which made him doubt his abilities with walking, which also made him worry somewhat about making it to the Namiah on time before it left. Be it that he had spent the last of his coin on drinks all around at The Screaming Barmaid, a local tavern not far from Hemnil's shop, he decided not to worry about it so much.

Ranyll will hold the ship for me.

Hemnil Redspear II had aged quite a bit since Oagthor's last seeing him over sixty-four years ago, as Hemnil had corrected him earlier, but his drinking ability was still on par with the best of them. Oagthor was hard pressed to keep himself sitting upright and it didn't look as though Hemnil was even feeling the brew, his eyes only slightly glossed over, the aged dwarf ordering another round of the special brew for the evening, something the top-heavy bar maid had called *Axle Grease.*

Hemnil mumbled something about greasing the bar maid's axle as she moved away from the two of them, Oagthor holding himself steady by grabbing at the table, the room starting to spin slightly.

"I take it from the white, pasty color of your skin, Oagthor, that it has been some time since you've had a good brew!"

Oagthor dismissed the idea completely, reaching for his mug, then realized that he was slumped over the table, his thick form sliding off his stool and onto the floor. He felt his whole body hit the floor and there were cheers all around, several other dwarves as well as some humans patting Hemnil on the back in congratulations.

"Well, there you have it, Oagthor! I'm the best this city has seen in some time at the drink. Take that back to your human, Axeblade!"

Oagthor tried his best to combat Hemnil with a comeback but all he could do was mumble spittle into his beard. The room spun even faster when he tried to focus, watching as the patrons around him flipped and turned upright on themselves in his eyes. Oagthor reached for the stool near him and righted it, pulling himself up onto his knees. He took a few breaths and, by the time he got back onto his stool, the bar maid had brought them another jug of Axle Grease. Oagthor looked at Hemnil, who had a wide grin on his face, through the curly, unkempt beard.

The younger dwarf shook his head, trying to get his vision back without it being blurred, looking at the patrons who were watching intently the two dwarves try to out drink each other, looking from one face to the other. Oagthor reached for his mug, closing his eyes this time to feel for it with his hands, his fingers moving across the table. Once he felt it in his grasp, he grabbed the mug's handle and lifted it to his lips, finishing what was left inside it in one, quick gulp.

"Fill it up! I'm not done with you yet, Hemnil Redspear…" he looked over to his old friend, "…. the SECOND!" The crowd around him erupted in equal amounts of applause and laughter, the bar maid filling both of their mugs to the brim with the warm ale. Without looking, Oagthor finished his and felt as though he were about to burst. His thick hands gripped the table and kept him upright. He looked over to Hemnil, waiting for him to follow. The older dwarf sat there, simply dumbfounded.

"You really don't know when to give up, do you Oagthor?"

Oagthor tried his best smile without erupting all over the table. The younger dwarf held his own.

If it was one thing Oagthor had on his side, he was hardheaded. Losing or giving up wasn't something Oagthor allowed to happen to him.

After two more jugs, Oagthor was stumbling out of The Screaming Barmaid, holding tightly to the boot straps of Hemnil Redspear II as he drug him out of the tavern, the older dwarf unable to speak; passed out stone drunk. The tavern inside erupted with cheers and applause, many chanting Oagthor's name, the dwarf finding the nearest alleyway to him.

He soon found it; it was away from the tavern a bit and, dropping Hemnil's boot straps, Oagthor made for a corner of the alleyway and let loose a thunderous upheaval of brew mixed with a few previous meals across the side of the building, holding himself steady with the wall near him. Once the nausea passed, the dwarf steadied himself and wiped his beard with his sleeve, moving back to the passed out Hemnil on the cobblestones not far from him.

Oagthor didn't have far to drag Hemnil and, not long after his moment in the alleyway, he had made it to The Tempered Sword, propping his old friend up against the door. He searched for Hemnil's keys but found none. Oagthor knocked twice and waited. There was no answer. The dwarf stood a few moments longer, waiting for a reply. Then, realizing that no one lay inside the shop, leaned Hemnil comfortably against the door and was soon on his way to the Namiah.

"…And a good evening to you, Hemnil Redspear, the second!"

The sun had not yet set into the Alvanus Sea and, though Oagthor felt better than he had, he still felt awful. The city of Goletta as well as the traffic in the city streets still spun around Oagthor, who now just relied on his sense of smell to find the sea, soon moving northwest to the docks, keeping close to the buildings so he could rest against them when he needed. The night lamps had been lit and there was fear deep in the dwarf that the Namiah might already be gone, though Oagthor did not have a real desire to even be on the vessel.

Just the thought of the captain with his treasure made Oagthor pump his legs a bit more, moving quicker through the city streets to, finally, the western checkpoint that led out to the docking area. He passed by the guards, who nodded to him as he moved by them, his eyes to the docks on the other side. It was a glorious sight to see, the docks at night.

Many of the ships had already settled in for the night, the lanterns on their ships lit and shining across the water's edge and beyond; even some of the cabins within the ships were lit and full of nightly movement, Oagthor looking for the Namiah, hoping it was still anchored at the docks that he and Ranyll had only left hours earlier. The dwarf moved closer out onto the docks.

It was still there. Thanks be to those watching above, Oagthor thought, his pace easing somewhat once he saw the vessel still in port. It was one of the more decorated vessels on the water; several lanterns hung from the forward mast and from the edges of the ship, which kept other ships from sailing into it when it was harbored, Oagthor noticed, all of the vessels docked having one and the same lanterns attached to the main boom as well as one hanging from the rear rudder. The captain's quarters were lit from what Oagthor could see but, as he approached, he saw no one inside. That's when he saw the captain leaning over the quarter deck, his eyes on the dwarf.

"Dwarf, where is Ranyll?" This comment stopped Oagthor in his tracks.

"Captain, has he not arrived yet?"

The captain shook his head. He seemed a bit upset but continued with the conversation nonetheless.

"The supplies that you ordered have been delivered and have been stowed away below deck. I half expected Ranyll Tolver with them."

Oagthor began to move away from the Namiah, already on his way to find the boy.

"I will have him back momentarily, captain. Do not leave without us!"

The captain shook his head. "The deal was for both of you to be here and ready by nightfall. Don't you see the time of day it is; almost nightfall. It would be in my best interest as well as yours to find Ranyll and bring him back before I decide to break the contract."

Oagthor continued to move away.

"Consider Ranyll and myself on the ship before nightfall."

"I hope you know where he is, dwarf, for your sake. My men are readying for the sea. We do not delay, no matter what the reason."

Oagthor did not respond though, once out of range, he muttered to himself.

"Curse my beard! Curse it! That boy! Ranyll, where are you?"

*   *   *

But Ranyll did not hear the dwarf's curse, nor did he hear a great many things that went on around him, intent on his purpose as he was, his eyes scanning for the doors that should be just in front of him.

It has to be here. That's just what the map says.

And, almost as if the map was correct down to the exact number of steps that he took, the locked double doors to The Halls of Ar Solon stood before him.

Ranyll rolled the map up and slid it in its scroll case, pushing it down into his pack. Again, he extracted the key from his breeches, finding the keyhole just in front of him. He did not take time to admire the ornate designs on the doors or the fine craftsmanship of the carvings on the walls just ahead of him, but took to his purpose, forever on his mind the thought of the Namiah leaving without him and his entire mission being for nothing.

I must stick to my purpose and not waver.

The keyhole was not hidden and the key fit snuggly into the opening, Ranyll turning it per the instructions on the map counter clockwise, two times around until the thick, wooden doors clicked and he could feel the tumblers give as the key went slack in his hand, Ranyll pulling the key out and placing it back into his pocket… and then he heard the most unnerving sound echo behind him that he had ever heard in his life.

Not far in the tunnel behind him, a sound carried to his ears that made his hand tighten his grip on his father's sword, though he knew it were already too late.

They had followed me all this way. They could have struck but didn't. They were waiting for something.

Ranyll turned around quickly, hearing the clicking sounds made by the daemon's claws in the darkness, soon catching a number of red slits that were the eyes that had been keeping up with him throughout the tunnels.

They were waiting for me to open the doors!

Ranyll dismissed the idea of using his sword and pulled at the doors, opening one wide enough to fit himself through. He pushed himself inside, leaning against the doors to shut them up tight when he felt the mass of daemons fall upon them on the other side, several daemon appendages sticking through the space between the doors to keep Ranyll from shutting it.

Ranyll took a downward swipe with his sword as it lit up brightly, severing a few limbs, but knew he couldn't stop them from coming in.

It was a trap!

Somehow, Ranyll knew that he had been followed, but by daemons, he could not comprehend how he had not heard them. He retreated further down the corridor, watching as the daemons pushed through the double doors, scattering themselves across the floors, some keeping to the walls and ceilings, clinging tightly with their sharp mandibles as they moved for him.

The hallway split into three different directions and Ranyll took the eastern passageway, running quickly down the hall, extinguishing the flame sword in the process with but a thought, pressing himself against the cold, stone wall. He took a deep breath and held it, listening. The daemons scrambled down the hallway he had just come from, stopping short for a moment in the main hall where the fork in the hallways occurred. In another moment, Ranyll heard them take another passageway and the sounds of the skittering daemons died away into nothing.

I lost them. They went through another passageway!

Ranyll tried his best to find his way in the dark, using the wall around him to navigate.

I wish Oagthor were here to help guide me through these halls.

However, Ranyll knew that would be quite impossible since he told the dwarf nothing about his underground plans. Quickly, he began to regret not asking for Oagthor's assistance.

*   *   *

"Where is that accursed boy?" Oagthor had followed Ranyll's scent all the way to the center of town, where there were five roads that intersected one another, but seemed to lose his trail right in the middle of the street. Though Oagthor was still drunk from the ale he and Hemnil had imbibed, the dwarf could sniff out even the cleanest inhabitant with a few, well-trained sniffs with his nose. And, with knowing Ranyll's scent from the caves years ago and smelling him in these last few days, he wasn't hard to find. Many times, the dwarf hated the gift of picking out scents, for it intensified with the more distinct odors.

The sewer system below the streets, for example, Oagthor thought, wrinkling up his nose in disgust. *That is one place my nose is not happy about,* he mused, watching as the street vendors moved past him with great carts, packing up their wares for the night.

"It's almost nightfall and this boy has yet to be found," he huffed, looking around at the various buildings that were at the center of the five-street intersection of the city. He wondered if Ranyll had gone into any of them.

"How could a human just up and disappear like that?" The dwarf moved over to a nearby building, a sudden wave of nausea on him, and leaned against the wall.

I need to remind myself to not try and out drink another dwarf again, Oagthor thought to himself, hoping that the nausea would pass so he could get on with his search. The sun was rapidly setting now, almost dipping into the sea. Just a sliver of the sun seemed to remain in the small chain of clouds that hung over the sea from some distance away, Oagthor admiring it for the first time in a long time. He walked a ways away from the building to get a better look at the sunset, something he had not seen in years, when he stepped on a metal cover on the ground. It seemed to be unlatched from the hole, shifting a bit with the dwarf's weight on it.

Oagthor just shook his head in disbelief.

Please don't say that Ranyll went down there. Whatever that boy did, please say he did not take to the sewers.

But as soon as Oagthor leaned down to the metal cover, he could already smell the faint traces that Ranyll's scent left on the metal covering, Oagthor lying his head on the cover before attempting to open it.

Please let it be locked.

However, much to Oagthor's chagrin, it wasn't. And there was another smell within the tunnel below, as well as the metal cover. It was something he hadn't had the scent of in some time, though he couldn't put his finger on it at the moment.

With much hesitation, the dwarf slipped his battleaxe free from its holdings on his back and slipped into the tunnel entrance, grabbing at the metal rungs to let himself down, his battleaxe in one hand as he went. He closed the cover behind him.

I'm going to kill that boy, Oagthor chanted inside his mind, the full scent of the sewer smothering any other smell within the tunnels, the dwarf soon losing Ranyll's smell altogether. He would have to, at this time, go by instinct.

Or follow the footprints in the dust on the ground, Oagthor remarked, looking at, not one set of footprints, but two moving ahead of him and turning off in another direction after a time.

Did Ranyll have someone else with him? Oagthor doubted that this was the case, for the other set of footprints, ones he couldn't decipher for some reason, seemed to follow just behind Ranyll's footsteps, many times stepping into the human's own footprints, leaving only one set for Oagthor to follow.

Whoever this person is, they know how to leave very little of themselves behind for me to follow.

Then the dread seemed to settle deep inside Oagthor's stomach. At first, he thought it was the warm brew starting to act up again within his belly and he looked for the nearest alley in which to deal with his weak moment properly, then he realized what could actually be happening.

What if there were dangers with what Ranyll was doing? What if someone had seen his purpose or knew of his magikal abilities, then he could be considered a threat to them and they would do their best to dissuade him from his present course; or worse, dispose of him completely.

Oagthor knew that there was something sinister happening around them and he quickened his pace to find Ranyll within the underground tunnels of Goletta.

19

Ranyll slipped silently without coming in contact with the daemons and made his way through the dimly lit halls beneath the city, lighting his flaming sword once he was far enough away from them, hoping to come upon a passageway or hiding place before the daemons made it to him. He knew that the secret book room lay not far from where he was at the moment. From what the directions had stated on the map, he knew it to be this way and only a few steps further.

Behind him, he could hear the faint pattering of the daemons as they continued their wicked parade in search of him. It had been some time since he had dealt with a daemon, yet Ranyll knew what the daemons were capable of.

All too knowing, he thought to himself, taking quick, well-placed steps, his eyes scanning the tunnel in front of him. Beneath the chattering of the daemons behind him, he swore that he heard another noise.

It can't be Oagthor, Ranyll reminded himself, *he was still getting the supplies that we needed for the voyage. He knew nothing of the secret chambers beneath the city. I hadn't a chance to tell him; that and their being separated had much to do with it.*

However, Ranyll recalled to mind a few instances where Oagthor had been able to make an entrance when least expected. Ranyll continued on until the smell of what lie ahead lay thick in his nostrils.

Ahead of him, still not completely visible with the light from his flaming sword, was the creature that the noise came from. A gelatinous form, cube-shaped, edged its way closer to him, its exterior shifting in the flickering light of Ranyll's sword, its transparent innards sucking into itself to propel its spineless form forward, the heavy sucking noise blowing an air of stench into Ranyll's nostrils that nearly made him gag.

Ranyll lifted the flame sword up above his head to get a good glimpse of the size of this gelatinous cube. He had been warned about sentries patrolling the passageways, but he never thought he would see one of these in all of his days.

A gelatinous cube!

The gelatinous cube took up the entire seven-foot by seven-foot passageway in front of Ranyll. Though the cubes Ranyll had been told about had always been said to be a clear, transparent color, this one seemed to take on a grayish sheen, almost waxy, with limited visibility through to the other side. Ranyll, however, could see through vaguely to the other side and saw the other side of the cube collapse in on itself, the side closest to him writhing and sucking closer to him as well, the human taking a couple of steps back in response.

In doing so, Ranyll could hear the daemons approaching not far behind him. Yet again, he seemed to be on the verge of a dead end on all fronts, not being given much of a choice on either end.

Ranyll reached his sword out at the cube, his sword tip touching the cube. The flames at the tip of the blade submerged inside the gelatinous creature and sizzled as they went out, the tip of the blade sliding into the cube, Ranyll feeling the weight of the creature moving throughout the blade to the hilt. The cube did not seem to take notice of the blade and kept moving towards Ranyll, more of the blade being submerged, over half of the blade in moments, Ranyll surmised, watching as the gelatinous form around his blade began to bubble and then sizzle, the inner form of the cube seemingly attacking the blade within moments of being inside the creature.

So it is true about their inner gelatinous forms, Ranyll concluded.

Their insides are their digestive system. He knew that there was a reason he had studied all of those tomes back at the checkpoint when visiting his uncle.

Ranyll could hear the daemons drawing closer. In moments, there would be scores of daemons on him and even his magikal blade could not protect him against the small daemon patrol that crept eagerly forward.

I have to get through it....through it without dying. The human flung his pack off his shoulders and dropped it onto the ground in front of him, digging through it as quickly as possible. He pulled out some rope, his bedroll and, finally, the crossbow that Hemnil had recommended to him, the old dwarf almost forcing it upon him at the shop. He hoped now that it would come to good use.

Loading a bolt into the crossbow's chamber, he laid the weapon down, tying the rope to the end of the bolt. In another moment, Ranyll had stuffed everything back into his pack and slung sheath and broadsword over his shoulder. Ranyll bundled himself up the best he could. He put on the gloves he had from his pack, tied his boots tightly around his legs, and laced his tunic up to the neck. Lastly, he tied his cloak around his waist at the hem so it would stick to him. Any pouches he had on his belt he slid back into the protection of his cloak for safekeeping.

The cube had come rather close to him in the amount of time it took him to prepare himself, Ranyll backing up against the wall of the passageway now, the gelatinous cube almost to the point of turning within the passage. Ranyll picked up the crossbow and looked deeply into the gelatinous cube, taking aim for the far wall on the other side of the cube. He pulled the lever and the bolt shot through, slamming into something solid on the other side. The rope was still connected and stuck through the cube, Ranyll testing it by giving it a light tug. The rope still held. Ranyll flipped his hood down over his head and tuck it in over his face, wrapping the rope around his left arm several times. He could hear the skittering of the daemons now but let go of it in his mind, turning back down the corridor away from the cube once before turning back at it in full stride.

He sucked in a deep breath and then leapt into the cube, hands and head first.

The daemons turned the corridor just in time to see their prey disappear into a thick, gelatinous shape. Several of them hurried after, only to get stuck in the cube as well, their claws clicking wildly trying to cut through the jelly-like creature that now pulled them into itself. Soon, they were swallowed whole, the remainder of the daemons on the outside watching as some of their own struggled hopelessly for an escape.

On the other side of the cube, the rope went taut, shaking every-so-often from the weight of the human trying to pull himself through. Ranyll's covered head soon emerged, coated in gelatinous waste, the hood of the cloak beginning to sizzle. Ranyll's gloved hands then came through and grabbed for the rest of the rope on the other side, the gloves beginning to sizzle now as well. Ranyll's breathing came in gasps as all of his clothing began to smoke and sizzle on him. He pulled his shoulders through, then gradually to his waist, grabbing up more of the rope in his hands for the final pull. Using both of his gloved hands, he pulled his legs out of the cube, crashing to the other side of the floor with a splat.

Ranyll stood up and ripped the cloak off of him, tossing it to the ground as it burned away from the acidic goo. He took a deep breath and bit his lip as he tore away at the rest of his outer garments; tunic, breeches, boots and, finally, his gloves, which seemed to almost disintegrate on his hands and he pulled the gloves off of his fingers.

He could feel the gelatinous insides of the creature still burning at his skin. Reaching into his pack on the floor, he pulled free a water skin and poured it over his hands, pouring the remainder over his head and shoulders and the other parts of the skin that burned, making a puddle of water on the floor for his feet to stand in.

He did not notice the figures standing just to the left of him in an adjoining corridor until they spoke. Two cloaked figures dressed in the robes of scribes, aged humans, stood on a set of steps right next to him, three heavily armored guards standing just behind them.

One of the cloaked figures spoke.

"What is it you want, young man? You have trespassed on sacred ground. Penalty for this is death. Speak, man! You have little time to explain yourself!"

Ranyll just stood there; still trying to recover from what just occurred when he reached back behind him, his sword not on his back. He looked on the ground next to him but it wasn't there either. He turned back to the gelatinous cube, which was already around the corner and could not be seen at all.

I have nothing to get it with, Ranyll thought to himself, searching through his pack for something, anything that he could retrieve his sword with. He was standing there with only his loincloth to cover him. The sharp voice of one of the scribes commanded his attention.

"Answer me, young man; on order of death!" That's when the scribe's cloak caught his eye. In one quick move, Ranyll wearing only tatters and looking like a poor sneak thief, he darted up a step, ripping the cloak off of the scribe, retreating back to into the passageway with it. The three guards followed after him, the scribe's still in awe at such a display.

Ranyll wrapped his right arm in the thick cloak and looked into the cube as he approached it, making out as best he could the location his sword might be stuck in.

If it's not already dissolved, Ranyll thought, wincing at the thought of such an idea. *If there's anything magikal about that blade, it should be resistant to such things,* Ranyll concluded to himself, slamming his cloaked right hand into the cube, his hand searching for a hold.

The three guards came around the corner, swords at the ready.

They seemed to be waiting for a chance like this to come, Ranyll agreed, watching the smiles come across their faces as they saw him at a dead end, huddling against the gelatinous cube.

Ranyll smiled back at them. "One moment, fine gentlemen! Just let me explain to you. As soon as I get this…."

One of them interrupted.

"Listen here, boy! We don't have to do anything of the sort. You had your chance. Prepare for death!"

Ranyll had to face a grim fact; these men had no notion of letting him live or of allowing him to explain. It would have been all too easy for him to simply say to them, 'My apologies, gentlemen, but I am nearly melting due to your gelatinous sentinel here', or a simple, 'Pardon me but I have lost something of value within this monstrosity before us. Could you help me to get it and then all will be clear.' But Ranyll knew that the time for formality had ended long ago when he was tasked with such a mission as this.

I hope that everyone with manners and time on their side will understand…

He could feel the pommel of his sword in his hands through the cloak. In one swift pull, his sword and a mass of gelatinous goo came flying out, the cloak on his hand coated in acidic goo. Ranyll flashed the guards a quick smile and tore off a scrap of untouched cloth from the cloak, cleaning the handle off before touching it. He brandished the blade before them, the sheath falling off into pieces on the floor, burning up the rest of the way from the digestive acid of the cube. The sword was still intact; in fact, it did not seem damaged at all.

In moments, the passageway was brightened from the flames on the sword that erupted in front of the three guards. They began to back away.

…but if they don't understand, then this should at least get their attention.

Ranyll called out to them, still out of breath from all that went on around him. He left the cloak on the passageway floor and began to move forward, back to the stairway.

"I suggest you put away your swords, gentlemen."

The guards, still transfixed on the flaming blade, managed to hear Ranyll after he said it a second time, the guards backing up to the wall where Ranyll's bolt still lie protruding from it, remnants of the rope hanging off the end of it.

Ranyll looked to the two scribes, who now stood transfixed as well by the flaming blade before them. They looked at Ranyll as he spoke.

"My name is Ranyll Tolver, scribes. I have come from afar in need of your assistance. You are the only ones that can help me. I must gain access to the Island of Dree."

A look of terror flashed across the faces of the scribes when they heard the name of the island, the cloaked scribe pressing his hand up to his opened mouth.

"You cannot be serious, young man! It is not a place one travels to."

Ranyll nodded in agreement.

He knew that the island was off limits to all of Kariyl, and all of Ar Solon for that matter. It had become a place complete with horror stories that rivaled those of Parthenian times, ages ago, when brutality had become the custom of the continent and the way of things. Yes, Ranyll knew of the dangers, especially of the ever-active volcano that became one of its primary features that kept many away; ash and dust for miles and miles. If you did survive against the unknown that lived there, the ash and dust would certainly be another challenge that stood in the way of safe passage into it.

"I wish I had another choice."

20

Kalir, Alyssia, and their convoy of checkpoint guards had rested the horses twice just off the main trail to Fell Whist and, as they moved away from the Reune Lake and the channels that connected to it, Kalir could make out the small dot in the otherwise flat landscape that was Fell Whist. It had taken them two days to get there through the snow at a fast pace. He smiled to himself when he thought of the times he had there, growing up, shortly after leaving Dradle as a young man without direction. He was soon flung into a great amount of responsibility with the rigorous training that Fell Whist had provided and was appointed his own checkpoint as the checkpoints expanded over the years.

It all seems so distant to me now, Kalir thought, looking over at Alyssia, who was on her horse as well, still bundled up tightly in her winter garb. Kalir kept his horse steady, watching as the rest of his convoy of men followed up just behind the two of them.

She and Dir'grar are the only things that I have to remember those times of youth, he reminded himself, recently setting out to rekindle some of his past now that he was able to travel.

That seemed to be the only good thing about traveling, he continued on, his eyes moving from Alyssia's deep, hazel eyes to her lips that, though were covered, could be seen through the transparency of the fabric she wore as a scarf to cover her from the cold. She caught the look in his eyes and matched it. Kalir could see her devilish smile under the scarf.

"Captain Ranolf, do we not have enough to attend to already? Being distracted from your present course will not do you or your men any good."

Kalir decided it was best not to continue on with the conversation, for he knew that it would only stir the desire he had already within him. He turned then to his convoy of men just behind him, though his mind still lingering on the nights with Alyssia, and got their attention.

"We are near Fell Whist, checkpoint guards! Before we move on, let us clean ourselves up and put on our armor so that we may ride into this great checkpoint and look the part of the men that they hired for the job!" Kalir slid himself off from his horse and began to loosen the strings of the sack that held his armor, pulling off the pieces, one at a time, so they didn't fall in the snow on the ground.

The eight checkpoint guards did the same, dropping down into the snow from off their horses, gathering their own armor together. Alyssia slipped off from her own horse and began to assist Kalir with the straps on the back of his armor, clasping the pauldrons just between Kalir's shoulders once he slipped on the light chain mail suit over his head. Alyssia pulled the straps tight on Kalir's shoulders, making sure it was snug. The captain could feel her breath on his neck when she spoke.

"So, you must give those at Fell Whist a show, captain? What happened to just riding into the town as checkpoint guards on a mission? Isn't that important enough?" Kalir nodded his head. He knew that Alyssia would say something, her not being much of a supporter of the idea of honor among strangers.

"It is a form of tradition for those that fight for the cause to represent the cause we fight for."

Kalir placed the greaves upon his shins and began tightening them on just behind his calf, pulling out the breastplate next. The armor had been polished and shined before leaving the checkpoint, but now it was dulled somewhat due to the cold weather, some of the parts even frosting over a bit and stiffening in the cold. The captain watched as the rest of his men assisted with each other's armor, nearly ready in no time.

He looked to Alyssia now, who seemed to be about to say something in return.

"Listen, I don't expect you to accept what I've done or been through in the last few years, but you can at least be silent if you have nothing else better to do than to question another's way of life!"

Alyssia refrained from saying what she felt; yet she did manage to say something when she helped Kalir with his vambraces, tying the cords snuggly across his forearm. The captain exercised the forearm braces back and forth until the oiled metal pieces began to move easier with his body.

"Are you offended by me, Kalir Ranolf? Do I say things that go against your character, my love?" Kalir could feel that she was baiting him and knew better than to let her rattle him. He grabbed her face and kissed her hard on the lips. Alyssia's hands grabbed for a hold on Kalir yet only found cold slices of armor across his body, her hands soon resting on his own warm hands on her cheeks.

The laughs and whimsical banter seemed to cease around them, the guards growing silent once noticing their captain locked in a love embrace of sorts. Kalir pulled himself away from the kiss, seeing Alyssia's lips still parted and wanting. He whispered into them before he let his hands fall away from her face.

"Whatever you're trying at, Alyssia, it will not work. I love you too much to fight like we used to. I do this for my men and for Ranyll's father, who wore the armor of the treaty until his death. I honor those that honor life and the crusade for it. That is all."

Kalir moved to his horse then, feeling Alyssia's hands fall loosely at her sides, his eyes now on his men, his voice ringing out as captain in the wintry morning.

"Checkpoint soldiers, for all that you have sworn to, that is what you will be when making our way to Fell Whist! I will lead you into the city and you will be my escorts; keep Alyssia here in the center of your protection and escort her as if she were the most valuable asset that we have here among us."

Kalir winked at her when saying that.

Alyssia was on her horse in an instant, carrying a smile on her face as Captain Ranolf slipped into the lead just in front of the checkpoint convoy; the men, also in their armor, made an entrance for Alyssia to move into, soon closing up the gap between them once Kalir's love interest began to keep a steady pace with the rest of them. She looked ahead to Kalir, who had just slipped his helmet on as they rode down into the snow-filled valley, his well-armored soldiers doing the same. The clang of their visors rang in unison and Alyssia was soon surrounded by a mass of shining metal upon a group of galloping horses, watching as Kalir kept the pace, his form shifting now and then to compensate for the weight of the armor upon him.

Only once did he look back and, in that moment, Alyssia could feel his stare though the visor was down and she couldn't see his eyes.

He loved me. Kalir loved me more than I could ever possibly imagine another loving me.

She had kept her promise to herself and held back her love for him until she found out how he felt; if it were the same as it had been all those years ago. It was true that they fought and argued; however, they loved fierce and free and, sometimes, she had to admit that it was too much for her. Both grew jealous of the world around them, scared that it would swallow up the other's love and leave them lonely in a world of strangers.

"It was more than what we had years ago," she claimed aloud, though nothing could be heard amid the hooves of the horses and the movement of the metal armor on the men around her. She did not have to worry if the thought had traveled to unknowing ears.

It was safe for the moment within the galloping of Kalir and I. He moves with great purpose.

The city of Fell Whist continued to get closer and closer until, soon they looked upon the great walls of the city and the great double doors that were pressed tightly against one other showed just ahead, keeping them galloping in. The horses were huffing and starting to froth at the hindquarters, but there was no more need to push them forward. They had made their entrance. Once the guards upon the parapets of the city saw the armor and the formation in which the checkpoint guards rode, they knew their duties. Captain Ranolf flipped his visor up from his helmet, holding his hand high out in front of him in salutation.

"Guards of Fell Whist! It is I, Captain Kalir Ranolf. I come here with urgent news and have escorts. We require a night's lodging and the stables for the night for our horses."

There were two guards directly above the great double doors and they nodded in understanding, throwing down a response in a throaty yell.

"Captain Ranolf, the captain of the guard, our tower captain is on his way to see to your needs as we speak. He shall be along shortly."

The captain nodded and turned back to his men, addressing them all at once.

"Remember, men, the first drinks are on me, but you must show some restraint in here. Once I am finished delivering my message, we shall be leaving. I want no one so drunk that you can't ride. Is that understood?"

The armored escorts nodded in understanding, a few giving out a verbal "yes, captain" to show further respect.

Captain Ranolf turned back to the gates and looked up, seeing not two men as before, but three now. The captain of the towers of Fell Whist, a human by the name of Marcres Trilt, looked down upon Captain Ranolf with a mix of displeasure and disgust. His nose wrinkled up as well as the edges of his mouth when he spoke down to the captain. Both captains wore the same type of armor, yet Captain Trilt's armor actually seemed worn with age and time, faded and covered in small dents.

"Why do you come here, Captain Ranolf? We have no use for you here. Send us your reports, nothing further."

Kalir just shook his head and, with a slight smile, returned back with, "Come, come, now, captain! Are you still sore about our last little wager?"

"A travesty at best, Captain Ranolf! If I ever catch you cheating at Black Starr, all of Kariyl will know it."

"With the mouth you've got, Marcres, I'm surprised they don't already!" Marcres' grim countenance broke with a few laughs and he patted his guards on the shoulders, giving them the okay to open the doors. The tension broke between the two captains and, as the double doors opened slowly in front of the captain and his guards, watched as Captain Trilt came out to meet them. He smiled even wider when he saw Kalir up close.

"Still as ugly as ever I see, Kalir. When are you ever going to grow that beard out and be a man?"

Captain Ranolf chuckled and slid off his horse, embracing his friend tightly, gripping his hand in a firm shake as the tower captain led Kalir's horse in first, the rest of the guards dissolving the formation and moving into a single file line. They let Alyssia move up just behind Kalir and the other captain.

Kalir smiled at Marcres and pulled his helmet off, straightening his hair the best he could.

"I guess the moment you get brave and get off the tower wall and face the rest of the world like a man."

"Well, I guess not everyone can be as lucky as you, with your own tavern and inn and the rest that comes with freedom."

Then Marcres stopped short in his sentence when he saw Alyssia.

"You show little honor, Captain Ranolf. Who is this you escort? I wasn't made aware that you kept company with fair maidens."

Alyssia simply rolled her eyes and slipped off her horse before Marcres could offer his assistance.

"I think you're eyes deceive you, captain. I may be fair, but I am not a maiden or a damsel in distress, so your talented tongue of deceit will not work on me."

Marcres slipped his own helmet off, seeing Alyssia without the restriction of the head piece. He was nearing the same age as Kalir or a few summers older, his face tanned and somewhat a little more gaunt than Kalir's. Yet, in between the great blonde locks of hair on his head and matching thick beard, a great set of blue eyes shimmered in their sockets, almost catching Alyssia off guard with their brilliance.

"Nor should it. If I know anything about Captain Ranolf, it is that he keeps interesting company. My lady, it is my pleasure."

The captain took Alyssia's hand and kissed it lightly, releasing it almost as quickly.

Alyssia, though hardened for a woman, softened a bit, and then returned to her previous state just as quickly as the scene happened, moving her horse forward herself, just next to Kalir's as they entered the double doors.

"And that is the only pleasure you shall receive from me, let that be known."

Marcres dismissed the comment kindly but locked eyes with Kalir, who seemed to understand everything in a moment that lay within their depths.

Where did I find here, Marcres, you may wonder? That story is a long one and, if I am correct about how the council feel about the news I am about to bring them, you may not have time for the telling, my friend.

The remainder of the checkpoint guard moved within the limits of the great checkpoint of Fell Whist, soon coursing into the main thoroughfare of the checkpoint, doing their best to keep together as the captain led them into the thick of the checkpoint to the nearest stables.

The captain, once looking through the guards with Kalir, looked back to their captain, a puzzling look on his face.

"Kalir! In all my years of knowing you, I have never seen you without your friend, Dir'grar. Times must be bad when this separation has occurred. I can only imagine that the news you bring is not good."

Kalir hated to say anything right away; that was, at least until he spoke with the council in Fell Whist. He just nodded to his friend of so many years and continued forward.

"Things are not good right now, Marcres. Something is happening again. I think we may be in danger."

Marcres moved closer after hearing those words. The bustle of the checkpoint around them seemed to drown out everything else, but Kalir's heart began pounding in his chest, slamming against his armor. He hated to be the bearer of bad news, yet it seemed that he was the only one to be able to bear the news, which gave him no comfort either way.

"What kind of danger, Kalir? From what?"

Captain Ranolf was led into a broad, rough wooden building that Fell Whist used for soldier stables, several stable hands moving in on them once they entered into the stable fully and they saw Captain Trilt with them.

Kalir shifted in his armor, feeling the tension between his shoulders beginning to build again as it had on the ride in. He only wanted to be in a relaxing tub of steaming water and out of this armor, yet he knew that he had much more to do before he could find any comfort what so ever tonight.

It is grim, my friend. There are daemons roaming the land again. They are looking for something and my family has something to do with it. Kalir wanted to say this and so much more but refrained from doing so. He already saw the concerned look on his friend's face and he didn't want to jump to conclusions and send the several around him spiraling without real control of their situation. He didn't know why, but Kalir felt that even speaking of the events that had come to pass so far would put him into immediate peril.

"Very unwanted danger, Marcres. Something we'd rather not see during these trying times here on Kariyl."

The other captain nodded and saw to it that the horses were taken care of, soon moving Kalir, Alyssia, and his men out of the stable and back into the streets, where many of the locals parted once they saw the shining armor of the checkpoint guards.

"Then I guess I should get you to the council members now instead of later."

Captain Ranolf nodded in agreement.

"That would be most appreciative, captain. Once I debrief the council on what is happening, I would be happy to help you lose some of your hard-earned wages at a table of your choice."

The captain tried his best to smile, but Kalir could see something within Marcres' countenance that he held back. Kalir admitted to himself that he had not being around Fell Whist for some time since receiving his rank as captain, but he also knew when Marcres was holding something back.

"What is it, my friend?"

The other captain was reluctant but folded when seeing Kalir's kind, concerned stare looking back at him.

"It is so strange that you appear here now, Kalir, for there is someone looking for you as we speak. No more than a moon's time had gone by when two dwarves from the east came to our doors, demanding that they take refuge here. They mentioned your name, Kalir. We hesitated at first until they showed us their cargo."

"And what cargo was that, Marcres?"

"A dying elf!"

Kalir felt his pace quicken just as quick as his heart had done when hearing those words.

Two dwarves and an elf, together? This can't be! This must be some kind of mistake. How did they know that I would be here?

But Kalir had no time to think on the subject for, in little time, the wooden doors of the council's cottage came into view through the crowds of the Fell Whist locals and, as they approached them, Kalir reached his hand out for Alyssia. She was at his side the whole time, for when his hand reached out next to him, hers took it and clung tightly to it.

"What is it, Kalir?"

Kalir swallowed hard and whispered to her.

"It's a sign, Alyssia. Something Ranyll told me about years ago. I just never thought it would come to pass. I doubted him then, just as I doubt it now."

"What is it a sign for?" Alyssia could feel the sweat from Kalir's hands coalesce in between both of their hands and, as she looked up at him, she could see small beads of sweat trailing down the side of his temples down the side of his jaw.

"The end is near! That is what Ranyll said. 'Uncle, the end is near when these three come to see you.' I laughed at him, Alyssia, and now it is here!"

21

"You are a curious, young man!" That was the only thing the scribe said to Ranyll as he was ushered through the doors behind the two scribes. After a brief introduction and Ranyll cleaning himself up so he could be more of a guest than a prisoner, he was lightly escorted to the secret writing chambers underneath the city. The guards led him through the doors just behind them and allowed Ranyll a change of clothes that were available after the scribes settled in their place within the room.

It was more of a library, yet the scribe members stated that they spent many of their hours writing within the confines of the hall.

"It seems fitting to do this; to write within the library that holds the great tomes of old! It is as if doing this gives rise to more ideas than a simple writing room is allowed to share!" This came from the aged human that had his robe stolen from Ranyll. He was garbed in another, Ranyll noticed, something similar to what he had worn before it had been disintegrated on the floor by the cube's digestive juices. Ranyll came to find out his name within the first few sentences the scribe spoke to him as he waited for some new clothing. Scribe Durb Filt seemed to sink into his robes as he walked, his wiry frame barely holding the great robes up as he made his way forward.

"Again, sir, I am sorry for taking your robe. I felt it of the utmost importance to do so."

The old scribe simply shrugged and chuckled a bit. "Not a problem, not at all! Actually, it was quite adventurous! It reminds me of the stories of old that I read lately, about a young man on a quest for great adventures on the high seas."

However, the other Elder Scribe, Enden Chois, did not seem so thrilled about the recent theft of the other elder scribe's robes.

"In olden days, young Ranyll Tolver, you would be whipped in public for dishonoring a scribe of the order."

Scribe Filt countered. "Yes, well we're not living in those days anymore, are we, Enden? That is why we chose a more sheltered way of life among these books and ancient scrolls, isn't it? You see, Ranyll, we were tired of being among the commoners and their simple problems. We knew there were more pressing matters in Ar Solon and we wanted to take the time to find them out. So we built this."

And with the opening of a simple pair of double doors, Ranyll saw the greatest thing his eyes had ever behold. The elder scribe led him into the great library of old, *from a greater time than him or his father Crin Tolver, back to his mother and father's parents and probably before*, he decided, looking up to the ceiling and back down again to what seemed to him the most accurate collection of history he had ever seen.

It wasn't simply a series of bookcases and intricate shelf work that made this place great or the smells of the old scrolls that were lined up on the walls, neatly and ordered by small tags that hung on the edge of each; it was more the feel of the place that excited the young man almost into a frenzy. It was as if he could feel the age of time here, relaxing within the confines of the room with the elder scribes, as if it were a real entity and not just an idea that floated around in all inhabitants' minds.

And Elder Scribe Filt saw this in Ranyll's eyes as he looked at one of the greatest libraries in all of Kariyl. He reached over and moved the young man forward with a slight push, allowing the guards to close the doors behind them, locking them up tightly. Elder Scribe Filt smiled, his wrinkled face growing a bit flushed in the cheeks.

"What is it, Ranyll? Feel something?" Ranyll looked over at the elder scribe and nodded, though he saw the look of recognition in the old man's eyes as well.

"Yes! Yes, I feel something in here. What is it, elder scribe?"

But Elder Scribe Filt didn't answer. He simply moved forward slowly, letting his new robes drag themselves over the series of rugs that were placed throughout the great chamber.

So Ranyll continued to look at the great rectangular room that was lined with shelves; not just of books, but of history. There were great shields, emblazoned with a fiery, red dragon and another one with a serpent made of ice that were displayed just to the left of him, while there were swords of different makes across the walls to the left. Within the great shelves in front of him, there were old texts in a glass case, even older maps of Ar Solon when it was still one continent, and even clothes and tools used from ages ago, something Ranyll had never seen.

Elder Scribe Enden Chois spoke up.

"They call this place an exhibition room, a collection of all things in one place. At least, that's what the elder scribes before us called it. We have a tendency towards tradition here, especially when things of this value are left to our keeping."

All of this and more was collected and maintained within this great room, for how long it had been here, Ranyll could only guess.

"And what was the purpose of this?" Ranyll hoped that the question did not offend. Luckily, the Elder Scribes seemed somewhat interested in Ranyll and his goings-on, so they humored him. Elder Scribe Enden Chois continued.

"The original purpose was to collect things that told a part of what we were before what we are now. You see, after some time, inhabitants lose sight of what they had come from and believe that we, the present, are what are and will always be. It is not until you look back," the elder scribe waved his hand out at the artifacts before them, "that you truly see who you are and what made you that you understand the meaning behind it."

Ranyll questioned further. "And what is the meaning behind it?"

Elder Scribe Filt, who was sitting now in one of a series of plush chairs in the middle of the room, motioned Ranyll to sit.

"Now, Ranyll, that is the question of all questions, is it not? How about we have a chat about that at a later time, once we understand your purpose behind this visit of yours. Would you like some tea?"

Time seemed to stand still just as the two elder scribes did as they listened to Ranyll's story of peril. The guards had resumed their posts by the door, two inside and one outside of the doors, and the elder scribes had set about the task of preparing tea for their visitor. Now, as the story concluded, some time and several cups of tea later, the two elder scribes placed their cups of half-consumed tea down in front of them on the table. The two old men seemed to process all of what Ranyll had said for some time, never looking to one another, but always looking with the same visage; their thin frames underneath the robes seemingly wanting to move about and not be able to sit still. Finally, Elder Scribe Filt looked to the other scribe and they both nodded, Filt then looking to Ranyll.

"I must say that what you have told us is one of the most adventurous stories we have ever heard. Ranyll Tolver, it is a pleasure to meet you, especially after all you have gone through."

Ranyll was unsure about what to say.

"So, does that mean that I can procure a copy of the Island of Dree for my travels? I really must be going. My ship is to sail…."

"We understand, Ranyll, we most certainly do. Let us not keep you from your task at hand, no matter how treacherous. However, once we do this, we cannot be responsible for anything ill-fated that happens to you, you see. We would hate to send you to certain doom, though that seems what you are asking us to do right now."

"How so?"

"In all the years that we have been alive and all of those chronicled by previous scribes, none have returned from the Island of Dree since it split from Kariyl over 220 years ago. The only thing that we have as a reference to the island is sailor's stories from taverns here in Goletta, and they are none too reliable."

"But does that mean that it's dangerous? Couldn't it just be that there is no interest in going to the Island of Dree?"

The two scribes were silent for a time and, eventually, one of them moved from their place at their chair. Elder Scribe Filt moved away from Ranyll and the other elder scribe for a moment and made his way over to a bookshelf on the wall. The other elder scribe began to answer Ranyll's question.

"You seem to come exactly to the right place for these answers, Ranyll Tolver. We are the only ones that have a map of the Island of Dree, as well as the only chronicle of any voyage there. It was damaged, you see, the captain's journal, from the water, among other things. But we were able to salvage information from what was legible. The rest, I fear, has gone to the grave with the captain and his crew of thirty-seven."

Elder Scribe Filt returned with an aged journal; a small, leather-bound book no larger than Ranyll's forearm that was almost damaged beyond repair. There were only a dozen or so pages still attached to the book, yet there were several that were stuffed into the book, some of them still retaining the page numbers written in hand at the top. The elder scribe laid it before Ranyll on the table after moving away the cups of tea, letting Ranyll look upon it.

The elder scribe returned to his seat and continued where Elder Scribe Chois left off.

"It tells of the voyage of an old warship named the Conqueror that, in the year 657, just a few short years after the War of the Races and during the skirmish between the Parthenians, they sailed to the Island of Dree to find the lost city of Dree that had disappeared off the face of Kariyl."

Ranyll had heard all of this before in stories his father had told him at bedtime.

"Yes, and they were taken by surprise when they found what was on the island. Yes, elder scribe, I know this story. Half of the children of Kariyl know this story because it was something that parents used to lull children to sleep and to keep them in their beds."

Both the elder scribes nodded in response.

"Yes, but it is the truth, Ranyll Tolver. It says so in the captain's journal. All of those flights of fancy with strange creatures and treasure and escape are all true. The stories your parents told you are true, truer than you can imagine!"

Ranyll stared down at the captain's journal for long moments, looking closely at the frayed edges of several of the pages that stuck out against the otherwise well-made journal, wanting so much to see for himself. But there were other pressing things at hand, he knew. Oagthor as well as the captain were waiting for him and he had matters at hand to attend to, more important things than treasure.

"So, elder scribes, why do you set this down before me? Do you want me to search out what this captain could not find, continue his journey, because you have heard my story and know my purpose. I cannot sway from the path I follow."

Elder Scribe Filt shook his head and seemed to want to apologize, his forehead wrinkling in response.

"No, no, Ranyll! We would not ask that of you, especially since you go with good intent. This captain, he went for gold and glory, something you seem to care little for. What we do ask though, in exchange for a rendering of the map of the island, is that you simply chronicle your findings for us. Tell us your voyage in a new journal so that we may know the truth as well as know what really lies on that island, or if anything even exists on there today."

Ranyll did not notice that, underneath the captain's journal, there was another journal just like it, only newly bound and filled with blank pages. Elder Scribe Filt handed the blank journal to Ranyll.

"Will you do this for us, Ranyll Tolver?"

However, Ranyll never had the chance to answer. There was a strong rapping on the other side of the door and the two guards inside turned to the sound, waiting. After the first knock, there came two more, *apparently a code*, Ranyll thought, watching as the two guards released the bolt on the door and let the other guard in. What Ranyll saw in the guard's features made him draw his weapon. Then the guard spoke and it only confirmed it further.

"Elder Scribes, we have daemons in the halls! I know not how they got through the passageways, but they have found a way and on their way here!"

Ranyll let the flame light his sword and watched as the elder scribes stood up, moving towards a nearby door, one of three that lay on the walls just behind them.

Elder Scribe Filt motioned for Ranyll to follow.

"Come with us, young man, you will be safe within the catacombs behind the great exhibition hall. We are certain."

"There is nothing certain when it comes to daemons. I would much rather fight them than have them chase me. I at least have a chance then."

The elder scribe nodded and the two scribes began to make their way to the exit door. Only a few moments went by before Ranyll saw the double doors shake at a force colliding into it on the other side. He looked at the guard that had just entered, moving by his side to defend the door.

"How many did you see?"

The guard, still shaken from the sight of the daemons, sputtered the words out.

"Two sets of ten. That's what it looked like; maybe a few more or less. It was dark within the tunnels, yet the torchlight caught enough for me to see that much. What do we do?"

The double doors shook violently then stopped. Soon, a clawing could be heard on the other side and the doors pressed themselves inward. Ranyll knew what they were doing.

They are clawing their way in. Once these doors are gone, we will have no way to hold anymore back. We must strike now.

"We must surprise them! We open the doors and attack them head on. I will begin the attack. The three of you take any that you see trying to get in. If we can contain them at the doors, then we can take most of them out. After that, we can fight off the few that are left within this room or in the hallways. That is, if your count was correct." Ranyll looked to the guard that had given him the count. The young man continued.

"We must fight fierce and quick! Each strike must count! Ready?"

The three guards, still hesitating, watched as Ranyll grabbed at the bolt on the door to open it. They all nodded their general readiness, though none seemed too sure about it.

Ranyll pulled the bolt across the door and opened the double doors just enough to get his blade through. The daemons began to push through but hesitated when they saw the magikal flame of Ranyll's sword blocking their way. Then it was too late.

Ranyll swept across the edges of the door with his sword, delivering death blows to all daemons that pressed upon the door, not waiting for them to strike back. The three guards soon took up their positions once the daemons moved around Ranyll, the daemons trying their best to find a way in. Once the slithery daemons moved away from Ranyll, they were met by the guards just behind him, sweeping them down from the top edges of the door. A few got through the doors and began to climb their way up onto the book shelves, tossing books and other items down onto the four that held fast at the door.

The two elder scribes stood, motionless, at the exit door and watched as three daemons crept up through their shelves of historical artifacts, snarling and clawing along, the old humans mesmerized by the creatures that had been told of in a great many stories now come to life in front of them. Ranyll saw this and called back to them as he fought of the daemons at the entryway.

"You must leave, scribes! Lock the door behind you and don't answer it until we say it is safe."

The elder scribes did as was told and moved into the exit door, bolting it behind them, the three daemons now on the door, clawing on it as well.

They must be here after the elder scribes and not me this time, Ranyll thought to himself, then thought better of it, watching as the three daemons behind him stopped what they were doing and came for him and the others.

"Behind us! There are three behind us!" Ranyll kept to the door and two of the guards turned to meet the daemons head on, striking them down in mid-air as well as on the ground, tossing their bodies to the side as they tried their best to keep the door partially closed so Ranyll could strike the rest of the daemons down from the space between the doors.

This seemed to work because no daemons replaced the ones that fell and, soon, there were only six or so daemons remaining, pressing for the door but not getting very far. Ranyll struck them down with his sword wreathed in flame, the blue flames soon turning to a brilliant white, slamming down into the last few daemons as they hit the floor, very little resistance against Ranyll and the magik that flowed through him.

Soon, the guards cleared the hallway entrance of daemons and pushed their corpses aside, tossing the carcasses of the three that had made into the room out into the hallway so the gelatinous cube could dispose of them. The doors were being checked for repairs by one of the guards and the two other guards patrolled the hallway together for anymore disturbances, both carrying torches with them at Ranyll's request. The guards had finished their patrol and the gelatinous cube had scooped up the still forms of the daemons by the time the guards finally allowed the elder scribes back into the room.

The two aged scribes just stared at the mess that had been made of their exhibition room and then at the exterior of the doors as the guard finished inspecting them.

"Centuries of silence and tranquility have been shattered this day. We have never been attacked before; ever!" Elder Scribe Filt seemed a bit flustered, yet it was not directed at Ranyll.

"Ranyll, I know it is not only you they are after. Many times, I mean many, many times, the daemons have had ulterior motives in their attacks, but never have I seen such intelligence in these creatures before."

"Then you have not dealt with these creatures as I have in the last few years," Ranyll added, trying to assist with the picking up of some of the fallen books and other items that the daemons had tossed down at them.

"They are most deadly. Just when you think you have them thought out, they surprise you."

Scribe Chois nodded his head in agreement.

"As we see today, Ranyll Tolver. Come, we must not dally! Let us get you to the map room so that you may get what you need and be on your way. After all, I am anxious to……." The scribe's voice caught in his throat. He swayed a bit and fell forward, Ranyll grabbing the old man up in his arms, dropping what he had in his hands to the floor.

"Elder Scribe Chois! What ails you?" But, as Ranyll looked down at the scribe's fallen form, he could see the small dart sticking out of his robes, silencing the old man forever. Already, the poison had run its course. The elder scribe's eyes rolled back into his head, a twinge of pain still on his face as his head lolled to one side, flat against Ranyll's arm.

Ranyll looked up to see the dark form against the far wall of passageway, moving in through the damaged double doors, the two guards in the hallway lying silent at their feet.

One guard still remained alive in the expedition room, yet the assassin moved quickly to change that. Before the guard could unsheathe his sword, the assassin flung out another dart, lodging it in open space of the guard's neck between his helmet and chain mail, dropping him to the floor before the guard could pull out the dart from his flesh.

Ranyll released the still form of the elder scribe and moved Elder Scribe Filt behind him and unsheathed his sword, exposing the glowing flaming sword out at the assassin. The form did not move. It remained in the doorway; still, motionless. It seemed to catch a sound on the air, however, waiting for something.

Are there more daemons, Ranyll thought, then discarded the idea altogether, knowing now that the assassin had waited for Ranyll and the guards to take care of the mess of the daemons, following just behind the gelatinous cube after it's clean-up. Then Ranyll knew what it was when he saw Oagthor's helm spiraling through the air at the assassin, the thick form of the dwarf moving past the two fallen guards in the hallway.

"Oagthor?"

The helm nearly made contact with the assassin, yet the lithe form moved out of the way from what would have been a death blow if the helm had made contact. The helm flew into the room and up into the bookshelves, slamming into a few books then falling down onto the ground harmlessly. But that gave Oagthor the advantage of surprise.

The hefty dwarf leapt at the assassin and wrapped his great arms around him and, picking him up, with one great heave he tossed him across the room into a nearby table. That gave Oagthor enough time to call out to Ranyll.

"Ranyll, get the human and find a safe place!"

Elder Scribe Filt took Ranyll by the hand and pulled him to the door.

"I know just the place. Thank you, kind dwarf!"

Oagthor nodded, still a little drunk, and side-stepped the other guard's body in the room, watching as the assassin stood up from the attack, still trying to recover from being tossed by a dwarf.

"If it's a fight you want, then it's a fight you'll get!" Oagthor Axeblade felt his blood churn within his limbs. It had been some time since he had this feeling, for he had spent much of his time sitting idly behind a table full of spirits and food to care about the sport of fighting. For the first time in a long time, it felt good to be himself.

22

Oagthor heard that latch click just behind him and knew for the moment that Ranyll was safe. He had passed by much of the carnage that the assassin had left in his wake but, as the dwarf looked on it now, he knew that the figure was here for more than just the little bit of death that it had taken from the guards and the elder scribe that lay still on the floor. Oagthor looked at the darkly clad form that seemed to stare him down.

The dwarf called out to the assassin.

"I knew that someone was following us in Simmer Lo, I just had no idea that you would make it this far without me finding you. Well, now I found you."

There was no response from the assassin. Oagthor didn't expect much from him, either. In fact, he didn't care if he said anything or not. The dwarf was not in the mood to interrogate anyone, so the idea of just killing this assassin was about the only thing that he had given himself as an option. He had already begun to feel the spirits inside him quell up and ask for another urgent meeting in a nearby alleyway, but he had no time for that now.

Oagthor Axeblade had tangled with many a foe throughout his years of travel, yet there was something that always felt awkward whenever a battle happened; it was those few moments before the battle that Oagthor didn't know what to do with. He could prattle on with his enemy, as he had before in a few drunken rages, yet he didn't feel that this was a moment where this should happen. The dwarf could simply begin the attack and rush his enemy, which had worked several times over in the caverns in Dardist when fighting a great many foes at once, yet this didn't seem a fair progression towards a successful win for him either, for assassins were always sly and had tricks up their sleeves.

And that is when he caught the smell off the assassin. He knew that there was a smell that he hadn't smelled in some time when he first opened the metal cover to go down into the sewer system, he had just forgotten it. As he caught the smell in his nostrils, he knew what he had to do.

"You're not getting past me, elf! Ranyll's going to continue on his quest and yours ends here, with me, you pointy-eared traitor!"

The movement was far too quick to see what the assassin did, yet Oagthor knew that a movement from the elf meant an attack, so he dove down behind a nearby table and flipped it over, using it as cover.

In another moment, there were three small darts sticking out from the floor from where he had just been.

Well, I guess that last comment did it for him!

And then Oagthor was up again, the table in his hands, using it as a battering ram against the elf assassin, who was already moving at the dwarf at an insane speed.

There's no way I'm going to catch him using basic battle tactics, Oagthor concluded, tossing the table at the assassin as one attack, bringing his axe down upon the form as a second attack. The assassin fell back against the far wall and let the table fly across the room, rolling away from Oagthor's second attack with ease, bringing a slender sword out from an unseen back sheath to strike.

Oagthor grunted in pain as he felt the tip of the blade strike under his armpit, tearing into the soft flesh beneath, the assassin striking in between his chainmail armor. The dwarf felt his blood begin to flow, though not as bad as he thought it would, down the side of his stomach and a trail of muddled, red blood stained his tunic and the edge of his breeches. Oagthor continued his movement towards the double doors he had come through earlier, feeling a small knife whizz past him as he rolled to the doors.

In another moment, the dwarf picked himself up and was out the doors and back into the main hallways.

I'll just wait until the assassin follows me out here! There's no way I can fight him in such an open space as that room was, Oagthor agreed, looking now at the narrow hallways in front and behind him.

There's no escape for him here. He'll have to fight me here and there's no hiding.

Oagthor felt under his arm and knew immediately where the assassin had struck him, feeling the small cut where the tip of the sword had entered in the flap of his chain mail under his arm. The warm blood flowed easily but had already started to clot up somewhat when the figure burst through the double doors, two swords now drawn and at the ready.

The elf was clad in all black and the material seemed to hug at the frame tightly, barely allowing for any free space in between the fabric and the wearer. The only thing protruding from the form in front of the dwarf was the small pack that was tightly cinched on the back. There were two sheaths within it and other items, though Oagthor had no time to see what else. The assassin was on him in moments, swords looking for further weaknesses in his armor.

Oagthor retreated a few steps and kept his back to the empty hallway just behind him, watching the other take the space back in only a few strides.

"Come on, elf! Let's see what you've got for Oagthor Axeblade!"

The elf assassin came for Oagthor.

*   *   *

Ranyll could feel his heart begin to nearly beat out of his chest. He had seen the elder scribe struck down in their conversation and knew that Oagthor Axeblade would not live if he couldn't get to him soon. But he couldn't leave the only elder scribe here by himself. If he did that and something happened to him, Ranyll would never forgive himself.

And all they know would be lost. This was one of the things that Ranyll was worried about the most. Just in the few moments of speaking with them, he knew that he and many others could learn a great deal from the many years that the scribes had been alive, yet none of that would occur now.

Not without my help.

Ranyll pressed his ear to the door that he had entered when Oagthor told him to leave, listening closely for any movement. He could hear Oagthor's voice and a flurry of movements, yet he knew they were still in the room with the elder scribe.

I must go and help him!

But Ranyll knew where his present task lay. All around him, maps from world and ages old were placed in glass cases, while many were rolled into scroll cases on the walls, lined neatly and evenly with dates and tags on all of them. There seemed to be at least a thousand maps all around Ranyll, some large, others small. He really didn't know where to start, yet he knew he had little time to finish. Elder Scribe Filt motioned to him with a quiet wave of his hand, pointing to a small scroll case that sat by itself on a shelf. The elder scribe took it from its spot and rolled it out, placing another blank scroll next to it.

Ranyll pulled out his set of quills and inkwell from his pack and began copying the map.

I must be quick.

*   *   *

Oagthor could feel himself growing tired, could feel the wind of ages pile up underneath his chest and keep him out of breath, huffing and puffing through the various battles that this assassin kept throwing at him. He knew, after three or four exact hits with his sword, the assassin would have him and he would not be able to defend anymore. Already, he could feel the soreness set in under his arm at the first wound, feeling the other across the knuckles of his left hand where he stopped the blade, yet the damage left caused his left hand to become useless; blood poured off his fingers and made his axe slick in its hold.

The dwarf's right arm was tired from the constant parry of the two blades the assassin kept aimed at him. The weight on Oagthor kept him from moving forward in an attack and it also kept him from moving as quick against the assassin's attacks, which cost him another wound across his right forearm, almost making him drop his axe in pain as the cut tore across his arm, a strong flow of blood spilling forth across the floor in front of him. The assassin stopped once he saw this, waiting for Oagthor to yield.

Yet, the proud dwarf refused. Binding the wound with a piece torn from his tunic he continued to defend, soon losing his ground in the well-lit tunnel, making his way into the darkness further behind him.

I must retreat or I'm dead to Ranyll. I will be no use if I'm dead.

Oagthor felt himself shift in his place and began to retreat down further into the darkness of the tunnel, only to see the assassin pass him and disappear into the darkness as well. He could hear the two swords clang together, seeing their slight spark in the darkness just ahead.

"Come out, you accursed elf! Come out and fight me!" But the elf assassin made no motion to leave from the darkness, trapping him from any hope of escape. It also made the dwarf more of a target and the assassin less of one, Oagthor not fully knowing where the assassin lay within the black veil of the tunnels ahead. For some reason, Oagthor had noticed that he could not see through the veil of darkness in these tunnels once he entered the secret entrance to the guild.

Must be magik, the dwarf mused to himself, cursing every last bit of magik that he had seen in the last few years. He looked into the darkness for the elf.

In frustration, Oagthor tossed his axe into the darkness. When he didn't hear it clang on the ground and instead heard it hit something and lie still, he thought he hit his target. Then the assassin came at him with such force that the kick the assassin delivered to his chest knocked Oagthor onto the ground. Oagthor felt the breath get knocked from him as he collided with the floor, his head spinning slightly, breaking his focus. He had seen the glint of the elf in the darkness and thought that he had struck him with his axe.

Something is messing with my abilities as a dwarf, Oagthor told himself. *How could I not see the elf in the darkness?* Then he knew the answer just as quick as he had asked it.

It was the garb that the elf wore. As the assassin moved closer to him, breaking from the darkness, Oagthor could see the garb shimmer in the last of the torchlight, almost turning into the night itself, making it hard for Oagthor to see the assassin, especially without light to catch the movement.

The dwarf lifted himself up from the ground and recovered as quickly as he could, ignoring the assassin completely, only focused on getting his axe back. He moved into the darkness of the tunnels and saw his axe not far ahead, apparently stuck in the wall.

But I didn't hear it hit the wall, the dwarf concluded, his feet now propelling him forward to his weapon. He reached out to grab his axe and realized why he had not heard it hit rock wall; it had been imbedded in a gelatinous cube. The dwarf didn't have time to turn away, his forward motion propelling him directly into the cube's sticky surface. Oagthor felt himself slam into the cube with full force, the gelatinous creature enveloping his right arm and right half of his face before he had a chance to slow himself down, his axe falling loosely into his hand.

The burning from the gelatinous ooze didn't occur until the dwarf ripped himself and his axe free from the cube. Slowly but surely, the gelatinous waste began to eat away at his tunic and other garments, soon dissolving the beads in his beard and some of his beard as well, the right side more than the left. He had not submerged his whole head, just the right side, the skin around his eye and forehead beginning to smoke. Just next to his ear, Oagthor could hear the hairs on his head sizzle in protest.

"Oh, no, please, no!" But Oagthor knew that he had made a grave error. He had little time left for foolishness.

I am about to feel real pain. He thought he had been bothered by the wounds the assassin had given him. He now felt the pain of the digestive juices of the gelatinous cube begin to burn into his skin.

The assassin watched from a distance as Oagthor howled in pain, dropping to one knee then to both, his axe tumbling out of his hand as he reached for his face. The secretion on his face soon began to smoke and the dwarf could feel the gelatinous waste burn around his eye, burning off his eyebrow, his beard completely on the right side, and then move to his lips and the right eye itself.

Nothing could be done. The pain was excruciating, even for a dwarf who had gone through much combat in his life and taken a great number of wounds. He felt himself melting from the outside in.

The assassin moved closer now, coming in for the kill, the two swords pointed and aimed at the ready, preparing to put the poor dwarf out of his misery. Oagthor watched as the two swords pressed themselves closer to him, almost at his neck now, coming in to make the final blow.

You shall not get the satisfaction, elf!

Oagthor listened behind him. The gelatinous cube was on his heels as well now, pressing against the tips of his boots.

In one quick movement, Oagthor reached into the gelatinous cube with his burning right hand and pulled forth a handful of the gelatin itself, tossing it straight at the assassin's covered face. It splashed against the mask and began to sizzle immediately, the assassin dropping his blades to try and take off the mask in time.

But the mask was well-tied around the neck, Oagthor noticed, for it took too long for the assassin to take it off. Soon, the gelatin was eating away at the assassin's face as well, the gut-wrenching cry of a woman echoing into the hallways, mingling with a dwarf's cries of pain.

Oagthor's cries of pain caught in his throat when he finally saw the mask fly off and a great mane of golden hair tumbled down the assassin's back, much of it melting off in the process.

"A female elf?" Indeed, it was an elven woman, and from what was still left of her face, she had been exquisite. She dropped to her knees as well, not far from Oagthor, trying her best to breathe through a half-melted face.

Oagthor did not wait to see the end result. The bones in his face were being burned into from the gelatinous goo and he couldn't see out of his right eye anymore, which he questioned whether it was there anymore or not. The dwarf made for the doors to the study, where they had began their battle, bypassing the fallen elf assassin, his right hand reaching out for the door handle to open it. That's when he learned that the skin had melted from other parts of him as well and he could now see the bones of his right hand. As he opened the door, he tumbled inside, still in shock from what was happening to him. He kicked the door shut behind him and dragged himself further inside the chamber.

"Ranyll, help me! Ranyll!" Oagthor cried out, the pain surpassing unbearable. The dwarf tried to lift himself from his position, using the plush chairs around him, but found it quite impossible to use his muscles anymore. He could feel himself dying. He called out to his friend one more time, this time louder than before.

"Ranyll, in the name of the Creator, help me!" Oagthor collapsed onto the floor.

*   *   *

Ranyll had almost finished the tracing of the map of the Island of Dree when he heard Oagthor's hoarse voice calling to him, then there was a thud, and all was silent. He dropped the quill and made for the door. He opened it and walked into the study, his sword at the ready, only to find Oagthor another victim. Ranyll approached him then turned back in disgust at what he saw.

On the other side of one of the chairs, Oagthor lay, half-melted from gelatinous secretion. The right side of Oagthor's face was sunken in and burned to the bone by the gelatinous juices that still clung to the dwarf's face, the eye in the right socket hanging limply out, lolling back and forth as the juices continued to eat their way through the dwarf's skin. Oagthor's right arm was burnt through as well, all the way up to the elbow, exposing nerves and bone in several places while the rest of the secretions still worked themselves deeper inside, his tunic in tatters.

Ranyll ran to his side immediately, placing his hands against parts of the dwarf's skin that were not yet burnt, his right hand pressed against the left side of Oagthor's face while his left hand cupped Oagthor's left hand in his own.

"By the mercy of the angels, Oagthor, what has befallen you?" But Ranyll did not wait for an answer. Immediately, he felt the magik flow within him, felt the tides of the healing power within him seep out from his palms and wake up from their slumber from deep inside the places that hid themselves all too well; his eyes closing, his thoughts reshaped poor Oagthor's face and arm, drawing a rough sketch of what he had looked like before the burns had occurred.

The dwarf did not move during the healing, which took some time. Ranyll could feel the severity of the damage as soon as he had put his hands on the dwarf, knowing that it would take most of Ranyll's powers to heal him. The same blue fire that had surrounded D'meir when he had healed Ranyll now surrounded Oagthor's wounds, healing first the great passages that carried the dwarf's blood, closing them up so no more life's blood flowed freely onto the floor and surrounding areas, Ranyll focusing then on the muscles and nerves within the body, first in the face then in the right hand, watching with his eyes, which had turned white, as the skin soon closed itself together and fell into place.

All of the skin grew back over the newly-formed bone, yet no hair grew back in its original place. Oagthor's face seemed repaired, yet the hair that had been singed off did not come back. Soon, though, the dwarf began to come to. Both of his eyes slowly opened and he could see Ranyll next to him, the human's hands placed firmly on his own face and hand, the human's eyes glowing white.

"Ranyll, what happened to me?" Oagthor reached up with his right hand to his face, feeling the soft, fleshy portion of his face where his beard was missing. He was still disoriented.

"You had an accident that almost cost you your life, Oagthor. Everything is fine now, or so it seems to be for the moment."

Oagthor glossed over his missing portion of beard and then looked at his hairless forearm down to his knuckles, which were white and hairless as well.

"By all that is sacred, have you gone to shaving dwarves now as one of your hobbies, Ranyll?" Ranyll scoffed at the comment and tried his best to help his friend up, though it didn't seem as though the dwarf were ready. Oagthor stayed motionless on the floor, looking up questioningly.

"What just happened?"

23

It was easily apparent to Oagthor what had happened once he saw the dead guards, dead elder scribe, and the remnants of the assassin in the hallway just outside the great exhibition room. Ranyll had apparently gone crazy and killed everyone in a fit of rage. The dwarf looked over at the young human as though he didn't know him at all.

"There's no way that you did all that, Ranyll!" Just the three guards would have been too much for Ranyll. Oagthor looked around, trying to place where he was on Kariyl, his mind missing the last few moments he had been alive. The dwarf tried hard, but he couldn't remember how he got here.

"It's just disorientation from the magik, Oagthor. It will pass in time and you will be fine. You'll see." Ranyll looked over at the dead guards and watched as Elder Scribe Filt leaned over the body of his lost friend on the floor.

"Who would do such a thing, Ranyll? We are here to bring peace and understanding. Enden would never try to harm another soul here on Ar Solon."

Ranyll could only imagine what Elder Scribe Filt was going through right now. The exhibition room was still a mess and the trusted guards had defended it with their very lives. Ranyll could only imagine who could do something like this. Then his thoughts jumped to the assassin.

"The assassin!" Ranyll's attention then went to the still form that lay outside in the middle of the hallway. He made his way into the hallway and stopped when he saw the remnants of the assassin, much of the face melted away. The form did not move.

It must have died from the burns; and in agony, no less. Ranyll looked closer at the figure's face, which was somewhat difficult for him due to the grotesque pose it was frozen in during its demise. Then he saw it; the slight curve of the jaw, the pale, white skin, almost like smooth marble. He could recognize those features anywhere, especially after spending some time with the race in Elvinisclar and Trayvilis. It was an elf!

Upon closer inspection, Ranyll pulled the matted hair away from the face and saw the pointed ears as well, confirming it with finality. But then there was more. The assassin was not a male. Just below the burnt skin, soft, rose-colored lips poked out from the face, the smooth chin and neck burnt through by the gelatinous waste that had been used as a weapon. Ranyll looked back to Oagthor in the exhibition room.

"You were almost beat by a girl?!"

The dwarf lifted himself up from the floor, immediately recovering from his maladies to stand over the assassin himself.

"That is no woman elf, Ranyll! I......" But the dwarf stopped himself short when he took notice of the finer features that lay behind the mask the assassin had worn.

"I... I knew it was an elf, but....I did not have any idea..." Oagthor's hand then went to his beard, or where his beard used to be. Ranyll's friend seemed to remember it all at once, piecing it together, the events in his mind. Ranyll moved back to the still form of Elder Scribe Enden Chois, helping to move his body with the other elder scribe's assistance.

"She and I fought, we did. Right here. That's how I lost my beard and the hair on my arm. I remember now."

Ranyll just smiled a bit.

"Don't worry, I won't tell anyone you were almost beat by a girl."

"She had an unfair advantage, Ranyll!"

"Alright. And what was that advantage.....height?" Ranyll waited for Oagthor's response, a smile forming on the human's face. But Oagthor did not respond. He just continued to stare down at the still form of the dead assassin with disbelief. Then the dwarf called out to him.

"Ranyll, take a look at this!" The dwarf pulled something from the elf's hand and raised it up into the light of the exhibition room for Ranyll to see.

"It's a ring."

*   *   *

Falwen Sanse stopped writing when the description of the ring played itself across the pages in front of him: a simple silver ring with small etchings across its surface, forming the ridges of a dragon's spine with scales all the way around the wearer's finger, finishing with a dragon holding its own tail in its talons and, in the dragon's mouth, a small pearl was placed, only the size of a fish egg, barely discernable without taking a closer look. But Falwen had gotten a look of a ring just like that, and not too long ago.

His mind jumped at the thought of a spy within the ranks of the Agnar Scribe's guild, yet he knew that it was very possible with the amount of things happening on the surface of Kariyl all at once. He knew he had to do something; and that something was to no longer sit at the table and write. He must act now or it would be too late.

The aged fisherman had known a great many secrets even before he came to his calling of The Chronicler, nearly four short summers ago. He had not been an innocent to the world and, though he had kept much from his family in order to keep them safe, his wife had always known that his past was filled with dangers untold; he was not dangerous himself, of course, but he had traveled with a great many brigands and ruffians during his time as a sailor on some of the greater ships that had ever sailed the Alvanus Sea. But Falwen Sanse felt that the need was rising before him where he had no choice.

Those that are trying to tear Ar Solon apart are not operating by the rules. It is time those that cherish this world do the same.

So, the Chronicler Falwen Sanse moved from his place at his desk deep in his underground chambers and rummaged through the desk drawer at his side, extracting the small hand dagger from it. He slipped it into his nightly robes and made his way upstairs, taking great care not to make any noise as he snuck out of his room.

Scribe Ostondilus Frews shifted slightly in his sleep but never noticed Falwen Sanse standing by his bed chamber until Falwen slipped the dagger to the dwarf's throat. The human scribe placed his hand onto Ostondilus' mouth to ensure that he didn't call out in the night and lifted the dwarf up out of his comfortable bed, leading him up and out of his room, walking just behind him, the blade of the dagger pressed tightly against the younger scribe's throat the entire way to the stables.

A considerable amount of snow had fallen and, as Falwen and Ostondilus traversed through it to the stables, the dwarven scribe fell several times, his unshod feet turning red with numbness as they shuffled through the thick snow before them. Falwen looked around at the quiet scribe's guild and searched the buildings for anyone that may be lying in wait besides Ostondilus.

After all, I have no idea who to trust here now. My security has been breached and it may not be safe for me to stay here any longer.

Falwen tossed Ostondilus down onto the stable floor, the horses whinnying a bit in their own stable area, shifting in their sleep. Once they shifted, however, all was quiet. Falwen leaned down at Ostondilus and ripped the ring off of the dwarf's fat finger.

"What is this, Ostondilus? Did you not think that I wouldn't notice this on you?"

The young dwarf put his hands up in protest. He was shivering but Falwen didn't seem to care at the moment.

"Wait, Falwen! Wait! I can explain!"

"I'm afraid that your explanation is not what I want."

The dwarf looked questioningly at the human.

"Then what do you want?"

Falwen pointed the dagger at the dwarf and then to the saddles that hung on the wall.

"I want you to get that horse ready. We have a long ride ahead of us."

"You don't understand, I have to be here when it happens."

Falwen shifted his gaze back to the dwarf.

"When what happens?"

"When the plan takes effect. That was the deal that was given to me to be in the Order."

"You play me as a pawn in your game so you can join some secret organization? My child has runaway because of what your order is doing! You don't think I see this? If you know so much about me, then why didn't you think about me finding you out?"

"I can't tell you that, Falwen. I was sworn to secrecy."

The Chronicler struck out with his blade, cutting the top of Ostondilus' hand open. The dwarf reeled back in surprise, bringing his wounded hand close to his body, holding his other hand out in defense against Falwen's blade.

"What are you doing?"

"Showing you that I don't care about your promises to others! You can die here for all I care!"

Falwen pointed the tip of the dagger at Ostondilus and the dwarf cowered before him. The aged human reached out and grabbed the small dwarf by his nightly robes, slamming him up against the stables. The horses whined for a moment but were still enough for the dwarf to hear Falwen's threats as they rose defiantly in his throat.

"Give me a reason not to kill you now, Ostondilus Frews, because I have no time for games!"

After seeing the seriousness in The Chronicler's eyes, the dwarf broke all ties that he had to the Order and told the secrets that lay deep within the confines of his mind. Falwen listened intently, yet he always felt the pull of his family in the forefront of the struggle within him.

I will find a safe haven for my family first. That is what I must do. Jannon is too far to get to now, but I will keep the others from harm. And this miserable dwarf will lead me safely to them or he will wish he had never crossed my path here in the Agnar Mountains!

The dwarf continued to explain his intricate part in the plan that was to upset all of Kariyl first then move to the rest of the continents once the Order of Emcrist had a firm grasp on the trading routes. During all of this, Falwen could feel the ring bearing into his palm, the sharp edges of the dragon's form on the ring digging into his flesh and he clenched his fist in anger.

*   *   *

"Ranyll, you must go now!" Elder Scribe Filt lifted the ring up to the light, watching as the lantern light within the room played tricks on the old man's vision, shifting shards of light across the small dragon's teeth on the ring. Gripped tightly between its teeth it held a mock Emcrist, a miniscule version of one of the ancient jewels said to be hidden somewhere on Ar Solon.

The elder scribe placed the ring in Ranyll's hand and ushered him to the door. In the time that it took for the three of them to clean up the mess in the chamber, several more armed guards had arrived, securing the doors the rest of the way and barring them with additional timber they had brought down with them on their second trip. The bodies of the guards as well as the elder scribe were being moved as the two humans and the dwarf spoke, somewhat closer than before when Ranyll had sat with the two elder scribes at tea. It seemed that the elder scribe wanted this information to remain secret.

"It's the Order! I had hoped that they were disbanded decades ago, but it seems that I was mistaken."

Ranyll shook his head, not understanding. He looked to Oagthor for answers but the dwarf seemed just as lost as him.

"What order? What is going on, Elder Scribe?"

"The Order of the Emcrist! They have found this exhibition room and were to know of the contents. If they sent that assassin, then they know all about this place. That means Kariyl is in great danger!"

The elder scribe seemed to go into a panic at the thought of this, trying his best to hold his composure as he moved across the room to one of the shelves on the wall. The old man continued.

"Many do not know of the Order of the Emcrist because very little was ever documented and kept safe long enough to be preserved." Elder Scribe Filt slipped a small tome from its place on the shelf and brought it to Ranyll, placing it in his hands. On the cover of the leather-bound volume, it simply read: ***The Emcrist Order***.

"This will tell you what you need to know for now. But you must leave. As you said, you are on a mission, one of the utmost importance apparently. If an order of this stature is following you as the dwarf says they did, then you have no time to waste!"

The elder scribe then looked to Oagthor and nodded.

"And you, my trusted dwarf, have seen much in here that few of your race have ever had the pleasure of seeing. I hope that you are this trust-worthy in spirit as this young man is when moving forward in your quest."

Oagthor cleared his throat and tried to run his fingers through his beard calmly but then felt the smooth skin on the one side of his face and thought better of continuing, so he simply smiled at the elder scribe.

"Ranyll and I have been through much, elder scribe. We have a deal now to hold true to this quest and see it out. And we shall."

Elder Scribe Filt nodded solemnly and ushered them through the guards that had arrived and to one of the doors on the other side of the entranceway that they had come through, though it had not been the door Ranyll and the Elder Scribe had hidden in earlier. The old man pressed his hands against the door and hesitated for a moment, thinking. A look of worry had suddenly crossed his face and he turned back to the two of them.

"Ranyll, Oagthor, you must understand something about Ar Solon. These are very trying times now. Kariyl faces a threat like none other. The Emcrist Order, they strive to find a weakness in the world and they have; for centuries they have made it a point to make a new history for the world and erase the old. But those that are right, true, and just have fought against the wrongs of the world."

The two of them looked at the elder scribe and seemed confused at the moment. They waited for him to finish.

"Do not repeat the mistakes of old. That is one thing that will send all of Kariyl spiraling to a halt. Make new choices. Do what is right and just."

Elder Scribe Filt opened the door and pressed for the two of them to make their way inside. Ranyll slipped the two tomes as well as his blank journal inside his pack and threw it over his shoulders, moving into the dimly-lit space of the tunnel ahead. Oagthor huffed a bit, still pressing his thick fingers against the bare skin where his beard had been.

"I still don't know how I'm going to explain this!"

Ranyll shifted the pack on his shoulders and checked the sheath at his hip, feeling the pommel of his father's blade resting against his side.

It has done more for me today that it has ever done, the young man thought to himself. He chuckled to himself when he looked Oagthor still tending to his pride and joy, the aged dwarf almost looking like a fattened human from the side.

"Whatever you do, I wouldn't tell the truth. Getting assaulted by a female elf might not go over too well with those on board."

"I wasn't assaulted! I defeated her, if my memory serves me correct!"

Elder Scribe Filt watched as the two travelers departed from the exhibition room and through the alternate escape route back out into the town of Goletta. He closed and bolted the door behind him and turned back into the room, watching as the remainder of the guards completed installing the new set of double doors. There were also some cleaning the floors with wet mops to get the stains of death off of the lightly-colored stones that the elder scribe now tread upon. He was about to assist with the last of the cleaning when he heard his name called out loud.

"Durb Filt!" No one had called him that since he had joined the scribe order. The only time someone had called him that while he wore the robes of the scribes was… the old man turned on his heels at the sound of the voice and stopped short when he saw who had spoken to him.

It had been some time since he had seen The One, but he would never forget the face or the voice for that matter. The One had taken the form of a human man when last coming to see the elder scribe and he did so again, the same form coming to him years later. Durb had almost forgotten of the promise he had made until this moment.

…When the time presented itself, the inhabitant reminded himself, hearing those words reverberate through his entire fragile frame

over and over, remembering all those years ago when The One had spoken to him.

And the world around the elder scribe had gone silent now, he noticed. The movement of the guards was gone and they did not stir from their places, frozen in position, neither blinking nor breathing. The elder scribe wished that he had been turned into the temporary statues as the guards had, but he knew that The One had come to see him and him alone.

The being that stood in front of the elder scribe wore what he had worn when they first met; dark black attire, close-fitting as well as a matching short cloak, which seemed to hug The One's shoulders rather tightly. He carried no weapon on his thick belt at his hip or any pouches.

He had need of nothing on this world; at least nothing of sustenance and form.

That's how Durb had felt when he first met him and he still felt that way now, looking at the being as he took the same seat that Ranyll had sat at only hours before. He gave the elder scribe a once over and leaned back into the chair, getting comfortable.

"The years have been kind to you, Durb!" The elder scribe could hear the condescending tone in The One's voice yet he nodded and stood where he was, answering back.

"Yes, I have been well-cared for by the guild."

"That's good to hear. I would hate to hear that they were anything but grateful for your long service to them and their cause, Durb."

Again, the elder scribe heard the tone, yet he did not answer back any kind of way except for with humbleness.

"I have done what you asked, great being, and have fulfilled the bond that we made."

"Of course you have! All I asked you to do is give up some of your great books in this library to a complete stranger! I'm sure that was hard to do for you." The One looked around at the great bookshelves full of tomes from long ago.

"But I don't think you'll miss them that much." The One leaned forward a bit, motioning to the chair in front of him.

"Sit, please! I know you must have had a trying day, with all the battling going on in here. Again, I did my best to get rid of that pesky assassin, but they are hard for my daemons to track. And feel free to call me Darien. I would hate for you to call me The One. It sounds so lonely, don't you think?"

"It is fine, Darien. The One, for….well, for the inhabitants, is symbolic due to it being a name that shows that you are one of a kind, that no being other than you will be called that."

"All that for such a simple name! I see where the learning goes with you, Durb. You don't miss a beat."

"Well, decades of research will go to waste if I can't have an intelligent conversation with someone."

The elder scribe could feel the sweat dripping down his back and small beads of it began to form around his brow and forehead. A feeling within him kept him weak, almost vulnerable mentally to Darien, exposed within every nerve of his body. Even his thoughts felt as though they were exposed to the being in front of him. The old man tried to gather his composure, but he found it quite impossible. He wiped his brow with the sleeve of his robe.

"That is very true, inhabitant! I hate meaningless conversations. So, with that said, I will get right to the point. You've done what I've asked, which I commend you on. It has been some time since we last spoke, and I was surprised that you remembered. My daemons spared your life as well as the other scribe's, though I can't take credit for the deaths that the assassin took, for she was not supposed to be here. Can you tell me a little bit about this assassin, if you don't mind?"

"Well, Darien, from what the two travelers spoke about, it was a female elf that was part of the Emcrist Order. She seemed to be sent to kill myself and the other scribe, which she did with ease until Ranyll stepped in and saved me."

"Saved you? Ranyll did that?"

The elder scribe nodded. The One stood up then, looking around the room.

"And he made a pact with you like I asked to chart out his journey so that you can see it once he returns?"

The elder scribe nodded again.

"Well, when he returns from his voyage, I will be delighted to read it. Then, maybe I can figure out what the bastard is up to!"

There was no trace of anger on The One's face yet, when he spoke those words, the elder scribe heard the frustration within the being's inflection.

"So, until then, Darien, what shall I do?"

"Oh, Durb, just do what inhabitants normally do. Enjoy your life here in the comfort of the scribe's guild until called for."

The One moved from his place near the elder scribe and walked towards the two double doors that were in the process of being placed onto their brackets by the still forms of the guards and disappeared into the darkness of the hallway, the movements of the guards soon sounding in the old scribe's ears again. Soon, the knots in his stomach began to loosen and he felt the overwhelming urge in his stomach to let loose his previous meals, which he did as soon as he stood up, his knees buckling under him as he tried to remain standing.

The guards came to his side but he dismissed them with a wave of his hand. He stood a moment longer and then moved away to continue on his task at hand. Yet, inside his mind, he could hear The One's voice calling to him.

I will be back sooner than expected, Durb. This time decades will not pass before you see my face again.

And then the inhabitant Durb Filt dropped to the floor as he was on his way to his chambers from exhaustion and was carried to his bed chambers by two guards that found him shortly after.

24

"What do you mean, you're dying?" Triggle had a difficult time grasping the concept, especially since he and Ilthen had saved the elf from an awful fate of becoming an elfsicle, yet Altina kept the idea of her death at a constant within the conversation, letting them know of the importance of what she had done. The elf just shook her head sadly.

Altina was able to travel after her brief rest and the two Miftles made it to Fell Whist, the grand human checkpoint to the west, just north of the Reune Lake. Triggle and Ilthen had begun frequenting there to trade their wares from Dardist now that the mining continued for the last few seasons, making their way in all directions to wherever their journeys took them as they worked with both the remnants of the faeries as well as the dwarves.

Once arriving in Fell Whist with Altina, they stayed at an inn for a day or so to rest, soon finding out that the elf's illness was far worse than imagined than when the Miftles first met her. However, Altina made it a point to have the Miftles deliver her message to the head of the checkpoint, ensuring that it was given to them before she rest further.

Soon, there were checkpoint healers at her bedside and they ended up moving her to a private chamber within the great tower of the checkpoint. The tower of Fell Whist loomed over all of the checkpoint area and was a watchtower that kept a constant visual over the land. Many that stood atop the watchtower could see in all directions; from the distant Reune Lake to the south as well as the checkpoints that dotted the wooded landscape around it to the Sinter Mountains in the East, blocking much of the fertile land around it with its jagged mountains.

There were several floors of the watchtower and, as Triggle and Ilthen waited patiently by Altina's bedchamber, they could hear constant movement within the hallways just outside her room. The window within the elf's room was closed, but both the Miftles could hear the snowstorm outside rattle the window panes; even the floors of the watchtower were covered with a slight chill from the coldness outside. Triggle seemed to take it to heart when even the magik in his pouches didn't mend the elf's pains.

What she had could not be mended with warm soup and rest nor could it be healed by any faerie magik, which both of us have. Triggle felt the small pouches on the belt at his waist. *This was something new altogether that I've never seen before.* The young elf scribe continued.

"There is nothing you can do for me now I'm afraid, Triggle. There is a poison running through my veins and, without the antidote given at regular intervals, I will die. That is how they keep us there, the scribes, in the keep."

Triggle shook his head. He knew for a fact that there was nothing in the Sinter Mountains except for a few knolls of grass and some jagged rocks. He had traveled there several times and had never come upon anything made by the inhabitants, let alone a keep.

"So they were keeping you in a keep?" The elf nodded to him.

"And there were many others that I did not know that were there before me. They told me of the effectiveness of the poison. One of their scribes that got away was captured and brought back to die before them. They said he suffered much before finally dying. I do not wish to go that way, my friends."

However, Triggle could not let go of the idea of something in the mountains.

"A keep, you say... in the Sinter Mountains?"

Ilthen interrupted, somewhat incensed now.

"For the love of Shilinda, would you stop it, Triggle! She said there was something there, so there must be something there! Elves don't just pop up from nowhere like she did."

"Ludicrous! That's what this is! They must have something that keeps the keep hidden in order to keep them there."

Altina pulled the blanket from the bed tightly around her neck. She was beginning to get the chills, even with being fed and well-clothed. The warmth from being in the watchtower did nothing to help her.

The poison is taking effect in my fragile limbs! I have little time to act.

"Yes, you are correct, Triggle. There is something there that keeps it well hidden. And there is not just a keep there, but a training ground. Humans, dwarves and elves are there, preparing for an attack. Many of them have already left from what the battle plans say, and are positioned in different places, waiting for the signal. Whatever those signals are, they are coming soon."

Ilthen had made more broth for them and lifted a small bowl to the elf's lips, letting her drink from it. Triggle had quieted down but he stood now, pacing around the room, deep in thought.

Ilthen returned to the questioning.

"Why do you say that, Altina?"

"Because the battle plan that I stole was in the midst of transit when I took it, which means that it was to be enacted out as soon as it was received."

Triggle piped up.

"Well, we've given it to the head of Fell Whist now. We should be hearing something back from them anytime. You've done what you came here to do, Altina Laese. Take comfort in that, at least, my fair elven scribe." The Miftle stood by her bedside and took her hand. Even now, Triggle could see the strength wearing away in the elven beauty. Her eyes had a milkyness over them that seemed to make them more glossy than usual, her eyes seeming to take comfort in her eye lids closing more and more often.

She's dying, you stupid Miftle, and there's nothing you can do about it.

Triggle had felt helpless many times in his life, yet this was one of his more trying times. He had never seen something just pass into oblivion like this. Faeries did not slip away as inhabitants did;

never. The heart of a faerie would burn up the shell of their former self, freeing it finally from the limited life that it had been given on Ar Solon, only to fly into another realm altogether. At least, that's what Triggle had been told when he was a youth. To see it happen, well, that was another story.

He knew that there must be something that he could do. He looked to Altina to help him.

"Altina, is there anything that I can do to help, anything at all?"

The weakened elf nodded. She took another sip of the broth that Ilthen had given her and handed it back, Ilthen at her side on the other side of the bed.

"Who do you trust, Triggle? Someone that is out there that you could contact from here."

Triggle took some time to answer. He looked to Ilthen for an answer and she began to think as well, going over a great many names in her mind. The Miftle knew that he knew a few humans that he could trust, but none that would be able to get her…. Wait!

"Kalir! Kalir Ranolf! He was a checkpoint guard during the daemon siege at Dardist and came to Ranyll's aide even when poor Ranyll and the others were outnumbered. Ranyll's uncle has a post not far from here."

Altina smiled slightly. She could feel the excitement in the Miftle's grip on her hand.

"Good! Now you need to send word out to him to warn the others. Get them away from the populated areas and find a place to hide and keep them safe. If he can reach others, then you must do this."

Triggle released Altina's hand as the last of the words came out of her lips and moved for the door that led out into the hallway. Ilthen continued to stay next to Altina and patted her on the hand.

"Thank you for giving him something to do, Altina. He has been waiting for a chance to help in any way that he can. He gets that way when he stays still too long. I guess it's all the journeying that we've been doing these last few summers."

The elf seemed to understand for she smiled slightly, reaching her hand out to Ilthen.

"The two of you have done more than you know, for me and the rest of Kariyl. I don't know how I could ever repay you."

The Miftle took Altina's hand and moved a chair close to the bed, sitting by the elf maiden. Long had it been since Ilthen was near an elf, but she still knew that they held a considerable amount of compassion for one another though they were all locked up within their kingdoms. These were the last moments of Altina Laese and the Miftle simply wanted to make it as comfortable as possible for her. Triggle did not see this nor did Ilthen want him to; *his heart was too soft and would take the elf's death rather harshly*, Ilthen reminded herself, still remembering some of the deaths that they had lived through with the other faeries that he had known for some years, lying still forever within the caverns of Dardist.

It seemed like an age ago, Dardist and all the battling with the daemons, Ilthen thought to herself, watching the elven maiden close her eyes, the poison coursing through her veins one final time.

You're death will not be in vain, Altina Laese! We will fight what evil took you still in your youth!

Ilthen could feel the ragged breaths that Altina took every so often and, as Ilthen got up from her position to get a healer, the elf kept hold of her hand, the last of her strength used on the action.

"Please stay with me, Ilthen Lendure. I do not want to pass on to the other world alone."

So Ilthen remained at Altina's side until she passed, the fragile elf exhaling her last words in Ilthen's presence; the elf desired the kingdom of her people. She did not want to be forgotten or left behind; she wanted to be buried with her family line back in Elvinisclar.

Ilthen only nodded with tears in her eyes when Altina said this, the pale beauty's eyes looking away as if she had seen those places in her last moments, her lips forming into a slight smile as her eyes grew blank and the warmth from her hand in Ilthen's grew cold. Triggle returned some time later, only to see Ilthen placing the elf's hands across her chest, the still form's eyes closed in the forever sleep.

Ilthen knew immediately what Triggle was feeling, so she contained her sadness for the moment and dealt with the other Miftle.

"She said her goodbyes, Triggle, and wants us to take her to her people in Elvinisclar. She thanked us, Triggle, for helping her in her time of need. Without us, she said that she would have died alone. I was with her when she passed."

Ilthen had seen many a dwarfs' death in the tunnels of Dardist in the years that she had lived there, so the numbness of death had been instilled within her; yet, when she had met Triggle and began to know better of his life and ways, she saw a Miftle that was free from the tyranny of life and death. It wasn't until the battle in the caverns of Dardist where Triggle saw true pain and death.

Triggle moved closer to the form of Altina Laese and placed his hand on top of her folded ones, the Miftle's eyes closing ever so slightly. He began to pray.

"Oh Creator, take this child and keep her safe, for she was not safe here on Ar Solon. Show her that the world here is not so horrible."

Ilthen was at Triggle's side then. She closed in on him, pulling him to her. Triggle felt her warmth and responded by drawing his hand forth from Altina and placed it upon both of their own hands clasped together.

"…and give us the strength to continue to have hope in our paths that move forward with a purpose that we have yet to see. I trust this prayer finds you."

*   *   *

"You cannot be trusted!" Falwen Sanse retorted, finishing up cinching the dwarven traitor's hands, binding each hand separately with a leather cord the Chronicler had found from the stables. He then slipped another leather cord around the knots in between the dwarf's hands and tied the other end to his own saddle, checking the supplies on third horse before they began their decent down through the Agnar Mountains. No one had seen or heard them that Falwen could detect as they left the Agnar Scribe Guild, so they continued on silently until they were far enough away not to be heard, Falwen holding his sword out at the dwarf.

"Say anything or cry for help, Ostondilus, and you will regret you did." But the dwarf said nothing; whether he was scared of Falwen or just did not want to put up a fight, the human did not know. The dwarf simply asked one question.

"Do you really think you'll get away with this, Falwen Sanse? They know you're the Chronicler, the teller of the histories that have yet to come for all of Ar Solon. They are the Order of the Emcrist; they have power beyond comprehension and pull within Kariyl that you could never imagine."

The Chronicler traveled for some time before answering, his hand held tightly to the leather cords that had Ostondilus restrained. The old man had not thought about that.

What if they are simply allowing me to leave and roam free in order to make me feel like I have a choice? What if me taking Ostondilus Frews is just their way of forever watching me? What if he was planted in the Agnar Scribe Guild to flush me out completely so that I'm exposed?

The Chronicler thought of these questions and many more before answering, letting them settle within his mind before he responded to the dwarf, who seemed to be in a somber mood and kept to himself.

"But there is one thing that they don't have that I do, traitor!"

"And that is?"

"A grand scheme given to me by the Creator! He alone controls the fate of us all, not the Emcrist Order!"

And, indeed, Falwen Sanse was following the grand scheme given to him by the angel Divlo, for the path was straight, steady, and not doubted within his mind. Of course, the inhabitant had doubts, but those were from the darkness that battled with the light of the grand scheme within his mind, forever making most inhabitants at odds within themselves, even when they were shown the path and the way.

The morning sun had yet to rise in the east, so it was unbearably cold for the two of them and the three horses that carried them and their supplies for the next couple of days. The snowfall the last few hours had been of considerable size, the horses sinking into the snow up to 7-8 hands before they touched the ground beneath.

The moon was the only form of light for Falwen and his captive, the human using his aged sight the best he could to guide them forward and toward the west, a good ways away from Simmer Lo. But Falwen Sanse was happy now, just at the idea of seeing his family whom he had not seen in nearly four summers.

I will get them to a safe place and then I will deal with the problem that lies within all of the inhabitants; the Emcrist Order!

It would take a few days just to get out of the Agnar Mountains, then nearly another ten day to get to Simmer Lo. Falwen had charted this out many times in his chambers, routing and rerouting himself through the shortest path to his family if ever there were a reason to go back.

In the satchel at his waist, he carried two empty tomes for his writing. The quill inside the satchel seemed to call to him at that moment, to issue forth another great command; an adventure in Goletta was taking place and it needed to be written. He could almost taste the salty air of the Alvanus Sea when he pictured Ranyll and Oagthor in his mind getting on board the Namiah with Test standing there at the ready.

It chills one to the bone to know that The One's creature of choice will be riding with such an important person in this world. And my son is there, as well, which brings me no comfort. However, this is the life of the Chronicler, the life of the scribe of the world, to know all and to do little about it. Well, Creator, that has got to change.

Falwen Sanse edged the three horses forward through the snow, holding at bay for as long as he could the urge within him to write. He didn't know how long he would be able to keep it at bay; already, the story was playing out in his mind. He kept sight of Ostondilus next to him, ever holding his aged weapon at the dwarf, the ring he had found on the dwarf tightly in his grasp.

'He did not let the great poisonous beast out of his grasp, for he knew the second that he did, it would bite him with all its might, delivering the death blow of ages that the great warrior could not recover from.'

The ancient tale of the great warrior Clestes then surfaced to mind, the quote still ringing in Falwen's ears from his childhood. Clestes had waged a war against the monsters of the old world and won, though he was poisoned by the final attack of the great serpent that watched the jewel of the world.

The Emcrist was that jewel, Falwen remembered, applying much of what he had learned within the guild to the old tales he had listened to as a child.

And Clestes had found solace in the face that, though he died, the world around him lived on and flourished, that his children were able to see their children and watch themselves grow old. Clestes gave all of that up to rid the world of the great ancients. It all played some part in the bigger picture.

For summer upon summer, Falwen could not decipher what the purpose of the inhabitants was, always just knowing that each was given a task and that was it. However, now the aged fisherman was finally beginning to piece it together.

The two continued forward in the snow, ever intent on Simmer Lo, wrapped tightly in their blankets for warmth against the cold. Neither the dwarf nor the human said anything to the other while they traveled that night or in the morning, both content with their thoughts, their minds on a great many things that shifted and swayed in the world.

25

Ranyll and Oagthor moved through the last of the tunnels, checking back every so often for anything that could be following them. Elder Scribe Filt had sent them on their own, with no guide. Oagthor was now leading the way. The dwarf huffed every now and then, looking over at Ranyll to show his displeasure at the situation. Eventually, the dwarf even said something.

"Do you mind telling me what just happened?"

"I had to have something that the scribes there possessed."

"So, instead of just going to them, you decided to break into an ancient scribe library and take it for yourself?"

"It wasn't like that, Oagthor."

"Well, I wasn't there, so I don't know what it was like. I was only there to save you from the assassin that's been following us since Simmer Lo."

"Since Simmer Lo? How did you know they were following us?"

The dwarf hesitated.

"I saw the assassin there."

"You saw an assassin and you said nothing to me?"

"I could say the same for you and your little excursion back there. By the way, what was so important that it almost cost us our lives?"

"A map."

"A map? Of the island?"

"Yes, it is of the island."

Oagthor pondered for a moment.

"I thought there weren't any maps of the Island of Dree."

"There's always more to the story, Oagthor. The guild had the only one in existence to my knowledge."

"So when was I going to play a part in all of this?"

"I thought I could handle it by myself. I knew little of the daemons or assassins that were following me. If my partner had been a little forthcoming in telling me about the assassin, I could have at least been aware and forewarned the guild about it."

"And exactly what could you have done against an assassin, Ranyll?"

By this time, the passageway ended and a simple, thickly-built wooden door stood in front of them. Oagthor went to knock on it when Ranyll stopped him.

"I would have taken you with me, Oagthor Axeblade! You would have been by my side like it was before, all those years ago, when we fought the daemons. But we are in the west, my friend, and dwarven kin are somewhat frowned upon here. In fact, they are barely tolerated. So, to bring you into the scribe's guild with me…"

"….would be a sign of disrespect to them. I understand, Ranyll. You did right by me, Ranyll Tolver." Ranyll let Oagthor continue what he was doing and Oagthor knocked on the heavy door.

There was no sound at first and then there was a grating of stone and the door unlatched from the other side and swung outward, revealing two guards of the scribe order in a small armory. They nodded to Ranyll and Oagthor and motioned them to another door just ahead of them.

Apparently, this building had been made as a part of the underground system, Ranyll thought, watching as the guards moved a wardrobe back in its place in front of the door, covering it completely. They looked at Ranyll somewhat menacingly, taking their posts by the wardrobe, watching as he and his dwarven friend left the room.

Once through another door, Ranyll and Oagthor passed a basic sleeping quarters for a dozen or so inhabitants, many of them occupied with sleeping soldiers, and then moved to the front of the quarters where the exit lay. Through the windows of the sleeping quarters, they could see the lamps lit outside in the Golettan square, which meant that they weren't too far from the docks. They made their way out quickly and quietly.

Soon, they were on the main cobblestones of the Golettan square, passing the metal cover both Ranyll and Oagthor had entered only hours earlier.

"Thank you for saving me, Oagthor. If you weren't there, I don't know what would have happened."

"Aye, Ranyll, Let's not be too quick to be thankful of the dwarf. I got myself in over my head and I paid for it."

The dwarf reached for the remnants of his beard and stroked what he had, not touching the bare skin on the other side at all.

"She would have killed me, Ranyll, if I didn't hit her with that substance in the cube. It was a blessing and a curse at the same time."

The two of them reflected for a moment at the situation and then both seemed to realize that there was no time to spare and began to run towards the docks, making their way outside of the Golettan streets and into the docking area after passing through the checkpoint.

Ranyll pumped his legs and continued forward, watching as Oagthor did the same, following just behind him.

"I hope that Captain Aaolos has not left us."

"He has every reason to do so: he's a pirate, for one, he's got my treasure, and he forewarned us that he would leave, so it gives me no comfort at all, Ranyll Tolver, to…" And the dwarf stopped running and speaking at the same time.

From a distance away, Oagthor could see down to the docks where the Namiah had been tied down and it was gone. The captain had been good on his word. He left them and took the treasure.

"Curse what's left of my beard! He left us!"

Ranyll stopped running as well and, though he could not see ahead in the darkness, he took Oagthor's word and took time to catch his breath.

"I'm sorry, Oagthor. I didn't know all that was going to happen to get the map. What do we do now?"

Oagthor, still winded, leaned up against one of the dock planks and looked out at the Alvanus Sea. Several vessels had left their moorings and there were only a few ships left that they had seen earlier that day. Many of them were well-lit with the bow and stern lanterns so as to be seen at night. Some were still close to the docks themselves while many of them were just small dots of light that disappeared into the ripples of the sea moments later.

"I don't know, Ranyll. That was our ticket to the island more than anything."

Then a voice from the darkness spoke.

"Ranyll? Ranyll Tolver?" A shadow broke from one of the shadowed areas near the end of the pier. Oagthor did not see the individual because he had climbed up from a smaller vessel that was moored to the docks.

Ranyll answered back in return.

"It is I, Ranyll Tolver. Who is it that asks of me?"

The pirate pushed himself into the dim light that was given off by the lanterns at the docks not far away. He was an older man, yet not as old as Falwen though older than Ranyll's uncle. He seemed in the later stages of his life, just over 40 summers, yet kept a youthfulness in him that the other pirates Ranyll had seen lacked.

"I am Fenwell Des'grees. I'm the Namiah's boatswain and I'm here to take you and your dwarf to the captain."

The boatswain pointed over into the water at a small rowboat that was tied to the docks. They would have to climb a rope ladder down to it, but they were on their way to the Namiah! Ranyll and Oagthor breathed a sigh of relief, clapping Fenwell on the back as he showed them the way to the small vessel so they could board it.

The dwarf piped up, smiling as he spoke.

"For a second there, I thought Captain Aaolos left us here."

Fenwell nodded in agreement and threw himself over the side of the pier, climbing down nimbly to the rowboat that lay in wait just underneath him. He landed down onto some of the rigging in the boat that cushioned his fall and motioned for them to follow, pulling the boat closer by holding onto the ladder connected to the dock. Ranyll climbed down first using the ladder, and then dropped down into the boat a few feet from it.

"The captain **did** leave the two of you, dwarf! I volunteered to stay behind until you showed, however long that may have been."

Ranyll nodded his thanks and assisted with helping Fenwell with hold the ladder as Oagthor made his way down the rickety device.

"And I'm not **his** dwarf! I'm not owned or rented, Fenwell the boatswain! I live a very rich life, without the likes of you, your captain, and all on your ship. I'm here for Ranyll and my treasure back and that is all!"

Fenwell looked over to Ranyll and they both held the ladder as still as they could for the dwarf, who had trouble seeing his feet which dangled on each ladder rung precariously as if they were about to slip off at any moment.

"Does the dwarf always talk this much?"

"Only recently."

The three of them took turns rowing to the Namiah, which had been only a small speck of light on the sea when they first started from the Golettan docks. After a few minutes of rowing, they could make out a shape, then after passing a few smaller boats along the way, they could make out the shape of the Namiah. The two lanterns were still hanging from the bow and stern, yet there were other lights present as well. A fair number of torches were moving about on deck and there were small slivers of light peeping out from the quarter decks below the deck.

In another few rows, the rowboat was pressed up against the hull of the Namiah, Fenwell standing up in the boat to grab the anchor ropes that were lowered down so he could tether them to their boat. The rowboat shifted in its spot in the water and was lifted up, Fenwell continually pressing an oar against the hull of the

Namiah to keep them steady. Oagthor shifted in his seat on the boat a bit, trying to keep himself steady as well.

As soon as the rowboat was brought up level with the lip of the Namiah's deck, crew hands brought them on board. Oagthor went first as Fenwell kept the rowboat from rocking further, the thick dwarf getting several crewmen to help him over. Ranyll was next. He stood up and reached out his hand and a crewman took it, pulling him over the deck rails to the deck.

"Thank you, crewman! I thought we were left for a moment."

First Mate Meekins smiled back at him slyly, keeping his grip on his Ranyll's hand a moment longer.

"That's an awful thought, Ranyll Tolver! The captain wouldn't dare do such a thing, especially after he gave his word. After all, what would the voyage be without its most interesting passenger?"

Test could feel the power of the magik flow through Ranyll's fingers and down into the tips of them, almost making Test shiver in delight. However, he kept his composure as the first mate and let go of Ranyll's hand with reluctance.

I have been waiting for this moment to meet you, young Ranyll. The time will come when I will get my chance to peel your flesh from your body. It will happen soon, my inhabitant, and I will take your head back to my master.

First Mate Meekins slipped into the crowds of crewmen that welcomed Ranyll and his dwarf on board, several others leading the two new visitors to the captain's quarters for the celebrational feast that Captain Aaolos always held on the first day of the voyage.

The Namiah broke away from the rest of the vessels on the Alvanus Sea and shifted its sails so that it pointed westward, soon vanishing from sight from those that watched from the Golettan docks. And so Ranyll Tolver's journey began to the Island of Dree, knowing little of what lie ahead except what lay in his dreams and in the items that lay in his possession from the elder scribes of Goletta.

*   *   *

The messenger from the Emcrist Order leaned on his walking staff, pressing through the snow to his next destination. Already, he had delivered fifteen scroll cases, knowing that there was still many more to be delivered by the weight of the bag that he carried on his back. He had travelled by foot from the wagon that delivered all the messengers two nights earlier, only to arrive at his destinations on time, always meeting with his contact at each point without a fuss.

The followers of the Emcrist Order are on their mark, that is for sure.

He walked up to the checkpoint tavern and inn and knocked on the door, waiting for an answer. The building was one of the better he had seen in his journey so far; brightly-colored panes of glass and such a celebration was being had inside that it made him want to stop for the night.

Checkpoint 18, I hear it's the best around for miles. A good night's rest and a few drinks in me would be rather nice, the messenger thought to himself, watching as the door swung open, a rather fierce-looking man answering the door. Marle Fibbs, bartender of the famous Happy Traveler, smiled at the sight of another from the Emcrist Order, displaying his own ring to the messenger as he took the battle plans from him, stepping aside for the messenger to enter, his bald head gleaming in the lantern light of the room.

"Can I buy you a drink, friend of the Order?"

*　　　　　　　*　　　　　　　*

Kalir bypassed the formalities that Fell Whist offered and urged his friend Marcres Trilt to take him to those waiting to see him. The captain of the tower did as was asked, leading Kalir and Alyssia up while the rest of the guards that had come with them went about their duties of having some much needed time away from their checkpoint. They soon disappeared from sight and Kalir was glad to be rid of them. The checkpoint captain's mind rang with all the warnings Ranyll had told him about all those summers ago.

This cannot be happening! Not now, not when all else is falling apart!

Alyssia could see the intense look on Kalir's face and still feel the grip of her hand in his, the captain of the lower checkpoints sweating from his forehead and base of his neck, small drips of moisture beading on his face and chin as well. She had never seen anything get to Kalir since all those years ago, when they had first met in Dradle.

Is it really the end to all things as Kalir says, Alyssia thought, watching as the captain of the tower led them through the last parts of the checkpoint city and to the entrance of the great tower. Marcres stopped them before they entered.

"As I said to you, Kalir, they brought with them a dying elf. I hear that she has passed now, I'm afraid, but the dwarves wish to stay by her side until you arrive, which is not a problem for now. Soon, though, the elf will have to be moved and taken to a place for burial."

Again, it was coming to pass, Kalir thought to himself. *Ranyll stated that one of them would pass away and, in that passing, would bring about an end like none had ever seen.*

Kalir did best to calm himself, mainly by grasping the pommel of his sword and holding on for dear life as they made their way up through the tower. Kalir had been inside the tower before numerous times, yet he saw the same look of amazement on Alyssia's face that he had years ago when he had been made a captain of the checkpoint guards.

It was upon the roof of the tower where the ceremony took place. Myself and three others were made captains that day, he remembered, feeling the weight of the armor now getting to him as he climbed the stairs up further into the tower. There were six levels of the tower, the first two they had already passed by, looking over at the small rooms that branched off on each level. If Kalir remembered correctly, it was within the fourth and fifth levels that the healer chambers were held, for those extreme cases that required a healer.

Of course, the term healer took a whole new meaning after Ranyll had shown his abilities to me, Kalir thought to himself, remembering the day that Ranyll showed his other abilities to him and Dir'grar.

The people in here claiming to be healers could not even be called that now, for they have no powers to heal, only ointments and salves that will reduce the pain but not cure the symptoms.

Marcres, Kalir, and Alyssia soon passed the third and fourth floors, finally stopping at the fifth and moving onto the fifth floor level, where there were a small number of doors down a rounded hallway that wrapped around the stairs to form a complete circle. They passed two doors and stopped at the third, Marcres opening the door before them. Kalir was the first to see inside the room.

The elf had been covered in a cloth wrap to cover the entire body, tied with laces across the top and the two dwarves sat at her side. Kalir immediately recognized who they were.

"Triggle, Ilthen, what are you doing here?"

Triggle jumped up from his place at the elf's side and ran to Kalir, who was still entering through the door. Triggle shook the human's hand numerous times before Ilthen prompted him to stop.

"My, it is good to see a familiar face, Captain Ranolf! It has been some time, has it not?"

Alyssia came in as well and Triggle nodded to her a simple hello, returning his attention to Kalir.

"We brought this young elf to get help… and to warn every one of things to come. I'm afraid we were too late to save the poor elf, though."

"And what of these things to come, Triggle?"

Kalir was still in awe that Triggle and Ilthen were there, having not seen them in the last several summers since the snow came.

Marcres interrupted, still standing in the doorway.

"Captain Ranolf, I believe it is best that we leave the dwarves and let them attend to their business."

But Kalir would not have it. He had come too far and, for the two Miftle faeries to put themselves out on account of an elf must be of some importance. Kalir hoped that what Ranyll had told him was false, but deep down inside he could feel that something was wrong.

"I will not hear of it, Marcres! They came too far and so did I. Let them tell me what they have to tell me!"

The answer Marcres responded with was the sound of his sword unsheathing behind Kalir and Alyssia. Kalir turned and immediately knew what was happening. Just behind Marcres, several armed guards stood, waiting for their captain's orders.

"It did not have to be like this, Kalir! I did not believe the dwarves when they said your name. They carried the message here to Fell Whist, which could only mean that the time has come and the Order of the Emcrist is ready to strike. When they told me that they had fallen upon the scroll case with the battle plans within it, I had trouble believing that they were not part of the Order."

Kalir argued in protest.

"But they aren't part of any Order of the Emcrist! And neither am I!"

Marcres nodded in understanding.

"I know you're not, Kalir... but I am! And now that you and your friends know about this, I can't let you leave here…at least not alive anyway!"

Kalir had trouble understanding what had just occurred, yet he did not hesitate drawing his weapon in defense of the other captain. Alyssia did the same.

"And how are you going to explain this to the head of the tower and the council here at Fell Whist of your treachery? You can't just kill another captain and get away with it!"

Marcres looked at Kalir slyly, as if it he had much more up his sleeve than Kalir gave him credit for. And the traitorous captain did, indeed.

"The head of the tower and the council have been dead for over a ten day. I've been carrying out my own orders these last few days to prepare for the rise of the Emcrist Order. By the time the rest of the guards find out that the head of the tower and the council were killed, the Order's plan will already be carried out and it won't matter anymore!"

Marcres pointed at Kalir's sword as well as Alyssia's.

"It would be best to put those weapons down, unless you want your death to be more painful than I was intending to make it."

But Kalir did not lower his weapon and neither did Alyssia. In fact, Triggle and Ilthen joined the ranks next to Kalir, pulling out their long daggers in defiance of Marcre's orders.

Triggle lifted his blade up and out to Marcres.

"You've tangled with the wrong person, captain!"

Marcres laughed and looked back to his men, who laughed as well at the small dwarf-like creature pointing his pint-sized weapon at them.

"What makes you think I'm scared of you, dwarf?"

Triggle just shook his head and grabbed for one of his pouches at his side.

"I am no dwarf, human!" The Miftle then dug into a pouch at his side and pulled from it a handful of dust, releasing it onto the ground in front of the captain and his guards.

In moments, a great fire sprung forth from out of nowhere, rising up between the two parties, sending Marcres and his guards back into the hallway, scrambling for cover. Kalir acted on the moment of surprise the Miftle had given them.

"Quick, up the stairs to the roof! That is our only chance!" If Kalir remembered correctly, there was another stairway on the outside of the tower that, though made of simple stones jutting out from the tower, could be accessed from the roof. Triggle took little time to think and grabbed Kalir's hand, pulling them through the fire without harm, Ilthen doing the same for Alyssia. Kalir guided them forward towards the hallway to the staircase, yet Marcres and the guards still stood in their way.

"Faeries! They're faeries, soldiers! Be wary of their magiks!" Triggle let out another fistful of fire dust, sending Marcres and his men back far enough so Kalir could access the stairs going up, pulling Triggle with him as he went. Ilthen and Alyssia followed quickly behind.

After two flights of stairs, Kalir found the access to the roof and pushed the door open with his shoulder, walking them out onto the roof. And what he saw there made him stop in his tracks. He did not try to block the door with anything or find the exit like he had intended to do, giving them a quick escape. Instead he just looked out at the landscape and saw that it was too late.

To points south and east of him, he could see it; the small shifting puffs of smoke from fires all across the Tirapoor Channel. And, in some instances, he could actually see the fires from a distance. The whipping of the wind, which blew snow into his face, did not chill him to the bone as it should have. What did chill him to the very core was the fact that Kariyl would never be the same again.

They set fire to the checkpoints! They are razing the towns as they go along the Channel! But where are my guards? Shouldn't they be fighting this?

But Kalir knew at once what the answer was when he saw Marcres come through the roof entrance, his armed guards immediately behind him. They did not hesitate as before. They came for him and those that were with him.

The inhabitants have betrayed themselves! All my checkpoints were compromised from the beginning. All were traitors!

Kalir gripped his blade for one final strike against all that was evil, against the hordes of traitors that took over what had been fought for since time began here on Kariyl, and for what all those that have died stood for ages ago. As he lifted his blade high over his head, he was not simply fighting for his life, but for the life of those he loved.

'Hold on to what you consider dear to you, for it may be the last time that you have it!', was what the angel said to me that day. The words have never rung more true than they did right now.

And so here ends
Part I of The Healer. Be
sure to read the
continuing adventures of
these characters in The
Healer, Part II, coming
soon to a retailer near
you!

Author's Note

I couldn't exactly leave Ranyll a young boy in the Forgotten Angel novel and never tell his story of how he came into manhood, now could I? Of course, with this telling, Ranyll also had inherited abilities, magikal ones, and his father's task at helping the inhabitants around him to a new level of understanding. This, of course, is why it was so important to tell this story, Book XXI and not tell Book XX…yet. So, fans out there please do not fret, you will be happy to know that Book XX is in the process and is on its way. However, that novel is a collection of short stories and only picks up the pieces and fills in the blanks between the two novels, Forgotten Angel and The Healer.

When I first started writing The Healer, even just the ideas for it, I knew that it was going to be a long storyline. There was so much to explore with Ranyll and the other characters. Plus, I had so many things on Kariyl that I wanted to explore, I felt that Ranyll should be the reader's own personal "tour guide". It became clear as I ended Forgotten Angel that Test would play a large role in this novel as well since he didn't get any face time in the previous novel. Originally, Test was set to come after Ranyll in Forgotten Angel; he just never made it into the book. Also, I had to tackle a number of other things.

First, I didn't want to write a 500+ page novel. It seemed that the story could get to the size of an epic, which isn't exactly what I wanted. There are a few novels in the Chronicles of Ar Solon that will be epics, but the smaller novels need to stay smaller, this being one of them.

However, that was not my call, I found out later when writing the book. Ranyll had a number of things to do and little time to do it.

Moreover, the back story about his father and Kalir as a younger man seemed somewhat important to what the whole theme of this novel was; which was this growth into becoming a man and understanding responsibility, even when the responsibility is not wanted, (such was the case with Crin Tolver, who wanted to be a father and a family man more than anything).

So, I'm writing this novel and, as I'm going through the chapter order of it, it spans out so large that I have to make a Part II and split it in half. Of course, Part I is not going to be a cliffhanger (I just lied right there), yet it does have some hard decisions that need to be made in Part II. And, to me, Part II is what really tests the characters and shows you what they're made of.

When you finally get a chance, (and I finish Part II, of course) you will be able to notice that the stakes have been raised when Part II begins and there is this urgency that is similar to the end of Forgotten Angel. The dynamics of Part I and Part II of the Healer have changed by the start of the second act. Many are in a race for time itself and seem to be clinging to something that's not there in a moment of despair. You see, we all make our own destiny; that is what many of the characters in these books do not realize until it is too late.

And, for The Healer, Part II, I want to showcase the characters in a new light instead of something that you've already seen. You can see that with the way the characters have changed so much since their last adventure in Forgotten Angel.

About the Author

Riley S. Brown has, for the last two years, been trying to change the pace of his life and has taken the proverbial bull by the horns. He has been working on outlining all of his epic fantasy novels; a collection of twenty-five novels all based on the world of Ar Solon that he had created when writing his first novel in the series, Book XIX: Forgotten Angel. He has self-published two novels and written two screenplays that are still being marketed. Riley has also worked as director, writer, and actor for numerous small productions his high school students have performed in front of an audience, taking an abundance of joy in seeing his students become something so much more than just a student.

Riley is also finishing treatments for several screenplays at this time as well. Two of them are horror films and another is a present day re-imagining of Lewis Carroll's *Alice's Adventures in Wonderland*.
He presently lives in Sarasota, Florida with his son Clover, mother and brother.

www.ingramcontent.com/pod-product-compliance
Lightning Source LLC
Chambersburg PA
CBHW050855130726
47900CB00013B/53